About the Author

Alexey Pehov is the award-winning author of The Chronicles of Siala, a bestselling series in his native Russia. His novel *Under the Sign of the Mantikor* was named 'Book of the Year' and 'Best Fantasy Novel' in 2004 by Russia's largest fantasy magazine, World of Fantasy.

Praise for *Shadow Prowler*

'An exciting take on classical themes ... the story is engrossing, the characters intriguing and dynamic; there are mysteries galore and the very real sense as we set out that far creepier things are waiting down the road. In short, a book I didn't want to put down.'
Chris Claremont, bestselling writer of *X-Men* and *Wolverine*

'Toothy, gritty, and relentless. Alexey Pehov sneaks up on you and fascinates with the wry voice of a young Moorcock. Clear space on your shelf – you'll want the whole series.'
E.E. Knight, bestselling author of the *Vampire Earth* series

'*Shadow Prowler* is a fresh, exuberant take on territory that will be familiar to all fans of classic high fantasy. Alexey Pehov introduces a cast of charming, quirky, unsavory, even loathesome characters in a fast-paced, entertaining adventure.'
Kevin J. Anderson, co-author of the bestselling *Dune* books

'It's not too often debut novels come with a legacy, but in this case it's a pretty impressive one ... If this were an English novel, we'd be reaching for the rest of the trilogy right now'
SFX Magazine

'*Shadow Prowler* reminded me of why I fell in love with fantasy in the first place'
Book Thing

Praise for *Shadow Chaser*

'The second instalment in Russian author Alexy Pehov's Chronicles of Siala trilogy includes all the facets of a true high fantasy novel'
Fantasybookreview.com

'Shadow Chaser is a novel of intricate plots, surprising twists and finely drawn characters that will not leave you when you put the book down. Shadow Chaser is truly something different in the world of fantasy, something special; it is something truly Russian, a fantasy that is gripping and haunting, fascinating and imaginative' Goodreads.com

Shadow Chaser

Shadow Chaser

ALEXEY PEHOV

TRANSLATED BY ANDREW BROMFIELD

**SIMON &
SCHUSTER**

London · New York · Sydney · Toronto · New Delhi

A CBS COMPANY

First published in Great Britain by Simon & Schuster, 2011
This edition published in Great Britain by Simon & Schuster, 2012
A division of Simon & Schuster UK Ltd
A CBS COMPANY

1 3 5 7 9 10 8 6 4 2

Simon & Schuster UK Ltd
1st Floor
222 Gray's Inn Road
London WC1X 8HB

www.simonandschuster.co.uk

Simon & Schuster Australia, Sydney
Simon & Schuster India, New Delhi

A CIP catalogue record for this book is available from the British Library.

ISBN: 978-1-84739-672-3

Printed and bound by CPI Group (UK) Ltd, Croydon, CR0 4YY

Acknowledgments

would like to say thank you to Robert Gottlieb, Trident Media Group, LLC, Olga Gottlieb, and Patrick LoBrutto for their invaluable help.

Shadow Chaser

1

RANNENG

In the fifteen hundred years of its existence, the city of Ranneng has survived a hundred rulers, six fires that wiped it clean off the face of the earth, a number of coups, rebellions, epidemics, and, naturally, wars. For those who don't know, Ranneng is the former capital of the kingdom of Valiostr, and it lost that noble title during the Spring War, when an armada of orcs came flooding in from the Forests of Zagraba.

Almost obliterated by the orcs and then rebuilt, Ranneng is rightly considered the most beautiful city in the kingdom. The old architecture; the numerous statues of the gods; the broad streets and fountains; the high, pointed spires of the watchtowers; and the swing bridges on the banks of the rivers—all of these attract large numbers of travelers, idle gawkers, merchants, and traders.

Inhabitants of the south of Valiostr who have never seen Avendoom are inclined to think that Ranneng is a very big city. Well, it certainly isn't small, but it's still nowhere near as big as Avendoom.

At the very beginning of the rule of the Stalkon Dynasty, the king founded the University of Sciences by royal decree, and now people come here to study from almost all the northern kingdoms. Opposite the venerable university there is a huge park, and a walk through this small forest that thrives within the city limits to the Upper District of the city will bring you face to face with the massive bronze gates of the school of the Order of Magicians.

This is where future sorcerers master the fundamentals of their trade, and only then, after five years of rigorous training, do they set out for the school in Avendoom to further refine and improve their magic art. Thanks to the magicians' school and the university, the old capital is known as the City of Learning.

It would be impossible to find a better site for founding a city— Ranneng is conveniently located on five hills at the precise intersection of the major trade routes in the south of the kingdom.

Poets love to sing the city's praises for its beauty, but Ranneng has one substantial shortcoming: It is much closer to the Forests of Zagraba than Avendoom and therefore much closer to the orcs—if they should suddenly have the morbid desire to go back to war, they can get here much more easily than they can to the Cold Sea. And that's why five hundred years ago we acquired a new capital. The orcs had taught men to be cautious.

The Stalkon Dynasty was certainly determined not to be taken by surprise again, and the king and his entire court moved north to Avendoom, farther away from the land of forests and the potential dangers lurking in them.

But, with your permission, I will end my brief historical and geographical excursion, since we have finally reached the gates of the city.

It was late morning and the people from the surrounding villages and towns were heading for the gates in order to buy, sell, steal, find work, go to college, visit relatives, listen to gossip, or simply gape for lack of anything better to do. The crush was so bad that I wasn't hoping to get into the old capital before evening.

The din of the crowd was absolutely indescribable. There were hundreds of people talking, shouting, bellowing, and arguing, foaming at the mouth as they claimed the right to push their way through to the entrance ahead of everyone else. A fight sprang up over a disputed place in the queue beside a cart loaded with turnips. The Ranneng guard tried to restore order, but they only made things worse and only served to focus the crowd's hostile attention on the hapless guardsmen.

A serious scrimmage was brewing, and the air had a distinct smell of burnt Garrak pepper. The small group of soldiers regretted ever getting involved in the brawl.

"What's all this nonsense?" the moody-looking character who answered to the name of Loudmouth asked irritably. "I can't remember seeing a jam like this at the Northern Gates. Everybody always piles in through the Gates of Triumph."

"Then what are we doing stuck here?" Hallas hissed angrily, holding one hand against his cheek.

What could be worse than a sullen, cantankerous dwarf who's angry with the whole wide world? Only a sullen, cantankerous dwarf who's angry with the whole wide world and also happens to have a toothache. Hallas's tooth had started aching the evening before and it was causing him dire agony. But the insufferable gnome had dug his heels in and refused to let anyone pull out the lousy tooth, saying he wanted to have it done by a respectable barber and not horse doctors, in which category he included Deler and Kli-Kli, who had offered their services as healers.

"These gates are closer to the highway!" Loudmouth exclaimed.

"They may be closer," Hallas said gloomily, plucking at the tangles in his beard, "but did it never enter your thick head that I'm about to expire from pain here?"

"Stop whining," Deler muttered. "Hold on for a bit longer."

The gnome gave the broad-shouldered dwarf a dark look, with the clear intention of thumping him on the nose, but instead he muttered: "Why's it taking so long?"

He watched as the guard allowed a cart loaded high with cages of chickens in through the gates.

"They have to inspect everyone, tax them, find out what they've come for," Kli-Kli squeaked.

"What incredible zeal from the municipal guard. Why now?"

"Who can say," the little green goblin said with a shrug.

"Perhaps we could try the other gates, Milord Alistan?" Honeycomb asked hesitantly, with a sideways glance at the leader of our party.

The knight pondered the suggestion for a few seconds and then shook his head: "They're more than an hour away."

Hallas's face turned crimson and I was suddenly afraid that he was about to have a stroke.

"An hour!" he snarled. "I can't hold out that long."

And the gnome started riding determinedly toward the gates.

"Where's he going?" Loudmouth asked, but Alistan only laughed and set his own horse moving after Hallas. There was nothing else we could do but stay with them.

At first the people gaped at us in fascination, but then, realizing that we were jumping the queue, they started murmuring.

"They'll kill us! I swear by Sagra, they'll kill us!" Marmot muttered. But the gnome drove on heedlessly through the indignant crowd, yelling like an old-time cobbler for them to make way.

"Halt, gnome! Ha-alt!" cried a guardsman with a halberd. "Where do you think you're going? Don't you see the queue?"

The gnome opened his mouth to let the soldier know what he thought about him and his family back to the seventh generation, but in some miraculous fashion Miralissa was suddenly there beside him and she edged him out of the way.

"Good morning, honorable sir. Why the delay?" the ashen-haired elfess asked with a smile.

The guardsman immediately lowered his voice and even tried to straighten his uniform tunic. Like all the rest of us he knew—because his mother had told him when he was a little baby—that you always had to be polite to elves; light or dark, it makes no difference. If, that is, you don't want to end up with a dagger under your ribs when some denizen of the forest decides that you just happen to have insulted him—or her.

"What's so good about it, milady? Just look at what's going on. We have to check and recheck everyone. And all because the Nameless One's been up to his tricks again. They say a few weeks ago he attacked the king's palace!"

"You don't say! The Nameless One?" Uncle chortled incredulously into his thick gray beard.

"The Nameless One, as large as life! And five thousand of his followers. If it wasn't for the guard and Alistan Markauz, they'd have killed His Majesty!"

"Five thousand, you say?" Uncle chortled incredulously again and scratched his bald head.

"Folks is saying as it was five," the talkative soldier said, slightly embarrassed—apparently he'd only just realized that five thousand was quite a large number.

"My, my," chuckled Uncle. Like all the rest of us, he had been in the palace on that memorable night when the Nameless One's supporters decided to test the resolve of the Royal Guard.

"But what's that got to do with the queue at the gates? The attack was in Avendoom, but the gates are in Ranneng!" Hallas exclaimed in exasperation.

"The king, may he reign for a hundred years, has given orders to increase our vigilance. So we're doing our best."

"If an army of orcs went tramping past them, they wouldn't even notice," Kli-Kli whispered quietly in my ear.

The goblin was right, because it was highly doubtful that your average guardsman would be able to recognize a supporter of the Nameless One even if he walked right under his nose. As yet, the traitors who sympathized with Valiostr's main enemy didn't actually look any different from perfectly peaceable citizens.

The crowd at our backs started murmuring more loudly.

"What is all this?"

A dour-looking soldier wearing a corporal's stripes came toward us from the gates. He was obviously not in the mood for pleasant conversation.

"Hang on there, Mis," the talkative guardsman said, ignoring the corporal's rank. "Can't you see the lady elfess is inquiring after the news?"

The corporal almost fell over when he got a good look at our motley group. A green goblin with blue eyes; three dark elves; a dour knight; nine warriors, one of whom appeared to be an angry gnome; and a dwarf in an absurd bowler hat. Plus a skinny rogue. Not the kind of company you meet in the city every day of the week.

"A-ah . . . ," the corporal drawled, trying to choose the right words. "Well, if that's how it is . . ."

"We don't wish to detain you," said Miralissa, with another smile. "May we pass?"

An elf's smile can put a man who isn't prepared for it into a prolonged stupor, especially if it's the first time he has seen those two sharp white blades protruding from over the lower lip.

"Of c-course you can p-pass," said the corporal, gesturing toward the gates so the guards would let us through. "But remember, only the municipal guard and elves have the right to carry weapons within city limits."

"But what about nobles and soldiers?" asked Eel, raising his eyebrows in surprise as he broke his silence for the first time.

"Daggers and knives of an acceptable size—that's the only exception."

"But we are in the king's service! We're not a detachment of mercenaries."

"I'm sorry, but the law's the same for everyone," the corporal responded.

I'd heard about this law. It had appeared about three hundred years earlier, when brawls used to flare up in Ranneng with the speed of forest fires. Those were troubled times, with three noble houses squabbling over power; when the king set aside his important affairs to intervene in the fracas, there were more bodies in the streets than on the Field of Sorna after the battle between the gnomes and the dwarves.

Half of the counts, barons, marquises, and other riffraff with royal blood running in their veins expired right there in the streets. Unfortunately the other half were left alive, and the houses known as the Boars, Oburs, Nightingales, and their supporters still nursed their grudges against each other to this very day.

And so anyone who walks round town carrying a blade the length of a man's palm or, Sagot forbid, a crossbow, risks a large fine and a couple of days' rest in an uncomfortable prison cell. This has had quite a remarkably sobering effect on noble gentlemen. After spending a little time in places that were damp and unbearably bleak, their lordships became as meek and mild as lambs . . . for a while.

"But that can't be right," Lamplighter exclaimed: His very heart and soul protested against the idea of such a law.

Mumr, our beloved Lamplighter, was never parted from his immense bidenhander, and now it seemed that in Ranneng the master of the long sword would have to hide his fearsome weapon and make do with a short-bladed knife.

"I'm not asking what business has brought you to our city and which house you intend to serve here," the guardsman said, giving us a suggestive look.

"We have no intention of entering service with the noble houses," Milord Alistan snapped.

"It's all the same to me, milord knight," said the corporal, raising his hands in a conciliatory gesture. "If you choose not to serve, then don't. That's your right. It's just that the first thought that comes into my head when I see a band of people bearing arms in the city is that one of the houses has hired itself a few more cutthroats."

"Is there unrest in Ranneng again?" Miralissa asked, tossing her thick ash-gray braid behind her shoulder.

"Just a bit," the soldier said with a nod. "The Nightingales and the Wild Boars had a set-to just recently in the Upper City. There were two barons slit open from neck to navel. Mmmm . . . I beg your pardon if I have affronted you, lady elfess."

"No, indeed, and thank you for answering my questions, kind sir. So, may we pass?"

"Yes, milady. Here's a paper for you, it will help you to avoid questioning by the patrols." The corporal took a rolled-up document out of a wooden case hanging at his hip and handed it to the elfess. "It says that you are newly arrived in our glorious city. Welcome!"

"This is for you. For services rendered," said Egrassa, leaning down from his horse and putting a coin in the corporal's hand.

"Why, thank you, kind—," the guardsman began, but when he saw what coin the elf had given him, he broke off and froze, like a statue in the royal park.

It's not every day that a corporal got to hold a full gold piece in his hand. I had a feeling there would be a party in the guardhouse that evening, and not a single guardsman would be left standing at midnight.

We left the delighted guards and rode in through the gates . . . with our weapons, though we would have to be careful about carrying them around.

From the lane that began at the city gates, we turned onto a broad street leading into the very heart of the city. The inn to which Miralissa was taking us was located on one of the hills, and as we made our way there I turned my head this way and that, studying the surroundings.

On a small street that began with a monument to the defenders of Ranneng who fell in the Spring War, we were stopped by a patrol of guards, but they left us in peace when they saw the paper that the corporal had given us.

"All right," said Loudmouth. "I have to go and see how my relatives are getting on. See you at the inn!"

"Greetings to the girlfriend!" Arnkh shouted, not believing his story about relatives, but Loudmouth had already melted into the crowd, leaving his horse in the care of Lamplighter, who was rather annoyed to be given this gift.

The people were as thick on the ground as gkhols in an abandoned graveyard.

"Is this some kind of holiday?" Lamplighter muttered, surveying the crowd with a not entirely friendly glance.

"Certainly is!" replied that know-it-all Kli-Kli. "Exam week at the university. The whole city's making merry."

"Very clever of us," I said drearily. "I can't stand crowds."

"I thought you were a thief," the goblin said.

"Well, so I am," I replied, not quite understanding what he was getting at.

"I thought thieves loved a crowd."

"And just why should I love a crowd?"

"I thought a crush was handier for stealing purses," Kli-Kli said with a shrug.

"That's a bit below my level," I snorted. "I don't deal in purses, my dear fool."

"Right, you deal in Commissions," the detestable goblin giggled. "But you know, Harold-Barold, I reckon that pilfering purses with coppers in them from the pockets of halfwits is better than the Commission you have now."

"Go and annoy Hallas," I snarled.

Kli-Kli had pricked me in a sore spot. Okay, there was no point in crying over spilt milk. I'd accepted the Commission—I must have been slightly insane at the time—and now there was no way back.

"Harold!" Lamplighter shouted, jerking me out of my moody reverie. "What's got you so miserable?"

"That's just his usual state of mind," the king's jester interrupted arrogantly. "Our Dancer in the Shadows has been far too glum and gloomy recently."

"But then, someone else has been far too cheerful and chatty," I muttered. "Make sure you don't regret your blathering later."

"Loudmouth's the one who blathers," Kli-Kli retorted. "All I ever do is speak the truth."

"And you also quote the prophecies of goblin shamans who guzzled magic mushrooms," I teased the jester. "All their prophecies about a Dancer in the Shadows aren't worth a rotten sparrow's egg."

"Too late to get stubborn now. You accepted the title of Dancer in the Shadows, just like in the prophecy. The *Bruk-Gruk* has never lied!" Kli-Kli began testily, but then he realized I was only teasing him and lapsed into offended silence.

Kli-Kli's weak point is his beloved goblin *Book of Prophecies*, which he knows from cover to cover. And now, you see, I wasn't Harold the thief any longer, but a walking prophecy, who was destined to save the kingdom and the entire world. Yeah, sure. If I had my way, I'd rob it, not save it.

"Kli-Kli," Arnkh put in, "why don't you tell us if this little book of yours by the shaman Tru-Tru . . ."

"Tre-Tre, not Tru-Tru, you great ignoramus!" the goblin interrupted the bald warrior resentfully.

"Written by the shaman Tre-Tre," Arnkh went on as if nothing had happened, but the goblin interrupted him again: "The *great* shaman Tre-Tre!"

"All right. Written by the great shaman Tre-Tre. So, is there anything in it apart from your beloved prophecies?"

"For example?" The native son of the Border Kingdom seemed to have succeeded in catching the goblin off balance.

"Well, for example, a cure for a gnome's toothache?"

Hallas, who had drawn level with our little group again, heard the conversation and pricked up his ears, although he tried to pretend he wasn't interested at all.

Kli-Kli spotted this and gave one of his now-watch-what-happens smiles—a clear sign that he was about to play one of his rotten tricks.

The jester paused so theatrically that Hallas started squirming in the saddle with impatience. When the gnome's fury was just about to reach the boiling point, the goblin spoke.

"It does."

"And what is it?" I asked, tugging desperately at my bridle and trying to steer Little Bee out of the space between Kli-Kli and Hallas.

As sure as eggs were eggs, the goblin had some rotten trick in mind, and I had no wish to be caught in the line of any heavy objects when the bearded gnome decided to spill the royal jester's blood.

"Oh!" Kli-Kli declared in a mysterious voice. "It's a very effective remedy. In principle it could have been applied at the very beginning of Hallas's ailment, and the tooth would have stopped hurting immediately. I swear by the great shaman Tre-Tre's hat, Harold, it's the truth."

"Then why didn't you say anything?" the gnome roared, setting half the street fluttering in alarm.

Uncle turned round and waved his fist at us, then pointed in Alistan's direction and ran the edge of his hand across his throat.

"Cut the clowning, Kli-Kli," Marmot said good-naturedly. "People are looking."

"All right, not another word," the goblin promised solemnly, gesturing as if he were locking his mouth shut.

"What d'you mean, not another word?" the gnome asked indignantly. "Deler, tell that green-skinned lout that if he doesn't give me the remedy, I won't answer for myself!"

Kli-Kli gazed at the gnome with his blue eyes and said with a very doubtful air, "I'm not so sure you'll like the goblin remedy for toothache, Hallas."

"Can't you just tell me, Kli-Kli?"

"You won't use the method anyway," said Kli-Kli. "And I'll simply have revealed a goblin secret for nothing."

"I promise that I will use your method this very moment!" said the gnome, struggling desperately to hold himself back from wringing the goblin's neck.

A broad smile split Kli-Kli's green face from ear to ear, making him look exactly like a wickedly contented frog.

I worked away even more desperately with my bridle, holding Little Bee back until I was beside Lamplighter, and the goblin and the gnome were ahead of me. My brilliant maneuver did not go unnoticed by Marmot, Deler, and Arnkh, who repeated it precisely. Hallas and Kli-Kli were left on their own: None of us wanted to be caught between the hammer and the anvil.

"Remember, you promised to use the goblin method," the prankster reminded the sick man. "Well then, in order to cure a sick tooth, you have to take a glass of ass's urine and hold it in your mouth for an hour, then spit it out over your left shoulder, preferably into your best friend's right eye. Your toothache will disappear instantly!"

Hallas gave the goblin a baleful glance, spat juicily on the ground under the hooves of his horse, and urged it on. I think Kli-Kli was rather upset. Like everyone else, he'd been expecting thunder and lightning.

"Tell me, friend Kli-Kli," I asked the downhearted goblin. "Have you ever tried that remedy yourself?"

The jester looked at me as if I were demented: "Do I look like an idiot, thief?"

I just knew he was going to say something like that.

"Behold and tremble, Harold," said Honeycomb.

"I am trembling," I said, with my eyes glued to the Fountain of the Kings.

And what a sight it was! I'd heard a lot about this fountain before, but this was the first time I'd ever set eyes on it.

The huge column of water fifty yards high was regarded as one of the sights of Ranneng. The fountain took up the whole square; its roaring jets of water soared way up into the sky, and then fell back down to earth, shattering into a watery haze that shrouded the entire area. The droplets of water and the rays of the sun merged in a passionate embrace to create a rainbow bridge that sliced the sky above the square into two halves and came diving back down into the fountain.

Those in the know said that when the dwarf master craftsmen created this miracle they had a little help from the Order. It takes magic to produce a rainbow that appears out of the spray every day of the week in any weather. It looked as if I could reach out my hand to touch the seven-colored miracle and feel all the airy fragility of this bridge in the sky.

"Magnificent," Arnkh sighed contentedly, catching the fresh spray on his face.

Late June and the first half of July had been so hot that even a hardened warrior like Arnkh had taken off his beloved chain mail a couple

of times during our journey. And for someone from the Border Kingdom who has been used to wearing armor almost since the day he was
born, that is a very serious concession indeed.

Fortunately, over the last few days the heat had abated a little, but it
was still hot enough to make me worry about my brains boiling in my
skull. So it was sheer bliss for our group to stand beside the fountain,
where the air was so cool, fresh, and clean.

"No halt here!" Alistan announced without even glancing at the
marvelous sight.

So much for our rest. When I thought about the long journey under
the summer sun waiting for us after Ranneng, I felt really bad. In the
name of a h'san'kor, what was wrong with the weather this year?

"What's wrong with you today?" an indignant voice asked right in
my ear. "Here I am fluttering about like a lark in front of a cockerel to
get your attention, and you might as well be deaf!"

"And did you say anything interesting, chatterbox?" I asked.

"Chatterbox!" the jester snorted. "I wasn't simply talking talking, I
was extolling the beauties of this glorious city."

"I don't see much beauty around here at the moment," I muttered,
looking round the street.

It was just an ordinary street. Little old two-story houses with battered, peeling walls, although I had to give the locals some credit—not
all the buildings looked totally decrepit. But I definitely couldn't see
much beauty. If I hadn't known I was in Ranneng, I would have thought
this was the Outer City of Avendoom.

"Wait a bit, we'll get to the park in a moment; the trees there are just
like those in the Zagrabian forest!"

"Have you been here before, then, Kli-Kli?" asked Lamplighter, who
had ridden up to us on his roan horse by the name of Stubborn.

Loudmouth's horse was trudging after Stubborn, flicking her ears in
protest at being dragged in such a perfunctory manner.

"Yes, I was here once," Kli-Kli mused, smacking his lips. "I was on a
mission for the king."

Hallas almost choked in surprise. Forgetting all about his sick tooth,
he stared at Kli-Kli and said: "Don't go telling me fairy tales, goblin.
I'll never believe the king could trust you with important business."

"Baa!" said Kli-Kli, sticking his tongue out at the gnome.

"Never mind, tell us your silly story anyway, it'll ease the boredom. Are we never going to get to this inn?" Marmot said.

"Why, there's no distance left at all. We just go through the park into the Upper City, where the university is, and the school of magic and all the rest of it. A fine district it is. We haven't got far to go now."

The goblin was simply playing the clown and waiting to be asked again.

"Come on, get on with it," said Lamplighter.

"Just let me think where to start," Kli-Kli agreed graciously, and put on an important air, as if he really was thinking.

"Harold, hold Invincible for me while I take my jacket off," said Marmot.

"All right," I agreed, and Marmot tossed his ling across, onto my shoulder.

Marmot's shaggy tame rat by the name of Invincible took a sniff, grunted, wheezed, and settled down on my shoulder. It was incredible, but apart from Marmot I was the only one in the entire party that the ling didn't bite; he even allowed me to stroke him when he was in a generous mood.

I couldn't fathom just why the long-haired rodent from the Deserted Lands took such a great liking to me. But when I saw the way the rat howled and tried to bite Kli-Kli's finger every time he reached his hand out to it, I chuckled merrily, which greatly annoyed the goblin.

"You promised us a story, Kli-Kli," I reminded the goblin.

"Ah, so I did! Right, then: A year ago the Oburs and the Wild Boars decided to conclude an alliance and give the Nightingales a bloody night of it. There was a fine old brawl all set to break out in Ranneng, and that was not in Stalkon's interests. They would have started with the Nightingales and finished with His Majesty. And so I was sent."

"And our truly fearless little friend defeated them all!" Deler chortled.

"You dwarves don't have even a spark of imagination," Kli-Kli snorted. "I was sent here to make the Wild Boars fall out with the Oburs and vice versa, to make sure that those noble gangsters never thought about concluding an alliance again. . . . And that's just what I did!" There was a distinct note of pride in the goblin's voice.

"And how did you pull that off?" I chuckled, handing the ling back to Marmot.

"I used the same plan as you did in that business with the Horse of Shadows. Set everyone against everyone else."

"Set everyone against everyone else? What's he talking about, Harold?" asked Lamplighter, puzzled.

"Don't bother your head about it, Mumr," I said: I didn't want to get into that story just then. "And how did the Oburs and Wild Boars take to your plan, Kli-Kli?"

"You know, Harold, it's strange, but they really didn't like my plan at all!" the jester giggled. "Especially the Oburs! Those noble gentlemen were so upset when they heard that one of the Wild Boar counts was marrying his daughter to a Nightingale that without thinking twice they set up a really lively betrothal party for the Wild Boars. And the Wild Boars gave tit for tat by slitting the throats of a couple of Oburs. The mayhem that broke out in the city then ended any more talk about an alliance. The nobles of the south carried on squabbling among themselves, and my king had no need to feel concerned for the safety of his throne. The threat of rebellion and civil war was postponed indefinitely, and the whole kingdom came to thank the jester for the peace and tranquillity of Valiostr."

"Well, isn't our fool a fine lad after all!" Arnkh chuckled, jangling his chain mail.

The nobles of the south are like a fishbone stuck in the king's throat. Painful to swallow, and if you try to spit it out, you're likely to make things worse. Because if their lordships aren't watched carefully, they might turn around and strike a deal with the western provinces, and that would be the end of the throne. As soon as the squabbling and intriguing comes to an end, the nobles—and especially the nobles who have formed an alliance—will start looking for something else to do with their armed men.

During the time of our present king's father there was an unpleasant incident when the western nobles decided to overthrow the dynasty. They were annoyed, you see, because the king didn't want to give away the Disputed Lands to Miranueh. Fortunately, that time the rebels got nowhere. The royal guards surprised them by turning up when they weren't expected. And the nobles of the south failed to support the revolt of their neighbors to the west: The Wild Boars, Nightingales, and

Oburs were too busy with each other to take any notice of any appeals to take part in a conspiracy.

We were riding through the park, with its giant oaks. I could hardly believe that trees that size grew inside the city limits. There weren't any big trees in Avendoom, even in the grounds of the royal palace, not to mention the other districts of the city. With the cold weather that the winds bring us from across the Cold Sea and the Deserted Lands, all the trees are taken for firewood the moment winter arrives. The folks from the Port City and the Suburbs would soon have reduced all these trees to nothing but stumps.

The road started rising uphill and we emerged from the park to find ourselves in the area of Ranneng immediately around the university and the school of the Order. The houses here were a bit newer and more handsome than the ones we had ridden past earlier. But even so, the streets were still swarming with people. More people than there were fleas on an unwashed dog, that's for sure.

The inn, separated off from the street by a fence, was a large, respectable-looking establishment of three stories.

"Well, blow me!" Deler said with a whistle as he surveyed our temporary residence. "If the building's that big, then the kitchen must be huge, too. And a huge kitchen is a sure sign of good food! What do you think, Hallas?"

The gnome merely cast a mournful glance at his partner and kept his mouth shut.

"You're right there, Deler," boomed the giant Honeycomb. "We've had enough of that lousy grub Uncle and Hallas dish up. Oh, I could just do with a suckling pig and horseradish!"

"And you shall have one, dear sir. You shall quite definitely have a suckling pig! And even two! I hardly think one would be enough to satisfy a mighty warrior like yourself!" replied a potbellied, red-cheeked little man who had appeared from out of nowhere. "Good day, Lady Miralissa. I'm glad to see you again in my most humble establishment."

"And I am glad to see you alive and well, Master Pito," the elfess replied with a polite smile. "How are things at the inn?"

"We get by well enough and just about make ends meet."

"Don't give us the poor mouth," Ell said with a smile. "You've put on weight in the half year since we were last here."

"What do you mean?" the innkeeper protested, brushing aside the comment from Miralissa's bodyguard. "That's just from the worry of everything! Oh! Tresh Miralissa has brought some new travelers to my establishment! But where are the ones who were here last year? I can only see their lordships Egrassa and Ell."

"They are no longer with us," Miralissa replied reluctantly.

I didn't know this part of the story, but from the fragmentary phrases that the dark elfess had let slip in conversation with me, I realized all the companions who left the Forests of Zagraba with her, apart from Egrassa and Ell, had been left behind in the snows of the Needles of Ice. Only three elves and Uncle's platoon, who had accompanied Miralissa to Avendoom, had escaped alive from the Deserted Lands.

"What a catastrophe!" the innkeeper exclaimed, wringing his hands. "How could that have happened?"

"Why don't you show us our rooms, Master Pito?" Egrassa suggested.

"Oh!" said the innkeeper, realizing that he had touched a sore spot. "I beg you most humbly to forgive my curiosity. Please follow me, good gentlemen. I've already given one of your companions his room. And poured beer for him!"

"Who have you given a room to, good master?" Markauz asked suspiciously, narrowing his eyes and lowering his hand to his sword.

"Have I done something wrong?" the innkeeper asked in dismay, stopping dead on the spot. "He arrived and said he was with you and—"

"Who arrived?" Count Alistan interrupted him.

"Why, I arrived, Milord Alistan, I did!" said Loudmouth, emerging from the door of the inn with a mug of beer in his hand.

"Oho!" said Arnkh with a sharp intake of breath. "You move like greased lightning! I expected you this evening."

"How's the girlfriend?" Lamplighter asked as he walked past Loudmouth and then disappeared through the door of the inn without hearing his reply.

"I didn't go to see any girlfriend," Loudmouth protested feebly.

"Of course not. You went mushroom-picking," said Marmot as he followed Mumr inside.

"Come in, gentlemen, come in!" said Pito, feeling firm ground under his feet again. "All the rooms have been made ready."

Kli-Kli gazed round at the group with his blue eyes and asked: "Nobody objects if I stay in Harold and Lamplighter's room, do they?"

Of course no one objected.

The main hall of the inn was the size of a city square; there were chandeliers with candles up under the ceiling, sturdy chairs with carved openwork backs, long benches, and stout tables. There was a huge owl carved out of a single tree trunk hanging on one of the walls, a staircase leading up to the second floor, a bar counter, and a strong oak door leading to the kitchen.

"Do you have many guests, Master Pito?" Count Markauz asked, taking off his leather gloves and tossing them onto the nearest table.

"No one, apart from you."

"How so?" asked the captain of the royal guard, raising one eyebrow in amazement. "Is business really going that badly?"

"Don't be concerned, milord!" the innkeeper said with a cunning smile. "Tresh Miralissa paid the inn's expenses for two years in advance."

"We decided to make the Learned Owl what you humans would call our headquarters," Egrassa said. "My cousin paid Master Pito not to take in any other guests, and with no one else staying here we can feel perfectly at ease."

"Master Pito," said Mumr, leaning on his huge bidenhander, "how about some beer?"

"Why, certainly!" the innkeeper said keenly.

"And a bath to go with the beer," Uncle put in.

"And a piglet," Honeycomb added.

"Everything will be ready in literally five minutes!" said the innkeeper, dashing to give instructions to the staff.

When we were all fed and refreshed, I walked to the farthest table, leaned back blissfully against the back of a chair, and hesitated for a moment before taking out the plans of Hrad Spein. I hadn't been able to study the maps of the deep labyrinth of burial grounds properly. But now at last I had a free moment to take a close look at the scrolls that I had worked so hard to get.

"Harold, stop poring over those papers. You'll have time for that later. Are you coming with us?"

"Where?" I asked, looking up at Kli-Kli.

"To take Hallas to the barber."

"We're not seeing him off on his final journey. What do you need me for?"

Kli-Kli moved up close, looked around conspiratorially, and whispered, "Deler says the gnome's terribly afraid. We might have to hold him."

"Then take Honeycomb," I said, trying to get rid of the jester. "He's big enough to restrain five gnomes."

"Honeycomb won't lift his backside off his bench now," the goblin said in a disappointed voice. "Arnkh, Lamplighter, and Marmot are going off for a walk round the city, the elves and Alistan aren't here to ask—they're busy searching for provisions for the next stage of the journey. And Loudmouth and Uncle will swig beer until they burst. Who else can I ask but you?"

"Eel," I said, nodding in the direction of the swarthy Garrakian.

"He's already coming with us."

"And you don't think he'll be enough?"

After the long journey I wasn't exactly burning with desire to go anywhere.

"Come on, Harold! Deler especially wants you to come."

I snarled at the goblin, but I still picked the papers up off the table, wrapped them in drokr, and put them back in my bag.

"Let's go!" Hallas hissed when Kli-Kli and I walked over to him.

"Harold," Miralissa purred, "don't forget to leave your crossbow at the inn."

Name of a h'san'kor! I'd completely forgotten about my little darling!

I really didn't want to part with the expensive and very necessary item. Without my crossbow hanging at my back I felt naked and defenseless.

"And leave your blade as well," said Ell as he watched me hand my weapon to Uncle.

"Yes, Harold," Uncle confirmed, "you'll have to forget about the knife, too."

"We'll give you something a bit less obvious. How about a fork?" Kli-Kli giggled.

"But why do I have to leave the blade?" I asked, ignoring Kli-Kli's jibe and looking at Miralissa's yellow-eyed k'lissang.

"It's longer than allowed."

I was reluctantly obliged to leave the knife in Uncle's care, too.

"Honeycomb," said Marmot, addressing Uncle's deputy, "throw my bag over here; we can't let Harold go wandering the streets without a weapon." Marmot caught the bag when it was tossed to him, rummaged in it, and fished out a dagger in a simple, well-worn sheath.

"Here, take that."

I took the weapon and pulled it halfway out of the sheath.

"Ruby blood?"

"Canian forgework. Good steel."

"Ooh, look at that! Just like Alistan's sword!" the jester exclaimed with an admiring whistle when he saw the red shimmer of the blade.

"Thank you, Marmot," I said and regretfully handed the knife back to the warrior. "It really is magnificent steel, but it's too noisy. Don't you have anything simpler?"

"We've got any amount of blades. Here, take mine," said Lamplighter, handing me a dagger.

"That'll do," I said with a grateful nod and fastened the weapon to my belt.

If anything happened, I had a razor in a secret pocket and a bag with a whole arsenal of magical tricks that I'd bought just before I left Avendoom.

"Kli-Kli!" said Alistan, going up to the jester. "Are you sure you haven't got anything you shouldn't have?"

The fool looked as if he had been accused of royal treason, and flung open the flaps of his dark cloak to reveal a wide belt with four heavy throwing knives hanging on it, two on the right and two on the left. I couldn't remember him taking one of them out of its sheath in all the time we'd been traveling.

"That's it? You haven't got anything else hidden away?"

"I'm as empty as a bottle of wine in the hands of a drunkard," Kli-Kli replied in a sincere voice.

"All right," said Alistan, apparently taking the goblin at his word. "But remember you can get into trouble if you're too sharp-tongued with the guards."

"I won't forget," said the jester, with an air that made it quite clear Alistan didn't need to tell him that soldiers had no sense of humor.

The goblin started rooting in his numerous pockets and pulled out a tangle of knotted string. I remembered he had wagered with us that he would work terrible goblin magic with that thing. But so far, all he had for his pains was a crazy jumble of string and knots. Kli-Kli caught my glance and winked merrily.

"Warn me when you want to test that," I told him. "I'll cut and run for the next kingdom."

The jester gave me a glance that said his faith in me was destroyed forevermore and stuck the bundle of string back in his pocket.

"You'll be surprised yet, Harold, when I let my shamanism loose."

"Marmot!" said the taciturn Eel, holding out the scabbards containing his "brother" and "sister." "Take good care of them."

"Of course, old chap, of course," Marmot replied, taking the two blades from the Garrakian.

"Come on, Harold, or I'll expire of the toothache right here on the floor!" the gnome grumbled on his way out of the inn.

2

THE GNOME'S TOOTH

So where are we going?" asked the jester, skipping along beside me.

The goblin's short little legs were not adapted to the pace that Hallas had set for our party.

"To the barber's. As if you didn't know."

"I know we're not going to the cobbler's, Harold. I asked *where* are we going? We've seen lots of barbers in the last hour!"

"Then you're asking the wrong person, you should try Hallas."

"Thanks, but I don't want to die young. He's a bit out of sorts today, and I don't intend to ask him any questions."

"Well, if you don't want to ask him, just shut up."

"Ooh!" the goblin exclaimed, offended, and went dashing off to pester Deler with his questions, but the dwarf gave him almost exactly the same answer as I had.

"You know, Harold," said Eel, speaking for the first time since we left the inn, "I'm starting to get a bit bored with this walk."

"And you're not the only one," I sighed.

We walked round Ranneng for the best part of an hour in search of the right barber. Just how the gnome was going to choose the *right* one out of all the barbers available was a mystery to us. But all the barbers we had already visited obviously didn't merit that title.

Hallas's rigorous standards for the man who was going to pull out his tooth left the disappointed barbers with empty pockets and the gnome with the toothache. Hallas had a whole mountain of reasons for rejecting one barber after another.

This barber's shop was too dirty, that barber's prices were too high, a third one had blue eyes, a fourth one was too old, a fifth one was too young. The sixth one was too sleepy, the seventh one was strange, the eighth had a stammer. There was no way to satisfy all the gnome's petty whims.

As soon as Hallas got close to the next barber's shop, in some magical fashion his steps grew slower and slower and he started creeping along like a drunken snail, trembling all over. A blind Doralissian could have seen that the gnome was frightened.

"People are looking at us," the Garrakian muttered.

"They've been looking at us ever since we left the inn," I muttered in reply. "What can we do about it?"

We were a curious-looking group, so people had no qualms about gaping at us. First of all, of course, everyone looked at the goblin—a rare sight in the cities of the kingdom. But as soon as people noticed the gnome and the dwarf, they forgot all about Kli-Kli. You might catch the occasional sight of a goblin, but gnomes and dwarves walking along peacefully side by side was something you never, ever saw.

"Harold, look!" Kli-Kli exclaimed, tugging on my sleeve.

"Where?" I couldn't see anything interesting.

"Right there!" said Kli-Kli, pointing toward a shop selling vegetables. "Hang on, I'll just be a moment."

Before I could even open my mouth, the goblin had dashed off to do his shopping.

"What's wrong with him?" Deler asked, puzzled.

"Everyone has his own weaknesses," I answered. "Some don't like to get their teeth pulled out, and some love carrots."

Hallas turned a deaf ear to the remark about teeth and uttered an exquisite groan.

"Stop that!" Deler shouted heartlessly at the gnome. "It's your own fault. You miserable coward."

"Who's a coward?" Hallas snapped back. "Gnomes aren't afraid of anything! It's your beardless race that are the cowards! Locking yourselves away in our mountains and sitting there trembling like an aspen leaf in the autumn wind!"

"Then why don't you get your tooth pulled out?"

"I told you, you thickhead! They're all bad barbers!"

"All right, but why are you dragging that sack around with you?" asked Deler, refusing to leave Hallas alone. "Can't you just leave it somewhere? What have you got in there anyway, the gnomes' book of spells?"

"It's my sack! I'll carry what I want!"

The gnome and his sack were inseparable. Hallas dragged it around with him wherever he went. Even Kli-Kli hadn't been able to find out what was in it. Deler was dying of curiosity, he had no idea what it was. And I didn't know what kind of treasure the gnome kept in the sack, either, but ever since he got it from his relatives in the fort of Avendoom, he had been fussing over his property like a chicken with the very first egg it ever laid.

"Here I am," said Kli-Kli, crunching happily on a carrot as he walked up to us. "Well then, are we going to get this tooth pulled out, or are we going to wait for it to fall out on its own?"

"What business of yours is my tooth? I'll do what I like with it!"

"The Large Market's not far from here. There's bound to be a barber there," Kli-Kli suggested.

The Large Market really was large. No, that's not right. It was immense! An immense space with an immense number of goods on offer. And there were more people than you could count striding along between the rows of stalls.

"Buy a horse! Genuine Doralissian bred! Just look how gracious she is!"

"Apples! Apples!"

"The finest steel of the north! The finest blades of the south!"

"Buy a monkey, good sir!"

"Thief! Stop that thief!"

"Catch him!"

"Best quality Sultanate carpets! Moths can't touch them!"

"Hey! Be careful, that's Nizin Masters porcelain, not your granny's old clay chamber pot!"

"Sunflower seeds!"

"Milord, our establishment has the finest girls in this part of Valiostr! Come on in!"

"Mama! I want a biscuit!"

"Stop shoving!"

"Reins, bridles, saddles! Reins, bridles, saddles!"

"Get your pies here!"

The hubbub was worse than at the gates when we were trying to get into Ranneng. Eel was saying something to me, but I couldn't hear him because a fat woman was howling in my ear and holding a fish up under my nose that was at least a month old and had a stupefying stench. I brushed the tradeswoman aside and dashed to catch up with the others.

Hallas, whose brain had obviously been completely addled by the pain, led us into the thick of a crowd of people watching a fairground show right in the middle of the market. The gnome had never been known for his courtesy toward others, and now he elbowed his way through the crowd, stepping on feet and swearing coarsely like a long-time inhabitant of the Port City. In just a few seconds the popularity of the race of gnomes plunged to an all-time low, well below prices for manure.

Somehow we managed to make our way through the crush and then Kli-Kli couldn't resist climbing up on the stage, turning a cartwheel, standing on his hands, grabbing a flaming torch out of the juggler's mouth and sitting on it, jumping up and climbing a post to the high wire, walking across to the other post, spitting on the strongman's bald patch as he was lifting a weight, and then swanning off to thunderous applause.

"Still amusing yourself?" I asked the goblin gloomily when he caught up with me.

"And you're still mumbling to yourself and expecting the worst, are you?" said Kli-Kli, giving as good as he got. "You have an idiotic out-look on life, Harold! Let's get going, or we'll get lost in this crowd."

The goblin went dashing on ahead—his small size made it easy for him to weave his way through the crush. People stepped on my feet twenty times and made at least ten attempts to foist things I didn't want on me—from a sponge to a mangy, squealing cat that was on its last legs.

Some inexperienced thief tried to slip his hand into my pocket, but I dodged aside and held Lamplighter's dagger against his stomach, then pressed the young lad back against the wall of one of the shops.

"Who's your teacher?" I roared at the pickpocket.

"Eh?" Cold steel against your stomach doesn't really encourage clear thinking.

"I said, who's your teacher, you young pup?"

"Shliud-Filin, sir!"

"Is he in the guild?"

"Eh?"

"Are you having difficulty hearing me? If so, you'll never make a good thief!"

"Yes, my teacher is in the guild, sir."

"Then tell him to show you who you should rob, and who you'd better leave alone until you have a bit more experience!"

"A-all right," said the lad, petrified. "Are you not going to call the guard, sir?"

"No," I barked, putting the dagger back in its sheath. "But if you come near me again . . . You take my meaning?"

"Yes." The lad still couldn't believe that he had got off so lightly.

"Then clear off!"

I didn't have to say it again. The unsuccessful pickpocket darted away from me like a startled mouse and was lost in the crowd in a moment. I watched him leave. In the distant days of my youth I used to clean out punters' pockets until I was picked up by my teacher For, who taught me the mysteries of the supreme art of thievery.

"Harold, are you planning to stand here much longer?" asked Kli-Kli, bounding up to me. "We're all waiting for you! And who was that young lad you were having such a relaxed conversation with?"

"Just a passerby, let's go."

Deler, Eel, and Hallas were waiting impatiently for us in a small open area free of trading stalls.

"There's a barber's!" said Deler, jabbing a thick finger toward a shop. "Forward, Hallas!"

"Forward? Do you think I'm a horse, then?" The gnome really didn't want to go.

"Go on, go on," I said, backing up the dwarf. "You'll see, you'll feel better stra—"

I gazed hard into the crowd and never finished the phrase. Over beside the rows of horse traders, I'd caught a glimpse of a painfully familiar figure. Without thinking twice, I went dashing after Paleface, paying no heed to my comrades' howls of surprise. My eyes could still see the face that I'd spotted just a second before. I had to catch that man, no matter what, and dispatch him into the darkness if I got a chance.

Along the way I almost knocked a tradesman off his feet and tipped over a basket of apples. Taking no notice of the abuse from all sides, I pulled my dagger out of its sheath and held it with the blade along my forearm, so that the weapon would be less obvious to the people around me, and I ran over to the spot where I had seen my old acquaintance just a second earlier.

"What is it?" asked Eel, springing up beside me like a shadow. "You look like you've seen a ghost!"

"Yeah," I answered, without taking my eyes off the crowd. "A ghost. But, unfortunately, a live one."

"Who was it?"

"An old enemy," I said gloomily, putting the dagger away in its sheath.

"There are so many people here . . . you could have been mistaken."

"Yes . . . ," I said after a pause, and ran my eyes round the market again. "I hope I imagined it . . ."

But I couldn't have imagined it! That man had been far too like the hired killer Rolio. As we walked back, I kept glancing round all the time, but I didn't spot anyone who looked like Paleface.

The gnome and the dwarf had disappeared, and the goblin stood alone, hopping from one foot to the other.

"Harold, what's happening to you? Are you well?" Kli-Kli asked, looking solicitously into my eyes. "Who was it you saw that sent you galloping across the market like a herd of crazed Doralissians?"

"Oh, no one. It was a mistake. Where have Deler and Hallas got to?"

"The dwarf dragged the gnome into a barber's shop," Kli-Kli answered. "And what kind of old acquaintance was it, if he deserves your knife blade under his ribs?"

"Paleface," I replied tersely.

"Oh!" the goblin said, and paused. He had heard plenty about this character. "Did he see you?"

"You know, my friend, that's the very question that's bothering me. I hope not, otherwise there's trouble in store, and not just for me. The character that Rolio works for would be glad to finish us all off."

"The Master?" the goblin guessed.

"Yes."

"What are you talking about?" Eel had never heard about any Master.

"Don't bother your head about it," I told the warrior. "Let's just say you could get something sharp under your shoulder blade at any moment. As soon as Hallas gets his tooth fixed we'll go back, and then Alistan and Miralissa can rack their brains over what to do next. I said we shouldn't come into Ranneng!"

"The halt was absolutely necessary. You know that perfectly well."

"You're very talkative, Eely-beely! Is there some reason for that?" Kli-Kli asked.

"Go and grin at someone else, Kli-Kli," the Garrakian said good-humoredly. "Let's go. Deler might need help."

"I'm warning you now," I said hurriedly. "I didn't volunteer to hold the gnome!"

It was annoying that the goblin and the Wild Heart both turned a deaf ear to my warning. I wonder why in certain situations certain people suffer from a selective loss of hearing. I sighed bitterly and trudged toward the barber's shop, following my comrades.

Hallas, bright red in the face, came leaping toward us out of the door of the shop, almost knocking the jester off his feet. The goblin only just managed to jump out of the way. Deler came flying out after Hallas. The color of the gnome's face would have put any beetroot to shame.

"What's happened?" I asked.

"That . . . !" the gnome roared so loudly that everyone in the market could hear him and pointed back at the door of the shop.

"Shut up!" Deler hissed, pulling his hat down over his eyes.

"I told you, shut up! Let's get out of here!"

"But what's happened?" I asked again.

"That cretin who slept with a donkey wants money!" the gnome roared.

"Errr . . . ," said Eel, who didn't understand a thing, either. "It's quite usual to pay a barber money, isn't it?"

"But not three gold pieces! Have you ever heard of anyone taking three gold pieces for a rotten tooth?"

"No, I haven't."

I hadn't, either. Three gold pieces was a lot of money. For that much you could get all the teeth of half the army of Valiostr pulled out.

"Let's go, Hallas!" Deler persisted.

"Hey, you! You damned swindler! Come out here! I'll break all your teeth out for a copper! And I'll wring your neck for free!"

"Hallas, shut up and let's get going!" the dwarf yelled, unable to control himself any longer.

"Eel, stop both their mouths, before the guard arrives!" I whispered to the Garrakian when I saw a crowd of idle onlookers starting to gather round us.

The barber made the mistake of looking out of his shop.

"I do beg your pardon," he babbled, "but I extract teeth using spells bought in a magic shop. The procedure is absolutely painless, that's why my price is so high."

"Hold me back," Hallas told us, and went dashing at the barber with his fists held high.

The barber gave a shrill squeal and slammed the door in the furious gnome's face. Deler hung on his comrade's shoulders and Eel jumped in front of the gnome, who was charging like a rhinoceros. I pretended that I wasn't with them at all, but simply standing there taking a breath of fresh air.

Some public-spirited individual had called the guards, and about ten armed men were already making their way through the crowd in our direction. They hadn't wasted any time. The Ranneng guard were obviously far more conscientious about their work than the guard in Avendoom. No doubt the frequent clashes between Wild Boars, Nightingales, and Oburs kept the servants of the flexible and corrupt law in a state of constant battle readiness.

We didn't have time to slip away.

"Problems?" the sergeant of the guard asked me.

"Problems? No, not at all. No problems," I answered hastily, just hoping that Deler would somehow manage to stop the gnome's mouth.

"No fairy tales, if you don't mind!" the soldier said harshly. "Tell me why that half-pint is yelling like that."

"He's having a bad day."

"And that's why he feels like slugging a respectable barber, is it?" another guardsman chuckled. "A deliberate breach of public order and incitement to affray. Are you going to come quietly or . . . ?"

It doesn't matter where the guards are from—spend a bit of time in any city and you get to know all there is to know about their kind. Even a Doralissian could tell what it was the lads wanted from us.

"We're not going anywhere, dear sirs," said Eel, coming to my assistance and leaving Deler and Kli-Kli to take care of Hallas.

There was something in the Garrakian's eyes that made the guardsmen take a step back. A wolf facing a pack of yard dogs, that was the thought that came to my mind when Eel blocked their way.

They had the advantage of numbers and—even more important—they had their halberds against our daggers. A very powerful argument in a fight, it must be said. But it was clear that they were still having doubts.

"Oh yes you are, dear sir," the bold sergeant hissed through his teeth, adjusting his grip on his halberd. "This isn't your Garrak; we observe the law here!"

Eel's lips trembled into a barely visible smile.

"If the law was observed in my country the way it is here, there'd be more criminals in Garrak than there are bribe-takers in the guard."

"Just what are you hinting at?" asked the sergeant, narrowing his eyes malevolently.

Eel gave another faint smile and swayed back thoughtfully on his heels. His hands dropped to the hilts of a pair of Garrakian daggers.

The gesture didn't pass unnoticed by the soldiers and they all took another step back, as if on command. Hallas had finally shut up, and now he was staring around in amazement at the guards and the crowd watching us, unable to believe that his quarrelsome nature could have attracted so many people.

"Gentlemen, gentlemen!" said a man who suddenly emerged from the crowd and walked up to the guards. "These are my friends. They're not from these parts, and they haven't had time yet to get used to the laws of our glorious Ranneng!"

A sharp nose, blue eyes, light brown hair, about my own age. He had an open, slightly roguish smile and was dressed like a prosperous townsman—probably that was why the sergeant answered him instead of sending him packing.

"They're disturbing the peace and insulting the keepers of public order," said the sergeant, with a hostile glance at the Garrakian.

"Of course, of course," the man whispered sympathetically, carefully taking the sergeant by the elbow and leading him off to one side. "But you understand, they're from the country, and my friends were never taught good manners. This is their first time in the city. And that thin one over there is my aunt's nephew, so he's a relative of mine," the man said, jabbing his finger in my direction.

"What's that goon doing?" Hallas asked in amazement.

"Dragging us out of the shithole that you dug for us," Deler explained to the gnome.

Hallas had enough wits not to start another argument.

"I was supposed to make sure they didn't get into any trouble," the man explained to the soldier. "Put yourself in my place, sergeant! If anything happens my aunt will tear my head off and she won't let me back into the house!"

A silver coin passed from the stranger's hand into the hand of the commander of the guard.

"Well . . . ," the sergeant said hesitantly. "We still have to perform our duty and carry out our responsibilities."

Another coin changed owners.

"Although," said the guardsman, starting to soften a bit, "although, following a brief reprimand I could quite well release your . . . mmm . . . respected relatives."

A third silver piece disappeared into his grasping fingers.

"Yes!" said the sergeant with a resolute nod. "I think the Ranneng guard can find more important business to deal with than punishing innocent passersby who haven't quite settled into the city yet. All the best to you, dear sir!"

"All the best."

"Let's go, lads," the sergeant said to his soldiers, and the guard immediately lost all interest in us and disappeared into the crowd.

The idle onlookers realized that the show was over and busied themselves with other matters. The market started buzzing again and no one paid any more attention to us.

The man came up to us, smiled, looked into my eyes, and said: "Hello, Harold!"

The only thing I could do was reply: "Hello, Bass."

"Hello, Harold."

"Hello, Bass," I answered lazily, half opening one eye.

"Still asleep?" my friend asked.

"Yeah."

"I'm hungry," said Bass, slapping himself on the stomach.

"So why tell me?"

"Well, you're my friend!"

"Sure as daylight, I'm your friend. But it's time you learned to earn your food some other way than playing potbellied small fry at dice and cards!"

"Ah!" Bass sighed in disappointment and sat down on the edge of the straw mattress. "Just because you're twelve and I'm only eleven, it doesn't mean that you're cleverer than me."

"Well, if that's not so, why are you nagging me about food?" I chuckled.

"There's a job."

"Well?" I stopped studying the ceiling and sat up.

"This man won a lot of money from Kra at dice . . ."

"How did you get in there?" I asked in surprise.

They didn't like to let us into the gambling den. Kra didn't make any profits out of juvenile pickpockets like us. We just got under everyone's feet and cleaned out the decent customers.

"I managed it," said Bass, screwing up his blue eyes cunningly.

Bass had earned his nickname of Snoop. He could get in anywhere at all—it was another matter that my friend quite often got in trouble for these escapades of his.

"Well, what about this man?"

"Ah! Well, basically, he was playing Kra at dice and he won three gold pieces!"

I whistled enviously. Only once had I ever managed to fish a gold piece out of someone's pocket on the street, and Bass and I had lived in clover for two whole months. And this was three all at once!

"Do you think you can get them off him?" I asked Bass cautiously.

"I don't think so, but you could," my friend admitted with a sickly smile.

"Right," I said morosely. "And if something goes wrong, it'll be me they grab, not you."

"Don't worry about that," Bass declared nonchalantly. "This character looks like a real goose. If anything happens, I'll help. We're a team!"

He was right there. We'd been through a lot together in the two years we had known each other and lived in the slums of the Suburbs. And there had been bad days as well as good ones in that time.

Compared with me, Bass wasn't too good at delving into people's pockets on the street. He didn't really have any talent for lifting purses, and that burden was always laid on my shoulders. But then Snoop did have other talents: He could sell a bill of goods to the Nameless One himself, con and swindle his nearest and dearest, fix a game of dice or cards, and point me in the direction of a man with a pocket bulging with coins.

"All right," I sighed. "Where is this golden gent of yours?"

"He's sitting in the Dirty Fish, guzzling wine."

"Let's go, you can show me," I said reluctantly.

We still had one silver coin and five copper ones, and there would have been no point in risking my neck if not for the three gold pieces. For that kind of money it was worth getting up off the mattress and going out into the cold.

We slipped out of the crooked old hovel that was home to more than twenty souls. The people who lived there were all homeless tramps, like us.

Avendoom was in the grip of early spring—there was still snow lying on the ground, the nights were still as fiercely cold as in January, when many people who had no roof over their head froze to death in the streets, but despite the cold weather, the unfriendly gray sky, and the snowdrifts everywhere, spring was in the air.

There was an elusive smell of opening buds, murmuring streams, and mud.

Yes, mud! The mud that appeared from out of nowhere every year in the Avendoom Suburbs. But of course the mud was a mere trifle, a minor inconvenience and nothing more. The important thing was that soon the weather would be warm and I would finally be able to throw away the repulsive dog's-fur coat with tears in five places that I'd stolen from a drunken groom the year before.

It had faithfully kept me warm all winter long, but when I wore it I was less agile and quick, and that enforced clumsiness had got me into trouble more than once. The week before I'd very nearly ended up getting nabbed by the guards because my feet got tangled up in the thing.

The Dirty Fish, a crooked old tavern, was right in the very center of the Suburbs, beside Sour Plums Square. No sane man would ever go to the Fish to fill his paunch—the tavern's sour wine and abundant bedbugs were enough to frighten away any decent customers.

We halted on the other side of the street, opposite the doors of the tavern.

"Are you sure your man's still in there? What would he be doing in a puke hole like that with three gold pieces? Couldn't he find a better place?"

"Obviously he couldn't," Bass muttered. "He's there, and he has two jugs of wine on the table in front of him. I don't think he could have guzzled all of it while I ran to get you."

"You simply don't know how good some people get at guzzling wine," I retorted. "He could be more than a league away by now."

"Harold, you're always panicking over petty details," Bass snorted. "I told you, he's in there!"

"All right," I sighed, "let's wait and see."

So we waited in the frost. Bass and I leapt up every time the door of the tavern opened, and every time it turned out to be the wrong man.

"Listen," I said, losing patience after two hours' waiting, "I'm frozen to death."

"I'm almost frozen solid, too, but that man's definitely in there!"

"We wait for another half hour, and if he doesn't come, I'm clearing out of here," I said firmly.

Bass sighed mournfully.

"Maybe I should go and check?"

"That's all we need, for Kra to give you a good thrashing. Stay where you are."

The frost was licking greedily at my fingers and toes, so I stamped my feet and clapped my hands, trying to warm myself up at least a little bit. Several times Bass wanted to go into the tavern to check how the owner of the three gold pieces was getting on, but every time, after wrangling with me for a while, he stayed where he was.

"Maybe the guy's had too much to drink?" my friend asked uncertainly; I could feel my fingers turning to icicles.

"Maybe . . . ," I replied, with my teeth chattering. "I don't want anything anymore except to get warm."

"There he is!" Bass suddenly exclaimed, pointing to a man who was walking out of the tavern. I studied him critically and gave my verdict: "A goose."

"I told you so," my friend said with a sniff. "Oh, now we'll really start living!"

"Don't be in such a hurry," I said, watching our future victim's progress. "Did you see where he keeps his money?"

"*His right pocket. That's where his purse is.*"

"*Let's go.*"

We tried to behave so that he wouldn't take any notice of us. Trying to get into his pocket just then would have been asking for trouble. There weren't many people about, there was no way to approach him without being noticed; all we could do was wait for a convenient moment.

"*Are you sure he's drunk two jugs of wine?*" *I hissed, keeping my eyes on the stranger.*

"*Why?*" *Bass hissed back.*

"*He's walking very steadily. Not at all like a drunk.*"

"*There are different kinds of drunks,*" *Bass disagreed.* "*You could never tell if my old dad was drunk or not, until he picked up a log and started chasing after my mother.*"

Meanwhile the man was wandering through the winding streets of the Suburbs without any obvious goal, like a hare circling through the forest to confuse his tracks. We kept our distance and tried not to let him see us until he reached the Market Square. There were plenty of people there, and it was quite easy for us to move up close behind him.

I gave Bass a quick nod, and he darted off to one side.

I tried to breathe through my nose, match the rhythm of the man's steps, and stop trembling with nerves. My fingers were chilly and not as nimble as usual. I would never have taken the risk if the man hadn't had three gold pieces in his pocket.

Someone pushed me in the back and for a second I found myself almost pressed up against the man, so I accepted this gift from the gods and lowered my hand into his pocket. I felt the purse immediately, and grabbed it, preparing to scram, but just at that moment the stranger grabbed hold of my hand. "*Got you, you little thief!*" *he hissed.*

I gave a shrill squeal and tried to break free, but the man was a lot stronger than me, and my hand didn't even shift in the grasp of his bearlike paw. The thought flashed through my mind that I was in for really big trouble now.

Bass came dashing up out of nowhere and gave the big lunk a smart kick on the leg. He howled and let go of me.

"*Let's get out of here!*" *Bass shouted, and legged it.*

Without bothering to think, I followed him, clutching the purse. I could hear the furious guy dashing after us.

"Thieves!" he yelled. "Stop those thieves!"

We wormed our way through the crowd and dashed out of Market Square onto a narrow little street. But that damn lunk was right there behind us all the way.

It was hard to run, the fur coat kept getting tangled round my legs, and the tramping feet of our pursuer kept getting closer and closer. Bass was showing me a clean pair of heels and the distance between us was gradually increasing. I groaned in disappointment: I would have to abandon the fur coat that I had acquired with such a great effort. I stuck the purse in my teeth and started unfastening the buttons as I ran along. The warm coat slipped off my shoulders and fell into the snow. Immediately it was much easier to run—I strode out and caught up with Bass.

"Into the alley," I shouted to him, and turned sharply to the right.

Bass followed me, and our pursuer, who was just about to grab me by the collar, went flying on past. Now we had at least a chance to disappear in the labyrinth of the Suburbs' winding side streets.

"Oh, he'll wring our necks!" Bass panted with an effort.

I didn't answer and just speeded up even more, hoping very much that my friend's prediction would not come true. We turned another corner, hearing the man threaten to pull our arms off. I was almost exhausted, but the cursed stranger didn't seem to know what it meant to get tired.

Suddenly a pair of hands appeared out of some hidey-hole, grabbed Bass and me by the scruff of our necks, and dragged us into a dark, narrow space. Bass yelled out in fright and started flailing at the air with his hands, and I followed my friend's example, trying to break free and give whoever had grabbed us a kick.

"Better shut up, if you want to live!" someone whispered. "Keep quiet!"

There was something about his voice that made us fall silent immediately.

Our pursuer went hurtling past, stamping his feet and setting the alley ringing with choice obscenities.

The man who had saved us still didn't release his grip, he was listening to the silence, and I tried to take advantage of the moment to put the purse with the gold pieces away in my pocket.

"No need to bother," said the stranger. "I don't steal from pickpockets."

"I'm not a pickpocket!" I protested, my teeth chattering from the cold. I was feeling the loss of the fur coat.

"Not a pickpocket? Then who are you?" asked the man who had rescued us.

"I'm a genuine thief!"

"A thie-ef! Well, well. I swear by Sagot that you might just become a good thief, with my help. Or you might not, kid. Let me have a look at what I've caught today."

The man opened his hands, walked out into the light, and inspected Bass and me closely.

"Well then, who are you?" the stranger asked.

"I'm Bass the Snoop," Bass said with a sniff.

"I'm Harold the Flea," I answered, studying our unlikely rescuer.

"Well now," the man said with a smile. "And I'm For. Sticky Hands For."

"Harold, do you know this goon?" Hallas asked, rousing me from my reminiscences.

"Yes, he's an old . . . friend of mine," I muttered.

"Very old," Bass said with a smile. "Glad to see you alive and well, Harold!"

"Likewise," I said in a none-too-friendly voice.

"How's For?" Bass asked, apparently not noticing my cool tone.

"Alive, by Sagot's will."

"Is he still instructing the young?" Bass asked with a smile.

"No, he's a priest now. Sagot's Defender of the Hands."

Bass whistled.

"Listen, Harold," said the gnome, whose patience had run out. "Maybe you and your friend could talk some other time? Thank you very much for the help, kind sir, but we have to be going."

"Deler," I said to the dwarf. "Give him his money back."

Amazingly enough, the dwarf delved into his purse and handed Bass three silver pieces.

"Hey!" Bass cried indignantly. "I don't want your coins. I was just helping a friend!"

"Everyone can always find a use for coins," I said. "Keep well. Ah yes, if you're interested, Markun is no longer in this world."

"And is that all?" he said, spreading his arms wide in protest. "Aren't you even going to talk to me? Are you just going to walk away when we haven't seen each other for more than ten years?"

"No time, my friend," I said curtly.

"How can I find you, Harold?" Bass shouted after me.

"I don't think we'll meet again," I said, looking round at him. "I'm only passing through. I'll be leaving the city soon."

And so saying, I turned away and hurried after Hallas. Kli-Kli couldn't resist asking: "Was that a friend of yours?"

"Yes . . . That is, no . . . maybe."

"Brrrrr," said the jester, shaking his head. "Is that yes or no? Make up your mind."

"Leave him alone, Kli-Kli," Eel advised the goblin.

"What have I done?" Kli-Kli asked with a shrug. "I only asked. Listen, Harold, are you so elegantly polite and considerate with everyone, or just the chosen few? I'm just asking to bear it in mind for the future, so I won't be too surprised when you tell me to get lost in such frank and charming manner when we meet."

"Chew your carrot!" I growled.

He grunted resentfully and took my advice, biting off a huge piece.

And just then we heard a loud howl ringing across the market: "Honorable sirs! Honorable sirs!"

"Does he mean us?" Eel asked, turning round just in case.

"Honorable sirs, wait!" shouted a decently dressed young lad, running toward us and waving his arms desperately in the air.

"He definitely wants us," said Eel, and stopped.

"What in the name of the underground kings does he want?" Deler muttered, narrowing his eyes suspiciously.

"Let's go," said Hallas, shoving his partner. "If we stand around waiting for everyone who starts shouting, we'll never get to the barber's before nightfall!"

"And if we keep walking, he'll run after us, bawling his head off," I objected reasonably. "That's one piece of luck we can do without."

"Uhu," said Kli-Kli, sinking his teeth into the carrot. "Hallas, your sleeve has ridden up your arm."

The gnome swore and pulled down the sleeve of his brown shirt to cover the tattoo of a red heart with teeth—the emblem of the Wild Hearts Brigade.

"Honorable sirs!" said the lad, breathing heavily. He was obviously worn out from chasing after us.

"What do you want, young man?" Hallas asked with a menacing

frown. "Don't you have anything better to do than go around yelling for all the town to hear?"

"I wanted to suggest—," the young lad began, but Deler interrupted him again:

"We're not buying!"

The dwarf and the gnome turned away and walked on, without even listening to what the poor panting fellow had to say. I shrugged. This youth was not going to sell anything to the gnome.

"Wait!" he shouted. "Aren't you the one looking for a barber?"

Hallas froze with one foot in midair, then slowly lowered it and turned in our direction. The expression on the gnome's face did not bode the young lad any good.

"How much?" the gnome asked, unfolding his fists.

"Free!"

That stopped our bearded friend dead in his tracks and set him thinking hard. He grunted, scratched the back of his head, and said: "I thought I heard you say that I can have my tooth pulled out absolutely free of charge. Is that right?"

"Absolutely right!"

"It's nonsense!" Deler rumbled. "Nothing's ever free!"

"That's what I think, too," said Hallas, giving the young lad another dark look.

"No, honorable sirs, I'm not lying! They'll do everything for you at the faculty of healers in the university without taking a single coin. And they're not barbers, but absolutely genuine healers. Luminaries of science. Professors!"

"Mm, is that so?" Hallas asked, still suspicious. "And don't these professors of yours have anything better to do than go around pulling everyone's teeth out?"

"But this is examination week at the university," the student explained. "The professors tell the senior classes how to treat ailments, and demonstrate at the same time, and then they ask questions to see how well we've learned it all. I happened to overhear your conversation with the barber."

Hallas sighed, and thought, then sighed again, narrowed his eyes, and said, "Lead on."

Naturally, they hadn't sent a cart for us, let alone a carriage, so we had to trudge all the way back on our own two feet.

Suddenly Kli-Kli gasped in fright and tugged at the edge of my jacket.

"Harold, look! Heartless Chasseurs!" he hissed in a theatrical whisper, pointing at the soldiers.

There were five of them, dressed in white uniform jackets and crimson trousers, walking toward us.

"What are we going to do?"

I wondered if Kli-Kli was in a real panic or just playing the fool.

"Smile," I hissed through clenched teeth, and stretched my lips out into an idiotic grin.

The Heartless Chasseurs walked past without even giving us a glance and Kli-Kli gave a sigh of relief.

"Phew!"

"Why were you so frightened of them?" I asked the goblin.

"Well, you know, after Vishki . . . ," Kli-Kli replied anxiously.

"Vishki? Calm down, Kli-Kli," Eel said with a smile. "I don't think the magicians have been broadcasting the fact that we escaped from them. They were up to no good in that village, and they'll keep quiet to avoid attracting unwelcome attention. Take no notice of these chasseurs, they're simply quartered in Ranneng and they don't know a blind thing about us."

The immense bronze gates of the University of Sciences were standing wide open in welcome to all who approached from the park that flourished between the Upper City, the university, and school of the Order. From a distance, we could make out an emblem on the gates, the mark of an ancient and venerable institution—an engraving of an open book, entwined with grape leaves.

The park in which the university stood was huge, magnificent, and beautiful. Once we were in it, I felt as if I had fallen into the magical forest of my childhood dreams where the oaks propped up the heavens with their green crowns the whole year round.

We followed our guide in through the gates and turned onto one of the shady stone pathways leading past the gray faculty buildings and into the heart of the university.

"Why aren't there any people here?" Deler asked curiously, gazing around on all sides.

"The students are either at their practical studies or taking the final examinations, or they've already gone off for vacation, honorable sir."

"And this—" Deler clicked his fingers, trying to remember the word. "—healing faculty of yours. Where's that?"

"Ah. The healing faculty's beside the morgue, so we won't see any of the students until we get there."

"Beside the morgue?" Hallas asked warily.

"That's in case they get it wrong when they pull your tooth out," Deler said to taunt the gnome. "So they don't have to carry the body too far."

"What are you croaking about, you ugly crow?" Hallas asked, and swore. "You dwarves are all like that, no good for anything but croaking misery and death. You croak away the centuries, and we dig the shafts and galleries for you."

"You dig them for us? Why, you can't make a single decent thing with your own hands. You're born mattockmen and you die mattockmen."

"That's enough," Eel barked. "Stop squabbling!"

A group of students was sitting on the grass under the trees and leafing lazily through their books.

"They're from the literary faculty," our guide said disdainfully when he caught my eye. "Bohemians."

Kli-Kli grunted theatrically at the sound of that word.

"What are you grunting for?" I asked him.

"You don't know what bohemians are!" Kli-Kli answered back. To prevent repetition of "but."

"Believe it or not, but I do," I disabused him. "My teacher's collection of books could rival the Royal Library."

"I don't really believe that. An educated thief is an absurdity."

"Oh, sure. Just like an educated goblin. What do you read in Zagraba apart from your Tre-Tre's books?"

"The great Tre-Tre," Kli-Kli corrected me automatically. "We have many ancient books, Harold-Barold. A lot more than you think! Many people would barter their souls just to get a glance at them."

Through the trees we saw a yellow three-story building with a broad stairway, covered as thickly with students as the Field of Sorna was with gnomes.

"An examination?" Deler asked, gazing round at the students leafing through their books.

"Yes, today the second year have anatomy," the young lad said with a frown. "Everyone who passes will go to the Sundrop to celebrate. So there'll be a right royal carousal tonight!"

Deler chuckled as if he had already started celebrating: "Hey, my friend Hallas! You've gone rather pale. Not scared, are you?"

"Gnomes don't get scared!" Hallas said proudly, and started climbing the steps on stiff legs.

"Let's just hope he doesn't faint," Kli-Kli whispered to me.

We walked into the building, down a long corridor crammed with excited students, and found ourselves in a hall.

The floor here sloped steeply away toward a desk, beside which a gray-haired teacher was making about twenty students watch as he hacked through a body lying on a stone table with something halfway between a saw and a knife.

"Professor!" our guide shouted out. "I've brought him!"

The professor looked from his attempt to saw open the poor corpse's skull and squinted at us short-sightedly.

"Well, at last! What a lot of them there are!"

"He's the only one with a bad tooth," Deler said hastily, pointing at Hallas.

Hallas shuddered and narrowed his eyes as he glared at the dwarf.

"A gnome? Hmm . . . Well, that will be instructive," said the professor, putting down his saw. "Come on down, respected sir, come on down."

"Go on, don't be afraid," said Deler, giving the gnome a push. "Harold, are you with us?"

"No," I said, "I think I'll just sit here on the bench."

"That's a mistake, think what a performance you'll miss!" said Kli-Kli, skipping happily down the steps after Deler and Hallas.

I sat down on one of the benches and started observing from a distance as they sat Hallas in a chair standing beside the table with the corpse on it. The professor washed his hands and picked up something that looked like an instrument of torture.

"Who was that man, your old friend?" Eel asked as he sat down beside me.

"You mean Bass? Is there some serious reason for your interest in my past?"

Eel paused before replying. He's the silent type, sometimes he doesn't open his mouth even once the whole day long.

"Both, to be honest. It's a strange coincidence that we ran into someone who knows you. You suddenly spotted an old enemy. And then, just a few minutes later, an old acquaintance of yours turns up. Just recently I've started feeling wary of any kind of coincidence or chance event. And, pardon me, but I don't trust anyone but myself. I'm feeling a little concerned about this Bass who suddenly showed up out of nowhere."

I knew Eel's iron character—it was practically impossible to disconcert him with any sort of surprise—and so the words "a little concerned" on his lips meant a great deal.

I paused, trying to gather my thoughts, because I didn't like talking to people about my life. The less other people knew about you, the better protected you were against all kinds of surprises.

For had hammered that wisdom into my head a long time before, and as time passed I came to realize that my old teacher was absolutely right. No one in Avendoom knew about Shadow Harold's feelings and attachments, and no one could put pressure on me by using my friends and dear ones. Because I didn't chatter much and minded my own business, I wasn't too worried about suddenly being stabbed in the back.

But I trusted the tight-lipped Garrakian.

Eel was probably one of the few people with whom I was not afraid of opening up and pouring out my soul, knowing that he would take everything he heard from me to the grave with him.

"We were friends ever since we were kids," I began. "We lived in the slums of Avendoom, and we went through a lot together . . . hunger, freezing winters, raids by the guards. . . . We survived all sorts of things. . . . Bass and I looked out for each other and more or less managed to make ends meet until a master thief took us under his wing. His name was For. . . .

"That man taught us a lot. . . . For used to say I had a natural gift for thievery, and maybe he was right. Bass wasn't quite so . . . When were living on the street, I was the one who picked people's pockets, not him. My friend had a different passion—cards and dice. For eventually gave up on my friend, and Bass got more and more involved in gambling."

I frowned. I still found remembering this episode from the past as painful as ever.

"A couple of times he got himself into nasty situations when he was completely wiped out. Back then For was a major figure in the criminal world of Avendoom and he was able to get his pupil off the hook. But everything has to come to an end sometime. One day Bass got into really serious trouble—my friend found himself owing a large sum of money to Markun, a man who was the head of the Avendoom Guild of Thieves for a long time. Bass didn't tell me or For anything about it. He just took our money and disappeared. He stole his teacher's and his friend's gold. Then the rumors spread that Markun's lads had left him floating under the piers, but the body was never found. For these last twelve years For and I thought that Bass was dead. So you can imagine how amazed I was to see him in Ranneng, alive and well."

"Yes indeed . . . ," Eel grunted. "Let's hope that your meeting really was just coincidence. . . . You're not planning to meet up with him for a talk?"

"No," I replied without even thinking about it, and the conversation fizzled out of its own accord.

Eel and I turned our attention back to what was happening down by the lectern.

The professor was clutching the instrument of torture in one hand as he lectured the students.

". . . As you can see, the dental system of gnomes is rather similar to the human dental system. But there are certain differences. The structure of the skull and the alveolar appendages is not quite the same in gnomes. This race has a straight bite, and fewer teeth than humans— only twenty-four, twelve in each jaw. They have no canines and only one set of premolars. Unfortunately, my friends, I am not able to show you the teeth of orcs or elves. But believe me, they are absolutely identical, which proves just how closely related the two races are. The hyper-development of the lower canines has led to the development of a rather specific bite in the elves and the Firstborn—when the mouth is opened, the lower jaw is displaced. . . . But I am digressing. The reason that has brought our patient to us today is the fourth tooth on the upper right. I am inclined to believe that the factor that induced the pain was abrupt hypothermia of the entire organism. But here, of course, it would be better to take a case history, because suppositions will not get you very far. I remember I had a case in which my patient . . ."

"I think this will go on and on for a very long time," Eel chuckled.

The Garrakian wasn't the only one who thought so. Several of the students were looking quite frankly bored. Kli-Kli was gazing curiously at the glittering knife left lying beside the corpse, and Deler was yawning desperately, covering his mouth with his massive hand. Hallas was squirming impatiently in the chair, his color gradually changing from pale to scarlet. Just as the talkative professor started analyzing the tenth clinical case from his own practice, the gnome's patience finally ran out.

"Aaah! I swear by the ice-worms!" the gnome roared, then he leapt up out of his chair and set off resolutely in our direction.

"Where are you going, dear sir?" the professor exclaimed in amazement. "What about the tooth?"

All the students, suddenly roused from their lethargy, started gaping wide-eyed at the gnome.

When he heard the question, Hallas stopped, turned round, and made an indecent gesture to everyone there. The poor professor clutched at his heart. Pleased with the effect he had created, the gnome strode on toward the exit with his head held high.

"And where to now, Hallas?" Deler asked.

"To a tavern! Maybe drink will do something to ease this damned pain. . . ."

The gnome strode in determinedly through the door of the Sundrop tavern. It was probably the worst of all such establishments in the Upper City. Although it was so close to the university and the school of magicians, the characters who gathered there were by no means the most trustworthy types.

My cautious glance immediately picked out a table with five Doralissians and a table with men wearing the badge of the Guild of Stonemasons. The Doralissians and the masons were eyeing each other dourly, but had not yet moved on to active hostilities. I was inclined to think that things wouldn't get as far as a fight until the lads downed another five jugs of wine.

Another danger zone in the bar room of the Sundrop was the tables where a dozen or so Heartless Chasseurs were sitting, apparently celebrating a leave pass. They cast sideways glances at the Doralissians and the stonemasons. The soldiers' faces were set in an expression of gloomy determination to batter the faces of both groups if they tried to stop them having a good time.

Of course, there were plenty of ordinary folks in a more peaceable frame of mind, but there was definitely tension in the air and the innkeeper was dashing about like a lunatic, trying to defuse the situation.

"Hmm . . . ," I said, trying to shout above the din. "Maybe we should find somewhere a bit calmer?"

"Don't be afraid, Harold, you're with me!" Hallas declared, taking a seat at the only free table, which was right beside the bar.

I wasn't afraid. I had no doubt that if the regulars of this tavern suddenly found themselves in the Knife and Ax, they would faint in sheer fright. But why were we here? What was the point in sticking your nose into a bear's den just for the sake of a fight? We needed to take good care of ourselves.

A serving wench appeared in front of us as if by magic.

"Beer for these four, and something very, very strong for me," said the gnome.

"We have wheat liquor and krudr—Doralissian vodka."

"Mix the liquor with the krudr, add some dark beer and a bit of Gnome's Fire," the gnome decided after a moment's thought. "Do you have Gnome's Fire?"

"We can probably find some, sir."

If the serving wench was surprised by this strange selection, she didn't show it.

"Listen, Hallas," Deler said to the gnome, "if you want to commit suicide, you don't have to drink garbage. Just tell me, and I'll dispatch you to the next world at the drop of a hat."

Hallas adopted a rather unusual tactic in response to this jibe—he ignored it.

"And no beer for me, please, just carrot juice," Kli-Kli put in.

"We don't serve that here."

"Well, some other kind of juice, as long as it tastes good."

"We don't have any," the serving wench said, not very politely.

"How about milk? Do you have milk?"

"Beer."

"All right then, beer." Kli-Kli sighed disappointedly.

"Fancy finding people like this in such a place!" said a familiar voice.

Lamplighter, Arnkh, and Marmot walked up to us. Invincible jumped off Marmot's shoulder, thudded down onto our table, and started twitching his pink nose in hopes of finding something tasty to eat. Kli-Kli thrust a carrot at the ling, but the beast just bared his teeth. He didn't give a damn for the goblin's attempts to make friends with him.

"What wind blows you in here?" the gnome asked the new arrivals in a none-too-friendly voice.

"I can tell you're not very pleased to see us," Arnkh laughed as he took a seat.

Mumr and Marmot followed their companion's example, although Marmot had to take a chair from the next table, where the goat-men were sitting. The Doralissians looked the warrior over dourly, but they didn't bother him, deciding that it wasn't worth risking their horns and beards for anything as petty as a chair.

"He's not pleased to see anyone today," Deler replied for the gnome.

"Have they pulled that tooth out?" Lamplighter asked.

"Listen, Mumr," Hallas said irritably, "go tootle your whistle and leave me alone."

"Oo-oo-ooh, things are really bad," said Lamplighter, shaking his head with disappointment.

"Why hasn't it been pulled out?" asked Arnkh, joining in the conversation.

"I changed my mind!" the gnome suddenly exploded. "I'm allowed to change my mind, aren't I?"

"All right, Hallas, all right," Arnkh said good-naturedly, trying to calm the gnome down. "So you changed your mind. What's all the shouting about?"

The serving wench brought beer for us and the fiery mixture for Hallas. She took the order from the three Wild Hearts who had just joined us and went away again.

"So how do you come to be here?" I asked Marmot, who was feeding his ling.

"Arnkh dragged us out for a walk round the city. It's a lousy little town. And we dropped in here to wet our whistles."

"And did you see anything interesting in the city?" Kli-Kli asked, sniffing cautiously at the beer he had been served: It was obviously not much to his liking. "Hallas, why aren't you drinking?"

"And you?" the gnome snarled back, staring at his booze as if there was a dead snake floating in it.

"I'm sniffing it!" Kli-Kli retorted. "That's quite enough for me!"

"Me, too."

"Well now, the krudr smells even worse than the goats," Lamplighter chuckled.

"Well, how do you like the race of gnomes?" Deler asked with a cunning grin as he took a sip of dark beer. "Afraid of having a tooth pulled on, so they order a brew of fire and they're afraid to drink that, too."

"Who's afraid, hathead? On the Field of Sorna we weren't afraid to break your horns for you, and you think we're afraid to drink this water? Watch!"

Hallas poured the liquid down his throat in a single gulp, without pausing for breath. I shuddered. One drop of the explosive mixture that the gnome had ordered would have been enough to fell a h'san'kor.

Our bearded friend drank, grunted, banged his mug down on the table, focused his wandering eyes together on a single point, and flared his nostrils as he tried to figure out what he was feeling. We all gazed at him in genuine admiration.

"That's dis . . . ," the gnome said, scorching us all with the indescribable aroma of that repulsive mixture. "That's dis . . . disgusting, may the Nameless One take me!"

"Are you alive?" Deler asked, squinting warily at his friend.

"No, I'm already in the light! The only time I've ever felt this good was when you dragged my butt off that Crayfish Duke's scaffold! Wench! Another three mugs of the same brew!"

"Well then?" Marmot asked after a pause. "Shall we drink to Tomcat?"

"May the earth be a feather mattress to him, and the grass his blanket!" said Lamplighter, raising his mug.

"May he walk in the light," said Hallas.

"A good winter to him," said Eel.

We drank in silence, without clinking glasses.

That's the way it goes: Some are already in the light, and some are still alive. Tomcat had been left behind in the ground beside the old ravine in Hargan's Wasteland, the first to die of those who had set out to escort me to Hrad Spein. I hoped very much that the Wild Hearts' scout would also be the last one to die during our journey.

Time passed imperceptibly, people came and people went; the stonemasons, Doralissians, and chasseurs kept filling themselves up with wine. Two hours later, when I had my third mug of beer standing in front of me, and Hallas had the eighth mug of his fiery "remedy," an old man with a whistle appeared out of nowhere and started playing a jolly djanga.

Those who were most sober and could still stand firmly on their feet got up and started dancing. Arnkh grabbed a serving wench by the arms, setting her squealing in indignation and then in delight, and launched into the swirling dance. The stonemasons sang along merrily, the Doralissians banged their fists on the table, and we stamped our feet, trying to keep time with the music. Only Hallas paid no attention to the general merriment and systematically drank his swill.

A gnome or a dwarf can drink as much as an entire crowd of men and still not get drunk. But Hallas had had more than enough, his speech was getting noticeably slurred, his nose had turned red, and his eyes were glittering. The apotheosis of the cure came when he made a confession of genuine love to Deler.

"Hey you! Hatface! What would I do without your ugly mug to look at?" the gnome muttered drunkenly and tried to kiss his friend. "Wench! Hic! The same again!"

A little more time went by, and my comrades were no longer even thinking of going anywhere else. They had a new entertainment now—Mumr and Marmot were trying to stare down the Doralissians. Each side was trying to drill a hole in the other. The stonemasons, realizing that they might have acquired new allies, started getting a bit livelier, and the chasseurs started wondering whose side to take in the fight ahead.

The gentlemen students came pouring into the tavern in a jolly crowd to celebrate passing their exam. Hallas fell into a doze on Lamplighter's shoulder and Deler heaved a sigh of relief—the irascible gnome had finally shut his mouth.

Rather unexpectedly a quarrel sprang up at our table about the cuisines of the various races of Siala. The dwarf thumped himself on the chest and said that no one knew how to cook better than his race, to which Kli-Kli replied by suggesting we should wake Hallas and ask his opinion on the matter. Deler said rather hastily that it probably wasn't worth waking him up, gnomes didn't have a blind notion about food in any case—it was enough to remember the chow the gnome had cooked up during our journey.

"In general, the goblins are masters at preparing any kind of food," Kli-Kli claimed.

"Right, only normal people can't eat your grub," Lamplighter snorted.

"It's hard to call you Wild Hearts normal people," Kli-Kli objected. "I'm sure you eat all sorts of garbage on your raids into the Deserted Lands."

"There have been times," Lamplighter agreed. "I remember once we had to eat the meat of a snow troll, and that, I tell you, is some chow!"

"Aw, come on, now," Kli-Kli said impatiently, taking a sniff at the beer in his mug to pep himself up. "What kind of exotic food's that? Troll meat! Ha!"

"Have you tried anything more unusual, then?" Eel asked the goblin.

"Sure I have!" Kli-Kli declared proudly. "We even have an old drinking song about food like that."

"Right then, give us a blast," Mumr suggested.

"No, don't," said Deler, waving his hands in the air. "I know what you greenskins are like. Worse than those bearded loons! If you start to sing, you'll have every dog within a league howling."

"It's an interesting song. It's called 'The Fly in the Plate,'" the jester said with a grin.

"Drink your beer, Kli-Kli, and keep quiet," Lamplighter warned the goblin in a threatening voice. The little ratbag sighed in resignation and stuck his nose into his mug.

"Good gentlemen!" said an old fellow who had come up to our table. "Help a poor invalid, buy him a mug of beer."

"You don't look much like an invalid," growled Deler, whom the gods had not blessed with the gift of generosity.

"But I am," the beggar said with a tragic sigh. "I spent ten years wandering the deserts of the distant Sultanate, and I left all my strength and my fortune behind in the sand."

"Right," Deler chortled mistrustfully. "In the Sultanate! I don't think you've ever been more than ten yards away from the walls of Ranneng."

"I've got proof," said the old man. He was swaying on his feet a bit; he'd obviously already taken a good skinful that day. "Look!"

With a theatrical gesture the old man pulled something from under his old patched cloak, something that looked a bit like a finger, only it was three times bigger and it was green, and it had thorns on it, and it was in a small flowerpot.

"What kind of beast is that?" Deler asked, moving back warily to a safe distance from this strange object.

"Ah, these young people," said the old man, shaking his head. "Haven't been taught a thing. It's a cactus!"

"And just what sort of cactus is that?" the dwarf asked.

"The absolutely genuine kind! The rare flower of the desert, with healing properties, and it blossoms once every hundred years."

"What a load of nonsense!" Arnkh pronounced after inspecting the rare flower of the desert suspiciously.

"Aw, come on, buy grandpa some beer," good-natured Lamplighter put in.

"And not just grandpa," Hallas muttered, opening his eyes. "Me, too! Only not beer, but that stuff I was drinking already. My tooth's started aching again!"

"Go to sleep!" Deler hissed at the gnome. "You've had enough for today."

"Aha!" the gnome snorted. "Sure! Some old-timer can have a drink, but I can't! I'm going to get up and get it for myself."

"How can you get up, Hallas? Your legs won't hold you."

"Oh yes they will!" the gnome protested. He moved his chair and stood up. "See!"

He was swaying quite noticeably from side to side, which made him look like a sailor during a raging storm at sea.

Hallas took a couple of uncertain steps and bumped into a Doralissian who was carrying a mug full of krudr back to his table; the entire drink spilled on the goat-man's chest.

The bearded drunk glanced up at the Doralissian towering over him, smiled sweetly, and said what you should never say to any member of the Doralissian race: "Hello there, goat! How's life?"

On hearing what his people regard as the deadliest of insults (the word "goat"), the Doralissian didn't hold back: He socked the gnome hard in the teeth.

When Deler saw somebody else hit his friend, he howled, grabbed a chair, and smashed it against the Doralissian's head. The Doralissian collapsed as if his legs had been scythed away.

"Mumr, give me a hand!" said Deler, grabbing the goat-man under the arms.

Lamplighter rushed to help him. They lifted up the unconscious Doralissian and on the count of three launched him on a long-distance flight to the chasseurs' table.

The soldiers accepted this gift with wide-open arms and immediately dispatched it homeward, to the table where several rather angry goat-men were already getting to their feet. The Heartless Chasseurs didn't have as much experience as Deler and Lamplighter in the launching of unconscious bodies, so the Doralissian fell short of the target and came crashing down on the stonemasons. That seemed to be just what they had been waiting for. They jumped to their feet and went dashing at the chasseurs, fists at the ready. The Doralissians ignored the brawl between the soldiers and the masons and attacked us.

Kli-Kli squealed and dived under the table. Knowing the incredible strength possessed by the mistake of the gods that is known as a goat-man, I grabbed the legendary cactus plant off the table and threw it into the face of the nearest attacker. The owner of the cactus and my target both cried out at the same time. One in outrage, the other in pain. The old-timer dashed to rescue his precious plant from under the goat's hooves and the Doralissian made a repulsive bleating sound as he pulled the prickles out of his nose.

By this time the fight had become universal. Everybody was fighting everybody. There were beer mugs flying through the air, aimed at any dopes who were still getting their bearings. One almost caught Marmot in the head, but he ducked just in time.

The wailing landlord tried to halt the destruction of his property, but he got a punch in the face from one of the goats and collapsed under the bar. Another beer mug went flying into a group of students and they dashed to attack the chasseurs.

"Harold! Stop getting under my feet!" Deler growled as he made a beeline for the next enemy. He took aim and kicked him between the legs.

I jumped back from the table, leaving the Wild Hearts to take the bumps and the bruises, since that was their job anyway—to protect me from all sorts of unpleasantness.

Eel, Lamplighter, and Marmot lined up in wedge formation and took on anyone who came within striking range. Eel doled out his punches sparingly and precisely, and anyone who was still standing after an encounter with the Garrakian was left for Lamplighter or Marmot to finish off.

The ling on Marmot's shoulder flew into a fury and squealed piercingly, trying to bite anyone he could reach with his teeth. Then, realizing that if he stayed on his master's shoulder he would miss all the fun, Invincible jumped onto the nearest enemy and sank his teeth into his nose.

"Harold! Out of the way!"

Arnkh pushed me aside, grabbed one of the chasseurs by the sides of his chest, and butted him in the face. Then another met the same fate. And another. The bald head of the warrior from the Border Kingdom was a truly fearsome weapon.

But there's always a ballista for every dragon. One of the stonemasons crept up on Arnkh from behind and smashed him over the head with a bottle that shattered into smithereens. Arnkh swayed on his feet and the stonemason, encouraged by his initial success, swung back his fist with the broken bottle.

Kli-Kli darted out from under the table and kicked the enemy on the knee with all his might. The stonemason dropped his weapon, cursed wildly, and tried to grab Kli-Kli by the scruff of the neck, but the nimble goblin slipped between the man's legs and gave the stonemason a hefty kick up the backside.

I added my own modest contribution with a sweet punch to his stomach. The enemy doubled over and Kli-Kli promptly repeated his blow to the fifth point, while I chopped him in the throat with the side of my hand. The lad rolled his eyes up resentfully and collapsed on the floor.

"Are you all right?" I asked Arnkh, holding him by the shoulder just to be on the safe side.

"Yeah," he mumbled. "Who did that to me?"

"There he is!" said Kli-Kli, pointing to the man lying on the floor.

"Give him a kick for me, please," said Arnkh, wincing, and Kli-Kli promptly did just as his comrade asked.

"It's getting too hot around here. Time to be leaving," said Lamplighter. He had a huge black eye.

"Screw that!" Deler panted as he fought off two Doralissians at the same time with a chair. "The real fun's only just beginning! Are you just going to watch or is someone going to help me with these goats?"

"You'll pay-ay for calling us goa-oats!" one of the Doralissians bleated, bringing his fist down on the short dwarf's head.

Deler skipped aside, smashed the chair into the ribs of the Doralissian who was trying to hit him, and jumped back out of the way, yielding his position to the "heavy cavalry" in the form of five bellicose chasseurs. The lads in red and white hung on the Doralissians' shoulders like bunches of grapes and set about pummeling their faces with military thoroughness.

A free space had opened up around Eel—no one else wanted to risk going up against the Garrakian. Maybe I just imagined it, but the warrior seemed a bit upset by this turn of events. He'd only just got into the swing of things!

"Can you stand?" I asked Arnkh, lowering him carefully onto the only surviving stool.

"Don't worry about me! I'm not a porcelain plate," he hissed, and frowned as he touched the lump on the back of his head.

"Those students are lively lads!" Marmot exclaimed. He had finally finished pounding his fist into the face of the largest stonemason and now he was observing the rough-and-tumble in the next corner of the tavern with academic interest.

The students had approached the fight in typically inventive, daredevil fashion. By turning over several tables, they had constructed an improvised barricade and then laid down what the gnomes call covering artillery fire, using beer mugs. After that they launched themselves, roaring in unison, against the Heartless Chasseurs and their sympathizers.

One of the fallen tried to crawl to the door and slip away. But he was too late. The door came flying off its hinges, and the guards appeared in the tavern.

"Nobody move! You're all under arrest!" one of the soldiers shouted, but he immediately took a beer mug to the helmet and slumped to his knees.

The guards were offended at not being taken seriously, and a stonemason who was about to launch a bottle in their direction fell with a crossbow bolt in his leg.

"Let's scram!" shouted one of the students.

The most quick-witted individuals started leaving the Sundrop via the broken windows.

After a brief moment's thought, Marmot dragged a frightened serving wench out from under the bar.

"Where's the back entrance?" he asked.

"That way!" the girl said, nodding toward the kitchen.

"Let's clear out, lads!" Marmot called as he dashed in the direction indicated.

Moving in close formation, our entire group followed his example. In the course of the tactical withdrawal Lamplighter and Deler took the opportunity to batter the face of the last Doralissian still on his feet.

"By the hundred sublunary kings!" Deler exclaimed, slapping himself on the forehead. "We've forgotten Hallas, burn his rotten beard!"

The tavern was already crammed with so many guards that they outnumbered the brawlers, and Hallas had to be dragged out from under the very feet of servants of the law.

The gnome had more or less snapped out of it and he started hobbling toward the back entrance, supported by Deler and Mumr. We slipped through the kitchen, frightening the cook on the way, and out into a dark back alley. Deler sang the dwarves' military march and Kli-Kli backed him up in a shrill little voice. Lamplighter grunted contentedly. The lads had really enjoyed the little set-to.

We must have been sitting there with our beer for quite a long time, because it was dark outside. Once out in the alley, we started scuttling away from the tavern, but then Hallas stopped dead in his tracks and yelled: "My sack!"

Shoving aside anyone who tried to stop him, the gnome went dashing back to the tavern.

"What an idiot!" Marmot hissed.

"He'll get into trouble! As sure as eggs he will," said Deler, preparing to rush after his friend.

"You stay where you are!" Eel snapped. "I'm not going to drag two of you out of the slammer."

Deler muttered an obscenity through his teeth. But he stayed where he was, staring impatiently at the bright rectangle of the open door. That minute seemed like an eternity. . . .

Eventually Hallas appeared, carrying his beloved sack.

"It's a pity that goat didn't smash your stupid head in!" Deler exclaimed, but there was a note of relief in his voice.

"Let's go," Eel said tersely, assuming command of our small unit.

"Marmot, you didn't forget your mouse in the tavern, did you?" Kli-Kli asked in alarm.

"I'll forget you before I forget Invincible," Marmot growled.

"Oo-oo-oh, you're mean," said the goblin, offended. "And it's been a bad day today all round!"

"And why's that?" Arnkh asked in surprise. "By definition you don't have any bad days."

"Well, think about it," said Kli-Kli, trying to match Arnkh's stride. "We wandered into the city and spent the whole day staggering around, Hallas still didn't get his tooth pulled out, and tomorrow we have to move on."

"Absolute disaster!" Marmot said.

"Hey," Hallas sighed in distress. "I forgot something."

"What else have you forgotten now?" Mumr asked in annoyance. "You've got your sack."

"I forgot my pipe! My pipe! It must have fallen out of my mouth when that damned goat poked me in the face!"

"Why, that's excellent," said Deler, who couldn't stand tobacco smoke. "Now you can take a break from smoking."

"It's a briar pipe," Hallas exclaimed, continuing his lament. "A family relic! Maybe I should go back for it?"

"Just you try it. Then you can sort things out with Uncle yourself," Eel warned the gnome.

"All right," said Hallas, spitting on the ground. "I've got a spare in my saddlebag."

"How's your tooth?" I asked the gnome. Hallas hadn't done any howling for a suspiciously long time.

"It's gone, Sagra be praised!"

"What?"

"That goat thumped me so hard he knocked the rotten thing out!"

"There now, Hallas," Deler laughed. "See what a noble barber you found for yourself. Thick-headed, with horns and a little beard, too! Why, just like you!"

The dark alley rang to loud roars of laughter, and Hallas laughed along with everyone else.

Three times guards who had been put on the alert went running past and we had to hide in the shadows of the buildings. Eel decided not to take any risks, and we took a long detour to avoid running into the guardians of public order, who were as ornery as wasps in early autumn. Eventually we came out onto the street leading to the Learned Owl.

3

We got back to the tavern without any adventures. When I say without any adventures, I mean nothing terrible happened on the way home: Mumr didn't try to conjure the call of a deliriously happy donkey out of his reed pipe; Hallas didn't get into an argument with anyone; Kli-Kli didn't hike up the skirts of any venerable matrons, sing vulgar little songs, or make faces at the guard; and Eel didn't slit anyone's throat out of the kindness of his heart.

Walking through the city with my comrades was like dancing a djanga with the Nameless One on a bone-china plate suspended over a chasm full of boiling lava—at any moment the sorcerer might roast you alive, or the plate might shatter, leaving you to take a rather unpleasant bath.

"Home, sweet home!" Kli-Kli sang as he slipped in through the gates of the Learned Owl. "Hey, get off! That hurts!"

These last remarks were addressed to Eel, who had grabbed the jester's shoulder in a crayfish-tight grip.

"Don't move," Eel whispered. "There's something wrong here. Harold, do you notice anything?"

"It's too quiet," I replied, looking round the dark courtyard. "The lantern over the door isn't lit. I think it's broken. . . . There's not a single attendant, and this morning they were as thick as flies in the yard. The only lights are on the ground floor."

"Trouble?" Marmot's dagger jangled quietly as it slid out of its sheath.

"I don't know," Eel muttered, letting go of Kli-Kli and taking out his daggers. "But somehow I don't recall seeing any crossbow bolts in the wall this morning."

That was when I noticed the bolt sticking out of the wall of the inn, which was brightly lit by the moonlight.

"Split up," Deler commanded. "Harold, you're a thief, creep across and try to take a look in the window. We need to find out who came visiting."

I may be a thief, but I'm not suicidal. I didn't get a chance to say that out loud. A dark silhouette stirred in the shadow beside the door, a pair of amber-yellow eyes glinted, and a voice asked: "Where have you been all this time?"

My heart tumbled into my boots and lay there like a frightened rabbit, skipping three beats—I thought the color of the messenger's eyes had changed to red, and I didn't recognize Ell's voice straightaway.

"What's happened, Ell?" Kli-Kli asked, and was just about to go dashing over to the elf, but he was stopped by Eel's cool command.

"Don't move, Kli-Kli."

The goblin froze on the spot and looked round at the Garrakian warrior. Eel hadn't put his daggers back in their sheaths yet.

"Don't you recognize Ell?"

"Come out into the light, Ell, if you wouldn't mind," the Garrakian said softly instead of answering the goblin.

Far too softly and calmly! Eel was as tense as a taut bowstring, poised to discharge its arrow at the enemy.

Why did he suspect the elf?

A stupid question. Like me, the warrior surely remembered Miralissa telling us that some of the Nameless One's servants could change their shape so that they looked like your friends, or even make themselves invisible. It was one of those creatures that Tomcat and Egrassa had killed near the shamans' camp during our journey.

"What's wrong, Eel?" the elf asked in a rather unfriendly hiss.

The Garrakian didn't trust anyone, but for an elf unjustified mistrust is a serious insult. So serious that it can even lead to a duel. But Eel wasn't easily frightened, he knew what he was doing.

"Just come out into the light, that's all. You know as well as I do what strange things have been happening to us recently."

Ell stopped arguing and did as he was asked. He cast a quizzical glance at Eel. Swarthy skin, black lips, ash-gray hair with a fringe falling down over his yellow eyes, a pair of huge fangs, a black rose—the emblem of his house—embroidered on his shirt, a heavy elfin bow, and the inevitable s'kash behind his back. Miralissa's k'lissang gently extended his lips out into a faint mocking smile.

"Well? Do I look right?"

Eel maintained a gloomy silence, studying the elf's face. Almost casually Deler darted to the left and Arnkh to the right, outflanking the dark elf.

"If I wanted to stop you, you wouldn't get ten steps," said the elf.

What's true is true. Unlike Miralissa and Egrassa, Ell had no knowledge of shamanism (magic is a matter for the higher clans of the elfin houses), but he was a superb shot. All seven of us would have got an arrow in the eye before Kli-Kli could even say "Boo!"

"Yes, it's you," Eel said with a nod, and put his daggers away in their sheaths, while keeping his eyes on the elf's bow. "Sorry."

I couldn't hear any remorse in the proud Garrakian's voice.

"Praiseworthy caution." Ell's lips curved into a genuine smile.

"What's happened?" Kli-Kli asked with a sniff.

"Go inside, Miralissa will tell you everything. Then one of you can relieve me. . . . We have to find Honeycomb, too."

"Where's he gone off to?" asked Deler, as puzzled as all the rest of us.

"Ask Miralissa," the elf said curtly, and disappeared into the darkness.

"He's hiding in the shadows. Ha! But see the way his eyes glow! A blind man could spot him, and a gnome certainly could," Hallas declared boastfully.

"You're wrong," said Eel, shaking his head. "He wanted us to see him. Never underestimate an elf, gnome."

Hallas grunted, tugged on his beard, and walked into the inn, but I didn't think he had changed his opinion about an elf's skill when it came to lying in ambush. I followed him in and froze in the doorway—the floor was wet with wine that had soaked into the boards. The reason for this disgraceful state of affairs was a large wine barrel on a stand, into which some swine had fired five crossbow bolts. Naturally, all the wine had spilled out onto the floor, almost flooding the inn.

There were lots of bolts stuck in the oak door leading to the kitchen, and we saw at least as many in the walls. Most of the tables and chairs had been overturned or moved. And there were six bodies lying beside the bar counter.

I recognized one of the dead—it was the innkeeper, Master Pito. I could tell that three others were members of his staff. The final two were unfamiliar to me, and they had been slashed with a sword instead of shot with bolts like the master of the establishment and his employees.

Miralissa, Egrassa, and Alistan were standing in the very center of the large room. Milord Markauz was impassively cleaning the blood off his Canian-forged battery sword, while the elves were talking to each other in low voices. Uncle was sitting on the bar, clutching a beer mug in his left hand. The sergeant's left shoulder was bandaged up and there was blood seeping through the white material.

"So there you are, rot your souls!" he swore as soon as he saw us. "In the name of the Nameless One, what are you doing wandering the streets when I need you here? I'll tear your heads off, damn you, you assholes. Do I have to carry the can for all of you, may a stinking goat dance on your bones!"

"What happened?" Deler asked guiltily.

Quite uninhibited by Miralissa's presence, Uncle proceeded to say what he thought of us in a style that we would understand, one best suited to conversation between stevedores in the Port City. The only more or less normal words I made out in his monologue were "have," "on," "go," and "to."

No one risked trying to interrupt him, and when he finished blowing off steam the sergeant finally condescended to explain. . . .

Alistan, Uncle, Loudmouth, and Honeycomb had been the only ones left in the inn. Less than an hour after we left, a group of strangers with crossbows had broken in and without any explanation started trying to dispatch everyone to the next world.

Honeycomb had pulled Uncle off his chair just in time, and the sergeant had taken a crossbow bolt in the shoulder instead of the heart, but the unfortunate Master Pito and his staff had been riddled with bolts. Honeycomb and Uncle had made a dash for the safety of the kitchen and Alistan had followed the two Wild Hearts, after first putting his sword to use and killing two enemies who had already emptied their crossbows. The Wild Hearts had barricaded the oak door of the kitchen, and the attackers had not even attempted to break it down.

But Loudmouth had been unlucky—when his comrades retreated to the kitchen, he was on the other side of the hall with three crossbows trained on him.

"When we came out after they left," Uncle continued, "the whole wall where those bastards caught him off his guard was studded with bolts, and the floor was covered in blood."

"I don't see his body," said Eel, nodding toward the dead men lying beside the bar.

"We didn't see it, either."

"You think they took him with them? But what for?"

"I don't know, perhaps he's still alive."

Alive? Miracles are too rare in this world to hope that things could have worked out like that.

I had no doubt at all that Loudmouth was dead. If the attackers had killed the harmless innkeeper without the slightest qualm, they would surely have shot an experienced soldier on the spot. As for the body . . . who could tell what they might need it for? Yet another irretrievable loss for our little band. Good-bye, Loudmouth.

"What did those men want?" I asked Miralissa, setting aside my thoughts on the death of one more of our comrades.

"The Key, Harold. They took the Key."

Things were getting worse and worse! Fortune and her little sister Lady Luck were definitely not on our side today.

"What Key is that?" asked Deler, who, like the rest of the Wild Hearts, knew nothing about that story. Miralissa and Alistan had not thought it necessary to tell the members of the team about the elfin relic.

"Without the Key it's doubtful if I can even get into the heart of Hrad Spein," I explained to the dwarf. "Basically, if we don't have it, we might as well not go anywhere, we can just sit here and wait for the Nameless One to arrive in Ranneng. No Key, no Rainbow Horn!"

"Shtikhs!" Deler swore in gnomish, and his frown darkened even further. "And how could they have found out about this key of yours?"

"Who knows?" said Egrassa, taking the slim silver crown off his head and tossing it onto a table in annoyance. "Human cities are full of talkative little birds. Someone knew, someone blabbed, someone heard and took action. We've lost one of the most important elfin relics!"

About fifteen hundred years earlier, when the elves and the orcs had only just finished building the upper halls of the Palaces of Bone (that was after they stopped even visiting the lower levels of the ogres), both races regarded Hrad Spein as a holy place and would not risk spilling each other's blood in the labyrinths. But their hatred had proved too strong and war had broken out under the ground, too. The palaces had become deadly places for the Firstborn and the elves. And ever since those ancient times Hrad Spein had been a dangerous place, filled with many things that even ogres spoke about only in whispers.

To this day no one knows who (or what) founded those Palaces of Bone so deep under the ground at a time when the race of ogres was still young.

It was only later that the ogres transformed Hrad Spein into burial chambers (and then their bad example was followed by the orcs, elves, and men), but no one has yet worked out what the original purpose of the underground labyrinths was.

The race of ogres occupied the lower levels and started to construct their own, but they lost their minds and their reason, becoming stupid, bloodthirsty animals. The elves and orcs took the ogres' place, but they were smarter than their predecessors and didn't go down into the gloomy depths of the lower level of Night. In fact, they didn't even risk going down into the former realms of the ogres, fearing that they would awaken the ogres' dark shamanism.

But the blood of the two younger races drove them on to do what reason had prohibited. Blood and hate were the two edges of the sword that slashed the rip in reason's defenses.

The elves and the Firstborn realized just in time that they must get out of the path of the evil that had awoken in those deep underground halls, and before it could break out, the elves blocked its path with Doors on the third level, cutting off the passage from one level to another.

The Doors were created using the magic of the dark elves' shamans and the light elves' magicians. In order to lock them, the elves needed a magic key, and for help in making it they turned to the dwarves, to whom they lied that they were sealing up the palaces so that the orcs could not get in. The Key had sealed the Doors forever, and there were very few bold enough to venture down into the depths of the palaces by the roundabout route, a route which, for some reason, the evil could not follow.

After the Doors were locked, the Key had remained in Listva, the capital of the dark elves' kingdom, for a very long time, until this past year when the House of the Black Moon had taken the Key from the House of the Black Flame and given it to Miralissa.

She had taken the artifact to Stalkon, knowing that the party setting out for Hrad Spein would not be able to complete its mission without it. The route through the Doors on the third level was the quickest and the safest—or, rather, the least dangerous.

"Without the Key I'd have a better chance of sticking my head in an ogre's mouth and taking it out safely than completing my jaunt around Hrad Spein successfully. The whole business is getting more and more hopeless. Does anyone have any idea what we should do now?"

"Wait," Egrassa answered, mechanically running his finger round the hoop of silver lying in front of him. "Now we're going to wait. . . ."

"Wait for what? Is someone hoping that these lads will be stupid enough to give us back the Key, along with a sincere apology?"

"What Tresh Egrassa says makes good sense, Harold. Don't start getting agitated," said Uncle, raising his beer mug to his bearded face.

"I'm not getting agitated."

"Good, there's no need. Honeycomb went after the thieves."

"Honeycomb?"

"Who else? We couldn't wait for you clunkheads," the sergeant growled. "The elves weren't here, I'm wounded. Milord Alistan is a knight, not a tracker. You were all gadding around the taverns and getting into fights. Honeycomb was the only one left."

"Has he been gone long?" asked Marmot.

"Yes, about two hours. . . ."

"Hallas, enough sitting around," said Deler, making for the door. "Ell asked us to relieve him; he could still overtake the big bruiser."

The gnome and the dwarf went out.

"I thought you always carried the Key with you, Lady Miralissa," said Kli-Kli, interrupting the lingering silence.

This time there was none of the jester's usual snickering and tittering. Even the resolutely cheerful goblin understood the fix we were in.

"My mistake, jester."

An elf admitting a mistake! This was something new. They usually accuse other people of making the mistakes.

"No one's to blame," Milord Alistan reassured Miralissa. "We had assumed no one would know that we had the Key."

"We should have assumed differently!" said the elfess, and her eyes flashed. "I was careless and I am to blame! I didn't even bother to erect a defense round the artifact!"

"How could they even have heard about our arrival?" Egrassa said thoughtfully.

The dark elf seemed to be reading my thoughts. There was only one answer to that question—they had been waiting for us, and waiting for a long time.

"Someone reported that we were here," Alistan replied to the elf. "We were in open view as we rode through the city. There are hundreds of eyes, they could have been watching out for us. . . ."

Eel strode across the room and leaned down over the bodies of the strangers. He studied the dead men's faces for a long time and then calmly checked their pockets and their hands. Why their hands?

"They're soldiers, all right. No doubt about it," the Garrakian declared.

"We can see for ourselves that they're soldiers, not priests of the goddess of love," Uncle snorted. "The question is whose service these scum were in."

"If they had simply shot us, I would have assumed one of the noble houses had decided to liquidate our group because they thought we'd been hired by their rivals. Then this would have been a warning," Alistan said after a long pause.

Some warning! A warning is when they break your finger and promise to break your arm the next time, and after that your neck. But when they shoot you full of crossbow bolts, that's not a warning.

"These dead men were followers of the Nameless One," said Eel, tossing two rings onto the table. "Look what I found on them."

I picked up one small circle of metal and turned it over in my hand. A ring in the form of a branch of poison ivy—the crest of the Nameless One. As worn by his servants when carrying out the will of their lord.

"Clear enough." I put the ring back down on the table and wiped my hands.

When I touched that ring it was probably the first time I had ever felt revulsion for an object made of pure gold. Even if there had been an entire trunk full of the things lying there in front of me, there was no way I would have purloined them. Stalkon was right when he condemned men who serve the Nameless One to be boiled alive.

The sorcerer's followers are fanatics, putrid filth, vile weeds in the garden of our kingdom, and the king's Sandmen, the ruthless gardeners, take real pleasure in pulling them up by the roots.

A man I didn't know came into the room and Miralissa introduced him as the late Master Pito's nephew.

"What a terrible disaster, Tresh Miralissa! May the gods punish the accursed murderers!" the heir wailed, wringing his hands despairingly.

"They will, Master Quidd, you may be certain of it," said Miralissa, patting the new owner of the inn on the shoulder to raise his spirits. "I shall make certain that the villain responsible for all this does not go unpunished."

"Thank you," said Quidd, nodding gratefully to the elfess.

"Does the guard know what has happened?"

"No, and they won't find out," the innkeeper replied. "Those spongers are only good for collecting taxes and taking bribes. But when something like this happens, they're never anywhere to be found."

"Then you better have the bodies removed from the hall before someone happens to look into the inn."

"Yes," Quidd said with a mournful nod. "Yes indeed, I'll see to it. I'll go and fetch my assistants, Tresh Miralissa, we'll take the dead men to my house and then the women can do what must be done. Prepare them for burial . . . ," Quidd said in the same sorrowful voice. "But with your permission, I'll have the two enemies buried at the back of the inn, beside the cattle yard."

"Just as you wish, Master Quidd."

Uncle finished his beer and came across to us.

"How's the shoulder?" Arnkh asked him in a rather guilty voice.

"It'll heal in no time at all. Thanks to the elfess—she used her shamanism on it. In a week it'll be as good as new."

"I feel sorry for Loudmouth," Kli-Kli sighed.

"Don't be in such a hurry to bury him, greenface! Maybe he's still alive," Marmot told the jester. "The Nameless One's men wouldn't have hauled away a dead body, they took him alive, I can feel it in my heart."

Maybe they did . . . and maybe they didn't . . . the absence of Loudmouth's constant nagging and grousing had left a gap in our little band.

The minutes crept by and the drops of time dripped onto the red-hot coals of anticipation, but none of the gods even tried to make them fall faster, to turn the drops into rain and quench the heat of the fire.

Quidd came back with his assistants, loaded the bodies onto stretchers, and carried them out of the inn.

Hallas looked in twice. The first time he reported that all was in order and the second time he took two mugs of beer. When Uncle asked what Deler and he were going to do with booze on watch, the guileless dwarf replied laconically: "Drink it." The sergeant frowned, but decided not to argue.

Meanwhile Alistan ran a whetstone along the edge of his sword with an imperturbability that persons of the royal blood might have envied. Apparently he wanted to make it the sharpest sword in the universe.

The count's example proved infectious. Eel took out one of his two blades and set to work. In my opinion, sharpening a Garrakian sword is an unnecessary waste of time. The narrow, elegant "brother" can slice through elfin drokr without the slightest effort, never mind plain ordinary silk.

I asked Uncle where my beloved crossbow and knife were. The sergeant jabbed one finger toward the farthest table, where all our weapons were heaped up.

What's to be done if I don't know how to use those yard-long lumps of metal they call swords, poleaxes, and all the rest? A crossbow, now, that's a different matter altogether—with my miniature friend I could easily hit the target at seventy paces. In any case, the art of using all those sharp things for stabbing and slicing is no business for a decent thief. Where would I go waving a sword about, I ask you? In a fight with the guards? Much better to run for it than wait for some beer-soaked guard to stick a piece of metal in your belly. I wasn't made for fencing and dueling, although thanks to For and his "secret battles" I have a pretty good understanding of all that.

Marmot was stuffing Invincible with yet another portion of grub—it looked as if the warrior was trying to fatten the little beast up. Arnkh, Uncle, and Egrassa had started playing dice to pass the time, and the elf had already won six games.

Kli-Kli was whispering to the elfin princess with a perfectly serious expression on his face. When I tried to go over to them, he gave me a rather unwelcoming glance, so I left them in peace. So did the goblin and the elfess have secrets of their own now?

Lamplighter was playing a quiet, sad melody on his reed pipe, and I was the only one left with nothing to keep me busy, so I decided to do something useful. I took the maps of Hrad Spein out of my bag and studied them until Ell walked in.

Miralissa raised one eyebrow inquiringly, but he only shook his head. "I didn't find it."

"No trace of the men?" asked Alistan, looking up from his sword.

"On the contrary. I followed the men who stole the Key right across the city and found them, but they were already dead."

"How's that?"

"Absolutely dead, all of them. Stuck full of arrows. If those men were carrying the artifact, someone took it from them. Six bodies in a dark alley. No Key, no Honeycomb, and absolutely no tracks. As if someone had swept them away with a broom. I looked, but it was useless. . . ."

The men who attacked us had fallen into an ambush themselves? So who had finished them off—their own side? Or had a third party joined in? But if so, who?

"I hope nothing bad has happened to Honeycomb and he has better luck than our Ell," Uncle muttered querulously.

"Mumr, Marmot," Milord Rat said in a quiet voice, "relieve Hallas and Deler."

Lamplighter put down his reed pipe and went to carry out Alistan's order.

The gnome and the dwarf burst into the inn, occupied the bar, and set about annihilating the strategic supplies of beer while they recalled their friend Loudmouth, may he dwell in the light, with a few kind words.

Everyone else went back to their own pastimes, casting occasional worried glances at the door.

I went back to studying my papers. But the cursed labyrinths of the Palaces of Bone absolutely refused to stay fixed in my memory, and I barely managed to make myself remember the route through the first level to the steps that led to the second. Eventually, when it was already after midnight and our patience was all but exhausted, Honeycomb showed up. Without saying a word he took a mug full of dark heavy beer out of Deler's hand and drained it in a single swallow.

"I found them," the young giant laughed, wiping his mustache with the back of his hand. "They're in a house in the southern district of Ranneng."

"The southern district?" Miralissa said with a frown. "There's nothing there but the mansions of the higher nobility!"

"That's right . . . Hallas, another beer."

Honeycomb handed his mug to the gnome, who filled it without a murmur.

"Did you find out anything about Loudmouth?"

"Not a thing. He disappeared into thin air," said Honeycomb, taking another swig of his beer.

"So what happened? Ell wasn't able to find you."

"No?" said Honeycomb, glancing at the elf.

"I found nothing but bodies. . . ."

"Ah yes! When I left the inn, I was about ten minutes behind our killers. And there were guards dashing around all over the Upper City, so I had to keep my head down. Anyway, I was a bit late reaching the scene of the fight. When I got there, there was nothing but dead bodies and a dozen lads with bows walking out of the dark alley. I had to make the best of it, so I followed them."

"Did they say anything?"

"No . . . ," Honeycomb said after thinking for a moment. "But later, when the killers met another man, he said that now the Master might be pleased with them."

"The Master?" Miralissa asked in alarm, casting a warning glance in my direction.

"That's what they said." Honeycomb shrugged and took a swig from his mug. "I had to follow them for quite a long time, and then hang about for even longer in a little hidey-hole while they waited for the man. They gave him the item that was stolen from you, Tresh Miralissa, took their money, sang the praises of the Master, and went on their way."

"And what about the man?"

"He went off in the opposite direction, so I had to choose who to follow. I decided the stolen item was more important and followed the man. A cunning pest, I tell you; I almost lost him."

"Did he notice you?" Miralissa asked anxiously.

"Oh no . . . He couldn't have."

"Why didn't you finish him off, if he had the Key?" the gnome asked in a disappointed voice.

"There were four others with him. Bodyguards. And he looked like a dangerous enough specimen himself. I even thought he might be a shaman—his skin was so pale."

"Did you say pale?" I exclaimed.

"White. As white as chalk."

Could this be my old acquaintance Rolio? If so, then it really was him I'd seen at the Large Market. The Nameless One's followers had done the job for Paleface, and the Master's servants had simply lain in waiting for their prey in the dark alley, shot the thieves with their bows, and taken the Key. Tonight the hired killer had done what the Master's shaman had failed to do fifteen hundred years earlier in the Mountains of the Dwarves, and now the Master would at long last hold in his hands the artifact he craved so badly.

"Carry on, Honeycomb," Egrassa said.

"Carry on with what?" Honeycomb asked with a shrug. "I'm not Tomcat, may his soul dwell in the light, I'm about as good a tracker as Hallas is a jeweler, but I managed to stick with the lad to the end. He's in a huge mansion in the southern district of the city. And that's the whole story."

"What kind of house is it? Where exactly is it located?"

"The darkness only knows where it's located. I've never been in this city before. I only just managed to find my way back here. But I can recognize it. It's not a house, it's a palace, and it has fancy gates, with some kind of birds on them."

"That's great! Now we'll break those birds' little wings!" said Hallas. He stuffed a piece of bread in his mouth and reached for his battle-mattock.

"Where do you think you're going in such a great hurry?" Uncle asked, watching the gnome curiously.

"What do you mean? We have to get that Key back from them."

"With one incomplete platoon? Without knowing who we're going up against? Without knowing how many guards there are? Get a grip, Hallas! That smack you got in the teeth must have been too hard," the dwarf quipped.

"Sit down, Hallas," Alistan said quietly, and the gnome, who had been on the point of starting a brawl with Deler, went back to his seat, shamefaced. "We need to find out who we're dealing with before we get into a fight."

"Who we're dealing with? I think I can probably answer that question for you, Milord Alistan," I blurted out without thinking, and then bit my tongue, but it was already too late.

"Have you become a visionary, thief?" Count Markauz asked me.

"Oh no, Your Grace. It's all much simpler than that. The man who took the Key from the Nameless One's men who attacked us is my old friend Paleface. And Paleface, as you recall, serves the Master. I think we can assume that whoever lives in that house is another one of the Master's errand boys, like Rolio."

"Well now, that is logical," Miralissa agreed, and snapped her fingers in annoyance. "So this Master has thwarted us yet again. . . ."

Alistan chuckled scornfully, making it very clear that he found my reasoning unconvincing.

"I beg your pardon, Lady Miralissa," Eel drawled, speaking for the first time. "Just recently the lads and I heard you talk about this mysterious Master. Could you tell us a little more about him? We feel like blind kittens—we don't even know which direction danger might strike from."

"I think Harold can tell you more than I can."

The Wild Hearts all turned to look at me.

"Mumr, pour me some beer," I said to Lamplighter. "This is going to be a long story."

"Well, I've already heard it, so I'll be off to bed," Kli-Kli said with a yawn.

"I'll hit the hay, too," said the gnome. "Just tell me tomorrow, that is, today, where this Master's head is, and I'll give it a tap with my mattock, so he won't bother us anymore."

"You're a great hero," Deler snorted.

"Sure, not like certain dwarves who wear stupid hats on their empty heads," said the gnome, and walked out before Deler could come up with a worthy reply.

I had a potbellied mug of beer in front of me, and I began my story. . . .

"Mmm, yes . . . ," Deler grunted when he had heard me out. "This is an interesting business we've got involved in, right, Uncle?"

"Don't whine," the sergeant told the dwarf. "You knew what you were getting into when you left the Lonely Giant with us."

"I did," Deler agreed with a nod. "We've seen worse in our time. Survived ogres in snows of the Desolate Lands, went hungry for weeks at a time, walked all the way to the emerald green Needles of Ice. We won't retreat now just because of some creep."

"No, we won't, dwarf," Alistan declared quietly. "We have nowhere left to retreat to. There's a good chance that the Key will leave the mansion before the night's over. Are there any volunteers?"

"I'll catch up on my sleep in the morning," said Marmot, taking Invincible off his shoulder and handing him to me. "Take care of him. I'm with you, Honeycomb."

"Wait, I'll take a stroll with you," said Egrassa, getting up from the table. He took his s'kash and walked out of the tavern with the two Wild Hearts.

"Mmm," Deler drawled thoughtfully. "Am I imagining things, or did Tresh Egrassa really take a sword with him?"

"The law of Ranneng does not apply to elves, Deler," Miralissa said with a smile. "We can carry weapons wherever we wish."

The dwarf grunted in disappointment and muttered to himself, but not loudly enough for Miralissa to hear: "If you've got long pointy teeth you can carry a ballista around if you like, but they won't let an honest dwarf take his own ax into town."

I picked up the dozing ling and went off to bed.

4

The next morning I was woken by Invincible's shrill, furious squealing. At first I was too sleepy to understand what was going on, but as usual divine enlightenment struck me out of the blue. The answer was very simple—I could hear Invincible squealing because a certain little green stinker had decided to annoy the formidable little mouse.

"Ai! He bit me! I swear by the great insane shaman Tre-Tre, the little rat bit me!" the goblin roared.

"You only got what you deserve. And when Marmot finds out you've been teasing his little friend he'll tear your head off."

"You're a fool, Harold," said Kli-Kli, licking his terrible wound.

"Oh, no. I beg your pardon," I said, getting up off the bed. "You're the fool here, not me."

"True, I am a fool," Kli-Kli agreed amiably. "But then, I'm wise, too. And you're just a fool."

"And how did you get to be so wise?" asked Lamplighter, who was listening to our conversation.

"What do you mean?" I snorted as I put on my shirt. "He was dropped on his head as a child, and ever since then he thinks he's a wise fool."

"Maybe I am only a wise fool, but you, Harold, are a genuine fool. And you know why? Because a wise man knows he's a fool, and that makes him a wise fool. But people like you, who think they're the cleverest and wisest of all, don't even realize what absolute fools they really are."

"What wonderful reasoning," I remarked, feeling slightly confused. "Did you ever think of becoming a professor of philosophy at the university?"

"Oh, what big words we know," said the little goblin, who found this exchange very amusing. "Phi-lo-so-phy! It must have taken ten years for a fool like you to learn that word. And as for reasoning, I can prove to you that you're a fool in no time at all. Do you want me to?"

"No."

"That's because you're a fool," the goblin snapped back. "Are you afraid?"

"I just don't want to hear any proofs from the king's fool. You're an idle chatterbox, Kli-Kli."

"I'm an idle chatterbox? No, I'll prove to you that you're a fool who doesn't listen to wise men," said the goblin, getting furious. "Look here. Proof number one. Who would ever take on a Commission to get the Rainbow Horn?"

"A fool!" I said, forced to admit that the green midget was right.

"Oh, you grow wiser by the hour," the jester said with heartfelt sincerity as he bound up his bitten finger with a handkerchief.

The handkerchief wasn't exactly fresh and clean, and it had very vulgar little blue flowers embroidered along its edges.

"To continue," the green bedbug said, "proof number two! When you refused to accept the authenticity of the goblin prophecies about a Dancer in the Shadows, that is, about you, you acted like the greatest fool of all time, didn't you?"

"I acted like an intelligent man. Why would I want to be in any of your ludicrous prophecies? I became a fool when I allowed you to call me the Dancer in the Shadows."

"Oh!" he sighed disappointedly. "Now you've started turning stupid again. But never mind, you may be a fool, but you accepted the name, and now there's no way you can get out of it. The prophecy will be fulfilled."

Kli-Kli simply adored the *Bruk-Gruk*—the goblin *Book of Prophecies* that's supposed to predict every important event that will ever take place in Siala. And supposedly there's a special cycle of predictions called "Dancer in the Shadows." The goblin insists that these fairy tales are about me, but I don't want to have anything to do with any crazy goblin shamans. The last thing I need for a happy life is to find that I'm the hero of some silly book.

"And how did he accept the name, Kli-Kli?" Mumr asked.

"How, Lamplighter-Mamplighter? Very simply. Because he's a fool."

Something must have got stuck in the goblin's brains. He's obviously going to repeat that word all day long now, like a green parrot. Lamplighter wasn't satisfied with this answer from Stalkon's personal jester, so Kli-Kli kept up his harangue: "I'll tell you. The prophecy about the Dancer in the Shadows says that this dancer, who will definitely be a thief, will save the entire world from a nasty villain. But before he does that, a whole heap of events and signs have to happen. There are all sorts of ways you can recognize the Dancer, that is, our very own much beloved, absolute fool Harold, also known as the Shadow. First the Dancer has to bind demons using the Horse of Shadows, then he has to kill a purple bird, and then take up the name."

"And what's all this got to do with Harold?" asked Mumr, puzzled.

"Oh, it's hard work talking with you fools," said Kli-Kli, stamping his foot and pretending to be angry. "We can say that Harold bound the demons, can't we?"

"Not me, the magicians of the Order bound the demons."

"That's not important," said Kli-Kli, brushing aside my objection. The jester was riding hard on his favorite hobbyhorse—the prophecies of the crazy magician Tre-Tre, may the light be a curse to him!

"Did the Order bind the demons with your help? It did! Has the sign come to pass? It has! Was there a purple bird in Hargan's Wasteland? There was, and not just one, either!"

"If goblins call those flying monsters birds . . ."

"It's a literary expression, my lad. You don't know a thing about art. So, was there a bird?"

"Have it your own way," I sighed. I couldn't be bothered pointing out to this cocky small fry that the creatures spawned by the Kronk-a-Mor used by the Nameless One's shamans should be called nightmares, not birds. "Okay, so there was."

"Right! And you have a name now, don't you?"

"Aha! Ever since I was a child. They call me Harold."

"Pah, you're hopeless! Are you really a total numbskull or just pretending so well that I can't tell the difference? I'm not talking about the name you were born with, I mean the name you were granted from above. Dancer in the Shadows—that one! You agreed that I could call you that. And so you accepted the name."

Yet again I cursed the day when I told Kli-Kli that he could call me that. The only reason I did it was to make the little pest leave me in peace, but instead he started yelling out loud for all to hear that the sign had been fulfilled. And now I could expect more, equally stupid goblin prophecies.

"And what prophetic sign do you have lined up next?" I asked the goblin scornfully.

"Next?" The jester screwed his eyes up, gave me a cunning look and declaimed.

> When the crimson key departs
> Like water soaking into sand
> And the Path is lost in mist
> There is work for a thief's hand.
> He meets at night with Strawberry
> But who will be helped by the key?

"Right," I said, and couldn't help laughing out loud. "It's like I've always said: Your crazy shaman Tre-Tre ate too many magic mushrooms for breakfast."

"Let's have a few less unjustified insults, if you don't mind!" said the goblin, baring his teeth at me. "Tre-Tre was my people's greatest shaman! Artsivus and his Order can't hold a candle to him."

"Maybe not, but I'd rather let someone else decide that. Have you even figured out what that little jingle of yours is all about? I didn't understand a thing."

"That's because you're a fool," the jester reminded me yet again. "It's a prophecy, so you get to understand it when it happens. But it's about to happen any minute, because the crimson key has departed. Or to put it in normal language, someone has walked off with our artifact."

"That key of yours? Is it crimson, then?" Lamplighter asked.

"Well, no . . . ," said Kli-Kli, confused by the question. "It looks more like it's made of crystal. . . . All right, Harold. Go and fill your belly, you and I have got a job to do."

"I only have one job to do, Kli-Kli, the one I swore on Tomcat's grave to finish. I'm going to get the Rainbow Horn, hand it over to the Order, grab my honestly earned loot and charter of pardon, and start living the good life. Nothing else concerns me, unless, of course, it happens to be a threat to my life or a chance to pick up some money."

"But we do have a job to do," Kli-Kli said very seriously. "Mumr and Eel are going to relieve Marmot and Egrassa."

"I don't see the connection. What's that got to do with me?"

"In the first place, you can give Marmot his ling back. . . ."

"I can do that here," I said, interrupting the goblin.

"In the second place," Kli-Kli continued imperturbably. "Miralissa has asked you to take a look at the house and say if you can get inside and filch the Key from under the very noses of the Master's servants."

"Filch it? From under their noses?" I asked like an echo. "Me?"

"Yes, you! You're our thief, aren't you?"

There was nothing I could say to that. I picked the mouse up off the pillow, put him on my shoulder, and said: "Let's go. Do you know the way?"

"Honeycomb came back this morning and told me. Eel's coming along. Lamplighter, are you with us, too?"

"Yes."

"All right then," I said to the goblin as I walked out of the room. "But there'll be no strolling round the city until I get my breakfast."

"You'll get your breakfast. Master Quidd laid the table ages ago."

Birds were singing their song of summer joy, flowers were blooming, the sky was blue, the grass was green, the sun was shining. If I could have forgotten that the Key had been stolen from right under our noses and we still didn't know what had happened to Loudmouth, it would have been a wonderful day.

"Do we have a long way to go?" I asked the goblin.

"Not very," the jester muttered.

He was holding on to my sleeve with his right hand and hopping along on one foot, amusing himself and all the passersby. I couldn't tear myself free, because the jester had a grip on my shirt sleeve like a tick on a dog's ear, so I had to try persuasion. But my polite and heartfelt request to stop playing the fool and walk on two feet like normal people was refused. Then I tried to ignore the hopping goblin; after all, I couldn't fight him in the public street, could I?

"How far is not very far?" I asked my companion after another unsuccessful attempt to tear my sleeve out of his tenacious fingers.

"About an hour," Kli-Kli replied indifferently, and hopped over a stick lying on the ground.

I groaned.

"We're going to the southern part of the city on Motley Hill. It's quite a walk to get there."

"For some it's a walk, for some it's an excuse to skip about and play the fool," I remarked.

But Kli-Kli was all set to hop on one foot for the entire hour. "I'm so sorry they didn't give us the carriage today," the king's jester quipped, hopping neatly over a puddle.

The little creep had lied. It was no more than twenty minutes from the inn to our destination.

The street leading up Motley Hill was an incredibly steep climb. By the time we reached the region where the big cheeses lived, I was drenched in sweat. But at least, Sagot be praised, the goblin finally let go of me.

"We could take a ride down the hill," the jester murmured dreamily when we were almost at the very top.

I followed the direction of his eyes. There was an old, dried-up cart standing outside one of the houses, with wooden chocks under its wheels to stop it accidentally taking off down the hill and crushing some unfortunate pedestrian.

"Don't even think about it!" I warned him.

"You don't understand a thing about lucky finds, Harold. A fool, there's no other word for it. Just look at that hill. We'd go flying along like a hurricane."

"I don't like this little idea of yours."

"What little idea? Flying along like a hurricane?"

"The idea that *we'll* go flying along like a hurricane. You may have decided to commit suicide, Kli-Kli, but there's no need to go tangling other people up in your crazy plans."

"Harold, you're a real bogeyman. Relax, there's no danger. Why bring up the subject of suicide?"

"Because, my little muttonhead, that hill is more than four hundred yards long! We'd get moving all right. And we'd pick up speed, too! Fly like a hurricane!" I said in a squeaky voice, teasing Kli-Kli. "But how are we going to brake, my little peabrain? Our bones would be scattered halfway across Ranneng!"

"Oh!" the jester said thoughtfully when he'd thought over my arguments. He glanced regretfully at the carriage. "I didn't think about that."

"Now who's the fool and who's the wise man?"

"You're the fool, I'm the wise man. Even a boneheaded Doralissian can see that. By the way, we've arrived, that's the manor over there."

The manor standing right on the very top of the hill looked about half the size of the king's palace, but I couldn't really see it properly from where we were standing. Most of the building was hidden by the thick crowns of the trees growing in the park around it.

The private area was surrounded by a tall gray wall with quaint little steel figures all along the top. I wasn't fooled by their appearance—first and foremost they were a barrier of spikes to prevent anyone climbing in over the wall. Their role as decoration was strictly secondary. And I had no doubt that after the spikes there would be dogs or garrinches or guards waiting for us inside. Maybe even all three of them.

The steel gates were covered with images of birds. Birds flying, birds singing, and doing all sorts of things. When I looked closely at them I realized they were nightingales. So whoever lived in this nest of vipers was a nobleman from the House of Nightingale.

"Impressive!" said Lamplighter, looking at the house appreciatively. "What do you think, Harold?"

"Difficult."

"How do you mean?"

"Difficult to get out of."

"But you're a master of your trade, aren't you?"

"Right . . . but that doesn't make the job any easier. Where are Marmot and Egrassa?"

"Probably pretending to be trees, and that's why we can't see them," Kli-Kli suggested. "They're hiding, Harold, hiding. Or do you think that two handsome fellows walking round and round a house wouldn't attract any attention?"

"Well, if they're hiding, you can look for them. I'm not going to play hide-and-seek."

Naturally, the goblin didn't find anyone. If an elf doesn't want to be seen, then he isn't. And the Wild Hearts, especially their scouts, have always been famous for their camouflage and their ability to hide even where it seems impossible. Marmot and Egrassa emerged like two phantoms from the clumps of bushes growing along the wall surrounding the mansion. I would never have thought that two sturdy warriors could have been sitting in there.

"You're late." That was how Marmot greeted us.

"I should think so. Even a h'san'kor would have trouble finding you!" I said, handing the joyfully squealing ling to his master. "Have you found out who the house belongs to?"

"No. How about you?"

"No," Eel replied. "Is everything quiet?"

"As a graveyard. At least, no one has left the house through these gates, but about an hour before dawn seven men went in. You're welcome to use our little lair. It's good cover, very convenient, and it's not visible from the road. There's a perfect view of the gates."

"Good luck," taciturn Eel said to the others, and started walking toward the bushes. He slipped in through a narrow gap and the branches immediately hid him from view.

"Come on, Harold. You'll stick out like a sore thumb hanging around here," Kli-Kli said.

I followed him in, comforting myself with the thought that until Miralissa found out whose house this was and she and Alistan came up with some way of getting into it, there was nothing for me to do. It made no difference whether I lay around here or sat around at the inn. True, there was no pestiferous Kli-Kli at the inn, but Miralissa *was* there. I would have been happier to be with the elf than an annoying clown. Ever since Valder's ghost saved me from the red flyer in Hargan's Wasteland, the dark elfess had been eyeing me with great interest. I hadn't told her or anyone else that I had the spirit of a dead archmagician living in my head. And after what happened at the wasteland I had pretended to be a complete fool, claiming I had no idea what had happened or how I'd been saved.

During the night Marmot and Egrassa had created a magnificent shelter. If you looked at the bushes from the road, you couldn't tell they'd been touched, but inside there was a cozy green lair with trampled branches and grass, quite big enough for two men. Of course, there were four of us, not two, but Kli-Kli was not very big, and I huddled up a bit and we fitted into the observation post quite comfortably.

Lamplighter immediately stretched out on the ground, picked a stalk of grass, put it in his teeth, and started staring through the branches at the clouds drifting across the sky. A fine occupation for a man who wants to fall asleep.

Eel set to work observing the gates leading to the house and Kli-Kli and I were the only ones left suffering from boredom. The fidgety goblin couldn't sit still for a moment, and the longer we stayed in our hideaway, the more fidgety he got.

The goblin counted the clouds floating past, too, but he soon got fed up with that, and less than five minutes later he started squirming about, kicked me in the side, and crawled over to Eel.

"Nobody?" Kli-Kli hissed curiously.

"No," the Garrakian replied tersely without taking his eyes off the gates.

"A-a-a-a," the goblin drawled in disappointment, then kicked me in the side again and went back to counting the clouds, taking no notice of the less than kindly glance I gave him.

Ten minutes later the whole business was repeated. He kicked me in the side, crawled over to Eel, asked his question, got the answer, said "A-a-a-a," kicked me in the side.

When he started for the third time I couldn't take any more.

"Kli-Kli, lie down, or I won't answer for myself!"

"I'm just going over to Eel for a moment."

A kick in the side.

I flew into a fury and swung my foot to kick him back hard, but somehow he managed to avoid it. He giggled in delight and stuck out his tongue. But I could wait for when he came creeping back!

"Nobody?"

"No."

"A-a-a-a . . . Oi!"

Just as Kli-Kli was about to come back to his place Eel pinned him to the ground with one hand, without even looking at him.

"Stay here."

"Why?"

"You've annoyed Harold enough already."

"But it's all in fun!" said Kli-Kli.

The warrior didn't answer him and the jester took mortal offense. He called me a sneak, but he didn't dare go against Eel, and stayed where he was.

The time dragged out endlessly. Mumr chewed his grass stalk. Kli-Kli fell into a doze, exhausted by doing nothing; my side went numb from lying on the ground, so I turned over onto the other one. But Eel sat, as still as he had been two hours earlier, watching the gates. There was no movement or any signs of life. The gates had to be very well guarded, since a member of one of Ranneng's militant noble brotherhoods lived there, but we couldn't see any guards.

Just as the third hour was coming to an end Eel sat up sharply and chuckled.

"At last!"

I started and carefully moved aside a branch to look out. Two guards, evidently from the personal bodyguard of the owner of the house (they had emblems of some kind sewn to their uniforms, but I couldn't make them out from that distance), were hastily opening the heavy gates.

"What's happening?" asked Kli-Kli, yawning widely as he woke up from his doze.

"The nest of cockroaches is stirring," Mumr muttered. "Harold, squeeze up a bit, I can't see a thing."

Horsemen came riding out of the gates. One, three, five of them. And Paleface, may the darkness take him!

"Rolio's with them!" I whispered.

"Where?" Kli-Kli almost tumbled out of the bushes straight onto the road to see the killer I'd told him so much about.

It would have been no laughing matter if the jester had ended up under the hooves of the horses. But Eel was alert: He grabbed Kli-Kli's leg and pulled him back into the bushes.

"Relax, lad."

"It was an accident."

"That's Paleface. The rider dressed all in black," I explained. My hands were itching to let the killer have a crossbow bolt, but unfortunately I didn't have my weapon with me. "Where are they going?"

"Ah, universal darkness! They'll get away!" Eel exclaimed. "I swear on a dragon, they'll get away!"

"And what if he has the Key?" I asked, pouring oil on the flames.

The horsemen rode off.

"Mumr, after them, quickly!" Eel ordered.

"But they've got horses!"

"And you've got legs! They won't gallop through the city, you can see they're riding slowly. Try to find out where they're going."

"All right," said Lamplighter, spitting out his grass stalk. "I'll try."

"We have to let Markauz and Miralissa know," said Eel, standing up and emerging from the bushes. "We still have a chance of intercepting them at the city gates."

"There are a lot of gates," Kli-Kli said doubtfully. "We'd better hurry."

But we never got to the inn. Or rather, we weren't allowed to. As soon as we reached the street we had walked up a few hours earlier, two men blocked our way. They were dressed in the modest clothes of craftsmen, with sullen faces and cold eyes. The lads looked very confident, and they had very good reason to be—each of them was holding a naked sword.

"It looks as though we were spotted at the manor after all," I muttered, taking my dagger out of its sheath.

A dagger against a sword is like a crossbow against a ballista. I couldn't speak for Eel, but I knew they would carve me into little pieces without the slightest trouble.

"Look behind us!" Kli-Kli squeaked.

Six men were approaching us from the rear. They were still quite a long way off, but each of them had a crossbow. And then I noticed that they hadn't come out of the manor grounds—the gates were still closed. They had arrived in a huge carriage.

"They're not Nightingales! They're the Nameless One's henchmen! We've been followed!"

Eel gave a low growl and pulled out his daggers.

"Harold, don't stand there like a fool!" Kli-Kli hissed as he watched the men with crossbows approaching. "Have you got your bag of magic bits and pieces?"

"No, I left it with my crossbow and long dagger."

The goblin groaned. "That's the most foolish thing you could possibly have done!"

I didn't argue with that.

Then suddenly I had a bright idea. I reached for my trump card—a magical vial full of potion. When it broke it should produce a flash, a loud boom, and smoke.

An absolutely useless little toy really, but I had got it for nothing, and I didn't want to just throw away a magical vial. I'd never had a chance to try it out. I'd stopped carrying the flash-bang in my bag in order not to confuse it with the other vials, and after I put it in the special pocket on my sleeve I'd forgotten all about it, because it weighed next to nothing.

"Close your eyes," I yelled to my comrades, and flung the vial down at the swordsmen's feet. There was a bright flash and a loud bang and a section of the street was hidden by thick, swirling white smoke. One of the men with swords cried out in fright.

"Stay behind me!" Eel ordered, and dashed at our stunned enemies in spite of their swords.

One of them was sitting on the ground in the smoke and rubbing his eyes in confusion. The lad had forgotten all about the sword that was lying a few steps away from him. The other one proved less timid. He swung rather clumsily and tried to slice Eel's head off, but Eel ducked under his sword, blocking it with his left dagger, and thrust his right dagger into the swordsman's neck.

The first lad was still sitting in the street rubbing his eyes, so I swung my foot and kicked him hard on the jaw. The would-be killer's teeth clattered and he collapsed on the ground.

"Take the sword!" Eel told me as he picked up the sword of the man he had killed.

I handle a sword about as well as a baker handles the wheel of a royal frigate, but in this particular case I didn't really have time to explain that to the Garrakian. As soon as the men with crossbows saw what had happened to their comrades, they broke into a run. Unfortunately my magical trick hadn't impressed them, and they were running toward us, not away. The most impatient of them fired at us and the bolt scraped across the road dangerously close to Eel's foot.

"They want to take us alive!" he growled.

"Follow me!" Kli-Kli squeaked, realizing that a spot where the air is filled with screaming crossbow bolts is not the right place for any respectable goblin to be.

The jester disappeared into the thick white smoke, I darted after him, and Eel covered our rear.

After ten steps, we broke out of the wall of smoke covering the street. The men with crossbows were firing without worrying about taking us alive anymore. The only reason our skins weren't full of holes was that thick wall of smoke. One bolt whizzed past my head and thudded into the side of the wagon with the props under its wheels. Kli-Kli wanted to take a ride, didn't he? It looked like his dream was about to come true.

"Harold, what was that stinking muck you tossed on the ground?" Eel asked me.

"A mere trifle that saved us a little unpleasantness! Stop, Kli-Kli!" I said, grabbing the goblin by the scruff of the neck. "Into the cart!"

"Don't be a fool!"

"Ah, but I am! In you go, wise man."

Without bothering to ask any questions, Eel tossed the protesting goblin into the cart. He realized that we couldn't outrun the crossbow bolts. Another few seconds and our hides wouldn't be worth a bent farthing. I jumped in after Kli-Kli.

"Harold, I hope you know what you're doing!" he said. I think it was the first time I'd seen the jester frightened. Even during the attack on the royal palace by the followers of the Nameless One, or at Vishki, or in Hargan's Wasteland, His Emerald Skinship had never turned that pale lettuce color.

With mighty blows Eel knocked out the wooden chocks that were holding the wagon in place, and it started rolling downhill. The cool-headed Garrakian even gave it a push, although that was quite unnecessary. The slope was steep enough, and our elegant vehicle was soon traveling at a terrifying speed.

"I-I-I th-think th-this was a b-bad id-deaa!" Kli-Kli stammered in fright as the wheels of the cart skipped and bounced over the stones of the street. He clung to the side of the cart with both hands, his eyes wide with terror as the houses rushed past.

People walking along the street jumped out of the way to avoid being crushed under the wheels, and rewarded us with choice obscenities and directions into the darkness.

Another bolt thudded into the back of the cart.

"Keep down!" Eel yelled, trying to shout above the rumbling of the wheels and the wind roaring in our ears.

We kept down. A deadly rain of crossbow bolts started falling on the back of the cart. Either there were a lot more pursuers than we thought or they were virtuoso marksmen. Not many of the king's soldiers could fire and reload as fast as that.

But even so, Kli-Kli stuck his head up, looked ahead, and exclaimed, "Oi!"

At that moment either of the goblin's eyes could have swallowed the moon. I was intrigued and decided I wanted to know what the wise man's "Oi!" signified.

Sad to say, the street ran on for another hundred yards and then made a sharp turn to the left. So there was an extremely unpleasant little surprise in store for us—our wagon was hurtling straight toward the wall of a house.

I looked back—our pursuers were seriously outpaced by the insane speed of our wagon, but they were still rushing after us, as stubborn as imperial dogs that have scented their prey.

"Let's jump for it!" I yelled.

The wagon was moving at an incredible pace, and if we were foolish enough to stay in it, we would end up smeared across the wall.

"If we jump, we could hurt ourselves!" Kli-Kli objected.

"If we don't jump, we're *certainly* going to hurt ourselves! Jump on two!"

"One . . ."

It was too late. The wagon caught up with the wall, or the wall caught up with the wagon, I don't know which.

We slammed into it.

The impact was appalling. Kli-Kli, who was balancing on the side of the cart like a tightrope walker, waiting for me to say "two," was thrown off into the air. He was lucky—unlike the jester, Eel and I were inside the cart.

When we hit, the world went dark. I thought a couple of rabid giants had come running down from the Desolate Lands, especially to dance the djanga on my ribs. I still don't know how my ribs weren't smashed. My ears were ringing, there were stars in my eyes, my left side was a solid mass of pain, and my head felt like it was made of lead.

I don't know how long I lay there like that. Maybe it was a second, maybe an entire age. The stars stubbornly refused to disappear and their crazy spinning was beginning to make me feel sick. And even worse, after the blow I could hardly even think, and only in short bursts.

After that it was like I saw everything that happened from the outside.

Kli-Kli was leaning down over me. The goblin looked completely unhurt, apart from a graze on his cheek and a tear in his cloak.

"Harold! Come on, Harold! Darkness take you! Get up! Get up!"

Why was he shouting like that? I'm not deaf. And where have all these planks come from? Ah yes! The cart!

"Get up, Dancer in the Shadows! They're almost here!"

May a h'san'kor eat his tongue! What is this jester pestering me about now? All I need is to lie down for half an hour, and I'll be as good as new. Let him go and pester Eel instead. Yes, I wonder how he's getting on.

I had to make a real effort to look away from Kli-Kli, who was trying to tell me something, and turn my head toward the spot where I thought the warrior must be.

Aha! Eel was there beside me, only an arm's length away. His face was covered with blood and he was leaning on the sword he had captured, trying to get up from his knees. I admired the Wild Heart more than ever. Our Eel was a stubborn lad, all right.

"Run, Kli-Kli! Warn them!" the warrior hissed.

Run? Who from? And warn who? When he heard the warrior's order, Kli-Kli's face clouded over in fright.

"I'm not going to leave you!"

"Go on, jester," I said. My voice certainly didn't sound any better than Eel's. "Warn everyone who needs to know and we'll have a glass of carrot juice together. . . ."

My throat was so dry, I could have drunk the entire Cold Sea dry, even though it is so salty.

"Try to stay alive, Dancer!" Kli-Kli gave me one last glance and disappeared from my field of view.

"Where has he gone to? Ah, yes, of course. He's gone running off somewhere to warn someone. He moved so fast, he must really want that juice. Well, good luck to him. And all the best . . ."

The Garrakian wasn't allowed to get to his feet. Some men surrounded him, knocked the sword out of his hands, and hit him on the back of his head. Eel fell down onto the ground and stopped moving.

I tried to get up, but my arms and legs wouldn't obey me and I closed my eyes to let these bad men know I was too well brought up to talk with people like them.

A thousand devils of darkness! We smashed into a house that was standing in the wrong place! Why couldn't it have gotten out of the way? Darkness! That wasn't what I should be thinking about.

"Is this one alive?" asked someone standing over me.

"Aha! But he's out cold," someone else said, and gave me a kick under the ribs.

I knew they were bad men.

"You halfwit. You let the shortass get away."

"Well, how much trouble can a goblin cause?"

"He can cause us a whole wagonload."

"Shall I send the lads after him?"

"Ha! Now you think about it. There's no way you can catch him, we'll never find him in the alleys now. No more talk. Load these two before the guards turn up and a crowd gathers."

They tossed me onto a hard surface. Someone swore, a door slammed, the floor jerked and creaked. It seemed like I was in a carriage. But why had they dumped me into it like that? The lads could at least have invited me to take a drive with them. I'm so polite and obliging, surely they didn't think I would refuse to get into the carriage?

I heard someone groan close to my ear. Eel?

I had to open my eyes to satisfy my curiosity. I discovered that I was lying on the floor of a carriage beside the unconscious Eel. The other people in the carriage were the lads with crossbows who five minutes earlier had been trying to shoot down Harold and his companions.

The orcs have a wonderful saying: "Curiosity led the goblin into the maze." One of the bad lads noticed that I had opened my eyes and exclaimed, "Hey, this one's come round."

I wanted to tell him that I hadn't done anything of the sort, and I had a name, but somehow my tongue wouldn't obey me.

"Then knock him out again," someone advised the crossbowman indifferently.

The last thing I saw before I plunged into nothingness was the bludgeon descending on my head.

5

CONVERSATIONS IN THE DARK

I walked along a wide, dark corridor with walls of rough-hewn stone, covered with either moss or lichen. There was practically no light at all and I had to keep my hand on the wall in order not to miss a sudden turn.

The ceiling danced up and down like an earthworm trying to fly. Three times I hit the top of my head against it, but then after I took a few more steps I could stretch my hand up as far as I could reach without feeling any obstacle—there was nothing but empty darkness and a slight draft.

A thousand questions came swarming into my mind. How had I gotten here? Where was I walking to? Why? What was I looking for in the darkness of this underground cellar? And was it really a cellar?

That didn't seem very likely, especially bearing in mind that every twenty-five paces my hand ran into a metal door with a small barred window in it. Twenty paces of crude stone and moss under my fingers, then they felt cold metal, dewed with the underground dampness. And then another twenty paces of stone. It all gave me the impression that I was on the lowest level of some immense prison.

The corridor seemed endless. Sometimes I heard groans and muttering from behind the doors, but mostly all there was behind them was a deafening silence. Who were the inmates of those underground cells? Prisoners, madmen, or the souls of people barred for all eternity from taking the path into the light or the darkness? I had no answer to these questions, and no real desire to find out who was actually in those cells.

As I walked past yet another door, I heard insane, cackling laughter from behind it. It took me by surprise, and I sprang away, recoiling to the opposite wall, and starting to walk faster in order to leave the insane prisoner behind as quickly as possible. But the sound of that laughter came after me along the walls and the ceiling, beating me on the back and forcing me to hurry on my way.

After three eternities, when I had completely lost count of my steps, I thought I caught a faint scent of the sea.

Yes, that was what the Port City in Avendoom smelled like, when the wind was blowing from the direction of the docks. It was the smell of salt and seaweed, of drops of seawater thrown into the air by waves crashing against the pier, the smell of the seagulls who meet the fishing boats in the evening. The smell of a cool freshness, the smell of fish, the smell of the sea breeze and freedom.

The inky blackness receded slowly, dreadfully slowly, revealing the ghostly outlines of the corridor. There was a timid beam of daylight shining down from somewhere up above.

I stopped and raised my head to look at the small spot of blue sky that I could see through a little window in the ceiling far beyond my reach. A ray of sunlight fell on my face and I involuntarily narrowed my eyes. I could hear a loud, regular sighing, as if a weary giant were resting somewhere nearby after a long day of hard work. The sea was somewhere close, and the sound of breaking waves was very clear.

The sea? But how was that possible? How could there be any sea here? Where was I then? And most important of all, *how* had I got here?

I certainly wasn't going to find any answers loitering, so I said goodbye to the light, dove back into the unwelcoming gloom, and walked on along the corridor. It took a long time for my eyes to adjust to the darkness and once I almost lost my footing and took a tumble. I stopped and stretched out my right foot, feeling at the floor.

Just as I thought.

Steps.

Unfortunately, they led downward, into a blackness that was even darker and more impenetrable (if that was actually possible). I stood there, wondering what I should do next.

Going down into the lower vaults of the prison was not a very attractive option. Sagot only knew what I might run into down there. And I could wander around in the dark for a very, very long time. There were only two things I could do: go back to the very beginning of my journey, or walk down the steps and look for a stairway leading up.

The first choice was actually more rational than the second, but I simply couldn't face the long and tiring journey back. Which meant I could only go on. I gathered myself and started walking down slowly. I didn't have an oil lamp, or a torch, let alone a magical light, and I had to grope my way along. On the way down, I kept one hand on the wall and counted the steps. There were sixty-four of them, steep and well worn. They led me into another corridor that was the twin brother of the first. The same inky-black darkness, the same cold, musty, damp air that sent shivers down my spine. The same walls of crude stone covered with rough moss or lichen, the same metal doors with barred openings. But there was just one difference, which I noticed when I started counting my steps. The doors in the wall were set a hundred yards apart instead of twenty.

It was a lot colder here than in the upper corridor and after a while I started shivering, without really noticing it. In the darkness I had to walk slowly; I was afraid of running into an unexpected obstacle or simply falling into a pit. When I had walked past seven doors on my right, the walls changed. The coarse stonework and the moss disappeared, giving way to solid basalt. Whoever the builders were, they had cut the rest of the corridor straight through the rock. I began to suspect that I had ended up in a prison built by gnomes or dwarves.

Far ahead in the darkness I caught a brief blink of light, like a tiny glowworm. I stopped, pressed myself back against the wall, and started gazing into the distance. The little light blinked again. From the look of it, it was probably the flame of an oil lamp that wasn't quite burning properly yet. The light was swaying gently from side to side in time with someone's steps and slowly moving away from me.

I didn't stop to think. A light meant rational beings, even if they might not be very kindly disposed toward unexpected visitors. I had to avoid getting too close to the unknown individual carrying the lantern, remain inconspicuous, and hope that my inadvertent guide would lead me out of this strange, confusing, and mysterious prison.

I dashed forward, ignoring the danger of stumbling over some unexpected obstacle and breaking my legs. Catching up with the stranger proved quite easy—he was plodding along with all the speed of an ogre gorged on human flesh.

As I ran, I passed a staircase leading upward (that was where the lantern-carrier had come from), but decided not to take it, because I didn't want to go stumbling through the dark again. When I got close to the man ahead of me, I could see from the hunched back, the shuffling walk, the wrinkled, trembling hand clutching the lantern, and the gray hair that he was definitely very old. He was dressed in old, tattered, dirty-gray rags. But I would have bet my last gold piece that some time long, long ago those rags had been a magnificent doublet.

The massive bunch of keys hanging on his worn belt jangled ominously in time to his shuffling gait. One hand was holding a bowl or a plate. The other was trembling slightly as it held the lantern out at arm's length, so that his shadow, enlarged several times over, danced on the wall.

I crept along several steps behind the old man, trying to keep two yards outside the boundary of the light. He shuffled his feet, groaning and swearing under his breath. Once he gave a hoarse cough. I was afraid he might fall to pieces as he moved, without ever reaching the place where his trek was supposed to take him. But, fortunately for me, the corridor suddenly came to an end and the jailer, as I had begun to think of him, halted with a grunt beside the final door. He put the bowl and the lantern down on the floor and took the bunch of keys off his belt.

Mumbling cantankerously, he sorted through the keys, until eventually he settled on one and tried it in the lock, but it didn't work. The jailer cursed the darkness and the father who had begotten him and started jangling the bunch again, looking for a key that would fit better.

At this point it dawned on me that when the old man started walking back, I would be right in his path, if I didn't make a run for that staircase in a hurry. But running in pitch-darkness without making a noise when I couldn't see the walls or the steps was a rather difficult proposition. The old man might be a slow walker, but even if he didn't follow closely enough to see me, he was bound to hear me.

He kept fiddling with the keys, and I tried desperately to think of a way out of this unpleasant situation. I could always smash the old man across the head, but then what guarantee was there that I would find the way back up without him? The new stairway could quite easily lead me into a new labyrinth where I would wander until the end of time. So attacking him was out.

There was no place along his route where I could hide—the lantern lit up the corridor from side to side, and no matter how hard I tried to squeeze back against the wall, a blind mole would be able to spot me. But opposite the door where the old man was standing, there was the doorway of another cell.

And I do mean *doorway*, because there was no door, just a pitch-black opening leading into a cell that had to be empty. The door was lying on the floor of the corridor, with its hinges torn off, formidable dents in its steel surface, and the bars on its window twisted and skewed.

I didn't know who they'd been keeping in that cell, but when I saw what the prisoner had done to the door, I didn't envy the guards when the creature broke out. And it was definitely a creature! No human being could possibly have made dents like that in a five-inch-thick sheet of steel (unless he'd spent three hundred years constantly hammering his thick head against it).

The old man finally found a key, picked the lantern up off the floor to examine his find in brighter light, clicked his tongue in satisfaction, and started playing with the lock. I slipped past him just two steps away and ducked into the dark cell.

The old man stopped trying to turn the key and sniffed the air rapidly, like a hunting dog that has caught the scent of a fox. But right then I wasn't concerned about the old man's eccentricities. I almost jumped straight back out into the corridor, because the empty cell stank as if an army of gnomes had been puking in it for the last ten years.

I covered my nose with the sleeve of my jacket and tried to breathe through my mouth. It wasn't easy, because the smell was so bad that my eyes started watering. And while I stoically struggled against the stench, the old man stood as still as a statue beside the door that he was trying to unlock.

Eventually the jailer took another long sniff at the air and shook his head as if he was driving away some delusion. Oh, come on, granddad! There's no way you can smell me through this stench! Not even if you have the nose of an imperial dog!

The old man started struggling with the stubborn lock again. Meanwhile I tried to keep the remains of my breakfast in my stomach. If I ever got out of these subterranean vaults, I'd have to throw away my stinking clothes and climb into a hot bath for a month.

The lock finally surrendered with a clang and the old man gave a triumphant laugh. There was a creak of rusty, unoiled hinges. He picked up the bowl and walked into the cell, lighting his way with the lantern.

I heard a faint clanking of chains.

"Woken up, have you?" the old man wheezed in a hoarse voice. "I expect you're hungry after three days, eh?"

The answer was silence. A chain clanked again, as if the prisoner had moved.

"Ah, you're so proud!" the old man laughed. "Well, well! Here's some water for you. I'm sorry, I forgot the bread, left it in the watch house. But don't you worry, my beauties, I will definitely bring it on my next round. In a couple of days."

He gave an evil laugh.

I glanced out of my hiding place, hoping to see what was happening in the opposite cell, but all I could make out was the dim glow of the lantern and the old man's back.

"Well, I'm off. Enjoy your stay. And drink your water. Of course, it's not peacock in mushroom sauce or strawberries and cream, but it's very tasty all the same!"

The old man walked out of the cell and the door creaked as it started to close.

"Stop!" Ah, so one of the prisoners was a woman. It was a clear, resonant voice, one used to giving orders.

"Well, I never!" the old man exclaimed in surprise, and stopped. "She spoke. What do you want?"

"Take off the chain."

"And is there anything else you'd like?"

"Do as I say and you'll get a thousand gold pieces."

"Don't abase yourself in front of him, Leta!" another woman said in a harsh voice.

"A thousand? Oho, that's a lot!" the old man croaked, and the door of the cell started creaking again.

"Five thousand!" I could hear a note of despair in Leta's voice.

The door kept on closing.

"Ten! Ten thousand!"

The door slammed with a crash, and I shuddered. That crash seemed to bring the sky tumbling down onto the earth. The bunch of keys jangled again, and I moved away from the wall beside the doorway, where I had been all this time, and retreated deeper into the cell, away from the light.

From my new position I would be able to see the old man's face— and I simply had to see the face of a man who could refuse ten thousand gold pieces in such a simple, offhand manner.

The key grated in the lock and the old man hung the bunch on his belt and turned toward me. What I saw frightened me.

Very badly.

The last time I had been so frightened was that night when I climbed into the Forbidden Territory and met the charming and hungry jolly weeper.

The old man had parchment-yellow skin, a straight, sharp nose, bloodless blue lips, a dirty, unkempt beard, and his eyes . . . His eyes terrified me so much that my knees started shaking. The old fogey had cold, agate eyes without any sign of pupils or an iris. How can you call two opaque pits of darkness eyes?

They were deader than stone, colder than ice, more indifferent than eternity.

Such things simply shouldn't exist in our world.

I couldn't withstand that gaze, and I staggered backward.

All the universal laws of misery united to place a piece of rubbish under my feet. And you don't need to be a genius to guess that the garbage made a deafening clang. To me it sounded loud enough to be heard on the other side of Siala.

The old man, as was only to be expected, froze on the spot and stared with those dead black eyes straight at the spot where I was hiding.

I couldn't think of anything better to do than to pretend I was a log or a lump of stone. In other words, I tried not to move, or even to breathe.

The old man drew in air through his nose and I prayed to Sagot that he wouldn't catch my scent. This jailer with two pools of blackness instead of eyes frightened me so badly, I could have wet my drawers.

The old man shifted the lantern from his right hand to his left and took out a weapon. What it resembled most of all was . . . Well, what can a large human shinbone sharpened at one end resemble? Only a sharpened bone, nothing else.

In the light of the lantern the bone looked yellow, except that its sharp end, which was shaped just like the point of a spear, was a dirty, rusty color—the color of dried blood. The old man grinned and I caught a glimpse of the yellow stumps of rotten teeth. He took a firmer grip on his strange weapon, raised his lantern, and moved in my direction.

Don't believe anyone who tells you that in the final few seconds before death a man's entire past life flashes in front of his eyes like a galloping herd of Doralissian horses.

It's a lie. A deliberate, barefaced, godless lie.

I didn't notice any visions passing through my mind in those few seconds. Who can pay attention to visions when his knees are knocking in sheer terror? The hideous old man had decided to do away with me, there could be no doubt about it.

Either the god of all thieves heard my prayer, or the smell, which I had almost managed to get used to, offended the jailer's sensitive nose, but either way, he stopped three steps outside the doorway of my refuge. The old man was looking straight at me, and the light cast by his lantern ended just five yards away from my feet. If the monstrous freak had taken just a few more steps forward, the light would have reached me.

I cursed my own careless curiosity. If I'd used my head, I would have pressed myself back against the wall and not just stood there like a statue in the middle of the cell, facing the doorway and hoping that the darkness would protect me from the old man's eyes.

Those black eyes gazed in my direction without blinking, and my heart pounded thunderously in my chest, louder than a blacksmith's hammer. I was amazed that the old man couldn't hear it. He stared for a long time. For a very long time, at least a minute, which felt to me like a year, during which I aged an entire century.

"Damned rats," the old man wheezed eventually. "Still breeding, the lousy creatures. What do they eat down here, anyway?"

He stuck his spear-bone away somewhere under his rags, shifted the lantern from his left hand to his right, and shuffled off down the corridor toward the stairway. Once he was gone, all I could see was a small piece of the corridor and the door of the cell in which the two female prisoners were languishing. The farther away the old man moved, the dimmer the light in the corridor became.

I didn't do anything insanely stupid like trying to creep along behind the jailer. Any desire to leave my stinking cell had evaporated the moment I saw his eyes. It would be better to wait and then make my way slowly and quietly to the stairs, even if they did lead into pitch-darkness.

So I stayed where I was.

What if, instead of going up the nearest stairway, I walked to the one that had led me into this corridor and then staggered back to the place where I had come round, and looked for a different way out? I didn't feel too lazy to cover the immense distance back anymore. I was prepared to do anything at all, up to and including flattening the Mountains of the Dwarves, just as long as I didn't meet that old man again. The sound of shuffling feet faded away and a deafening silence filled the corridor. But there was still light! The light of the lantern hadn't completely disappeared. There was a thick, deep twilight in the corridor. . . .

The old man had stopped before he got to the stairway. But why, darkness devour him?

Keeping my eyes fixed on the doorway, I took a careful step to the left, then another, and another, and another.

And then I almost had a heart attack! On my word of honor, no one had ever managed to frighten me so badly twice in such a short time before.

The monster hadn't gone away at all. He'd stretched his withered body out on the floor and he was looking into the cell. If I'd stayed in the same spot where I'd been standing only a few seconds earlier, I wouldn't have noticed him. And if I'd done something even more stupid and moved toward the doorway instead of stepping to the left, I would have come face-to-face with him. And now this monster in human form was staring intently at the very spot where I had just been.

What a cunning devil! How furtively and silently he had come back! He had even duped me. May the darkness drink my blood—it had all been a pretense.

As the old man got up off the floor, his hand dived under his doublet and whipped out his weapon. My back was instantly soaked in cold sweat.

In only two heartbeats the old man leapt into the center of the corridor, stood facing the doorway, and with a movement almost too quick to see, flung the bone at the spot where he thought I was standing. The bone whined as if it were alive as it flew through the air and shot right across the cell, crashing into the far wall with a dull thud and falling to the floor.

My would-be killer grunted in surprise and scratched the back of his head thoughtfully.

"It really is rats," he said in a rather disappointed voice. "Oh, what a bone I've wasted! I'm not sticking my nose into this dump until that smell's gone."

Muttering and swearing, he set off in the direction of his lantern. The sound of shuffling feet receded, the corridor turned darker, and soon the impenetrable darkness returned.

I tried to calm the insane pounding of my heart, which was all set to jump right out of my ribcage. I'd been lucky. If I hadn't moved from my old spot that bone would have been stuck in my chest. The old man had thrown it so quickly that I couldn't possibly have dodged it; I wouldn't even have realized what had happened.

I had been saved by good luck, the help of Sagot, and the caprice of fate. My heartfelt thanks went to all of them for allowing me to keep my life.

The old man's footsteps faded away. My eyes had become so used to the darkness now that I could make out the contours of the doorway. It was very, very quiet all around me, but my fear was still as strong as ever. I was quite simply afraid to move a muscle. What if this was just another cunning trick? I'd already seen how silently he could move. He could easily have pretended to be leaving, taken the lantern away, and could be waiting for me now in the darkness of the corridor!

Waiting . . . in the darkness of the corridor. . . .

A cold shudder ran between my shoulder blades and down my back. I distinctly felt the hair on my head move. That cursed old man with his cursed black eyes was as tricky as a dozen orcs and he could quite easily be waiting in ambush, ready to send me on my final walk into the light.

"Stop, Harold, stop! Stop thinking about it, otherwise the fear will seep into your very bones! A few more thoughts like that, and you'll start to panic. You're a thief. The calm, calculating master thief known as Shadow Harold. A menace to every rich man's treasure chest. The Harold that little green goblins with sharp tongues call the Dancer in the Shadows. You've never given way to panic while you were working, so don't give way to it now! Keep calm. . . . Keep calm. . . . Calm your breathing now, that's it. . . . Breathe in, breathe out. . . . Well done! Now get out of here, before things get even worse."

I don't know if I muttered these words myself or if someone invisible whispered them in my ear, but, with an angry snarl and clatter of teeth, the fear retreated.

Wandering about unarmed in the dark is an absolutely crazy idea, so I held my breath and walked to the back wall of the cell, where the bone had fallen to the floor. I felt around blindly with my feet for a long time, trying to find it. My eyes were watering from the stench and my nose felt as if someone had emptied a wagonload of Garrakian pepper into it, but eventually I found the bone and picked it up.

It was heavy! As I weighed the weapon in my hand, I immediately felt safer. If, Sagot forbid, something went wrong, at least I would have a weapon. I stuck it under my belt and cautiously peeped out of the cell into the corridor.

Nothing and nobody. Black darkness.

I couldn't see the light of the lantern; the old man must have already reached the stairway. After the stupefying stench of the cell, the stale, musty air of the corridor seemed like refreshing nectar of the gods to me.

I couldn't get those cursed black eyes out of my mind—I knew they would haunt my nightmares forever. Ah, if only Eel was with me. . . .

Eel! How could I have forgotten about him!

The veil of forgetfulness fell away and all the previous events of the day flashed through my mind. I remembered what had happened that morning.

First the walk to the mansion and estate of the unknown servant of the Master, then the attack by supporters of the Nameless One, our escape on that absurd wagon, and the crash into the wall before we were taken prisoner and I lost consciousness. And then I had come to in the corridors of this underground prison.

But if I was here, then what had they done with the Garrakian? And why had they left me on the floor of the corridor and not put me in a cell, like the other prisoners? And there was another strange thing—I didn't feel as if I'd gone flying into the wall of that house at full speed. . . . My arms and legs were all sound, my side wasn't smarting. I felt as if I could easily sprint a hundred yards with the guards chasing me.

Was I asleep? It didn't really feel like it. So I had to find Eel and set him free. He had to be somewhere around here. Poking my nose into every cell was pointless—there were too many of them. And I could easily run into serious trouble if I opened the wrong one. I couldn't tell who might be waiting for me inside. The best idea was to steal into the watch house and take a look at the register of prisoners—there had to be one of those in a prison, even if the warders here were old men with black voids where their eyes ought to be.

I set off along the corridor in the direction of the stairway, but stopped before I had taken ten steps. The women prisoners! How could I have forgotten about them? The women must know what prison this was. And there was no way I could just leave them to the mercy of that cursed old man. Maybe I ought to try to let them out, since the Nameless One's supporters hadn't touched the lock picks in my pocket.

A blizzard of contradictory thoughts immediately started swirling around in my head.

"Harold, you're not a knight on a white horse from some sickly sweet children's fairy tale," whispered a voice with a slightly cynical tone. "Take your arms and your legs and scram, get as far away from there as possible! You won't save the women anyway."

"Oh, yes I will!" retorted a different voice. "Could you just leave someone to rot in the dark if you had even the ghost of a chance of saving them?"

Oho! So I had not just one, but two inner voices! Plus my own voice, and Valder's as well! Four in all! It was time to book a room with padded walls in the Hospital of the Ten Martyrs.

"Yes, I could," the first voice replied. "Wandering around in the dark with two women who are half dead from starvation is sheer lunacy. We'd never make it."

"Say what you like, but I'm at least going to try to save them."

"All right," the first voice said to the second after a pause. "But afterwards don't say I didn't warn you. But then . . . What if we can grab ourselves the ten thousand gold pieces that woman offered the old man? Ten here and fifty from the king when we deliver on the Commission . . ."

I went back to the cell where the female prisoners were languishing.

Very carefully, so that I wouldn't make the slightest sound, I put the lock pick with the triangular notch into the keyhole and tried to turn it. It didn't work. Hmm, let's try the one with four prongs and the size zero-one-eight groove. Right, now . . . that was it! Or at least, something in the lock had given a quiet click.

This wasn't a simple lock, though. It had at least nine springs and two secret ones. Catch one of those by accident and you had to start the job all over again. It must have been made by dwarves. The short folk had done their usual good job, and now it would cost me no end of effort to get the door open. I would have to work on a lock like that for anything from two to fifteen minutes.

"Don't be in such a hurry. Think. These women weren't afraid of the old man," I suddenly heard a voice say inside my head.

I shuddered. It wasn't one of my own "inner voices," the sides of a stupid quarrel with myself, it was the voice of Valder, the archmagician who had died several centuries earlier and had now found a refuge inside my hospitable head, which welcomes anyone at all who wants to come in.

"Do you think so?" I thought in fright.

"Yes. Did that old man frighten you?"

"Do you really have to ask?"

"Me too, although I saw it all with an entirely different vision, but while they were talking the women's voices didn't even tremble. So should we really . . ." Valder's whisper inside my head stopped for a moment. "Should you really go barging into the spiders' den?"

"What is this place where I've . . . where we've ended up?"

"I don't know. I can't remember." It was the first time I could recall the magician not knowing something. "Suddenly we were here, that's all. . . . As if someone had just dropped us here. . . ."

"Suddenly we were here? That is, some kind individual just snaps his fingers and bang!—here I am in prison?"

In my mind I wished away the zealous clicker's fingers, together with the rest of his hand. That would teach him to go sending decent people off to Sagot only knew where!

"What should I do?" I asked Valder, just to be on the safe side.

"It's your head," the answer came back. "You decide what you should do."

"Oh no, I beg your pardon! Thanks to you, it isn't just my head anymore!" I snapped back at the archmagician. "You climbed into it without asking permission, and now, if you would be so kind, since you have no intention of disappearing from it, advise me. What should I do?"

This time the answer was silence. The damned archmagician had disappeared, just as he had done before. It was as if he didn't even exist. But I wasn't going to be fooled like that. Valder only pretended to be dumb until some genuine magical danger threatened my skin. He had already got me out of several really tight corners, and I had no doubt that he would do the same again.

Some people might say that the archmagician and I had a mutually advantageous collaboration going, with Valder saving me from dangerous situations and me offering his soul rest and temporary forgetfulness in a corner of my mind. Well, now, everyone who thinks that's great can just shut his mouth and keep it shut! They just don't know what it's like sharing your own head with another person, even if he did die a long, long time ago and he doesn't interfere in my business until things are looking really desperate.

It's a very unpleasant feeling, being able to sense someone else inside yourself and remembering things that never happened in your life. Although I can't deny that if the archmagician hadn't been with me, my eyes would have been eaten away by death-worms long ago.

"All right, the darkness take you. You can keep your damn mouth shut until you turn blue!" I swore under my breath.

I had no time to make any decision about what to do, though. I suddenly heard the sound of footsteps approaching from the direction of the stairway. Whoever the newcomer was, he was walking with a firm, confident stride, and walking in my direction. I thought how strange it was that all the jailers were in the mood for wandering the corridors today. For had always taught me to be afraid of people who strolled blithely through places where you ought to tiptoe and avoid attracting any unnecessary attention. If he was so noisy, it meant he wasn't afraid. If he wasn't afraid, it meant he could be dangerous. If he could be dangerous, he was someone I ought to avoid if I possibly could.

I had always tried to follow my old teacher's wise advice, which was why I was still alive and well. I had no intention of doing anything different this time around.

I ducked into the cell with the open doorway. It already felt like home—the stench crept up into my nose, but this time I was able to adjust to it much more quickly than before. I stood where I could see the door of the female prisoners' cell, and listened to the approaching steps.

The footfalls were only about five yards away from my sanctuary. Three . . . two . . .

The newcomer had a dark-lantern and although I could see an orange crescent in the dark, I couldn't make out anything else around it. There was just the outline of a shadow in the darkness that had scarcely paled at all.

The newcomer stopped and the door gave a pitiful creak. I stared as hard as I could, but it was impossible to see anything in the pitch-black darkness. All I could do was keep my ears open.

The newcomer walked into the cell and I heard a chain jangle again. "Hello."

This time it was the second woman who spoke first.

"The most important thing is always to be polite, is that right, Lafresa?" the unexpected visitor asked in a mocking tone. The moment I heard that voice, I wished I was a thousand leagues away!

Darkness! A h'san'kor and a thousand demons! May they roast the soles of my feet on a frying pan! May I be caught red-handed every time for the rest of my life! Now I was really in trouble.

I recognized him. I had only heard his voice twice before, but both times I really wished I wasn't there. It was the Master's faithful servant, the one they called the Messenger.

"And what else do I have, apart from politeness?" The woman's voice sounded bitter. "Or did you expect me to start begging you to spare my life?"

"Only the Master can spare your life," the creature replied bleakly. "I am merely the Messenger who carries out his will. And as for not begging me . . . you will. If I want you to. You certainly will, Lafresa."

The woman didn't answer.

"Well, now," the Messenger chuckled, without waiting for an answer. He sounded quite human now. "I see Blag is keeping you on nothing but water."

"I'll rip his heart out!" Leta hissed furiously.

"I don't think that would do him any harm," the Messenger chuckled. "You ought to know how to deal with Soulless Ones. It's simpler to cut Blag's head off than try to tear out a useless organ. . . . Although I can offer you some hope—you may soon be able to carry out your threat, my dear Leta. I've been thinking more and more often about making you into the same kind of Soulless One as old Blag. Our mutual friend needs an assistant . . . for various kinds of . . . pleasures."

"You were always fond of foul jokes, slave!" the woman replied contemptuously.

Now I felt delighted that I hadn't tried to save their lives. Anyone who talked with the Messenger on equal terms was no companion for me.

"And for all your short life you have been distinguished by tremendous conceit," the Messenger parried mockingly. "You took too much upon yourself, my dear Leta, as did the lovely Lafresa here, and you have paid for it."

"I have always been faithful and carried out all the Master's orders!" Leta retorted furiously.

"Always? Come now, Leta! Don't try to deceive an old friend. There's only you, me, and Lafresa here; you can feel free to tell me how you managed to bungle such a simple task."

"We did everything just as the Master ordered! For the good of—"

"Don't give me any speeches about the good of the cause! Leave that for the priests and those tawdry peacocks who call themselves noblemen. Come on, tell me why your purple cloud didn't work!" the Messenger barked. "Why does the Master still not have the Key?"

A purple cloud! Was the Master's faithful dog talking about the shamanic storm? It certainly sounded as if he meant the abomination that had almost wiped out our group in Hargan's Wasteland.

"I don't understand how it happened," the woman said in a tired voice. "You know I did everything carefully and correctly, just as I was told. The servants killed all of the Nameless One's shamans—they were hunting the travelers, too—then we used the brew they had prepared and concealed the spell with a storm so that, darkness forbid, the Order would not get wind of anything, and we sent the magic off on the right wind. Everything was carefully calculated, and no one should have survived. Neither the elves nor the elfess had enough knowledge to oppose me. They couldn't have destroyed the cloud!"

"But they did!" the Messenger retorted implacably.

"It wasn't them," Leta argued. "You can smell the shamanism of the dark elves and the Firstborn a league away, and there was nothing."

"Don't make excuses!" Lafresa exclaimed shrilly. "He's nothing but a servant."

"It wasn't them," the other woman insisted stubbornly, taking no notice of what Lafresa had said.

"Not them? Then who? In the name of the Font of Bloody Dew, tell me who!" the Messenger hissed.

"I don't know. Someone powerful. And probably a magician, because we couldn't sense anything. Someone you didn't take into account."

And his name was Valder. It was my acquaintance who had shattered the purple cloud into a million tiny shreds and saved our group.

"Stop lying! You're walking a knife edge as it is. Everything was taken into account. Everything! Or do you expect me to believe that there's a magician hiding among those ants? Player from Avendoom didn't say anything about any powerful magician. Nobody from the Order went with the group, he made sure of that!"

"I don't trust Player," Leta muttered. "He's a fox who could mess up our plans at any moment."

"Immortality and knowledge make a magnificent incentive for loyalty."

"If he's so loyal to our cause, then why is the thief still alive?"

"The plans have changed."

"That's stupid!"

This woman would have done better to follow Lafresa's example and say nothing, if she wanted to live a bit longer.

"Just a little more and I'll rip your tongue out, girl! It's not for you to discuss the will of the Master."

"No threats, please, Messenger! I knew you in another life, servant of the Master, so save your eloquence for the sheep. You'll find them much easier to frighten than me!"

"Oh, yes, they're much more compliant than you are. But you're no different from them. You're just as mortal, although you can remember all your previous lives. But we're not talking about the servants, we're talking about you and your friend here. You made a mistake, you failed to justify the Master's trust, and that's why you're here, waiting to pay the penalty."

"Is that why you came? How low the one they now call the Messenger has fallen! Well, I'm ready to die," Lafresa declared proudly.

"Have you any last words you would like to say?"

"No."

Leta laughed hoarsely and hysterically: "Unlike you I can always return to the House of Love. But you, my dear J—"

The man suddenly started wheezing. Now that was something we'd seen before. When this character got upset, he liked to grab the nearest person within reach round the neck.

"Ne-ver," he hissed quietly. "Do you hear me? *Never* dare to speak my real name! Yes, thanks to Lafresa I was born in the House of Pain and the House of Fear, and I can never even touch Love, but now I am in the House of Power, and it is not for a little louse like you to speak my name!" The wheezing gradually became a gurgling, and then I heard the soft thud of a falling body—our messenger was a very affable fellow.

"If I had my way, you would never leave this cell, Lafresa. I haven't forgotten. So when you meet the Master you can thank him in person for sparing your life! You're lucky, there's a job for you to do."

"What can I do for my lord?" The surviving woman's voice didn't even tremble. She wasn't saddened in the least by the death of her friend.

"You are one of only a few who can be trusted with the Key. You will take it and bring it here."

"The Key?"

"Have you become hard of hearing? The artifact is in the hands of one of the servants. You will bring it back, or is that too difficult for you?"

"No . . . it's not difficult. But why me?"

"You ask the right question. Leta could have been in your place. And any feeble human, even without your abilities, could have brought this thing to the Master, but the problem is that . . . the Key has been attached. The elfess has already worked her shamanism and now the bonds will have to be broken. Apart from you there are only five others who are capable of that. And to anticipate your question, the reason *you* have been chosen instead of them is as follows: Player is too busy in Avendoom and the others are too far away. And they would require a lot of time to prepare before they could even begin. . . . Knowing your natural gift for Kronk-a-Mor, I make bold to presume that you won't need any preparation. Or almost none . . ."

"When does the Master need the Key?"

"In two weeks at the most."

"It will take me four months to get to Ranneng from here."

"You will be there the day after tomorrow. Collect the artifact, break the bond, bring it to the Master, and then, perhaps, our lord will forget your annoying blunder. Do you understand?"

"Yes."

"Good."

"I shall need time. I have to wait for a propitious conjunction of the stars, otherwise the bonds will not break."

"You have no time. Try not to make a mess of this."

"Take off my chains."

I heard a quiet clicking sound.

"Take the lantern and get out of here."

"Gladly," the woman responded.

"Remember, this time you'd better not make any mistakes, or it will be a long time before you see the House of Love again."

"I shall remember your words, Messenger."

I saw that the woman was short, with bare feet, but I couldn't get a look at the features of her face. If this Lafresa was going to turn up out of the blue at the Nightingales' mansion to collect the Key, somehow or other I had to get there in time to stop her. She walked off with the Messenger following her.

I waited for the sound of their footsteps to fade away.

"Harold, now you've stopped thinking altogether," Valder remarked sulkily.

"Well, you're a real chatterbox today," I replied to the archmagician. "What's the problem?"

"Did you hear what he said? It takes four months to get to Ranneng, but she'll be there the day after tomorrow." Then Valder disappeared again.

Ah, darkness! By the time I got to the city, the Key would probably already be gone! And I couldn't warn Miralissa or Markauz, either. The only thing I could do—much as I loathed the idea—was follow those two and . . .

And what? Stop them? Or ask them to take me along?

Sagot, show me the way! I walked out of the cell and then, keeping one hand on the wall, set off toward the staircase, in the same direction the Messenger and the woman had gone earlier.

I tried to walk quickly and silently—as far as that was possible in the pitch-black darkness.

The pair I was following were fifteen yards ahead of me. I didn't dare move any closer to the Master's servants because I was afraid of being noticed, and I judged how far away they were by sound. As soon as their steps sounded quieter, I sped up and moved closer to the pair in front of me. If I overdid it and the sound started getting louder, I stopped and waited before carrying on.

We walked on like that until they came to the stairway. Then I had to wait for Lafresa and the Messenger to walk up before I could follow them.

It took me a long time to climb the stairs. In the first place, it was just as dark as ever, the steps were completely different sizes, and I had to feel my way along, so I could only move at a snail's pace. In the second place, the stairway itself was very long: At first it went upward, then it started spiraling round and round, and it went on and on and on.

I felt as if I was going to offer up my soul to Sagot right there on that accursed stairway and, naturally, I lost sight of the pair I'd been following all this time.

When the steps finally ended, I peeped out cautiously into a corridor illuminated by widely spaced smoking torches. No one. No Messenger and no Lafresa. The massive stone-block walls were almost completely covered in soot, and the arched ceiling was far from clean, too. Here and there it still bore traces of genuine whitewash, but to my inexperienced eye they looked decades old. No doors in the walls, nothing but inscriptions in some language that I didn't know—either ogric or the language of the Firstborn, I don't have a clue about the writing of either race.

I hadn't walked very far, perhaps a hundred or a hundred and fifty paces, when the corridor ended at another stairway, but this time there were only twenty steps at most. At the top of the steps the thick darkness started again. I put my foot on the first step, and my nose was immediately assailed by a faint, moldy odor of dust and decay.

"Oh, no," I muttered to myself. I walked back a little way along the corridor and took a torch down off the wall.

The flame trembled and spat sparks in the draft that somehow managed to find its way into the underground maze. Then I walked up the steps into a small hall and swore out loud—I didn't like what I saw one little bit.

There was a skeleton lying stretched out on a crudely built wooden table. I could tell straightaway that it wasn't human. To judge from the fangs, it had probably been an orc or an elf. And it had a rusty hatchet stuck in the top of its skull.

I'm not afraid of dead men, especially the kind that lie still and keep their mouths shut. I'm not even really worried by the wretches that members of the Order call "the arisen" and the simple folk call "wanderers" or simply "the living dead." They're fairly clumsy creatures, harmless as long as you keep away from their hands and teeth. And try not to get under their feet in general.

The living dead do exist, that's a fact. But I'd never heard of living skeletons before. How can bones move if they have no muscles, tendons, pads of cartilage, and all the rest to connect them?

Two answers immediately came to mind: Either some idiot was jerking the bones about on strings, or the shamanism of the ogres was responsible—and that, of course, was entirely possible.

Anyway, I had no time to figure out why the skeleton lying on the table was jerking its legs about rather friskily and apparently trying to get up. I was concerned with a different question: Would it be able to do what it wanted and would that be dangerous for me?

The skeleton jerked its legs and tried to stand up. But it was getting nowhere, because some kind soul had pinned its spine to the table with huge iron staples.

I have to admit that curiosity is a failing of mine. I walked a little bit closer. The creature immediately turned its head in my direction and hissed. I swear by Sagot that it *hissed*, even though it had no lungs or tongue or any of the other things that decent people are supposed to have in order to make sounds.

The black holes of the eye sockets, with a myriad of crimson sparks swirling in them, were trained on me. "Free me, mortal!"

I was dumbfounded for a moment. If skeletons had learned to speak, it was time for me to move into the cemetery—the end of the world had to be near.

"Not in this life," I replied grimly, and backed as far away as possible.

The dead creature lowered its head onto the table and hissed in fury, like oil poured onto a red-hot skillet, then started writhing and jerking about. It really put its heart into it (except, of course, that it didn't have one), and the table started shifting across the floor.

"I shall free my-self an-y-way!"

Every syllable was accompanied by a sharp jerk that set the table shuddering. The staple at the dead creature's waist started to yield ever so slightly.

I decided it would be better to go on my way and not tempt fate. The creature's spine was pinned down along its entire length, and it would have to jerk for at least a week. But the most important thing was to make a start. The first restraint had already yielded, and the others would follow. Water wears away stone, as they say. I wasn't going to hang about to observe what would happen when this thing broke free.

For the next few minutes after that, nothing strange, let alone unpleasant, happened, for which Sagot be praised and glorified forever! The floor rose up a very slight incline and the torch lit up the dreary gray blocks of stone gleaming with the underground damp, and the inscriptions scrawled on the walls by someone's careless hand. The ceiling retreated to a great height, so that the flame of the torch could no longer pick it out of the gloom. A slight echo appeared, doubling the sound of every step I took, and I had to walk almost on tiptoe.

The Messenger and the woman had dissolved into the darkness, and now there was no way that I could possibly catch up with them.

"Start with the Lower South Level," said the Messenger's voice, spreading along the corridor. I dropped the torch on the floor and stamped it out with my foot. "The Master has no more need of them."

"Can I . . . ?" asked Blag, his voice trembling with excitement.

"I don't care what you do, Lost Soul," the Messenger replied, and every word was full of contempt. "If you want to eat them, then eat them; if you want to carve trinkets out of their bones, then do it; but first do as I have told you."

"Of course, my lord! Old Blag will take care of their bones. Oh, yes! He'll take care of them."

The voices seemed to come from all around me. They enveloped me, so that I couldn't tell where the speakers were. I was sure that the Messenger and the old man weren't in the corridor, or they would definitely have seen the light of my torch. It sounded as if they were talking somewhere behind the wall, but I hadn't seen any door while the torch was still alight.

"Permit me to say, my lord . . . Please forgive me if it is none of my business . . . but you shouldn't have let that girl go."

The sound of Blag's voice was coming from right above my head now. Were they walking on the ceiling, or what?

"Just do as I told you!" the Messenger snapped. "Otherwise you'll find yourself back in the place the Master found you, feeding the worms again!"

Blag started muttering in fright and the section of wall directly in front of me slid to one side, revealing a room that was lit by a lantern. I didn't even have time to jump aside; the secret door opened so suddenly that I was caught in the circle of light. Blag was coming out into the corridor and he saw me.

I swear on Kli-Kli's head that I saw a momentary flash of amazement in those black pools of eyes. The old man grinned, baring his rotten teeth, and I flung his own weapon—the bone—at him without bothering to think.

I must say that I'm no great master at throwing ordinary knives, let alone bones. But this time someone must have guided my hand.

I didn't hit the old man, but I did hit the oil lamp in his hand. It exploded, and the flame threw itself on Blag like a polecat crazed with hunger. The old man howled, dropped onto the floor, and started rolling around, trying to put out the fire. The flames enveloped him completely, devouring his clothes and his flesh. I stood there, completely spellbound by this terrible sight, and only noticed the frenzied gleam of a pair of amber-yellow eyes at the very last moment.

A black shadow sprang at me, I instinctively jumped back, and the clawed hand extended to tear out my heart missed.

Almost missed.

The claws ripped open my shirt, and then a clump of pain exploded somewhere in the region of my stomach. I think I just had time to yell before the world splintered into a thousand excruciating shards.

6

FRIENDS AND ENEMIES

The black night of the universe and the icy fire of magic. A world within a world, a dream within a dream, a drop within a drop, a mirror within a mirror . . .

I've been here once before.

When was that? An eternity earlier or an eternity later?

Ah yes! I think I remember—it was in the distant future, on that day when Miralissa bound the Key of the Doors of Hrad Spein to my consciousness. On that memorable evening I fell through into the black night of Nothingness, into a dream of a dream, filled with fiery flakes of the crimson flame of Kronk-a-Mor.

But unlike last time, this time I felt cold . . . very cold. . . .

My body was racked by agonizing cramps. The only things I could feel were the cold and the pain. But which of these two evils was causing me more suffering? Just at the moment I couldn't give a rotten damn; all I wanted, with every nerve in my body, was to get out of there to somewhere a bit more welcoming and a bit less mysterious. But this time nothing came of my futile efforts to escape from Nothingness. There was no dark elfess there to help me, I was absolutely helpless and freezing . . . colder and colder.

Cold-cold-cold-cold-cold . . .

After a while I had the feeling that a tangle of gluttonous leeches had invaded my stomach, inflicting a pain more appalling than anything I could have imagined. If not for the cold swirling of the sharp, prickly snowflakes, constantly distracting me from the hot coals blazing in my belly, the pain would have driven me out of my mind. There was no question of actually looking at what the Messenger's talons had done to my stomach: I was afraid I would pass out if I even caught a glimpse of it.

The pain pulsated and increased, doubling and multiplying inside me, like the infinite reflections in the mirror maze of a dream. It unfolded its sharp petals all the way through my body, driving me to the brink of insanity. Now I knew what the most terrible torture of all is.

Through the silent swirling dance of the fiery snowflakes I could hear a regular tapping sound, but it took me a while to realize that it was my teeth beating out a tattoo in honor of the master of this world—the fiery snow, bringer of an icy death.

The wind of the darkness, the wind that had once brought me dreams of the past, dreams of those who were long dead—men, elves, gnomes, orcs, and many other creatures—sprang to life, flinging sharp crystals of icy fire into my face.

I tried to dodge away, or at least protect my face against the snowflakes with my hands, but my pitiful efforts only infuriated the leeches of pain in my stomach. The moment they sensed that I was busy with something else, that I had stopped trying to control them, they started gnawing into my guts, and I howled out in pain and horror.

They pulsated in unison, breathing together, but if you knew that they are not all-powerful, they could be defeated.

But the cold was pitiless, heartless, and indifferent to everything alive. This thing was trying to put me to sleep, to bring me false warmth and peace, to carry my mind off into the river of eternal forgetfulness and dreams that flowed into the sea of Death.

I'm cold! Sagot, I'm so cold!

In the darkness the fiery snowflakes swirled together into a gigantic pillar of flame, falling on my hands and melting, turning into crimson steam.

The black Nothing of magic, the world of dreams and phantoms of the past, has its own, different, laws.

"Greetings, Dancer!"

Just like the last time, I had missed the brief instant when they appeared in front of me. They glided toward me—my old friends, the living shadows, the mistresses of Nothing. I thought of them as First, Second, and Third. Three shadows, three friends, three sisters, three lovers . . . They hadn't changed at all since our last meeting and our last dance, which had helped me get out of here the last time. Perhaps I might be able to escape with their help this time, too?

"Hel-lo, la-dies." My teeth were chattering and words were hard to pronounce.

"Do you not know, Dancer, that some dreams are as dangerous as reality?" There was a note of sadness in Second's voice.

"D-dreams are d-dangerous?" I recalled all the nightmares about the past that I had seen in the last month. "Yes, I sup-pose I kn-now that . . ."

"Then why do you summon them to yourself, Dancer? Prophecies and destiny cannot protect you forever."

First and Third did not say anything.

"I did not wish to ap-pear in your d-dream world," I said, trying to make excuses. "I d-don't even know how I ended up here in this cr-cr-crimson snow."

"You think our world is a dream?" the First Shadow asked in amazement. "That is a mistake, Dancer. Our world is far more real than yours—it was the first of all to appear. The world of Chaos had served as the basis for thousands of others when your kind started creating and destroying shadows. It is not a dream, and we are not a dream, and you are not in a dream now. . . ."

"And you are dying, Dancer," said Third, joining in the conversation. "You are dying because you wander too often through dreams that are too dangerous for you as yet."

"I d-don't und-derstand what you . . ." The cold was lulling my mind to sleep.

"Dreams can kill," First murmured. "Once you believe a dream is reality, you don't just see it, you start living in it. And then how dangerous it becomes! The one who did this to you was in your dream—"

"Or you were in his," said Second, interrupting First.

"That's not important now. You believed and so you received this wound . . ."

The Master's prison is a dream?

The reminder of the wound and the sincere sympathy I could hear in the shadow's voice made me take a look at my stomach.

I really shouldn't have done that. I didn't know why I was still alive. Wounds like that guarantee a quick passage into the light with no chance of ever coming back to see the blue sky.

The leeches of pain started gnawing on me twice as viciously, and I was unable to hold back my scream.

"There, Dancer, now you see how dangerous uncontrolled dreams can be?"

"How d-did . . . How did I g-get here?"

"We should ask you that—you entered our house of your own free will."

"I d-didn't want to come here! I wanted to g-go home!"

"Now our world will be your home forever. In Siala you would have drawn your last breath ages ago. You can only stay alive here."

"I n-need my world!"

"Your world?" Third began swirling round me, scattering a shimmering curtain of crimson snowflakes. "Why is it better than this one? Can you do this there?"

Third moved close, until she was almost touching me, and I caught a brief glimpse of a woman's face. Then she merged into me, and I felt a wave of warmth run through my body, and the leeches of pain unclamped their suckers with a rasping groan of disappointment and drifted away into the black night to find a weaker and more accommodating victim.

In an instant Third was beside her sisters again, and I stared in astonishment at the spot where only a second ago there was a terrible, gaping wound.

Nothing. No wound at all. My torn and bloody shirt was the only reminder of the Messenger's blow.

"Is your world capable of that, Dancer?"

I shook my head in bewilderment. Nobody, not even the Order, can make healthy, unbroken skin appear where there was a hole the size of a man's fist, gushing blood, with guts spilling out of it. In Siala only the gods can pull off tricks like that.

"Then why are you so eager to go back there?"

"I have b-business to finish," I blurted out. "And ap-part from that, it's t-too cold here."

First laughed, and the snowflakes responded to her laugh by bursting and turning into little sparks. Then they fused together into the ravenous beast whose name is fire, and in an instant it had devoured the black night and surrounded us with a dense cocoon of heat.

The shadows remained as impenetrably black as ever.

"Well then, Dancer, is that warmer?" First asked mockingly.

"Yes . . ." I didn't have the strength to feel surprised. Just how omnipotent were these three? And why were they so interested in my humble person?

"Are you staying with us?"

"What d-do you want with me?" I asked, playing for time as I warmed up.

"You are the Shadow Dancer. The first Dancer who has appeared in more than ten thousand years! And you can do things that other people cannot. You still don't know what you are capable of. We need you, this world needs you, and you will breathe into it the life that has gone to other worlds, thanks to your kind. Without you our home will die!"

"Without me my world will die," I tried to shout above the vicious roar of the flame. "It's my duty . . ."

"Your duty?" Second said sarcastically. "A thief talking about duty."

"I have to go back and finish a job," I insisted stubbornly. "I accepted a Commission, and until I carry it out, I am not free to follow my own wishes."

The shadows put their heads together and started talking quietly. Had I really managed to persuade them? My place was not in this world, a world of emptiness filled with fiery snow or hot flame. Surely they could understand that?

"All right, you can leave," Second announced. "We have waited for thousands of years, we will wait a little longer. You will come back to us in any case. He who has found the way to the primary world always returns. Now go!"

"Which way?"

"Forward."

I cast a wary glance at the wall of fire.

"You know that I cannot pass through the fire without you."

"True. But this time you must pass through without our help. We shall not always be beside you. A djanga with shadows will not always lead you through the traps of the House of Power. The time will come when you will have to fight it singlehanded."

"The House of Power?" I exclaimed. "You said 'the House of Power'! And do you know about the Houses of Love, Pain, and Fear as well?"

"Yes, we know."

"And the Master? Who or what he is? You know about—"

"Yes, we know," Third interrupted me.

"Then tell me. It's very important!"

"A moment ago you were in a hurry to get away, Dancer, and now you are hungry for information," First answered my question coldly. "Information must be paid for, are you ready for that?"

"That depends on what you want for it," I said cautiously. You should never agree to anything until you know what price you'd be asked to pay in return.

"You will have to stay with us."

"Then your knowledge is not worth a bent penny. I won't have any use for it here."

"I'm sorry, but it will be a long time before your world is ready for this knowledge," Second answered me regretfully. "Forward, Dancer, the fire is waiting for you."

"Good-bye!"

"No, until we meet again, and soon, Dancer! Remember that a djanga with shadows does not always lead along the right road."

"Remember!"

"Beware!"

They shouted something else as well from behind me, but I could no longer hear what they said. The fire flicked its hissing tongues of flame at me, menacing me.

"You're mine!" roared the crimson fire.

"You're ours!" its ravenous tongues echoed.

I'm not much inclined to acting in a crazy, irrational fashion, but the time for it had clearly come now. So it's not always possible to pass through the flame by dancing with shadows? Well, some other way, then . . .

The fire scorched my face and my hair started crackling menacingly. The skin started to crack on the hands covering my eyes.

The last time only the djanga, the wild, crazy dance that I'd been whirled into by the three shadows, had allowed me to pass through the flames of this inhospitable world and get back to Siala.

This time I was on my own, face-to-face with the ravenous fire.

"You're mine!" the wall of heat droned.

"You're mine!" I barked back.

And without thinking about it any more, I jumped straight into the oven. The wall roared triumphantly as it embraced me. The pain from the burning unfolded into a crimson blossom, but my clothes and my hair didn't flare up. The flame was left howling in disappointment behind me. Before the silence came crashing down on me, I had time to realize that I had managed to break through the boundary between worlds without the help of any djanga with shadows. . . .

My head was buzzing, a herd of hedgehogs had settled in my mouth, the back of my head was throbbing. I hissed louder than a boiling kettle and forced myself to open my eyes. Everything was swimming about, so it cost me a serious effort to understand where I was.

"Good morning!" said a loud voice, and I started.

"Is this what you call a good morning, Eel?" I asked with a wry chuckle.

"At least we're still alive."

"How long have we been here?"

"We've been stuck in here all yesterday and all night. How's your head?"

"Don't even mention it," I told the Garrakian with a groan. "It's buzzing like an angry nest of hornets. They belted me pretty hard in the cart."

"I was starting to get worried. You had a fever and you were talking, but you didn't come round."

"I was having bad dreams," I muttered, recalling the walk along the gloomy corridors of the Master's prison and the mysterious fiery snow of the primary world of Chaos, which the shadows had said was on the point of death.

A dream! It was only the latest dream in a never-ending sequence of nightmares.

"How are you? You came off worse than I did," I asked Eel.

"I'll survive," he answered laconically.

Well, if a Garrakian says he'll survive, then he will.

I tried to move my arms, but nothing came of it—some rotten lout had tied them good and tight behind my back.

"Don't bother," Eel chuckled, noticing me trying to test the strength of the ropes wrapped around my wrists. "It's art fiber rope, not that easy to get out of. I fiddled with it for an hour, but it didn't get me anywhere."

Art is a kind of tree—stunted, twisted, and nothing remarkable to look at. But when its fibers have been properly processed, they make magnificently strong ropes. You can cut through them or gnaw through them, but you have to be extremely strong or extremely supple to snap them or twist your way out of them.

"Have they stuck us in a cell, then?" I mumbled rather dimwittedly.

I just couldn't shake off the visions of my dreams. I couldn't believe that the long walk through those underground corridors and the conversation with the shadows were just a nightmare.

"That's right. The Nameless One's supporters don't seem very keen to invite us to a formal banquet."

I looked round, trying to get a clearer idea of our place of confinement.

It had gray walls and a little window with bars up near the ceiling, dirty straw on the floor, and a solitary torch on the wall. At first sight it was a perfectly ordinary cell, not a very attractive place for a permanent residence. But there was one thing about it that was strange—in all my life, no one who had been in jail had ever told me that a cell needed to have two doors.

"Is the second a spare? In case the jailers lose the key to the first one?" I asked, trying to joke, despite the roaring that still filled my head.

The first door, which was wooden, and bound with narrow strips of steel, was directly opposite us. The second, which was completely made of metal, was on the left-hand wall of the cell and, unlike the first, it had a bolt here on the inside, not on the outside like any self-respecting prison door.

"What kind of nonsense is that?"

He followed my glance and shrugged his shoulders awkwardly.

"I haven't got a clue. Better pray to that Sagot of yours, ask him to help us get out of here."

"I think we'll be getting out of here soon enough, probably feet first." I was in a grimly talkative mood. "What are the chances of the squad finding us before the Nameless One's lads offload their surplus baggage?"

"If we were surplus baggage, they wouldn't have bothered to snatch us, they'd have finished us off right there in the street."

"True enough. They need us for something, but how long will that last? Kli-Kli got away, Sagot be praised, and I think enough time has gone by for Alistan and Miralissa to start doing something."

We heard a cock crowing loudly outside the little window.

"We're not in Ranneng," said Eel, "we're in the country, and Alistan is hardly likely to guess that he should look for us so far away from the walls."

"What makes you think we're in the country? Do you think there are no cocks in Ranneng?"

"Of course not, there are plenty, but I came round in the carriage, and before they knocked me out again, I managed to look out the window, and the landscape I saw was definitely not in a city."

Aha. That's nice to hear. Now we know for sure that the chances of finding us, in a cellar so far away from the inn, are nonexistent.

"You certainly know how to keep a man's hopes up," I sighed miserably.

All we could do was wait, hope for a miracle, and trust in Sagot and any other individuals who might be willing to help us. But the miracle was avoiding us, Sagot apparently couldn't hear us, and those other individuals didn't exist (at least, they were nowhere within a league of us). As the sailors from the Port City say, we had run firmly aground.

A bolt clattered and two men came in. The first was a short bald man of about fifty with broad shoulders, a purple nose, and icy blue eyes. He was wearing crumpled, grease-spattered clothes and a crooked grin plastered right across his repulsive face. The second visitor was . . . Loudmouth.

Alive and absolutely well.

For a second I couldn't believe it was him, I thought it was some kind of apparition or ghost risen from the grave.

When Eel saw who had come to visit us, his face never even quivered. But his dark eyes narrowed.

"I'll tear your heart out," he hissed through his teeth.

"I shall try to be careful and not fall into your hands," Loudmouth replied very seriously. "My apologies for the inconvenience that you have suffered."

Still speaking in the same icy voice, Eel told Loudmouth to take his inconvenience and stuff it you-know-where.

"A pity," the traitor said sadly. "I genuinely regret everything that has happened, but no one can choose his destiny. You have chosen your side and I have chosen mine."

"And did you make your choice a long time ago?" I asked gloomily, finally spotting what Eel had noticed straightaway—a little ring on Loudmouth's finger in the form of a branch of poison ivy.

Everything suddenly fell into place. He was the one who told the followers of the Nameless One where we were staying and where the Key was! And he must have helped them to track us down at the Nightingales' house.

How cunningly this bastard had worked everything! Right under our very noses, and nobody had suspected a thing! How could anyone ever think that a Wild Heart would be a servant of the Nameless One? It would be like saying the sun was green and ogres were charming creatures.

When he said he was going to visit relatives, he'd told his accomplices about us and then gone back to the inn. After that it was all very simple. The Nameless One's lads broke into the inn and shot the staff, Markauz and the warriors took shelter in the kitchen, and Loudmouth staged his own death and cleared out with his helpers and our Key. Who would ever have made the connection between a Wild Heart and the Nameless One? No one! And we would never have heard about Loudmouth again—he would have disappeared and our paths would never have crossed if the servants of the Master had not taken the Key from him.

"A very long time ago, Harold," he laughed. "You can't imagine for how many generations my family has been trying to help the lord return to Valiostr."

"But you're a Wild Heart. How could you do it?"

"Harold, I really do like you a lot, but don't talk to me about the Wild Hearts. I only gave them fourteen years of my life because the Nameless One ordered me and a few others of the Faithful to do it."

The servants of the Nameless One call themselves the Faithful? Ha!

"And are there many of you among us?" Eel asked in a voice that was monumentally calm.

"Very well, I will answer you, my old friend," the traitor said with a smile. "You can know that now, and you know why?"

"Because you'll never get out of this cellar," said the man with the purple nose, finally opening his mouth.

"Shut up!" Loudmouth snapped at his companion, then addressed Eel again. "There were six of us. The eyes and ears of the Nameless One among the Wild Hearts. Surprised? You'd be even more surprised if you knew their names. I'll tell you one of them, just for old times' sake. You remember Stump, Captain Owl's deputy? He was the leader of our group. Unfortunately the faithful one never returned from the Desolate Lands."

"It's a pity that you didn't stay there with him," Eel said in a dull voice.

This time the Garrakian was unable to disguise his true feelings. A hedgehog could have seen how shaken he was to discover that traitors had wormed their way into the Wild Hearts. It was unbelievable!

"I would have, if you hadn't saved my life," Loudmouth said with a nod. "Well, anyway, that's all in the past, and we'll have plenty of time to talk. In the meantime, I just came to visit and find out if there's anything you need. Give them water."

The final words were addressed to Purple Nose. Loudmouth walked toward the door, but I called to him.

"Loudmouth!"

"Yes, Harold?"

"Was it worth it?"

"Was what worth it? Fourteen years of life thrown away or serving the lord?"

"The second."

"You don't understand and you can't understand. Not you, or the Wild Hearts, with whose tattoos I defiled my body. For you the Nameless One is evil. Pure, unadulterated evil, and nothing more."

"My, what a fine talker you've become," Eel muttered.

"You're used to seeing Loudmouth whining and sleeping all the time, dissatisfied with the entire world, right?" He smiled again. "Loudmouth! If only you knew how sick I am of that name fit for a dog! For fourteen years I was a dog, for fourteen years I barked for your king. I have a name perhaps even more noble than the title that you conceal, Garrakian."

"Noble birth won't save you from me."

"Anything can happen, but it's not likely," our enemy said with a frown. "As for your question, Harold, it was worth it. From the very beginning. If not for the Rainbow Horn, the Nameless One would have crushed the Stalkon dynasty long ago."

"How can anyone hate a dynasty for all those hundreds of years? Your Nameless One really is insane."

"The Stalkons made him what he is. They took the name of the finest magician of the Order and blackened it in the eyes of the people. Everyone turned away from him, everyone he loved. Including his own twin brother, his wife, and his children! He had no other choice but Kronk-a-Mor and immortality. And now he wants to take his revenge."

"There's no one he can take it on. They all died ages ago, and his brother Grok has been lying in Hrad Spein for a long time."

"This conversation is not going to lead anywhere," Loudmouth said with a shake of his head, and walked out of the cell.

"Loudmouth!" Eel roared, and I started in surprise.

"Yes?" Amazingly enough, he came back.

"Remember, I'm going to cut your heart out!"

He didn't say anything, just glared intently at the bound Garrakian through slightly narrowed eyes, grinned crookedly and not very confidently, and went out again.

"Here's your water," said Purple Nose, putting two bowls down in front of us.

"And how do you expect us to drink with our hands tied behind our backs?" I asked him.

"Sorry, I'm afraid that's not my problem. I'm not suicidal and I'm not going to untie your hands. Find yourself another fool for that. But I can give you a piece of advice: You don't have to drink it, you haven't got much time left anyway."

"Why did you drag us all the way here? You could have finished us off in the street."

"You ask Rizus that when he comes to count your bones."

Purple Nose started walking toward the door.

"Hey, scumbag," Eel called quietly to the jailer. The Garrakian's voice simply oozed the contempt of a superior being for an inferior.

"Scumbag? Did *you* call *me* a scumbag?" said Purple Nose, clenching his fists.

He bounded across to the Garrakian, waving his fists in the air. Eel didn't look away, and Purple Nose couldn't bring himself to punch him.

"Do you want to know how you're going to die?" Purple Nose asked with an evil laugh. "Your neighbors in the next cell are going to eat you. I'll introduce you right now."

Purple Nose walked across to the metal door and pulled the squeaking bolt open with an effort. Behind it there was a massive forged-iron grille, blocking off the entrance into the next cell. I was unpleasantly surprised to see something that looked like tooth marks on the lower part of the grille. Someone had tried very hard to gnaw their way through to freedom, and I disliked that someone very much indeed. It's best to give creatures with teeth like that a wide berth.

Preferably at least a league wide.

"I haven't fed them for three weeks, so there won't even be any bones left. I'm leaving the door open so that you can enjoy looking at them. Once Rizus has had a talk with you, I'll be glad to turn the lever in the corridor, the grille will rise, and someone will get eaten, heh-heh!"

Purple Nose gave that repulsive chortle again and left the cell.

"What's in there, Eel, can you see?" I asked nervously.

"No, but I don't like this."

"I should think not, with a stench like that coming out of the place!" I agreed.

The smell coming from behind the grille made me feel a bit panicky. It wasn't really all that harsh, there was only a slight whiff, but it was quite enough to put me on my guard.

That was the way rotten meat smelled. Carrion. Corpses.

"The sons of bitches have got one of the living dead in there!" I exclaimed in horror.

"We seem to have arrived at the same conclusion."

I shuddered. To be eaten by a walking corpse brought back to life by the chaotic magic of the ogres that was still floating about above our world. What a terrible death!

Behind the grille it was quiet and dark. Not a single movement . . .

"If only my family knew how low I have fallen." Eel suddenly laughed for no obvious reason. "First I joined the Wild Hearts, now I'm behind bars and about to become breakfast for a lump of half-rotten meat! If my father found out, he'd have a stroke."

"What are you talking about?" I asked in exasperation.

The Garrakian looked at me and laughed bitterly.

"I became a Wild Heart about ten years ago, Harold. The Hearts were my new family, and the Lonely Giant was my new home. I renounced everything in my old life and I became someone for whom I used to have little respect, whom I basically despised. In Garrak we're not very fond of those you call Wild Hearts. You know why."

"Who doesn't know? Once upon a time in the hoary old days of Vastar's Bargain, the Wild Hearts crushed the Garrakian 'Dragon.'"

"For the nineteen years of my previous life I bore a different name. I changed my ancestral name, the name that my ancestors bore with pride, for the nickname Eel—what could be more terrible than that for a nobleman?"

I tried not to breathe, tried not to interrupt Eel's story in any way. According to Marmot, no one in the Wild Hearts knew who he used to be and what he did before he arrived at the Lonely Giant.

He had always kept his distance from the others, always been calm and cool, never talked much, and he was magnificently skilled with the twin blades of the nobility of Garrak. Eel was a mystery. Rock, Ice, Unapproachable, Tight-lip—those were the few nicknames that Kli-Kli had given the warrior.

It was rather surprising to find Eel pouring out his heart to me. He wasn't in the habit of making sentimental confessions, and some of the Wild Hearts still thought he would take the secret of his appearance at the Lonely Giant with him to the grave.

"My father is a Tooth of the Dragon," Eel went on. "Do you know what that means?"

A bemused nod was all I could manage. According to a centuries-old tradition, only a close relative of the king could become a Tooth of the Dragon, and that meant that Eel had royal blood flowing in his veins. He was no ordinary little nobleman, not even a duke. He was an archduke, directly in line to inherit the throne if the king's line should suddenly come to an end.

"My father, Marled van Arglad Das, cousin of the king of Garrak, is already the sixth Tooth of the Dragon in our family. A great honor, thief! The highest honor that can possibly be bestowed on a noble of our kingdom."

I've heard that more than once before. All a Garrakian nobleman needs from life is the supreme glory of preserving the honor of his family line, the ancient traditions of the nobility, and other similar nonsense that I really don't understand all that well. The noblemen of Garrak are total crackpots when it comes to the words "honor" and "loyalty to the king."

"I'm the eldest son in the family, so I was due to become a Dragon's Tooth, too. I was due . . ." Eel ground his teeth together.

"What stopped you?" I asked cautiously.

He looked at me, and I could see an entire lake of ancient pain splashing about in his eyes.

"What stopped me?" he repeated thoughtfully. He was obviously not there with me, but somewhere very far away, in the past. "Youth, overconfidence, and, I suppose, arrogance . . . In those days I thought I could take everything from life. The eldest son of a Tooth of the Dragon, the king's nephew—I had a fine military career waiting for me . . . I did everything that I wanted to do. I thought I was number one, the best at everything, and many other people thought the same. And anyone who held a different opinion went to his grave after a duel. I was untouchable and far too reckless. The favorite of the nobility, of the women . . . I! I! I! That 'I' was what ruined me in the end. . . ."

"What happened?"

"That's not important. It all happened many years ago. I made a mistake, disgraced myself, my father, my family, and my king. And disgrace can only be erased by death. So I died. Ulis van Arglad Das ceased to exist, and Eel took his place. . . . It was probably the best thing for everybody . . ."

He snorted.

"That night I died and preserved the honor of my line. No one ever found out that when the moment came, I couldn't plunge the dagger into my own throat and I remained alive. Nobody, not even my father, and especially not the king, although I think that my younger brother has his suspicions. . . . I left the country. . . . No ancestral name, and no way of ever going back to Garrak. I had nothing left, apart from my weapons and the ability to use them. I went to the far side of the Northern Lands and became a Wild Heart. I became that for which I, the first warrior of the Dragon of Garrak, had previously had little love or respect. Here no one asked about my past and . . . but I've become very talkative today," the Garrakian said, pulling himself up short. "I'm sorry for dumping all of this on you."

"Forget it."

"And you forget about this conversation. I should never have started it."

"But you did start it, after all."

He paused for a moment.

"I told you because I want to ask you to do something for me," Eel muttered, and looked up at the ceiling. "If I happen to die, and you survive, give my 'brother' and 'sister' to my younger brother. He has far more right than I do to carry the ancestral blades of the line of van Arglad Das."

"I don't think I'll be able to do that," I said after a pause. "The two of us are in the same boat, and we'll be eaten together."

"Just promise me," Eel said.

"All right, I promise."

"Thank you. I won't forget this."

Of course you won't forget it, I thought. It would be rather hard to forget anything in the amount of time that pitiless Sagra has measured out for us.

Someone twittered behind the grille separating us from the next cell. Eel and I both turned our heads toward the strange sound at the same moment.

"Did you hear that?" I asked the warrior in a voice that was somehow too loud.

"Yes," he answered morosely. "That's even worse than hungry corpses."

Worse than hungry corpses? Hmm! The Nameless One's followers couldn't really have stuck a h'san'kor in there, could they?

"Couldn't you just tell me and not make me even more nervous than I already am?" I asked.

"Look!"

Eel somehow managed to hook an overturned bowl with the toe of his boot and smash it into the grille, sending a shower of fragments flying into the air.

The sparrowlike twittering changed to a menacing hiss, and four creatures threw themselves against the grille from out of the darkness with all the fury and hatred of hungry demons. One of the vile beasts tried to bite through the iron bars, and the mind-numbing grating sound ran round the cell, bringing my skin up in goose bumps. I turned cold and started praying to Sagot that the barrier would withstand those teeth.

The bars held, but there were notches left in them. Those teeth were famous throughout the whole of Siala. They effortlessly reduced the old bones of dead men in graveyards to dust.

"Gkhols, may Sagot save us!" I screeched. "That bastard has tamed gkhols!"

Eel didn't say anything to me, he was studying the beasts that had come dashing to the bars.

Several long, weary, and rather unpleasant minutes passed. We observed them, and they observed us. The gkhols' interest, unlike ours, was strictly gastronomic.

Not many city dwellers, coming upon a gkhol somewhere in an open field, would realize just who the spirits of evil had put in their path. They are quite rare now, and can only be found in the most desolate spots in Siala: in old abandoned graveyards and burial sites. They are scavengers and corpse-eaters who prefer human flesh, preferably after it has been lying in the open air for a week or two, but they don't disdain other carrion. Gkhols, especially solitary gkhols, are cowardly, and so they're not terribly dangerous for a full-grown man, unless he happens to be stupid enough to fall asleep beside an old burial chamber. But a solitary gkhol will easily kill a child, even a ten-year-old.

The situation changes drastically when the corpse-eaters gather together into a herd after going hungry for a long time. When they are in a state of rabid hunger, the beasts simply go berserk. Every child knows the story of the two knights who set out for some war or other and ran into a dozen gkhols who hadn't eaten for a year. As you might expect, all that was left of the knights was their armor, and even that had been thoroughly chewed.

So what could two bound prisoners expect? Gkhols who hadn't had a bite to eat for three weeks wouldn't leave a single scrap of us behind.

One of the vile creatures had taken a grip on the bars with its little hands and was gazing fixedly at us, and the thick, sticky spittle started dribbling out of its mouth.

How come they had managed not to eat each other in there?

The gkhol cast a carnivorous glance at me, leaned his head over to one side, and twittered derisively. He reminded me of a fledgling of some exotic kind of bird. Although, in fact, that idiotic chirping is the only thing that gkhols and birds have in common. Gkhols actually look like very unhappy and fairly harmless creatures, even if they do have a few odd features here and there.

They are small, no larger than a newborn child, with smooth, ash-gray skin, huge bloodred eyes like saucers, a disproportionately large head and small body with a protruding belly, short crooked little legs, long thin arms, and wide-spaced yellow teeth. People who have never seen them before and don't know what it is they've run into are likely to feel sorry for them, or laugh, but certainly not feel afraid.

And that has been the death of many bold fools who have turned their back on such an apparently harmless creature when it was hungry.

"Eat!" one of them said suddenly, looking straight at us. "Eat-eat-eat! Eat! Aha! Eat!"

Like ogres, gkhols carry a few shreds of brain in their heads. The ogres, the only race from the Dark Age to have survived into our times, have degenerated from the most powerful race in Siala, the creators of the first new magic in the world—shamanism and Kronk-a-Mor—into stupid and extremely ferocious monsters. The gkhols, on the contrary, have grown cleverer and cleverer from century to century. But too slowly, fortunately.

They can remember and repeat single words just as well as parrots, and they are a lot more intelligent than the monkeys that can some-times be found in the show booths on Market Square.

"Eat!" the gkhol said to us one last time, and then disappeared into the darkness.

Two others followed the little talker's example, leaving the fourth to stand guard at the metal grille. The gkhol grabbed hold of it with his little hands, tugged at it a few times, and then hissed in disappointment.

"Just look at the little lad's claws," I said rather nervously.

How could I not be nervous, knowing that any moment Purple Nose could pull that lever and raise the barrier that was the only thing standing between us and a meeting with the gods?

"We ought to get some sleep, Harold."

I looked at Eel as if he was insane.

"No, I'm absolutely serious. Sleep, there's nothing we can do."

"Go to sleep, with neighbors like that? No, thank you!"

"Whatever you say." He closed his eyes.

This is a guy with nerves of steel. He could probably get to sleep with the Nameless One himself standing behind him.

I took another look at the gkhol standing on guard beside the grille. Demons of darkness! How much of that vile sticky saliva does he have inside him?

Noticing that I was looking at him, for some reason the gkhol started getting nervous, and he twittered. One of his friends immediately appeared out of the darkness to make sure that breakfast was not about to cut and run. Once he was certain everything was under control, he went back into his lair.

"Valder," I thought, trying to summon the archmagician, "Valder, are you there?"

No answer.

As far as I knew from my dream about the magician's former life, he really hated these vile creatures, but apparently this time the archmagician had no intention of interfering. A pity; I would have been delighted to see what a dry-roasted gkhol looked like. They're much more likeable that way than when they're still moist and alive.

I made a face at the gkhol sentry. He mirrored my efforts and made a face back at me, and I must say that the corpse-eater's effort was a lot better, and a lot more frightening.

A little more than four hours had gone by since I first made the acquaintance of the charming family of corpse-eaters, and Eel had still not condescended to wake up.

Meanwhile the gkhols had already changed their sentries twice. They deliberately stayed where I could see them, staring with those red eyes, sometimes hissing menacingly, twittering and drooling, checking the metal grille to see if it was edible, and generally making me more nervous than the detachment of corrupt guards who once caught me in a certain count's treasure house at an inappropriate moment.

Basically, the gkhols amused themselves until they got bored, and then the sentry withdrew into the darkness, but I could still feel the hungry gaze of those ravenous eyes on me.

The sun had been in the sky for a long time, its bright rays were shining in through the little barred window up under the ceiling of the cell and falling on the straw. Time slips through our fingers like golden sand, and no one can slow its pace.

At first I took no notice of the squeaking that came from somewhere above my head. But the gkhols and Eel did take notice. Alarmed by the unfamiliar sounds, the gkhols crowded against the grille, while Eel opened his eyes abruptly, as if he had never been asleep at all.

"Praise be to all the gods!" the warrior murmured joyfully, and his face lit up.

I turned my head to look at the little window.

"Invincible!" I exclaimed.

"Exactly. And that means that the lads have found us!"

"Hey! Is there anybody there?" we heard Marmot's voice ask.

"We're here! What took you so long?"

"Why didn't you hide another ten leagues away? Then we could have spent another week looking for you! Are you alive?"

"Yes!"

"Can you move?"

"Our hands are tied!"

"That's no problem. I'll send Invincible down."

"Find the door!" said Eel.

"That's what we're trying to do. There's a whole heap of the Nameless One's followers here. We're just finishing off their patrols. Right, see you soon."

Something glinted for an instant in the rays of the sun, and then a cobbler's knife landed blade first, sticking into the straw just behind my back. With a squeak, the ling leapt down intrepidly from the wall, landing in the straw and ambling toward us.

"Now what?" I asked nervously, watching the shaggy rat.

"Now we get the knife."

"I don't know about you, but I can't even move my hands, let alone reach for the knife. This damn rope!"

"Don't be in such a great hurry, Harold."

Meanwhile Invincible had darted across to Eel and started gnawing through the rope tying his wrists together.

"Surprised?" Eel chuckled. "Marmot's taught the ling all sorts of tricks."

"So I see."

I took heart, realizing that rescue was close at hand. Soon one of the Wild Hearts would reach the cell and open the door, and we would be free.

The minutes dragged by, and a feeling of alarm crept into my heart. Where had they got to? Had the lads really been spotted and forced to retreat? No, what was I thinking of! Wild Hearts didn't retreat and abandon their comrades. Any moment the bolt would clank and . . .

But the bolt didn't clank. There was no sound at all apart from the vicious hissing of the gkhols, who seemed to realize that their breakfast was about to make a run for it. Invincible gave a squeak of satisfaction and came toward me, and Eel began rubbing his wrists.

"Right, now we'll fight." The Garrakian grabbed the knife and sliced through my rope at a single stroke. Just at that moment the lock of the door clanked.

"At last!" I hissed. "Hey, what are you doing?"

Eel dashed back to his old place, grabbing up the ling and stuffing it into his pocket on the way. He put his hands behind his back, setting the knife along his forearm so that it wasn't visible to anyone else.

"Sit still and don't move!"

Unfortunately, Eel was right; it wasn't our rescuers who entered the cell.

Loudmouth, so imperturbable and so unfamiliar, so very different from the character that I was used to, leaned back against the wall farthest away from us, folded his arms across his chest, and fixed his eyes on an invisible point just above Eel's head with an air of absolute indifference.

Purple Nose stood not far from me and pointed me out to the third man.

"There, Master Rizus, this one's the thief."

Master Rizus was short, with shiny black hair and deep-set gray eyes. His thin-lipped mouth and perfectly straight nose indicated a man not given to listening to other people's opinions, and the unhealthy yellow color of his face put me in mind of the copper plague. He gave off an acrid smell of horse's sweat, and his rich clothes were badly creased and spattered with mud. He'd probably galloped for a day and a night without stopping in order to view my humble person.

"I shall ask you just two questions." For a man with such a delicate figure, his voice was exceptionally deep and low. "The way you die will depend on how you answer. Tell me the truth and you will die quickly. If you are stubborn, the gkhols will gnaw on your bones."

"By your leave, Master Rizus, I will explain everything to them," Loudmouth put in. "That way we will save a lot of time."

The man nodded reluctantly and hissed: "But be quick. You have ten minutes while I change out of my traveling clothes."

He went out.

"Friends . . . ," Loudmouth began.

"The Nameless One is your friend," I replied morosely.

"Perhaps so," said the traitor, not attempting to argue. "In case you have not already realized it, Master Rizus is a shaman and, I can assure you quite definitely, a very good one. He came to Ranneng especially to collect the Key for the Nameless One. I'm sure you can imagine how upset he was to discover that we didn't have the artifact."

We said nothing.

"All that Master Rizus wants from you is two honest answers to two very simple questions. If you answer them, I promise that I will kill you myself, quickly and painlessly. And then I shall make sure that you have a dignified burial."

"And what are the questions, if you wouldn't mind telling us?"

"I always knew that thieves were more amenable to a deal than other people," Loudmouth chuckled contentedly. "The first question is: Who killed the shamans who were preparing to attack our group?"

"You were with us then," I exclaimed in genuine amazement. "So how would we know? Some good people turned up, that's all."

"Good people are not capable of killing six of the Nameless One's best shamans!" snapped Loudmouth. "Now Master Rizus is the only supreme shaman he has left in Valiostr."

"Loudmouth, your Rizus is crazy. How does he think that we could know who knocked off his best wizards when we were ten leagues away in Hargan's Wasteland?"

Well, I couldn't really tell him that the Master and Lafresa were behind it all, could I?

Loudmouth clicked his tongue in disappointment and said regretfully: "Yes, I never really doubted that it wasn't you, or Miralissa or Tomcat. They're not up to it; this was done by someone of a much higher class."

"Then why do you ask?" Eel said.

"Don't look at me like that, old friend, or you'll drill a hole right through me. Master Rizus wants to know, and I have to ask. All right, then, the second question is: Where is the Key?"

"Get lost!"

"Let me deal with him," Purple Nose suggested to Loudmouth.

Loudmouth frowned angrily, but he didn't say anything.

Eel muttered something very uncomplimentary about the big brute's mother. The Garrakian's calculations proved absolutely correct. The quick-tempered executioner immediately forgot about me, grabbed Eel by the sides of his chest, and lifted him up off the floor.

"Why, I'll tear you to pieces! I'll—"

But Eel punched the man under the chin with his left hand and threw the knife with his right. It flew through the air and hit Loudmouth in the shoulder. I jumped to my feet and took great pleasure in pounding the traitor with my fists.

Eel appeared beside me, pushed me aside, pulled the knife out of our enemy's wound, slashed him across the leg below the knee, and knocked him to the floor.

"Rope! Look lively!"

Somehow we managed to tie the wriggling traitor's hands together with the scrap ends of rope.

I hobbled across to the door and looked out into the corridor.

"All clear!"

"Excellent! Don't take your eyes off that corridor!"

"For sure. Is he still alive?"

"Yes. Take the mouse from me."

I put the ling on my shoulder and as my eyes met the Garrakian's, I read the traitor's death sentence in them. Eel leaned down over him.

"I promised to cut your heart out, but I don't have the time for that now. Good-bye."

He gestured to me to show me it was time to leave the cell. Once we were in the corridor, he closed the door and pushed the bolt home.

"Don't tell any of our lads about Loudmouth," he said to me. "Let them think he died back in the inn. They don't have to know who the wretched villain really was."

"Okay."

"And don't say anything about what I told you about myself, either."

"Okay," I repeated.

"And another thing . . . no one must hear a thing about there being enemies among the Wild Hearts. This is not the time to be spreading alarm. When we get back to the Lonely Giant, I'll have a word with Owl myself."

"All right."

"I'm glad we understand each other," the warrior said with a nod, and tugged hard on the lever that I hadn't noticed in a niche in the wall.

A mechanism rumbled somewhere, raising the metal grille and letting the gkhols out. I shuddered, but I didn't feel sorry at all for the Nameless One's followers.

"Let's go," Eel said laconically, and hurried away without looking back. A guard jumped out of the watchman's room and the Garrakian wrung his neck with a single deft movement.

The door of the corridor opened and three familiar short figures appeared in the doorway.

"What did I tell you, Hallas?" the smallest one piped happily. "I said I'd find them first, didn't I?"

"Kli-Kli, is that you?"

"You humans have a strange habit of stating the obvious. Of course it's me, Harold!"

"You're the one thing I've been missing all this time."

"And I'm glad to see you alive and well, too," said the royal jester, making a face. "Oh, look! Gkhols!"

It turned out there was another cell full of the creatures. Apparently Purple Nose was even more of a pervert than I thought, and he bred them for his own pleasure.

The goblin completely forgot about me, went over to the grille with the crazed man-eaters raging behind it, and stuck his finger in, evidently wishing to get to know the vile creatures better. Fortunately for Kli-Kli, he had much faster reactions than the voracious little monsters, so he managed to pull back in time and the greedy jaws closed on nothing but air.

"Eel, your blades," said Deler, leaning his poleax against the wall and taking the scabbards with the "brother" and "sister" out from behind his back.

"You didn't happen to bring the crossbow, did you?" I asked the dwarf hopefully.

"I did, but Marmot has it, so keep behind us for the time being. Kli-Kli, are you going to stay here?"

"I'm coming. Oh look! A dead man! Eel, did you wring his neck? Why is he looking backwards like that?" the goblin jabbered excitedly.

"Cut the chatter, Kli-Kli," I growled at the goblin.

"It's hard work with you fools," Kli-Kli sighed, turning serious. "Well, are we going then?"

"It's high time! Our lads have been holding the exit for us," Hallas wheezed from under his helmet.

The gnome leaped out into the corridor, followed by Deler, then Eel.

Kli-Kli and I walked up a stairway and found ourselves outside the door, beside the gnome, the dwarf, and the man.

Master Rizus was lying there dead, with two black arrows sticking out of his back. Ell was standing there with his face painted black and green and his bow across his shoulder. Elves are not noted for magnanimity to their foes, and they're not above planting arrows in an enemy's back if he offers them such a magnificent opportunity.

"How did you manage to get him?" I asked the dark elf in surprise, with a sideways glance at the shaman's body.

He didn't look so menacing now. A skinny little man who had met his death from elfin arrows.

"Harold, are you blind?" Kli-Kli asked me mockingly. "Can't you see how he died? He was shot full of arrows."

"That's not what I meant!" I said with a frown of annoyance at Kli-Kli's slow-wittedness. "I want to know how he managed to kill a shaman."

"A shaman? Hmm . . . ," rumbled Arnkh, who had just walked up to us, covered from head to foot in iron. He gave the body a curious glance.

"He could be a hundred times a shaman, Harold, but when I fire an arrow under a man's shoulder blade without any warning, he forgets all about any shamanism," Ell explained. "Do you think we fight the orcs' shamanism in Zagraba with swords?"

"No, I don't. An arrow from out of the bushes, and the job's done."

"Quicker, may the darkness take you!" we heard Marmot shout from somewhere in the distance, and then we heard men shouting and the clash of weapons.

The ringing sounds of swords clashing were suddenly interrupted by screams and howls—Milord Alistan had joined in the battle with his sword of singing steel.

When we darted outside, it was all over. There was a new dent in Alistan's oak shield and the right sleeve of Marmot's jacket was torn, but no one had been hurt, which was more than could be said for the enemy. Three of the Nameless One's followers were lying dead and another was writhing in the bushes, groaning and clutching at his stomach.

Yes, this is no fairy tale. It's only in fairy tales that men die honorably and silently. In life they usually squirm and howl and bleed a lot. Blood was oozing through the wounded man's white fingers. He had been stuck as neatly as any pig.

Arnkh's sword rose and came down again. The man fell silent forever.

"Withdraw!" Markauz ordered when he caught sight of us. "This noise will bring the whole nest of them running!"

So we ran. That is, the jester and I ran. The others withdrew in organized fashion to positions that had been prepared beforehand and were guarded by the Wild Hearts who had not been involved in the fight, Honeycomb and Lamplighter, and a rear line support group consisting of Egrassa and Miralissa, armed with bows. I couldn't see Uncle anywhere. No doubt the platoon sergeant had been left behind at the inn because of his wound.

I heard shouting behind me, a crossbow bolt whistled through the air, and I took a dive, burying my nose in the ground and almost smothering the ling underneath me. Egrassa and Miralissa, joined by Ell, began returning the enemy's fire, aiming at the windows and doorway of the building. Three of our pursuers decided to chase after us and try their luck in honest combat, but they each caught an arrow in the chest and ended up stretched out on the ground. That discouraged any more of the villains from sticking their noses out from behind their stone walls.

"Is everyone all right?" Miralissa asked, pulling her bowstring with an arrow on it back to her ear.

Twang!

"If you don't count my nerves!" said Kli-Kli, as usual taking any opportunity to complain.

"There's worse to come," I muttered, getting up off the ground.

"Withdraw to the horses!"

Alistan's order was never carried out. Something white but, unfortunately, not fluffy took off from the top story of the building where we had been held in the basement for almost an entire day and night.

"Look out!" shouted Miralissa.

I dropped to the ground again, and everyone else followed my example, including the elves. A blinding white disk rustled through the air with a whistling sound and crashed into an unfortunate apple tree, shattering it into a thousand tiny chips of wood.

A shaman, darkness take me! There's another of the Nameless One's shamans in the house, but Loudmouth told us . . . Well, never mind what he told us! A fact is a fact: A sorcerer had just flung something rather unpleasant at us, and it was only by good fortune and the will of the gods that he had missed by a good ten yards.

Miralissa was already on her feet; she started whispering and spinning like a top in a spellbinding dance. Ah, if only the elfess had power over the ordinary magic of men and the light elves, instead of shamanism that takes far too long to prepare, then we might have a chance, but this way it's a game of cat and mouse. Or more like blind man's bluff in total darkness. Whoever was quickest would win.

Ell and Egrassa concentrated their fire on the window that the disk had flown out of.

"Milord Alistan!" Miralissa's cousin shouted before he fired yet another arrow at the window. "Get the men away!"

The dark elves' attention was completely focused on the window. They had totally forgotten about the door, and the Nameless One's followers immediately took advantage of the fact. Two crossbowmen darted outside with the clear intention of making holes in our hides.

"There's nothing we can do!" said Egrassa, taking another arrow out of his seriously depleted quiver. "They're yours!"

The shaman could not be allowed to concentrate on a new spell. If the hail of arrows relented even for a moment, a white disk would reduce us all to a bloody pulp.

"Marmot, the crossbow!" I barked, and surprised even myself by jumping up off the ground.

With no hesitation, the Wild Heart tossed me my little darling. Thank Sagot, it was already loaded.

One of the enemy managed to get a shot off first, squatting down and firing at me from a kneeling position. Without aiming. Don't anybody ever try to tell me that the Nameless One doesn't have any professional soldiers! The only place you find crossbowmen with that kind of skill is in the army.

I would have caught a bolt in my lung if Alistan had not covered me with his shield—the bolt thudded into this barrier that had suddenly appeared out of nowhere. I chose the crossbowman who hadn't fired yet as my target and pressed my trigger.

The crash was every bit as impressive as the shaman's spell, I can tell you! The poor guy was reduced to a charred firebrand, and the other one, who was hastily reloading his crossbow, had his right arm blown off and his face almost completely burned away. I think the only ones who took no notice of the devastation caused by my shot were Miralissa, who was still whispering a spell, and the elves, who were busy preventing the Nameless One's shaman from concentrating.

I hadn't even looked at what my crossbow was loaded with. A bolt with a fiery elemental!

"Marmot, the darkness take you! What did you load it with?"

"That was Kli-Kli!"

"Harold!" the goblin whined. "They all look almost exactly the same!"

"Almost! Surely you can see that there are three red stripes on these?"

"Don't be so stingy! The bolt may have cost five gold pieces, but this is no time to be cheap."

When the doorway was suddenly covered with ice and we heard howls of pain, Miralissa finally stopped singing her song and spinning round like a child's top at a fair.

The elves stopped firing and a white disk immediately came flying out of the window, as if that was all it had been waiting for. It was flying straight at us, and I swear I thought that this was the end!

But then the elfess's spell took effect, and a green wall flashed up in front of us for an instant. It flashed up and then disappeared, but the disk, either flung back or reflected, went flying back in the opposite direction. Unfortunately, it hit the corner of the house, and not the window where the shaman was hiding.

Fine fragments of stone shot off in all directions, striking down the Nameless One's supporters who had come darting out of the house. The magic shield protected us against being wounded or maimed.

Yet another disk, and another deflection back toward the house in which our enemy was lodged, but this time a green shield just like ours sprang up in front of the white projectile and it flew off to one side, demolishing a shed standing thirty yards from the building. Our horses whinnied in fright.

Another disk. And another. The Nameless One's shaman possessed far greater skill than the elfin princess. Our shield sagged and shuddered noticeably with every impact.

"Get away, you idiots! I can't maintain the defense for very long!" exclaimed Miralissa, pale from the effort.

"I'll help!" said Kli-Kli, and he started rummaging desperately in his pockets.

"Let's move back, Kli-Kli," said milord, reaching out his hand to grab the goblin by the scruff of the neck, but Kli-Kli took a tangled bundle of string out of his pocket and pulled on some inconspicuous little loose end.

The whole structure, woven for so long with such care by the jester, who had promised that he would show us some "terrible shamanism," instantly came unwoven and then dissolved into thin air in the most magical manner imaginable.

"Oi!" said Kli-Kli, gazing wildly at his empty hands: He evidently hadn't been expecting this effect. "Why did it do that?"

Miralissa surprised me by pulling me down onto the ground then covering her head with her hands, and shouting, "Get down! Quick!"

The sight of the elfess with her face buried in the dirt was highly persuasive: If she was willing to do what no dark elf would normally do (bathing in mud is not one of the main elfin pastimes), then there was no point in wasting any time on thinking.

I dropped to the ground for the third time in the last two minutes, noticing as I fell that the roof of the building had flown a good five yards up into the air and was falling back into the fountains of roaring flame that were pouring out of all the windows and doors.

Boo-oooom!

An incredibly powerful blast of heat roared past above us. The air was sizzling hot and impossible to breathe. It scorched my throat and lungs. My clothes didn't protect me either. The heat licked at my skin, even through my jacket, shirt, and trousers.

I didn't dare to raise my head until about twenty seconds later. The massive two-story stone house with a tiled roof no longer existed. All that was left was one wall that had survived by some kind of miracle. There were flames still roaring and licking at the stones. A broad spiral of black smoke was rising up into the sky.

Who would believe that could happen? He just pulled on a stupid piece of string, and suddenly there was nothing left! No house, and none of the people inside it, either.

Everybody, including me, was staring at the fire. I got up, dusted myself off, and glanced warily at the goblin.

"I . . . I . . . I didn't mean it!" Kli-Kli jabbered, retreating in the face of our none-too-gentle glances. "I never thought! Honestly! There ought to have been a little fog, that's all."

"Fog!" Deler roared. He spat the sand out of his mouth, jabbed his finger toward the ruined building, and asked acidly, "Is that your idea of a little shower?"

"But honestly, I didn't think that would happen!" the jester said with a guilty sniff. "My grandfather the shaman showed me that when I was little . . . I suppose I didn't tie forty-five knots in it after all."

The little jester's face was covered in soot and mud and it wore an extremely guilty expression.

"Kli-Kli," Miralissa sighed, wiping her dirty face with the back of her hand. "If you ever do anything like that again without warning me . . ."

The goblin started nodding so fervently that I thought his head would fall off his shoulders any moment.

In the distance we heard the sound of people hurrying toward the site of the explosion. It was time for us to get out while the going was good.

"To the horses! Quickly!" said Alistan, throwing his shield over his shoulder and running on ahead toward the spot where the horses had been whinnying only a few moments earlier.

I handed the ling to Marmot and tried to keep up with the captain of the royal guard.

"That was great!" panted Kli-Kli, running along beside me. "You can tell my grandfather was a shaman all right! I certainly showed them!"

There was not a trace of remorse in the goblin's expression.

"You almost roasted us along with them, you genius!"

"You're just annoyed because you're envious of my abilities," the jester replied.

I snorted derisively. Kli-Kli only pretends to be a fool and a windbag. In all honesty, the goblin is smarter than Master of the Order Artsivus, he just works on his image. But at moments like this I am almost ready to believe that the royal fool really does act the buffoon because he is so witless.

We ran past the smoking ruins of the shed and saw our horses beyond the apple trees. The poor animals were snorting and wriggling their ears in fright, and their eyes were wide with terror.

I greeted Little Bee with a gentle slap on her flank and jumped up into the saddle.

Alistan immediately set the horses to a gallop, and I had to focus all my attention on my riding, to make sure I wouldn't go crashing into some tree that just happened to turn up in front of me. It was only after we saw Ranneng come into view ahead and we approached the city walls that the weariness came crashing down on me with all the weight of the sky.

7

BRIGHT IDEAS FROM A GOBLIN

When our squad came flying into the yard of the inn on lathered horses, Uncle was waiting for us, striding nervously from one corner to another. His lips moved rapidly as he counted the riders and he smiled happily once he was sure everyone was safe and well. Honeycomb jumped down off his horse and started telling his friend in a low voice what had happened during our rescue. Uncle clicked his tongue in disappointment, regretting that his wound had prevented him from taking part in the battle.

I handed Little Bee's reins to a servant who came darting up and then sat down on the ground right there on the spot. I was reduced to a state of total exhaustion; the final ounce of strength had been drained out of me.

"Hey, old friend? Are you still alive?" I heard a sympathetic voice ask.

Glancing up, I saw Bass towering over me.

"And what are you doing here?"

"He's here on probation," the jester said, plonking his backside down on the grass beside me. "Or something of the sort."

"Something of the sort?" I asked like an echo.

Bass didn't say anything, just looked at me expectantly. What did he want? Meanwhile Kli-Kli pulled one of his beloved carrots out from under his new cloak, crunched on it, and then spoke with his mouth full.

"You ought to know that if it wasn't for your friend here, you and Eel would have been dead men," the goblin explained as he chewed. "He showed us where they were hiding you."

I gave my old comrade a quizzical look. He sat down warily beside me and started telling me what had happened. Kli-Kli occasionally forgot about his carrot and added his own weighty comments to Bass's story.

Apparently Bass had been on the street when we rode down on the cart, and had seen me and the unconscious Eel being loaded into the carriage. He hadn't tried to interfere (which was absolutely right—one man against a dozen is no kind of odds) but he had managed to follow the carriage outside the city all the way to the private country estate that was owned by the Nameless One's followers. Remembering his childhood nickname of Snoop I was not surprised.

After finding out where we were being held, Bass had set off back to Ranneng, but the gates were already closed, and he had been forced to while the night away outside the city walls. But in the morning Snoop had hurried straight to the Learned Owl Inn.

"And how did you know about the inn?" I asked, although I already knew the answer.

That day when we met him for the first time at the Large Market, he had simply followed our group. First to the Sundrop, and then to the Learned Owl. So he had known where to go for help. Although, of course, he didn't know that he would run into a practical, and deadly, elf.

Ell's first inclination was to let Bass's blood, in line with the old folk wisdom that says if you trust everyone who comes along, sooner or later you'll end up in the graveyard. But first Hallas and Deler, and then Kli-Kli—when he came back from his fruitless search for my own humble person—confirmed that they had seen this slob talking with Harold, who was now missing. So Ell had put away his knife, and Miralissa and Alistan subjected the informant to intensive interrogation.

I have to give the elfess her due—she suspected Snoop right up to the final moment, quite reasonably assuming that the person in front of her was either a top-notch swindler, or a follower of the Nameless One, or a servant of the Master, or darkness only knows who else. And so Bass was promised that, if he was lying, his eyes would be gouged out and every protruding part of his body would be sliced off in the most painful way possible.

Ell, Egrassa, and Honeycomb set off to reconnoiter the address given by Bass, and discovered that the house was absolutely teeming with characters of distinctly dubious appearance. And then the cavalry had arrived, in the person of almost all the rest of the group—Uncle had stayed behind to keep an eye on Bass and nurse his wound, which still hadn't knitted together, even after Miralissa's best efforts.

"Thank you." It cost me a certain effort to say that to him. "If not for your help . . ." There was no need to say any more.

"Peace?" he said, holding out his narrow hand and smiling uncertainly.

"Okay." I shook his hand. "But I need to have a serious talk with you." I was still angry with him for all those years when he hadn't let me and For know that he was alive and well.

"All right, but a little later on. You look like you need a couple of days' sleep. We'll see each other again."

Snoop set off toward the gates of the inn, but Ell sprang up in his way like an apparition of doom: "Where are you going, man?"

"You will have to stay, Master Bass," said Miralissa, who had appeared beside Ell.

"But why, in the name of a thousand dead goblins?"

Kli-Kli choked on his carrot in surprise and looked at my old friend reproachfully.

"Our business in Ranneng requires absolute confidentiality and I'm sorry, but we can't trust you, even though you have helped us."

"Are you going to keep me under lock and key?" asked Bass, his eyebrows rising in surprise.

"No, no need for that," Alistan Markauz put in. "We'll provide you with every possible comfort until our group leaves the city. There's food here in plenty, and we can find you a bed, so do stay."

"And what if I don't agree?" Snoop always was a stubborn one.

A crooked grin appeared on Ell's face.

"I advise you to agree," he said.

"But I can hope that when all your 'business' is over, you will let me go?"

"Of course," said Ell, without batting an eyelid.

Somehow, I wasn't entirely convinced. Elves are a practical race, and it would be simpler for them to slit Bass's throat out of genuine concern for the fate of our mission than to set a witness free to go wandering wherever his fancy might take him. I'd have to have a word with Miralissa when the time came, or her k'lissang could quite easily dispatch the rogue to the light. Ell was rather hot-tempered, and he had a short fuse when it came to things like that.

"Harold, my old friend, I'm so glad that you're alive!" said Hallas, putting his arm round my shoulder (the short little gnome could only do that because I was sitting on the ground). "Come on, I'll pour you a beer."

"All right, old friend," I said with a smile, getting up off the ground.

As I walked toward the door of the inn, I found myself thinking in surprise that I was changing despite myself. Shadow Harold, the master thief, the most skillful rifler of treasure chests in the whole of Avendoom, that solitary, morose character who never had any real friends and never showed his feelings to anyone, was changing. But for better or for worse?

Would I have called anyone my friend two months ago?

No.

I didn't have any friends, except for my mentor, teacher, and second father, For. And as for taking a friendly drink with anyone . . . That was something I'd never done.

A thief, if he is a good thief, has to be alone. No family, no attachments, nothing that would affect his work or his safety. And that was how it had been until just recently.

I was astonished to realize that now I could call those constant squabblers Deler and Hallas, that tiresome pest Kli-Kli, Miralissa, Lamplighter, and all the others my friends, and without the slightest hesitation.

As Eel and I quenched our thirst, we took turns in telling everyone (with the exception of Bass, who had been sent upstairs) what had happened to us. Naturally, without mentioning Loudmouth.

"At least there's one thing we can be happy about in all this, Harold," Arnkh said with a sigh. "The Nameless One's followers will leave us in peace now."

"We won't have any peace. There's still that Master of yours," Honeycomb boomed in his deep voice.

"But you must agree it's a completely different matter fighting on one front instead of two."

"Oh, for sure."

While they were talking I plucked up my courage and, when there was a pause, I said: "I had a dream . . ."

Alistan snorted suspiciously. He didn't take my "visions" very seriously. Kli-Kli groaned dolefully and grabbed hold of his head. But Miralissa nodded approvingly. I told them about the Master's prison and the Messenger's conversation with the mysterious woman.

"Interesting," the elfess said after a short pause. "You seem to have some special affinity for the Master. I must tell the chroniclers of the House of the Black Moon about this—perhaps they'll be able to learn something from it. But if your dream really is prophetic, then this Lafresa is dangerous for us. If she should manage to get hold of the Key first, all is lost. Somehow I have no doubt that this woman would be able to break the knots that bind the artifact."

I chose my words carefully. "Lady Miralissa, why can't the Master's servants simply deliver the artifact to their lord without waiting for this woman?"

"Yes, indeed," said Alistan, supporting me. "What could be easier than to deliver the glass bauble to where it's needed without having to rely on the witch?"

"The Key is attuned to Harold, and if it is delivered to the place where the Master lives without those bonds being broken, it could be too dangerous for our enemy."

"Wait!" The impassive Eel looked up from his food and stared at the elfess in amazement. "You know where the Master lives?"

"I can guess," the elfin princess replied reluctantly. "The Master, if he controls beings like the Messenger and endows his servants with such powerful magic, must be in a place where there is a concentration of immense power. And in a place like that, an artifact attuned to someone else would create such powerful turbulence in the flow of magic that the Master would be deprived of his powers and abilities for a long time. Therefore they have to destroy the bonds first, and only a highly experienced shaman can do that."

"A place of power, the House of Power," I muttered to myself, recalling the phrase that the Messenger had spoken to Lafresa.

"What did you say?" Miralissa asked sharply.

I raised my eyes from my plate and looked at the elfess in surprise. She was gripping the edge of the table so hard that her knuckles had turned white.

"I said 'the House of Power' . . . do you know something about it?"

I spotted the swift glance that Miralissa exchanged with Kli-Kli.

"The question is: Where did *you* hear about it?" she answered.

"In my dream," I said with a shrug, and then recited the list: "House of Power, House of Pain, House of Love, House of Fear . . ."

The swarthy elfess's skin turned paler and paler with every name. Kli-Kli choked on his custard pie and started coughing. Deler thumped the goblin on the back with all the generosity that his dwarf's heart could muster.

"I do not like your dreams, Harold! What else have you discovered?"

"Well . . . nothing," I said, rather surprised at the fervent insistence of this lady who was always so calm.

"Are you sure?" The amber eyes drilled into me, trying to draw out the innermost secrets of my soul.

"Yes," I replied quite honestly, without turning my eyes away.

She suddenly went limp and seemed to age. Wrinkles of fatigue appeared on her forehead and in the corners of her mouth; the fingers with the black nails reluctantly released their grip on the tabletop.

"What did I say?"

"That would take too long to explain, Harold. We don't have time for it just at the moment," Kli-Kli said hastily.

Was that a note of nervous tension I heard in the little goblin's voice?

I cleared my throat and stared down at my plate, still mechanically stirring my soup with the spoon and thinking that the jester and Miralissa had far more business and secrets in common than they showed. Secrets.

Nothing but secrets. They were dancing and prancing around me like the shadows from a flaming torch, but there was no way I could get a grip on them. More and more secrets, so many that soon I would drown in the murky stream. Who is the Master? Who is Influential, or Player? Why does the Master want the Horn? Is he the Nameless One's enemy, too? Why does the Master take such pleasure in playing cat and mouse with us? Who is the Messenger? What is that world of Chaos that I entered in my dream? What kind of strange dreams are these? What are the Houses of Power, Pain, Love, and Fear? And a thousand and one other questions that I don't know the answers to.

I didn't ask the elfess and the goblin any questions—Miralissa would only have fobbed me off with a seductive smile, and Kli-Kli would have pretended to be a total fool.

I had lost my appetite, but I stoically finished my soup, feeling the elfess's searching glance on me as I ate. . . .

"We need to have a talk, thief," Alistan Markauz said drily when I got up from the table.

"Of course, milord."

"Follow me."

He started up the stairs to the second floor of the inn, without even looking to make sure I was following. I walked up after him. Egrassa and Miralissa were already waiting for us in the room. Ell wasn't there; he had taken on the job of keeping an eye on Bass, who at that moment was dining in the hall and trying to teach Lamplighter how to play some card game or other.

"Have a seat, Harold," said Egrassa, pointing to a chair. "A glass of wine?"

"Yes, thank you."

I was immediately on my guard. The dark elves had never offered me a drink in their company before. Miralissa's cousin was exceptionally courteous today. And they say that elves are spiteful, wicked creatures.

But then, so they are.

Men have never really lived at peace with the dark elves of Zagraba or the light elves of the Forests of I'alyala. There has always been friction, through all the thousands of years that our two races have known each other. Fortunately, things have never gone as far as open war, but border skirmishes have been common, especially during the period after men first appeared in Siala.

The dark elves had concluded a treaty of peace and friendship with our kingdom, but before that the yellow-eyed race had never shown any great fondness for the inhabitants of Valiostr. And even now the elves were not helping us to resist the Nameless One out of the sheer kindness of their hearts. Elves have about as much kindness in their hearts as their closest relatives, the orcs.

That is, none.

The silence in the room dragged on. I eventually cleared my throat and asked:

"What did you want to see me about?"

The question sounded a little impolite, but what can they expect from a thief? Fine manners? I don't have them. . . . Or rather, I do (thanks to For), but I didn't want to use them at that moment. They're going to ask me again what it was that saved me in Hargan's Wasteland or how I found out about the houses.

"Be patient, thief," said Alistan Markauz, who was standing at the window. "We'll start as soon as Kli-Kli gets here . . ."

"Kli-Kli's already here. You can start, Your Grace!" The jester slipped in through the door, winked at me, and sat down on the bed. He was relaxed now, playing the fool, nothing like the lad sitting at the table downstairs who had suddenly tensed up when he heard my innocent phrase about the House of Power.

"Well now . . . I didn't talk about this downstairs, your friend is there, Harold."

"I think he should be locked up for the time being," Egrassa said with a glint of his fangs. "It's ridiculous that we should suffer the inconvenience of hiding in our own home."

"Everyone else already knows the news, so you and the Garrakian are the only ones left," Alistan Markauz continued, although it was clear that he shared the elf's opinion concerning Bass. "Ah, and here he is . . ."

Eel entered the room silently, nodded politely, and froze, leaning back against the upright of the door frame in a pose that reminded me of a statue from the beginning of the Age of Dreams.

With this latest arrival, the small room suddenly felt rather crowded.

"We have found out who owns the estate and where the Key is," Markauz said sternly, turning away from the window.

"Are you sure that it's still there?"

"It is in the city," the elfess answered for him.

"I beg your pardon, Tresh Miralissa, but how can you be sure of that?"

"I applied the bonds to the Key. I can sense it. If it was not in the city . . . But then you should sense it, too, as the one to whom the Key is bound."

"You must be mistaken, I don't feel anything apart from fatigue and the need to sleep," I muttered discontentedly.

"It's just that you're as thick-skinned as a herd of mammoths, Harold!" said Kli-Kli, taunting me as usual.

"Perhaps it's not there yet, but it will come. Especially when you find yourself close to the artifact. It's like a kind of itch. And the house where they are hiding it belongs to Count Balistan Pargaid."

When the elfess said that, Milord Markauz glared at me, as if he was expecting some kind of immediate response.

"So?" I asked stupidly.

Kli-Kli grabbed hold of his head in despair and started groaning as if all his teeth were aching.

"Harold, you've locked yourself away in your own little world and you can't see further than your own nose!" the goblin said. "Count Balistan Pargaid is the most influential individual in the south of Valiostr. The antiquity of his family line rivals the Stalkon dynasty, not to mention the fact that he is the leader of all the Nightingales and a very, very dangerous character. He is no ardent admirer of our king. He keeps a low profile, but give him a chance, and the Pargaids will advance their claim to the throne. And believe me, they have a serious right to that claim. Now that we know Pargaid is conspiring with the Master, I am doubly afraid for the king's welfare."

"Pargaid and his standard-bearers can put up eight thousand swordsmen, not counting all sorts of other petty riffraff. A force like that has to be taken seriously," Alistan rumbled.

It was obvious that he was not fond of Pargaid. But what is the love of a nobleman worth, anyway? They're always squabbling over land, sticking daggers in each other, slipping poison into each other's drinks, and then the simple soldiers are the ones who have to bear the consequences.

"His lands extend from here almost as far as the oaks of Zagraba, and as for gold . . ."

"All right. So we've found out who the estate belongs to. Now what are we going to do?" I asked, looking at Alistan.

He tugged on his mustache and answered reluctantly. "I don't think there's any way we can simply break into his house. Without a map of the patrols and without knowing exactly where the Key is . . . it would be suicide. The Nightingales' guards will be on the alert. It's a big house, and you won't be able to run round all the rooms. The risk is too great."

"You're absolutely right, milord. There's no simple way to get in there, and if we do get in, we need to know exactly where the artifact is."

"Kli-Kli has suggested a plan of how we can infiltrate the count's house."

Kli-Kli? Has suggested? A plan? I glared at the goblin in astonishment.

"Well?" he asked testily. "Do you think I'm incapable of proposing a brilliant plan?"

"You're capable all right," I said, making no attempt to argue. "Only I have absolutely no doubt that your brilliant plan will lead us all straight to the graveyard."

"All right, Harold. It's not a brilliant plan, just a few bright ideas from a goblin. So where was I now? It's no secret that the day after tomorrow Count Balistan Pargaid is holding his annual reception in honor of the great victory of the Nightingales over the Wild Boars two centuries ago. And we have a genuine chance of getting into the festivities—"

"I beg your pardon, Kli-Kli," Eel put in. "But I find it hard to believe that we will be allowed into the Nightingales' holy of holies for a polite how-do-you-do."

"Don't worry, Tight-Lip. They'll let us in, all right. Not only will they let us in, they'll actually invite us themselves! Balistan Pargaid is well known as a dedicated collector of antiquities, and that will be very helpful to us."

"Kli-Kli, have you really got some rare old book of your grandfather's stuck in your back pocket?" I asked provocatively.

"You're a fool, Harold. Show him, Lady Miralissa."

Without saying a word, the elfess handed me a bracelet. I turned it over in my hands, studying it carefully. Black steel, crudely forged, runes, writing in what I thought was ogric.

"Is this really what I think it is?" I asked, looking up at Miralissa.

"I'm not a mind reader, Harold." For a fleeting moment the black lips curved into a smile. "Yes, it is very valuable. The bracelet was forged by the ogres in the times before they withdrew into the Desolate Lands."

Yes, that was it. A piece of ordinary metal, not even a single ounce of precious metal, but the antiquity of the item, and the fact that it was one of the very few artifacts still surviving after the ogres, made it worth two or three hundred gold pieces. Serious money. Especially for someone in my profession.

"So we buy our pass into the house with this?" I asked the goblin.

"We've already bought it! While you were resting on that soft straw, we weren't just sitting about doing nothing. Count Balistan Pargaid has already been informed that this rare piece is in the city and he has politely forwarded an invitation for the Duke Ganet Shagor to attend his modest reception, and to bring his valuable treasure with him."

"Mmmm . . . ," I murmured. "I don't quite catch the connection between us and this duke."

"The connection's absolutely direct, Harold," Kli-Kli said, looking at me with a mocking smile. "Duke Ganet Shagor is none other than yourself, in person!"

That was the moment when I realized I was going to strangle the little blackguard for his stupid bright little ideas.

"Kli-Kli," I said, trying to speak in a quiet, ingratiating voice. "My friend, did you have too many magic mushrooms for breakfast again? What sort of duke will I make?"

"The perfect kind. You want to get into Pargaid's house? Then you'll be a duke," the jester snapped back.

"I don't know how to be a duke!" I exploded. "I'm a thief! A thief, not a nobleman and a high-society peacock! Couldn't you find anyone else for the job?"

"Who do you suggest, Harold?" Miralissa asked. "The Wild Hearts will not do, they are warriors. Anybody would recognize them as simple men straightaway. Milord Alistan cannot do it, he is known at court. Who does that leave? Only you."

"Why does it have to be a duke, why not an elfess or a miserly dwarf?"

"Because news about the collector has already spread through the city, and the collector is a man."

"But I don't know all those stupid noblemen's rules—etiquette and all that high-society stuff! I'll be spotted in the first five seconds!"

"Oh, Harold, don't make me laugh!" said Kli-Kli, sitting on the bed and swinging his legs to and fro jauntily. "Do you think those idle spongers will understand anything? You're a duke now, not just some lousy little marquis. Just put on your usual gloomy face, and no one will even come near you or ask you any questions. Just be haughty, cold, and smug, like Master Quidd's turkey cock, that's all!"

"You have no idea what you're talking about," I said, shaking my head. "This is a wild gamble."

"Our entire journey to Hrad Spein is a gamble," the jester said in a serious voice. "We have two days. I'm going to try to teach you something in that time. And I'll tell you your life story."

"Are dukes as thick in our kingdom as flies on rotten meat? Kli-Kli, fear the gods! Everyone knows who all the dukes are! Where are you going to get another one from? Overseas? With my accent even a Doralissian could tell that I've lived in Valiostr all my life!"

"Now, don't get so excited! There is one duke, the king's second cousin via one of his grandmothers. He's an eccentric, he lives like a hermit and hasn't left his castle for twenty years, so no one will recognize you as an imposter."

"But there are—"

"If I say no one, that means no one. Don't worry, I'll be there with you, and if anything happens—"

"No!" I snapped.

"No what?"

"No. You won't be there with me!"

"And why's that?"

"Kli-Kli, you're a walking disaster with two skinny little legs! If you go with me, we'll definitely never get out alive!"

"I'm going with you, Dancer in the Shadows, that has already been decided. And in any case you'll need a retinue and prompter. In case you didn't know, dukes don't go out visiting all on their own."

"A fine retinue! A little green fool!"

"Precisely, a fool, you fool! Who's going to take any notice of you when a jester appears in the house?"

Hmm? Well, I had to admit to myself that the goblin was talking sense there—if he pulled a couple of his rotten tricks, everybody would be keeping their eyes on him.

"They could recognize you as the king's jester."

"No chance!" he retorted. "The chances of meeting a familiar face among the Nightingales are very slim. And anyway, all goblins look the same to you humans. It will all go off perfectly, no one will suspect a thing. Master Quidd has already obtained garments appropriate for the occasion. You will be accompanied by Egrassa. And the other six lads, as a guard of honor."

"I'm sorry, but any child could see through your plan! I don't look like a nobleman, I don't look like a duke, and no matter what you say, a single question about heraldry, and the truth will be obvious! I swear by Sagot, this will be a disaster! We'd do better to risk breaking into the house! I repeat, goblin, we have absolutely no chance."

"Not only do we have no chance, we have no choice, either," the goblin sighed. "Or do you have some other duke in mind?"

"I do," Eel said unexpectedly.

Everyone turned to stare at him.

"You can't be a duke!" Kli-Kli objected after a pause. "You're a Garrakian! And Ganet Shagor isn't!"

"I can help with that," Miralissa put in. "Applying a different likeness is hard, but it's worth trying, and after all, Eel really does look more like a nobleman. What do you say, Eel?"

"I think I can play the role of a nobleman successfully, my lady," the Garrakian said dispassionately.

I gave a sigh of relief and nodded gratefully.

"Don't get your hopes up, Harold," Kli-Kli said with a menacing frown. "You'll still have to go to the reception."

"Kli-Kli is right," Miralissa confirmed. "You're the only one who can sense where they are hiding the Key."

"But Lady Miralissa, you said you could sense that the Key was in Ranneng."

"I can tell that it is in Ranneng, but only you can point out the precise spot."

I sighed. "During a reception, servants wait outside for their masters."

"Yes, and that's why you will not be a servant." The goblin's blue eyes glowed in triumph. I was afraid even to ask what brilliant ideas the fool had gotten into his little green head this time.

When he realized that I wasn't going to ask who he wanted to turn me into now, Kli-Kli said: "We'll make you a dralan."

"Kli-Kli, all the high-society people will have steam coming out of their ears if he has a dralan with him."

It's no secret that those who once used to root about in the mud and now bear a noble title are not much liked by those who inherited their titles from their noble forebears.

"That will only make everything all the more amusing." The little green fool will do anything for the sake of amusement.

"What do we have to do at the reception?" I asked, bowing to the inevitable.

"Drink sparkling wine, eat pheasants, and make intelligent conversation about the weather."

"Not that, Kli-Kli! What do we really have to do?"

"You have to try to find out where Pargaid is hiding the Key. Don't worry, Miralissa says that as soon as you're close enough, you'll feel your connection with it."

Well, if Miralissa says so. . . . But I'm afraid the dark elfess is wrong this time. Why didn't I feel the Key when we had it?

"I just have to find out where it is?"

"Yes. I don't think you'll be able to take it with so many people around," the elfess said.

Well . . . I pulled off trickier jobs than that in my young days, and I'll manage to steal this thing one way or another.

"There is one other little problem, Tresh Miralissa. Paleface could come back at any moment, and he knows what I look like. Did Lamplighter manage to find out anything about where Rolio went off to?"

"The assassin left the city in great haste along the southwestern highway. We must hope that he will not come back in time for the reception."

"You will have to take the risk, thief."

I wish you could take it, Milord Alistan. This is an absolutely wild adventure! If you ask me, it would be easier to take the manor house by storm.

The next day I was simply unbearable, and I made Kli-Kli regret his brilliant idea of turning me into a dralan. But Miralissa and the goblin completely disregarded my argument that a commoner who had only recently been promoted to high society didn't need to learn all this stuff.

I never realized that being a nobleman was so complicated. Only someone with noble blood flowing in his veins could possibly keep all those absolutely stupid and unnecessary things in his head.

I learned the correct way to pick up a wineglass, bow, behave at table, pay compliments, maintain a significant silence, challenge someone to a duel, and to discuss eternal philosophical themes, horses, hunting with falcons, military parades, jousts, heraldry, and all sorts of other trash that has no place in the daily life of a self-respecting master thief. By the end of the day the excessive load of superfluous knowledge had given me a splitting headache.

Duke Shagor's coat of arms happened to be a hedgehog on a field of purple, and the effort of trying to make sure I wouldn't make an absolute fool of myself turned me as prickly as an entire herd of my noble lord Eel's heraldic beasts. By the end of it all, the mere sight of Kli-Kli was enough to set me hissing and spitting like an angry tomcat, but even so he and Alistan kept hammering the knowledge into my head—it turned out that every dralan had to know all the ancestors of the lord who had granted him his noble title.

A family tree is no joke, I can tell you. Remembering who married who, when, how, what for, and how many little children they had, and then who married who, when, how, what for, and so on to infinity . . .

Eventually I got Eel's new relations totally confused and I mixed up his grandaunt, the most benign Duchess de Laranden, with the second cousin of his grandnephew by his sixth half sister, who was married to the uncle of his mother's twelfth sister via the father-grandmother-grandfather line. Kli-Kli spat in annoyance and said I was hopeless if I couldn't remember such a simple little thing and stomped off to the kitchen, leaving Arnkh and Lamplighter, who had been splitting their sides with laughter while I suffered the torment of my training, to make fun of me.

"If I had that many relatives, I'd run away from home!" Arnkh gasped through his laughter.

"You did run away," Mumr reminded the man from the Border Kingdom.

That set Arnkh laughing even louder, and he almost spilled a mug of beer on his chain mail as he wiped away his tears.

An hour before we had to leave I suddenly got the shakes and started walking from one corner of the inn to the other, like a garrinch in a cage. I had the feeling that we were tempting fate with all our subterfuges and all this was not going to end well. "I swear by Sagot, we're going to run into big trouble," I thought. "And all thanks to Kli-Kli, may the orcs catch him!"

"Marmot," I said to the Wild Heart who was training his ling, Invincible, "did you see where the jester got to?"

"Take a look in your room; I think he was doing something in there."

Well, of course the considerate goblin was preparing my costume for the reception. I still hadn't seen my gala outfit. Kli-Kli had refused point-blank to show it to me, obviously out of concern for the state of my nerves. All the other characters in the masquerade had already been given their new clothes: green vestments for the Wild Hearts, with a gray hedgehog on a purple field sewn on the chest; Eel was decked out in a very expensive noble's outfit with a tall starched collar and wide, dark brown sleeves; and Egrassa had already changed into a blue and yellow tunic embroidered with a black moon—the symbol of his house.

I found Kli-Kli frantically trying to shoo a fly away from his bowl of cherries.

He looked so ridiculous I couldn't help asking, "Don't you ever get tired of playing the fool?"

"That's my job, Harold," the goblin sighed. "If I didn't play the fool, I'd still be at home, in Zagraba, studying to be a shaman."

"You don't regret it, do you?" I asked, taking a handful of cherries.

"Not really . . . Everything that happens is for the best. And anyway, if I wasn't here, who would protect you?"

"Me? Are you telling me that *you* protect *me*?" We'd been through this conversation a hundred times or more.

"Well, who does, if not me? You're only still alive thanks to me," the jester said, puffing himself up proudly.

"The things I have had from you, my little green prankster, include prickly thorns across my backside, cold water in my bed, a stupid prophecy, and the false title of a dralan, with a fancy peacock's outfit—a gift from the duke—to go with it. And by the way, where is my costume? I'd like to take a look at what you ordered for our obliging innkeeper to pick up for me. What am I wearing to the reception?"

"Ah!" said the jester, taking my point. "You'll soon see."

"Soon? Why not right now?"

"We still have one important thing left to do. Follow me, Dancer in the Shadows, and you will have your final lesson."

"You can go into the darkness! Is there no end to all this?" I asked furiously. "You tormented me all day long with that heraldry of yours. It's enough to drive the Nameless One crazy, let alone an ordinary thief. That's enough lessons for today!"

"You're not an ordinary thief. You're a master thief," said the jester, pointing his finger at me. "And I must at least show you how to dance in respectable company."

Every idea Kli-Kli has is crazier than the last one.

"Why not teach me to deliver babies, too? Dralans don't get invited to dance. And anyway, I know how to dance without any lessons from you."

"Yes, you do, some djanga or galkag or whatever." Kli-Kli gulped down a cherry, screwed up his left eye, took aim, and spat the stone out the window. "But noblemen's dances are quite different altogether. Come on, you don't want to mess things up just at the wrong moment, do you?"

I groaned, not for the first time that day, but there was nothing to be done and I had to tramp after the jester into the large open hall, cursing the day that had brought the two of us together.

All the Wild Hearts were gathered in the hall. Even Bass was there. He was frowning in puzzlement at the soldiers' rather strange servants' costumes but, fortunately, he didn't understand a thing.

"Hey, Deler!" Kli-Kli called. "Come over here!"

The dwarf broke off his quarrel with Hallas and waddled to us without hurrying. In his bodyguard's outfit he looked like a cow in the uniform of the Heartless Chasseurs.

"What do you want?"

"Listen, Deler, for the sake of the common cause, do us a favor."

"Well?" he said, squinting suspiciously at us as the idea penetrated that a favor is something you do for nothing—and dwarves don't like to do anything for nothing.

"Put your arms round Harold."

Deler's face turned gray.

"What do you . . . ? Kli-Kli, you're a friend of mine, but . . . I could punch you in the face—"

"You fool, Deler! This is a dancing lesson."

"A-a-ah!" the dwarf drawled as the light dawned, and he took off his bowler hat and ruffled up his ginger hair. "Then I'm too short for this; you need Honeycomb."

"Honeycomb," Kli-Kli growled, knitting his brows. "Honeycomb is such a great bear, he'll flatten Harold's feet."

"Well, Arnkh then."

"Arnkh?"

"Why not? I agree! This should be very amusing!" the bald warrior chuckled, getting up from the table.

Amusing? Somehow I didn't share this old war dog's passionate enthusiasm for launching into a dance.

"That's just wonderful! Right then, Arnkh, put your arms round Harold. Put your hands on his waist. On his waist. You know what a waist is, don't you? That's it! Now Harold, why are you standing there like a statue? You do the same. Right! Your backs! Hold your backs straight. What kind of paralytics are you, may the orcs take me! That's it! Now watch what you have to do."

The goblin performed a short series of intricate and absolutely bizarre steps.

"All right?" he asked when he got his breath back.

"It reminds me of a Doralissian jumping around after someone tipped red-hot coals down his trousers," said Hallas, expressing the general opinion.

The gnome's final words were drowned in laughter.

"Why, you dolts! This is the most fashionable dance there is right now!" said Kli-Kli, trying to shout above the laughter.

The laughter turned into a loud roar.

The jester snorted in annoyance and turned his attention to me and Arnkh.

"Don't just stand there as if you're frozen solid. Do what I do. Follow the count!"

I felt like an absolute idiot.

"And . . . One-two-three, one-two-three! Make the steps more distinct! Three . . . Straighten that back! Two-three! Harold, don't drag your foot! One-two-three!"

Arnkh crushed the toes on my right foot, and we almost fell down when Kli-Kli speeded up the rhythm.

Everybody just kept laughing. Lamplighter took out his reed pipe and started playing a tune for us. Master Quidd came to see the free show. The elves came down into the hall. Then Alistan showed up. Our beloved count had a very pleased expression on his face. Well, naturally; it's not every day that you see the likes of this. . . .

"One-two-three. Lift that foot higher. One-two-turn-three!" Kli-Kli just kept going, never falling silent for a moment. Arnkh stepped on my foot again, and I hissed in pain.

Finally it was over, and I caught my breath.

"Kli-Kli, why did you have to teach Harold to dance?" the elfess asked the goblin curiously. "After all, you know that Balistan Pargaid absolutely detests dancing, and there won't be anything of the kind at the reception."

"Ah, you—"

"Harold, I had to cheer you all up and raise the spirits of our troops!" the goblin whined, as if his feelings were hurt. "What are you so angry about?"

I controlled myself.

"Harold, you only have a quarter of an hour left to get changed," Eel reminded me.

The warrior was already decked out in his costume. A real duke, I swear by the light! Thanks to Miralissa's magic, his face had become less swarthy for the time being. His black hair had turned lighter, and now no one would ever have guessed that Eel was a Garrakian.

"Bah! Eel! We could crown you king of Garrak, dressed like that!" Honeycomb exclaimed admiringly.

Eel's cheek twitched at those words.

"Kli-Kli, where are my clothes?"

The goblin peeped out warily from behind Bass, trying to assess his chances of living to a decent old age, then made up his mind and blurted out: "Let's go, then."

"Where are you going?" Bass asked casually.

Ell suddenly appeared in front of Snoop and offered to escort him to his room. He laughed, got up, and followed the elf. Kli-Kli led me back to our room. My clothes were laid out neatly on the made-up bed. I cast a skeptical eye over them, turned to the jester, and growled. "Are you making fun of me?"

"I wouldn't dream of it," the goblin replied hastily. "What is it you don't like this time?"

"Those aren't clothes, they're a peacock's feathers!"

"All dukes are a bit like peacocks. These are perfectly normal clothes for noblemen. Not to mention dralans. Those lads like their outfits to be splendid."

"Alistan doesn't dress like that!"

"Alistan is the captain of the king's guard, not a dralan who has been invited to a formal reception."

"I'm not a dralan, and you know that perfectly well! And apart from that, I can't even imagine how to put all this on!"

"We'll soon manage that," Kli-Kli declared boldly, and started rummaging through the expensive rags with his tongue hanging out.

When the goblin led me across to the mirror, I was struck dumb. I was wearing a blinding white silk shirt with narrow sleeves and a lacy collar, under a dark plum velvet doublet with gold buttons and a high collar. And on the right side of my chest there was a coat of arms skillfully embroidered in silver thread: a plow turning over the soil in a field.

The breeches were rather tight, and therefore not very comfortable. High boots with an embroidered design, a belt that was one-and-a-half hands wide, a dagger of singing steel in an expensive sheath, with a handle of bluish ogre-bone—this absurd finery was topped off with a long satin cloak with a black lining, three ruby rings, a wide-brimmed hat with a green plume, and a massive plaited gold chain. If I fell in a river wearing that chain, there was no way I would ever surface again. Eel's costume was a lot richer than mine, but that didn't make me feel any better.

I looked at Kli-Kli and he opened his mouth to share his impressions with me.

"Not a word!" I said, cutting him short.

"But I—"

"Shut up!"

"All right, Harold." Kli-Kli submissively folded his little hands together like a priest of Silna.

To my mind I looked like a scarecrow in a vegetable garden. I could have gone off and started scaring crows straightaway. Clothes like this were definitely not for me.

"And how do you like my little outfit?" asked Kli-Kli, pulling off his cloak and spinning round on the spot.

The goblin had dressed himself up in something made out of scraps of blue and red and stuck a cap with little bells on his head.

"Colorful."

"Then it's just what's required!"

When we walked down into the hall of the inn, strangely enough no one laughed at my outfit.

"May the gods be with us. Let's go." Miralissa caught my glance of surprise and explained. "I'm going with you; I have to check the house for magical traps."

She had changed her usual gray and green elfin scout's outfit for a very stylish purple silk dress with a black iron brooch shaped like the moon. Her invariable braid of ash-gray hair had been transformed into a tall hairstyle in the fashion of Miranueh, and round her neck she was wearing a string of smoky-yellow topazes, which harmonized beautifully with the color of her eyes. From a professional point of view I can say that a set of stones like that would buy five years of good living, spending money like water on daily sprees and drinking sessions . . . but if you looked at her with an unprofessional eye, she looked absolutely stunning.

"Take this," she said, handing me the ogre bracelet. "When Balistan Pargaid asks Eel about the bracelet, you be there and give it to him."

"What?" I asked in amazement.

"It's no great loss, it has no value for us. But this is a chance to get close to the Key, if you can win our count's favor."

"No, that's not what I meant," I said with a frown. "Why should I have the bracelet, and not Eel?"

"I'll tell you on the way."

"The carriage is ready, Lady Miralissa," said the innkeeper, darting across to us.

"Thank you, Master Quidd," the elfess said with a gracious smile. "You have been a great help to us."

"Don't mention it, I do it for my deceased uncle's sake. You took revenge for his soul, and my entire family is indebted to you."

"Remember, Harold," the elfess told me as we walked to the magnificent carriage with a team of six Doralissian horses that Quidd had somehow managed to find, "we shall be in the house of a servant of the Master."

I just had to hope that everyone at the reception was a bonehead and no servants of the Master happened to remember that a goblin left Avendoom in the company of elves.

We were hoping for a miracle, making a Vastar's bargain with destiny. In the house of a servant of the Master. There was no need to remind me. I was only too aware of that.

8

t was already dark and the carriage drifted through the emptying streets and parks of Ranneng like a phantom ship from the old sea legends. Kli-Kli, the elves, Eel, and I were sitting on the soft benches, Lamplighter and Arnkh had taken on the job of driving our carriage, and Deler, Hallas, Honeycomb, and Uncle accompanied us on horseback.

Miralissa had strictly forbidden the Wild Hearts to bring any weapons with them except for daggers. The Nightingales were too afraid of spies and assassins from the Wild Boars and Oburs to allow strangers to enter their house with any large sharp objects hanging on their belts. Deler had immediately asked the elfess in a peevish, discontented voice: "But couldn't you avert their eyes, Tresh Miralissa, the way you did with the Ranneng guard, after we rescued Master Harold and Eel?"

On that occasion it had cost the elfess a serious effort to ensure that the guardsmen would not notice the weapons sticking out from under our group's clothes while they were riding through the town. The dwarf received a polite and chilly refusal, and he had to leave his beloved poleax at the inn. I hardly need to say that Deler was not particularly happy about this.

We came closer to the Nightingales' estate and I began feeling calmer as the nervous trembling that I usually suffer before starting any job passed off.

After all, I'd been in all sorts of risky situations before, hadn't I? Being a dralan for a while is a lot less dangerous than stealing the reward for my own head from the house of Baron Frago Lanten, the leader of the

Avendoom municipal guard. And it's nowhere near as dangerous as taking a stroll through the Forbidden Territory or going down into the burial chambers of Hrad Spein. Jumping into a pit swarming with vipers and then climbing back out—surely that's the very test for a master thief?

"As soon as you sense the Key, let us know and make your way to the exit," Egrassa warned me, checking the edge of his crooked dagger with his thumb.

"Got you."

He's right, there's no point in taunting demons any longer than necessary. The longer we hung about in the house, the more chance there was that we'd run into some kind of trouble.

I prayed hard to Sagot that there wouldn't be any bright spark at Balistan Pargaid's house who knew the real Ganet Shagor in person, or we'd find ourselves in a real mess that not even Miralissa's shamanism could get us out of. And we couldn't afford to forget about my old friend Paleface, either. He might have left the city without trying to settle scores with me, but . . . That piece of scum could turn up at the most inappropriate moment just as suddenly as he had disappeared.

"What are you thinking about?" asked the fool, jangling his little bells.

"The vicissitudes of fate and various possible kinds of trouble," I answered.

"Don't you worry, Dancer in the Shadows, I'm here with you!"

"That's what I'm afraid of."

"We're losing days," Miralissa said in a dull voice as she tidied away a lock of hair. "It's August already, and we haven't crossed the Iselina yet. If things carry on like this, it will be September before we reach Hrad Spein."

"You are mistaken," Egrassa disagreed. "The Black River is two days' hard riding from Ranneng, then it's two weeks to reach the Border Kingdom, and another three days from there to Zagraba. And then a week in Zagraba until we reach Hrad Spein. So we should be there in late August."

"These are not our lands, cousin," the elfess sighed. "The eastern gates of Hrad Spein lie in the territory of the orcs. We do not know how long it will take us to get through the Golden Forest."

And we don't know what we might run into on the way, either. Or how much time I'll need in Hrad Spein. Or if I'll be able to get the Doors open. Or if I'll be able to find the Horn in the labyrinth of the Palaces of Bone. Or get back out with it.

"Time will tell," the elf replied to Miralissa, and put his dagger back into its sheath.

Time! Accursed time. We lost too much of it in Hargan's Wasteland, and now we're losing more of it in Ranneng. If it goes on like this, we won't get the Horn back to the capital before the start of winter.

Meanwhile our carriage was ascending the memorable incline that I had ridden down in the cart only a few days earlier.

"We're almost there," Kli-Kli murmured with a shudder.

Oho! So even the goblin is feeling nervous! And there he was trying to reassure me.

"Right, Harold, you know what to do. Put on a miserable face and pray to that Sagot of yours to help you find out where the Key is."

Put on a miserable face?

"Will this do?" I asked, squinting sideways at the jester, and he gave me a thumbs-up.

"Whoa there!" we heard Arnkh say.

The carriage stopped. A man with a gold nightingale emblem on his formal uniform came up to the door.

"Name yourselves, my worshipful lords."

"His Grace Duke Ganet Shagor, the honorable Milla and Eralla of the House of the Black Moon, and Dralan Par!" the jester barked as crisply as a dozen royal heralds. "And, of course, the duke's favorite jester. That's me, in case you didn't recognize me."

Miralissa and Egrassa had changed their names for simpler ones, and that's something quite unheard of. The pride of the race of the Second-born does not, under any circumstance, allow an elf to use a name that is not his own. So today's event must be very special indeed, if two elves from the highest families of the House of the Black Moon decided to change their names.

Members of a noble family could attract close attention of an unwelcome kind, so for the time being the elves had dropped their proud *ssa*. And in addition, although Pargaid had never seen us, he could have heard from informers in Avendoom about the elves called Egrassa and

Miralissa who had visited the king, so we could hardly be too careful. The elves had changed their own names, but not the name of their house. For members of the elfin race, their house is absolutely sacrosanct.

"May I see your invitation, Your Grace?"

The jester insolently thrust an envelope under the guard's nose. The light blue paper bore an embossed seal with a clear image of a nightingale.

"There! Any more questions? Or do you want to make His Grace angry?"

"I beg your pardon," the soldier muttered in fright and started backing away, almost tripping over the scabbard of his own sword. "Proceed!"

Up on the coach box, Arnkh clicked his tongue to urge the horses on and the carriage set off, but then stopped again before it had even gone a yard.

Another guard came up to us. Unlike the first, he was dressed all in silk, not chain mail. His bald cranium could have been the envy of all the warriors of the Border Kingdom. He had a nose like a mountain eagle's beak, thick bushy eyebrows, ears that stuck out, and a long beard. His eyes were the color of blue steel, and they slid over us with a piercing gleam, remembering our faces.

"I beg your pardon, Your Grace, but may I take a look at the invitation?" this man asked drily.

"We have just been checked! You forget yourself, guard! You see a duke before you!" Eel snapped in a cold voice.

"My most humble apologies yet again, milord, but this is Balistan Pargaid's order, and this check is for your own safety."

"Give him the paper, fool!" Eel hissed. "Bear in mind that your conduct will be reported to the count, and I shall personally give you a flogging!"

"As Your Lordship wishes," the man said indifferently.

"Yes, the seal is genuine," he said with a nod after examining the letter carefully. "My most sincere apologies for the inconvenience."

There was not even a hint of regret in his voice.

"Take this for your pains," Eel said acidly, and tossed the man a copper coin. He automatically caught it and his eyes glinted in fury.

"Thank you, Your Grace," he said with a bow. "I shall remember your generosity."

The carriage moved on and the gates of the estate were left behind. Now we were driving slowly through a small park.

"There was no need to humiliate him," Miralissa said after a pause.

"In Garrak the nobility are not used to dealing politely with commoners. I do what my character requires," Eel said with an indifferent shrug.

"This is not Garrak, and that man is dangerous."

"I know, but even so I did what had to be done."

"That man is called Meilo Trug," the jester said in a quiet voice.

"You know him?"

"Yes, I saw him five years ago at a tournament held in honor of the birthday of Stalkon's younger son. He won the section for open combat on foot. A master of the long sword."

"He might have recognized you," I muttered anxiously.

"I don't think so. I was watching him from the grandstand, but it's not very likely that he saw me."

The carriage stopped in front of the mansion house, in which every window was brightly lit. The door of the house opened and servants with golden nightingale emblems on their clothes bowed low and respectfully to us.

Kli-Kli was the first to jump out of the carriage, and he immediately started making faces.

"Milord, noble gentlemen!" said a man clutching something like a massive, richly decorated mace or staff as he bowed to us. "In the name of Count Balistan Pargaid I am happy to greet you! Follow me, you are expected."

Eel nodded, which seemed to be exactly what the lad was waiting for. He swung round and led us into the building along a carpet runner. Kli-Kli overtook our guide and skipped along in front of him, jingling his little bells merrily. The herald tried to take no notice of the goblin twirling about right under his feet.

The reception hall began immediately inside the door, and it was bursting at the seams with guests. I didn't know there were so many nobles in Ranneng and the surrounding area! And this was just one of the warring parties! There were all the Oburs and Wild Boars, too, almost as many of them as the Nightingales!

The hall was crammed to the breaking point, groaning and screwing up its eyes at the bright colors of the guests' rich costumes, swooning over the vast diversity of hairstyles, choking on the smell of perfume. I glanced round the hall with a practiced eye, trying to keep an expression of disdainful boredom on my face. Yes, the valuables on the ladies would have made up a dragon's treasure hoard. There were plenty of spoils on display.

Thousands of candles were burning and it was as bright as day. Beside the fountain that had been set in the very center of the hall on somebody's insane whim, musicians were playing to amuse the gathered guests. There were servants darting about, carrying trays with goblets of sparkling wine. I could hear voices and jolly laughter on all sides.

The lad who had showed us in struck his staff on the floor three times and yelled so loud that I almost jumped out of my skin.

"Duke Ganet Shagor of the House of Shagor! The honorable Milla and Eralla from the House of the Black Moon! Dralan Par!"

"And the jester Krya-Krya, you simpleton!" Kli-Kli shouted, bowing elegantly to the guests.

People turned to look at us and bowed respectfully. The goblin skipped over to me.

"Now what?" I asked him, barely even opening my lips.

"Drink some wine and put on a clever face, and that's all that's required of you. I'll go and get to know the people."

Before I could open my mouth, Kli-Kli had disappeared among the ladies and gentlemen. Miralissa quickly got talking with a pair of rather tipsy ladies, speaking with surprising expertise about male elves and the intricacies of elfin fashion. She batted her eyelids and twittered away as recklessly as if she was a total fool, and if I didn't know her, I would never have guessed that this was all just pretense. The ladies listened to her, open-mouthed.

Egrassa walked along a wall hung with ancient weapons with the air of a connoisseur.

"Milord Shagor?"

A man dressed in a doublet of blue and black velvet approached Eel and me. Tall, with a neat black beard, a gleaming white smile, and quizzical brown eyes. His temples were already gray. His features were noble but perfectly agreeable. Lads like that are often used as models for heroes in temple frescoes.

There was something vaguely familiar about his face.

"Whom do I have the honor of addressing?" Eel inquired with just the slightest of bows. According to Kli-Kli, a duke doesn't really have to bother bending his back at all. I bowed rather more deeply.

"Count Balistan Pargaid. I am delighted that you have accepted my invitation," the man replied, bowing gently.

"Thank you for your kind invitation to this wonderful reception, count. Allow me to introduce my protégé, Dralan Par."

A faint nod. Dralans may be nobles of a kind, but they're not held in very high esteem.

"Do you always accompany the duke everywhere, dralan?" Balistan Pargaid asked, flashing his white smile.

"I like to travel, milord. And a journey with His Lordship is always full of adventures."

"Is that so?" Another polite and meaningless smile. "I hope that I have not dragged you away from more important business with my untimely invitation, duke?"

"Indeed, no. I was in need of a little diversion."

The gentle music drifted round the hall and the people on all sides glanced curiously in our direction, but merely bowed politely, without trying to join in the conversation.

"I was not in time to meet you in front of my house, but I have heard that you are traveling with elves. Forgive the indiscreet question, Your Grace, but what is your connection with that particular race?"

Before Eel had a chance to reply, the jester popped out from behind the wide skirts of a lady already well past her youth, who was languidly sipping wine. The goblin was holding a cream bun in each hand.

"Bed," he said.

"What?" the count asked, blinking.

"My master, may his backside sit on the Sea Cliffs for another two hundred years, travels with elves because they're good in bed. Pay no attention to the dralan. He just *travels*."

For a moment I was dumbstruck at such an audacious, bold-faced lie. I think that if the elves had heard what the goblin said, they would have gutted him like a fish, even though he was wearing a jester's cap. Eel received the news about his preferences with the calm composure of a genuine duke. Balistan Pargaid, on the other hand, chuckled and gave him a knowing look.

"One must have a little variety in one's life," said Eel, shrugging his shoulders casually. "Otherwise it simply becomes too boring."

"Well, naturally. Is this your fool, milord?" the count asked, examining Kli-Kli with interest.

"Is this our master, milord?" the goblin asked Eel in the same tone of voice, and stuffed both cream buns into his mouth, which instantly made him look like a hamster. Kli-Kli thought for a moment, and then spat both tasty morsels out onto the Sultanate carpet.

"My fool is sharp-tongued, but not trained in good manners, please forgive him."

Kli-Kli made a face and bowed very low to Balistan, almost burying his nose in the carpet.

"I could say that I am glad to be here, if only there weren't so many stuffed dummies around, dear count," the jester squeaked.

Count Balistan Pargaid laughed merrily: "Not every man would dare to call my guests stuffed dummies!"

"In case the count has failed to notice, then I must regretfully inform him that I am not a man, but a goblin," said Kli-Kli, jingling his little bells.

"Duke, your fool is amusing! Let me have him!"

"Don't sell me for anything less than a thousand gold pieces!" the jester exclaimed. "And don't forget to give me my share after the deal!"

"I'm afraid, count, that if the duke lets you have his fool, then my lord will become your bitter enemy. Believe me, Krya-Krya is a walking disaster!" I said, deciding it was time for me to open my mouth.

The count laughed again.

Meanwhile the herald struck his staff on the floor and announced more guests.

"Ah, please excuse me, Your Grace but, you understand, the obligations of a host. We will certainly find time to talk again, will we not?"

"Of course, count. Of course."

"Duke. Dralan."

Then all those idiotic bows again. If it goes on like this all evening, my head's going to fall off for sure.

"I'll take a stroll to the fountain. Let's meet by the stairs," Eel said, and walked away from us.

"Well, what do you make of him? I mean the count."

"Not now," the jester hissed out of the corner of his mouth, jumping up and down desperately and jingling his bells. "Can you sense the Key?"

Jingle-jangle! Ding-dong!

"No."

Kli-Kli grunted, disappointed.

Ding-dong! Jingle-jangle!

"Take some wine. Take a stroll!" Kli-Kli whispered to me, and disappeared into the crowd of Nightingales.

I looked around, but I couldn't see the elves or Eel. The longer this evening went on, the more wonderful it became.

With a casual gesture I halted a servant giving out drinks and took a glass of sparkling rosé wine from him, wishing that there was something else. I can't stand that Filand piss-water. One glass is enough to set my insides on fire, as if it had been spiked with poison.

"Would the gentleman like some sweet fruits?" An entire dish of foreign garbage sprinkled with powdered sugar was thrust under my nose.

"The gentleman would like you to clear off," I growled at the servant.

I started strolling round the hall with a bored expression on my face. People looked askance at me, as if I had brought a half-decomposed cat into the hall and dumped it in the main dish of the evening.

A woman passed me with her skirts rustling, almost rubbing up against me. Her face was hidden behind a veil.

"I beg your pardon, milord."

"Yes, of course, there isn't much room. I understand."

Another couple of steps, and the whole thing was repeated all over again, only this lady dropped her fan at my feet.

"I beg your pardon, milord, I am so clumsy."

I had to bend down, pick the fan up off the floor, and hand it to her. She smiled sweetly and dropped a curtsey, offering her plunging neckline to my delighted gaze. It cost me an almighty effort to leave milady alone. But if I hadn't the goblin would have given me the sharp edge of his tongue.

A few steps farther on a third milady appeared beside me, flashing her eyes flirtatiously in my direction.

"What is your name, milord?"

"Take no notice, my dear dralan! I'll rescue you!" A heavy hand fell on my shoulder and pulled me away. "Pardon my familiarity, but I am only a baron, my domains border on the Border Kingdom, and we are taught to use a sword much earlier than etiquette. Yes, and I think you are no great devotee of etiquette, either! However, allow me in any case to introduce myself. Baron Oro Gabsbarg at your service!"

I bowed reservedly.

He was a huge man, almost as big as Honeycomb, with a shaggy black beard, little black eyes, a red face, and a thunderous voice. What he resembled most was a bear. And like everyone else in this hall, beside his own crest (a black cloud belching out lightning on a green field) he had a brooch in the form of a nightingale pinned to his clothes.

"What do you think of this wine?" my new acquaintance asked me unexpectedly.

I told him the absolute truth.

"It's swill."

The baron laughed deafeningly and in his excessive enthusiasm he thumped me on the back, almost fracturing my spine.

"Ah, I like you! I've always said if only we had a lot more dralans in our kingdom, soon there wouldn't be a single namby-pamby left in the nobility. The moment you appeared in the hall, everyone said you were stupid and ignorant. But I can see that's not true!"

"Who said that?" I asked, trying to get my breath back after the baron's bearlike blow.

"All of these carrion-eaters," said the baron, gesturing round the hall without the slightest embarrassment. "What do you think they all do with their time, my dear fellow?" Oro Gabsbarg's little black eyes glinted in fury. "Tittle-tattle! They don't have anything better to do. These popinjays who dare to call themselves men pour scent on their handkerchiefs!"

I thought the baron was going to vomit on my doublet there and then.

"Can you imagine it? But I can see that you're a different kind, better than these puppy dogs," Oro Gabsbarg boomed contentedly and chuckled into his beard as he winked at me. "Well, didn't I just save you from those cunning little serpents?"

"I beg your pardon?" I didn't understand what he meant.

"From those demons in skirts! How did you like the way I shooed them off? The little widows. Their main pastime is dragging a new man into their bed. Well of course, bed is an essential and important business, but before you get round to doing your business, these ladies, who would be better called harlots, will stuff you with poison right up to your . . . What I was going to say is that all their husbands preferred to be stabbed to death by Wild Boars and Oburs. You must agree, it's better than putting up with a rotten bitch."

I nodded in agreement. The baron seemed to be in need of a grateful listener, and he had found one.

"The nobles are getting petty, really petty," the giant sighed plaintively. "They're not at all what they used to be. The nobility haven't had real blood running through their veins for ages; it's as thin as water. Of course, with the exception of you and me," he added hastily.

"Of course."

Despite his loud voice and not entirely elegant manners, I was beginning to like this man.

"How many swords has your duke got?"

Oro Gabsbarg's question stumped me. How many swords did Duke Ganet Shagor really have? And what kind of swords? The kind you hang on your belt, or the kind you command in battle?

Seeing my confusion, the baron uttered the bearlike roar that was his normal laugh.

"That's what sitting stuck at Sea Cliffs all the time gets you! Your lands are peaceful, Zagraba's a long way away, and you can't even remember how many warriors your lord has!"

"It can't be helped, my friend," I said with a shrug.

"Friend?" The baron gave me a curious look. "Yes, why not!"

He grabbed hold of my hand and crushed it in his palm. Thank Sagot, by some miracle my hand was still whole and undamaged after that handshake.

"And how do you feel about the Nightingales, dear fellow?"

"Er-er . . . ," I began warily.

"You don't feel anything," Shadow Harold's new friend, Oro Gabsbarg, concluded impassively, reading the answer in my eyes. "I confess from the very bottom of my heart," he whispered, leaning down to my ear, "I feel the same. But mum's the word, all right? Sh-sh-sh-sh!"

"Then what's that nightingale doing on your doublet?"

"Oh, you northerners," the baron murmured wearily. "Times are hard, dear fellow. My ancestral castle of Farahall is not very far away from Zagraba. Of course, there are still the lands of Milord Algert Dalli, Buttress of the Throne and Keeper of the Western Border of the Border Kingdom, but the Firstborn still manage to get through even as far as me. This year alone we wiped out two detachments of orcs, but a third one completely massacred one of my villages and then disappeared into the woods. I have a hundred and fifty warriors at my castle, plus another hundred scattered about in patrols. There aren't enough swords, the orcs find breaches in our defenses. There are rumors that the Hand of the Orcs is gathering an army. And so, my friend, I'd gladly be a butterfly, never mind a nightingale, if only Balistan Pargaid would give me fighting men!"

"I understand."

"You don't understand a thing, my dear dralan!" Oro Gabsbarg thundered with unexpected fury. "Pardon my harsh tone, but trying to tell you about our troubles is like trying to explain to a blind man what a catapult looks like! Your duke's lands are too far away from the damned forest, you cannot feel or understand the threat that constantly hangs over those of us who live in the Borderland. Since the Spring War the orcs have stayed put in the Golden Forest, but nobody's patience lasts forever, and any lesson is eventually forgotten."

He frowned.

"I've written to His Majesty three times and asked him to send me men. I'm rich enough to feed three hundred additional soldiers, but the king hasn't replied. I don't think he's to blame; the letters might not have reached him, or got lost. You know yourself how easy it is to lose a letter. My men were not admitted to the palace, they're too unimportant to be allowed to tramp across all that marble! And I can't get to the capital, I can't leave the lands of my ancestors for long. Not in times like these. . . . I only came away for this gathering because I was relying on getting the count's help, but obviously I was wrong. The border is uneasy, and if anything happens, we won't be able to hold out. . . .

So, instead of experienced warriors, I have to make do with my own militia raised from the local villages and mercenaries. Ganet Shagor is a relative of the king, isn't he?"

"A distant one."

"Do something for me, will you? If you're in the capital, have the duke tell Stalkon about this conversation of ours. The king's an intelligent man, he must realize that our southern border is coming apart at the seams."

"But there are the garrisons—"

"A bunch of idle, drunken guardsmen!" Oro Gabsbarg replied derisively. "Decades of peace have completely undermined discipline! A quarter of the fortresses are standing empty. And in another quarter of them the soldiers don't even know how to hold a sword. Yes, I'm prejudiced, yes there are some garrisons where they still haven't forgotten what orcs are, but the situation is de-plor-able. Absolutely deplorable. If, Sagra forbid, anything should happen, they'll push us back to the Iselina, or even further. Do you understand me?"

I nodded. I was sure that in Avendoom they didn't know any of this. Or, at least, the king didn't. Everybody thought that since the Spring War the border of the kingdom was unassailable and securely defended against incursions from the land of forests.

If the king found out how things really stood, heads would roll.

"Will you tell the duke what I said?"

"At the first opportunity," I replied quite sincerely. "And not just the duke, but the king himself. Just give us time to get back to Avendoom."

The baron's dark eyes were still fixed on me.

"I swear it."

"Wonderful! Thank you, my friend, I'll never forget this! Er-er, excuse me, dralan, but my wife wants me. You can see the way she's looking at me. She's a handsome enough woman, but the trouble is that she's too quick with her hands. Let me tell you a secret: She has a magnificent spiked mace. I swear by all the gods, I lose three duels out of five to her! So you can understand. . . . If you're ever in my parts, you must come and visit. Farahall is at your service!"

The baron bowed awkwardly and left me.

Well, the things that are going on in our kingdom!

Just then one of the wanton ladies started taking an interest in Eel. I went dashing to help him out, but someone else got there ahead of me: An old woman holding a little shaggy dog in her arms came to the Wild Heart's assistance. She brushed the latest little widow aside as if she simply wasn't there.

The seductress hissed something scurrilous through her delightful teeth to express her dissatisfaction and went on her way, greatly offended. The reason she left was clear enough: Milady was only a marchioness, she had a little coat of arms on a chain, but granny had an entire duchess's crown. The forces were unevenly matched.

"These young people nowadays! We used to have time for romance, time for courting, but nowadays? All they want is . . ."

And then the nice old lady pronounced a phrase that would have made a sailor blush. Eel's new acquaintance was certainly colorful, I would even go so far as to say amusing. Her black dress hung on her as loosely as on a coat hanger and her purple wig looked like some kind of misunderstanding. Her wrinkled face was covered with a layer of white powder as thick as a finger, and this charming get-up was rounded off by a well-fed little doggy with a blue silk ribbon round its neck.

"Countess Ranter at your service."

I wonder why everybody's so keen to offer their services today?

"I . . ."

"Oh, don't bother yourself, duke. I know perfectly well who you are. But then, so does everyone in this hall."

"The gossipers?" I put in, remembering what the baron had said as I came to Eel's assistance.

I earned a rather disdainful glance from the dear old lady.

"Is that what Oro the bear told you? What was he talking about with you for so long? But then, don't bother to answer, dralan, even my shaggy little Tobiander knows, don't you, my little one?" the countess cooed, addressing the lap dog, which was drooling in its sleep. "What can that beer-soaked barbarian possibly discuss? Nothing but swords, battles, and stupid orcs that don't really exist. Isn't that right, my little darling?"

"You don't believe in orcs, countess?"

"I do. But Tobiander is so impressionable! By the way, you look a lot younger than I thought you were, duke!"

"Really! You flatter me."

"Yes, when I saw you last, about forty years ago, you were marching around gravely under the table with a wooden sword in your hand. But now you don't look a day over thirty. Do northerners possess the secret of eternal youth?"

I gave a forced laugh. Eel remained icily calm. This damned old woman had seen the real duke! Even if he was only an infant at the time!

Don't worry, Harold! The duke has lived like a hermit, Harold! No one will recognize him, Harold! I'm with you, Harold!

May the demons gobble up Kli-Kli and his brilliant little ideas!

"My youthfulness must come from my ancestors, countess."

"Yes, and by the way, about them! You're not at all like your father. Not in the slightest! And I can't see a single feature of my dear second cousin in you!"

Her second cousin? Ah, that would be Eel's supposed mother. I quickly ran through the duke's family tree on his mother's side in my mind. Yes, that was it! There was an intersection with a branch of the Ranter family. A distant connection, but it was there.

"These are questions you had better put to my mother, dear countess."

"And how, may I ask? She has been dead a long time!"

Oops! Time to close down the conversation.

"Yes, a great loss," I put in, taking Eel by the elbow. "But allow us to take our leave, we have a lot of business to attend to."

And before she could say another word, we set off toward the broad marble stairway at the opposite end of the hall. I could feel the old lady's stare of amazement drilling into my back.

Never mind, she'll survive. And anyway, what did she expect from a dralan so recently separated from his plow? Polite manners?

I heard laughter break out on my left. Of course, it was Kli-Kli amusing the noble gentlemen. The jester was taking his work seriously, and all those dolled-up peacocks were chortling just like any ordinary commoners. The goblin sang songs, juggled three full glasses of wine, and asked riddles. All the jokes were too stupid for my taste, but they were a resounding success with the nobility.

"Upstairs," I said to Eel. "We'll check what's up there."

We walked up the stairs to the second floor and found ourselves on a balcony that ran right round the hall and provided a magnificent view. Two corridors started from the same point, leading into the depths of the building. The one nearest to me contained a lot of paintings in huge gilded frames, an entire portrait gallery, in fact.

Out of curiosity I walked up to the first canvas. Staring out at me from the picture with a sardonic expression was Count Balistan Pargaid in person. The next painting showed a man who was a copy of Pargaid. No doubt it was his father. I took another step in order to see the count's grandfather, and suddenly felt a strange tickling in my stomach. I started wondering what could have caused this nuisance, but then I remembered what Miralissa had said about the Key and the sensation I should feel.

The Key! I swear by Sagot, the Key was somewhere near!

"I felt something. Eel, cover me in case anything happens!"

I strolled on down the corridor, moving farther and farther away from the Nightingales' festivities, and found myself alone with just pictures, from which Balistan Pargaid's numerous ancestors gazed out at me.

The tickling in my stomach grew stronger. The Key was calling to me, luring me. I almost thought I could hear words.

"Here I am! Come quick! The bonds are calling you!"

There was not much farther left to go. The artifact was behind one of two doors on each side of the final portrait in the corridor. I walked up to them and stopped to examine the portrait, which had caught my attention. It cost me an effort of will not to gasp out loud.

The portrait was old. Very old. I could tell that from the way the paint had darkened, and the artist's style. Assessing the picture with the strictly professional eye of a master thief who has not disdained the theft of a few works of art in his time, I can state with certainty that the canvas was at least five hundred years old and, to judge from his costume, the man depicted in it had lived at least fifteen hundred years ago.

The man in the picture was over fifty years old, thin, with gray hair at his temples and gray streaks in his neat little beard. He had no mustache. His brown eyes gazed at me in genial derision. And I knew this fellow or, rather, I had seen him, even though he lived at a time when Ranneng was no more than a small village and Avendoom did not even exist.

Where have I seen this gentleman! But of course, in a dream! The dream in which this man killed the dwarf master-craftsman and tried to take possession of the Key, but met his death from an elfin dagger. I recall that he had a golden nightingale embroidered on his doublet.

So this was who Balistan Pargaid reminded me of! The family likeness between the present-day servant of the Master and the man whose life ended in the Mountains of the Dwarves was striking! What was his name, now . . .

"Suovik Pargaid," a quiet voice said behind my back.

I looked round. The master of the house was standing behind me. I hadn't even heard him walk up to me, although the floor was made of slabs of marble and not covered with a Sultanate carpet.

"I beg your pardon, milord. I saw the picture and was unable to overcome my curiosity," I said lamely.

"You have walked quite a long way, dralan," Balistan Pargaid said with a rather unpleasant laugh. "A-ah, here is our good duke!"

Fortunately Eel had sensed that something was wrong and he appeared from round the corner of the corridor.

"I trust that Dralan Par has not offended your ancestors, count? He has an interest in antiquity . . ."

"Oh, indeed?" the count asked.

Since when does an uncouth lummox like him take any interest in antiquity? said his eyes.

"Tell me, count, who is the subject of this portrait?" Eel asked, hastily switching the conversation to a less contentious subject.

"You do honor to my ancestors, Your Lordship! This is Suovik Pargaid, as I have already said. The third of the Pargaid line. Unfortunately, one fine day he set out for the Mountains of the Dwarves and never returned."

"How regrettable."

"He did a great deal for our family. But why do I keep talking of nothing but my ancestors? Come, let me acquaint you with my collection!"

The count took out an elegant key and unlocked the door nearest to us. It was a good lock, too, I would have to sweat long and hard before I could get it open.

"Make yourself at home, duke. And you too, dralan, go in. Well? What do you say?"

"Impressive."

"My little passion."

"Its value is not so very little, count," I said, looking round at Balistan Pargaid's collection.

"Oh! You know about such things?"

"A little. I am interested in antiques . . ."

"Well then, how would you assess the value of this set of trinkets, dralan?"

"About seventeen thousand gold pieces. But that is only an approximate figure."

"Oh! You really do know something about antiques. Sixteen and a half thousand, to be precise. Your Lordship, did you happen by any chance to bring along the trinket that I mentioned in my letter?"

"The bracelet? Yes, Dralan Par has it. He is the one who is interested in such things."

"Here it is, count."

I handed the ogres' piece of handiwork to Balistan Pargaid.

"By the way, how did you come to know that I had this little item?" Eel asked casually, as he examined a sword corroded with rust.

"Rumors," the count laughed, examining the almost obliterated ancient inscription on the bracelet.

"One of my servants, no doubt . . ."

"Yes, servants are an unreliable breed. But take my advice, duke: Nothing brings a servant to his senses like a good flogging. By the way, will you be in Ranneng for long?"

"No, I am just passing through and intend to go back in the morning.

"Simply traveling?"

"Yes," the Garrakian replied curtly as the count carefully studied the fascinating article from the Age of Achievements.

Walking up to the window, I saw the park painted silver by the moonlight.

"You have taken the precaution of installing bars on the windows, count."

"I'm sorry, what did you say, dralan?" asked Balistan Pargaid, inter-rupting his contemplation of the black bracelet for a moment. "Ah yes! To stop thieves. I have put bars in this wing. Here and in my bedroom. Although after my men skinned two thieves alive, the local guild of thieves decided not to risk any more of its members."

"I think that will not last long. You have a fortune here . . ."

"Well, time will tell."

It certainly will. I'm sure the bars are not the full story; the windows and, perhaps, even the doors are protected by a couple of magic sur-prises to give intruders a warm, or rather, hot welcome.

"How much do you want for it?" Balistan Pargaid asked, handing the bracelet back to me regretfully.

I weighed the bracelet in my hand, mentally taking leave of it for-ever. Ah! How I'd love to take its full value in gold from the count, but Miralissa said . . .

"Take it as a gift. It didn't cost me anything."

Balistan Pargaid made no attempt to refuse, which indicated quite clearly that he was a man of intelligence who took anything that hap-pened to be there for the taking. But he was rather staggered.

"Dralan Par!" It was the first time he had called me by my full name. "I am in your debt."

"Well then," I said, forcing a smile. "Let's get back to the hall quickly, or they'll drink all the wine while we're gone."

Balistan Pargaid smiled, carefully placed his new acquisition beside a battle-ax from the Gray Age, and nodded.

"And what is behind this door? Another little collection worth sixteen thousand in gold?" I asked the count when we had left the room.

"Oh no! This is my bedroom. I deliberately sleep close to my trea-sures," the count said with a laugh. "But let us go, or my guests really will think that I have forgotten about them."

Perhaps that really is his bedroom. But the Key is in there, too. I felt its call very clearly now. For a moment there I wanted to hit Balistan Pargaid over the head while his back was turned, then take advantage of the commotion to sneak into the room and steal the Key.

But I couldn't do that. Miralissa ordered me only to find out where the Key was, but not to touch it under any circumstances. . . . And if the dark elfess thinks that for the time being the artifact should not be touched, then that's how it's got to be.

In the hall the music was still playing, people were making idle chit-chat, and Kli-Kli had clambered up onto a table and was juggling four cream buns. By absurd coincidence a fifth landed on his pointed cap to general laughter and a storm of applause.

My attention was attracted by a woman in a bloodred dress, standing all alone beside the babbling fountain.

She was short, with light brown hair that just reached her bare shoulders, high cheekbones, a very slight crook in her nose, and pensive blue eyes. You couldn't really call her a beauty, but I could hardly take my eyes off her. There was something about her . . . I can't describe it in words. This woman literally radiated waves of power and attraction.

Power? I wonder if that's what I'm sensing, or is Valder sensing it?

Balistan Pargaid noticed my glance and smiled knowingly:

"Come, gentlemen, let me introduce you to my guest."

The female stranger smelled of fresh strawberries. She was not wearing any jewelery apart from earrings in the form of spiders with their legs tenderly embracing the lobes of her ears.

"Lady Iena! Allow me to introduce my dear guest. His Lordship Ganet Shagor. And this is Dralan Par."

The plump, attractive lips smiled, and the young woman bowed her head as she bobbed down in a casual curtsey.

"My respects to you, gentlemen . . ."

Her voice sent a chilly shiver running down my spine and I shuddered. It had been dark in the Master's prison, and I hadn't been able to see the Messenger's captive clearly. But I recognized her voice, even though she had not talked as much as the late lamented Leta.

Lady Iena and Lafresa were the same woman.

"What's wrong, dralan?" she asked me in concern, apparently having noticed how dumbfounded I was.

"Don't be concerned, milady. It's nothing to worry about. I am not used to attending such impressive receptions, that's all," I said awkwardly.

I wanted very badly to get out of that house as quickly as possible. While I was busy trying to be a dralan, I had completely forgotten that

Lafresa was also desperate to get hold of the Key. This was big trouble. We had really serious problems now!

"Is everything to your liking, milady?" the count asked.

"Yes, thank you. I am tired after the journey, please forgive me. Good night, gentlemen."

She left us and started walking up the stairs.

All this time Kli-Kli, who was standing some distance away, had been making faces at me and pointing desperately by turns at the white tablecloth on a small table with drinks and at his own face.

I gave a faint nod.

I don't understand.

Another jab of his finger in the direction of the white tablecloth, then at his face, and then a highly suggestive gesture, running the edge of his hand across his throat. What's he trying to tell me?

Kli-Kli gave a despairing grin and hurried across to us.

"Milord, of course I understand that the evening has been a success, and your dralan has even turned pink from drinking, but unfortunately Milla and Eralla, to their own supreme regret, will have to leave the gathering. They have developed an itch in a certain place, if you take my meaning. They are wondering if you will go with them or join them later?"

The jester's eyes simply screamed that it would be better for us to go with them. What could possibly have happened?

Eel yawned wearily, casually covering his mouth with his glove, and nodded.

"Unfortunately, count, I am obliged to leave your remarkable house. You know what these elves are like."

"Well then, if you are ever in Ranneng you must pay me another visit."

"Definitely. At the very first opportunity," said Eel, taking his leave of our host.

I don't think Balistan Pargaid has any idea of just how soon we'll be paying our next visit to his estate.

Kli-Kli went galloping on ahead of us, jangling his little bells and waving a soft roll that he had grabbed off the table.

"Make way for the highly talented jester of Duke Ganet Shagor! Make way!"

He carried on shouting like that until we were out of the hall.

"What's wrong, Kli-Kli?"

"Paleface is back."

I forced myself to keep on walking without looking round.

"Are you sure?"

"Oh yes! He arrived half an hour ago with that lady you were drool-ing over."

So that's where Rolio went! He was meeting Lafresa.

"Then we've left the party just in time."

"Did you find the Key?"

"Yes."

"The gods be praised!"

Our carriage was standing at the entrance. Miralissa and Egrassa were already inside it. The Wild Hearts on horseback made up a guard of honor.

As usual, old woman weariness arrived unexpectedly. I only realized how dangerous what I had just done was after I got into the carriage.

"Harold, did you find the Key?" Miralissa asked.

"Yes," Kli-Kli answered for me. "Can't you see that he's asleep?"

I sank down into the deep whirlpool of sleep before the carriage had even left the count's estate.

9

AND THE KEY WILL DECIDE WHO TO HELP

Don't even think about it, you're not coming with me," I hissed at Kli-Kli.

"That's what you think! But I'm coming anyway!" the jester retorted.

"I told you, stay here!"

"Harold, you can leave me here, but I'll still follow you, no matter what you do! And what's more, you've got my favorite medallion hanging round your neck now. If you don't let me come, then I'll take it back."

I gritted my teeth and gazed at the wall surrounding Balistan Pargaid's estate. Not for the first time in the last five minutes.

Night. Silence. The moon and the stars were hidden behind the clouds. Only the light from the large lanterns hanging beside the gate made it possible to see anything. Ideal conditions for my kind of work. The darker it was, the easier it would be to get the job done. Although when Kli-Kli's around, it's best to forget about words like "easy."

Almost a full day had gone by since we attended the count's reception, and now here I was, lying on my stomach beside the wall of his estate. This was the perfect time to steal into the mansion house and take back what belonged to us. To be quite honest, I'd wanted to take the risk and break into the count's home on the night of the reception, but Miralissa had insisted that we mustn't act in the heat of the moment. Even the fact that Lafresa had shown up didn't persuade her. When I told her about it, the elfess simply laughed and said that breaking the bonds was not that simple and the Master's envoy would have to wait for an auspicious conjunction of the stars.

While I was making genteel conversation with the nobility, the others hadn't wasted any time. Miralissa checked the house for magical surprises and discovered that all the windows on the second floor were protected by defensive spells. Egrassa got hold of a detailed plan of the house from somewhere (how he managed that, I have no idea!), and the Wild Hearts, who had smuggled a couple of bottles of fine wine from Master Quidd's cellar into the estate, got talking with five of the guards and found out the actual routes followed by the patrols, as well as their schedule. So now I was all set. All I had to do was get in, take the Key, and get out before it was missed.

Really, what could be simpler than that?

And then, when everything was ready, and I was all set to get started, Ell, Egrassa, Markauz, Eel, and Arnkh announced that they were going with me. Of course, I was indignant at the very idea and fervently opposed it. The last thing I wanted was an entire crowd tagging along!

"And what if they spot you? Who's going to cover you, Harold?"

"They won't spot me," I insisted stubbornly, but it was no use. The five of them set off with me, while the others started hastily packing all our things, so that when we got back we could leave the city immediately.

The elves dressed up in their dark green traveling outfits, smeared some dark gunk on their faces (which were already swarthy enough anyway), slung their s'kashes over their shoulders, and picked up their bows. Alistan set aside his sword of singing steel, armed himself with the battle-ax that had belonged to Tomcat, and dressed himself all in black, then he and Eel and Arnkh, who had pulled on a black tunic over his beloved chain mail, set off to protect poor little Harold.

His Grace was not at all concerned that this would effectively make him an accomplice to a burglary, a fact that was surely enough to dishonor any decent noble's line for the next ten generations. (But then, if you think about it, there was no real disgrace involved: Everybody knows that most noblemen steal on a much bigger scale than ordinary commoners.)

The elves swarmed up the wall like two shadows and froze on top of it, with their bows drawn at the ready, covering Arnkh, Eel, and Markauz as they clambered over the obstacle. Then the dark ones jumped down into the count's park and I was left alone. Egrassa had asked me to wait for a couple of minutes while they reconnoitered (meaning, while they got rid of anybody they came across). Well, I didn't mind, I wasn't going to weep bitter tears if the yellow-eyed archers took out a few patrols.

And that was when Kli-Kli showed up. I've no idea how the goblin managed to escape Miralissa's vigilant eye, but a fact is a fact—the jester was lying there beside me in the bushes, stubbornly arguing that without his help I didn't have a chance. The two minutes that the elf had given me were already long over, and I was still arguing with this little walking disaster.

"All right!" I said eventually. "You can go with me. But only as far as the house! If you make noise or get under my feet, I'll strangle you with my own bare hands."

Kli-Kli nodded.

"And if you fall behind, that's your problem," I warned him.

Without bothering to wait for an answer, I skipped out of the bushes, jumped up, and clung to the top of the wall with my fingertips. Fortunately, none of the count's servants had thought of scattering broken glass along the wall—which in my opinion left a serious gap in their defenses. If that rotten crud had been there, not even my gloves could have saved me. Finely milled pigskin is no defense against sharp glass. And in any case, the fingers of my gloves had been cut off—it's more convenient that way for working with locks.

I pulled myself up, threw my right leg over, and climbed on top, taking care not to impale myself on the spiky figures. I had to throw my arms out and bend my knees to keep my balance and avoid injury.

"Harold," Kli-Kli whined, jumping up and down desperately, "I can't reach!"

The goblin was too short to climb up on his own. I was seriously tempted just to leave him there. It would certainly have made things a lot simpler, that's for sure!

But I gritted my teeth in annoyance and started unraveling the spider's web. I had to help the goblin, otherwise Kli-Kli would never forgive me for abandoning him, and he'd throw a fit of hysterics right there under the wall.

"Hold on to the rope," I hissed, lowering the spider's web.

A shadow appeared beside me. It was Ell.

"Why the delay?"

"That damned goblin's showed up! Kli-Kli, set one foot above the other!"

"That's . . . what . . . I'm . . . doing!" the jester panted. Of course, he wasn't getting anywhere, just swaying from side to side, like a sack full of stones.

I tightened my grip on the rope, at the same time trying to keep my balance on the wall. The slightest deviation to the right or the left, and those spikes were waiting for me.

"Let me help," said Ell. And he gave me a hand, ignoring the spikes.

What a sight! Two shadows standing on a wall, trying to pull up a third. Fortunately for us, there was no moon or stars, and no spectators, otherwise we would have been in really big trouble.

Eventually Kli-Kli appeared on the top of the wall, panting hard.

"What are you doing here, goblin?" Ell's tone of voice wasn't exactly friendly.

"Obvious, isn't it? I'm taking a breath of fresh air. Why do they build such high walls around here? I wouldn't have bothered to come if I'd known. The villains! It's incredible! They deserve to be robbed just for that!"

"Leave the talk until we get down!" I said, stepping over the spikes.

The elf flitted down like a silent, weightless shadow and stood below me.

I had to hang on with my hands, on the other side of the wall, then open my fingers and drop onto the grass. Of course, I could have jumped, like Ell, but what for? Why risk my legs when there was no need? It would really mess things up if I broke anything.

Kli-Kli was still sniffling up on the wall.

"Kli-Kli!"

"Coming!" the goblin squealed, and came crashing down on top of me.

I managed to stretch my arms out and catch him just in time.

"And now explain what you're doing here!" said Ell, moving closer.

"I'm helping Harold. And don't you look at me like that, you'll drill a hole right through me."

"He'll stick to you no matter what we do, right, thief?" Ell said with a thoughtful glance at Kli-Kli.

"Only as far as the house," the goblin assured Ell hastily. "Just what were you thinking of doing?"

"Tying you up."

"I am the royal jester, and I will not allow any tusky-mouthed elf to tie me up! I'm warning you! I'll bite and I'll scream!"

"I'm wasting time with you two," I exclaimed angrily. "You can discuss what to do next without me!"

"All right, let him go with you." The elf had only two ways out of the situation. He could slit the goblin's throat, or let him go. "But remember, Kli-Kli, if anything happens, I'll personally skin you alive."

"No need for threats . . . I get the idea. Anything happens, and I'm done for!"

"Good luck, Harold, we won't be far away."

"What's happening with the patrols?"

It was very dark that night under the thick crowns of the trees, but I thought I saw Ell grin.

"We took out three of them, so the west wing's free." The yellow-eyed elf picked up his powerful crook-backed bow off the grass.

Fewer guards meant fewer problems. Now I had to run round the edge of the estate and make my approach to the windows of the west wing. It had to be the windows, because the central entrance was out of bounds—just like all the other doors leading in and out of the manor house, in fact.

According to Deler, who had drunk wine with the count's servants, there were guards standing watch at almost every door—the usual arrangement for people afraid of a sudden attack. That left the windows, and only the ones at the back of the house, because there was only one patrol there, and the chances of being spotted were far smaller than anywhere else.

It wasn't possible to break straight into the east wing of the house—there were bars on the windows of the second floor there. There was only one way to do it—get into the house through the west wing, walk along the incredibly long corridor to the balcony that overlooked the reception hall, and from there along the corridor with the pictures as far as the count's bedroom.

"Time to go. Kli-Kli, try to keep up!"

It was dark; the massive tree trunks in front of us were black silhouettes. And then the lights of the house came into view. The only lighted torches were beside the central entrance of the mansion house, and there were four guards standing there. Or, rather, one was standing and the other three were sitting on the steps and making conversation. I couldn't hear what they were talking about—I was too far away.

"They're not sleeping, the skunks," Kli-Kli hissed in disappointment.

"That's their job."

"Ah, no, I meant the ones in the house."

There was light in the second-floor windows. They weren't sleeping, and that meant I could run into problems. The Nameless One take those night birds! In my line of work there's nothing worse than people who don't go to bed when any decent law-abiding citizen ought to.

"Where to now, Harold?"

"See those little trees way over there?"

"Well?"

"We run over to them, then across to the wall of the building and up to the window."

"They'll see us!"

"Don't talk so much, and do what I do, then they won't see us. Or you can stay here in the park and wait for me, I don't mind."

"I think I can avoid attracting any unwanted attention," the jester replied quickly.

The open space between the park and the house was about forty yards across. Mostly short-cut grass and beds (or, rather, entire fields) of roses. I tried to run across all this as quickly as possible.

There was total silence all around, not a sound but the light wind that had sprung up, rustling the crowns of the trees. No birds calling, no crickets singing. Kli-Kli and I had to trail straight through the flowerbeds, trampling the bushes of white and yellow roses cruelly with our heels. I could just imagine the curses that the gardener would call down on our heads the next day! The roses took their revenge by surrounding me with the scent of cheap women's perfume. Disgusting!

The wall of the house suddenly rose up in front of me and I leaned against it in relief, catching my breath. Kli-Kli puffed and panted beside me.

"You scamper along faster than a royal messenger. I didn't know a thief's work was so hard."

"And nerve-wracking, too. Keep up!"

The wall stretched away to the right of us. I crept along in front, with Kli-Kli right behind me, almost stepping on my heels. Unfortunately for us, there was no grass. Someone had thoughtfully scattered little stones on the ground, so we had to move very carefully—as if we were walking over dry brushwood.

The darkness was pitch-black, as if we were deep underground. Of course, it was hard for anyone to make out Kli-Kli and me now, but the trouble with darkness is that you can't see the enemy, either. Just as we reached the corner of the building, a patrol of guards appeared out of the gloom. I froze instantly, and Kli-Kli blundered into my back with a grunt of surprise.

In the next three seconds I managed to do three things at once: pull my hood up over my head, stop the goblin's mouth with my free hand, and try to melt into the wall—there was enough shadow there to hide ten Nameless Ones.

To give Kli-Kli his due, he never even twitched.

The three guards walked slowly toward us, talking to each other. That would have been fine, but one of them was holding a torch. In a few seconds the goblin and I would be in plain view.

"And I says to him, why are you acting like such a bonehead? You lost, didn't you? So pay up!"

"And what did he say?"

"What did he say? He went for his knife, and—"

"Listen, Hart, if the captain of the watch finds out who killed Radish . . ."

"He won't find out, if you keep your mouth shut. And it's not my fault! Why bet on a cock fight, if you can't cover your losses?"

"Radish is a fine one, grabbing his knife like that. . . . He was always a fool, and he died a fool! I won't tell anyone, don't you worry."

"Thanks, friend," the first guard said with feeling.

I started slithering slowly along the wall, covering myself and Kli-Kli with my cloak. I had to take my hand away from the goblin's face, there was no other way I could load the crossbow. I held the little darling in my hand and tried to pull back the lever with as little noise as possible, drawing the string toward myself. A faint click told me that the bolts had slipped into position. If Sagot was feeling well-disposed, I'd have enough time to silence two of them, but that still left the third one, and the lad would have a sword.

The guards drew level with our flimsy cover and my finger involuntarily tightened on the trigger.

"Kind of cool tonight," muttered the one with the torch.

"We'll finish this round and drop into the guard room. I've got a little bottle tucked away there, 'specially for a moment like this."

"What if Meilo nabs us?"

"He won't," the first guard answered jauntily.

The lads tramped past us and went on their way. Not one of them even looked in our direction. After all, what danger could possibly be lurking over by the wall?

"Meilo? He'd nab his own father, never mind a thickhead like you!"

"There's no sign of Klos and his two."

"Klos and his lads were unlucky today, Meilo set them into the park—to protect milord from the savage squirrels!" the torch-bearer chortled.

"They should have been back ages ago. Maybe something's happened?"

"Of course something's happened! Do you think you're the only one with any brains? Klos has a little bottle of his own, stashed away under a tree somewhere. And more than one! I reckon the lads will be sleeping the rest of the night on the grass."

I'm afraid that after meeting Ell and Egrassa, Klos and company are never going to wake up again.

"Shall we go and look for them?"

"What for? Do you feel like wandering around in the dark?"

The guards' voices faded away into the distance.

"Phew," Kli-Kli sighed. "Are all guards born blind, or is it just them?"

"It varies. We're almost there."

All we had to do now was turn the corner and run along the far wall of the building until we reached the right window. I lay down on the ground and warily stuck my nose round the corner to check that the way was clear.

No one there.

There wasn't a single light on at this side of the house.

"Here."

I took out the cobweb and flung the free end of the rope upward, aiming at the balcony jutting out above our heads. The magic rope took a solid grip on the stone, without any grapnels or hooks. For my own peace of mind, I tugged on it a few times, checking the reliability of my stairway to the heavens. I couldn't pull it off—I certainly hadn't wasted my gold on that marvel.

"Stay here. Don't make any noise and don't even think of getting up to any tricks!" I said, glaring at the goblin menacingly.

"Yes, Harold."

"And no matter what happens, don't you dare climb up after me."

"No, Harold."

"If I'm not back in an hour, find Markauz and clear out of here."

"Yes, Harold." The little goblin looked like the most miserable creature in the whole of Siala.

"I'm going up. If anything happens, whistle. Only quietly."

"But Harold, I don't—"

"Kli-Kli, just do as I tell you."

"All right, Harold," the goblin agreed meekly.

I opened the clasp holding the cloak on my shoulders. It was a good cloak, no doubt about that, it was ink-black, like all my clothes, but climbing up a wall in it, especially a high wall, was rather awkward.

"Keep your eyes peeled," was my final instruction to the jester before I jerked on the spider web and sent it a mental instruction.

The rope shuddered and started lifting me upward. All I had to do was brace my feet against the wall and watch the balcony moving toward me.

About halfway up, when I was poised between heaven and earth, I heard a loud hiss below me, something between a red-hot frying pan and an expiring viper. I had to stop and look down. Kli-Kli had almost all his fingers stuck into his mouth and his cheeks were puffed out, as if he was trying to look like a bugler.

"What's wrong with you?" I hissed down at him.

"Danger!" said the jester, pointing in the direction from which we had just come.

There was a lone guard walking along the path that ran round the house. I don't know what he was looking for, but it certainly wasn't adventure. The lad was staring down at his feet, so he hadn't even seen the goblin standing there right in front of him.

Kli-Kli started dashing from side to side, not knowing where to hide, and I gritted my teeth in annoyance.

"Where can she be?" the guard exclaimed. I couldn't make out his face, but his voice was young.

Didn't I tell everybody I'd have problems if the goblin was with me?

"Hey! You there! What are you doing here?" the guard said, lowering his hand onto the hilt of his sword.

"Come here," Kli-Kli said, gesturing to the guard conspiratorially.

Sagot! What is that idiot doing?

The man started moving toward the goblin, without taking his hand off his sword or his eyes off the intruder. He was confused, because his enemy was so short and didn't attempt to run away or draw a weapon when he was caught red-handed.

"Come on, come on. I don't bite."

"Bah, you're that duke's jester!" the guard said, stopping right underneath me.

"Of course I'm a jester! Who were you planning on meeting here? A h'san'kor?"

I tugged on the rope, giving it the mental order to lower me down.

"What are you doing here, you little rogue?"

There was no more than a yard left to the nitwit's head.

The goblin kept one eye on my miraculous balancing act.

"Want a gold piece?" A disk of yellow metal glittered between the fool's fingers.

Kli-Kli's calculations were absolutely correct. There are some specimens of humankind who only have to be shown a coin and they completely lose their head.

"Yes!"

I wasn't surprised in the least to see him staring hard, desperately trying to follow the movements of the coin.

I hit him with both feet, aiming at the back of his head. He was wearing a light helmet, so the blow wasn't all that powerful, but it was quite enough for him. He slumped to his knees, clutching at his head.

I opened my fingers and fell onto him, pressing him down with all my weight.

"Finish him!" Kli-Kli squealed, jumping up and down nervously. "Finish him!"

"What a . . . bloodthirsty . . . goblin," I spat out, shaking my bruised fist.

The lad was surprisingly strong. I had to punch him twice on the back of his head, which was as hard as oak, and then jam my elbow into his temple before he condescended to quiet down.

I swung round toward Kli-Kli.

"What kind of trick was that you pulled?"

"I had to keep him busy while you were descending on him like the demon of vengeance."

"I mean, why didn't you whistle?"

"I can't whistle. I tried to tell you, but you wouldn't listen!" the goblin explained lamely.

There was a clank behind me. I drew my knife and swung round sharply, but it was only Ell. He was just wiping his dagger on the guard's clothes.

The dead guard's clothes. No one lives after he's had the best part of a yard of steel run through his heart.

"He won't shout now." The elf's yellow eyes glinted disapprovingly. "You always need to finish the job, Harold."

"Get it over with quickly, thief. There's no time," Alistan Markauz put in from out of the darkness. "Kli-Kli, I'll have a word with you later. Come with us. Ell, take the body's arms."

"Stop!" I told them. "The goblin's bound to get you into trouble. He's just one big headache."

"I won't get them into trouble!" Kli-Kli was offended. "If not for me, this dead man here would have spotted you for sure."

"Listen, fool, do you see those bushes over there? They're exactly opposite the window of the count's bedroom. You hide in there until I call you. I'll throw you the Key, and then you clear out just as fast as you can. Ell, you help him get over the wall."

"All right."

I jumped up, grabbed hold of the end of the rope, and the whole business started all over again. When I threw my leg over the railings and found myself on the balcony, there was no one below me any longer—no elf, no count, no Kli-Kli, no dead body. The spider web nestled back snugly into its usual place on my belt.

It was a small balcony that had been built for decoration, hardly even big enough for two people. The door, with glass panes set in a fancy wooden grille, looked like a rather frail, defenseless barrier for lads of my kind. But first impressions are deceptive—always expect some kind of dirty trick from such naked defenselessness. Fortunately I didn't even have to guess, or waste precious vials of spells, in order to expose any magic. Miralissa had said there were defensive spells on all the windows on the second floor.

I didn't know how they worked, but anyone who tried to climb into the house at night was in for a hot reception. The elfess had offered to create a runic charm so I could break through the defense, but I had politely refused. I'd been feeling very negative about runic magic just recently—ever since I read out an old scroll that I found lying about and drove all the demons into the darkness. (Well, almost all, Vukhdjaaz was an exception.)

And apart from that, I didn't want to experience the clash of shamanism with human magic at close quarters. And I couldn't count on Kli-Kli's medallion, either—it only neutralized shamanism, not the magic of men and light elves. I would have to dip into my own reserves in order to get into the house.

I opened the small green bag on my belt and took out a vial containing a powder as black as the night around me. The cork came out with a pop and I kept hold of it in my teeth.

I scattered a generous sprinkling of the powder straight onto the door, put the cork back in the vial, and put the precious little item back in my bag. In the meantime nothing had happened to the balcony door, and I was already beginning to think that this time the elfess was wrong. But no, blotches appeared where the black powder had landed. They spread out, merged together, and then disappeared with a flash.

That's done.

As I expected, the door was locked. For some reason people are never desperately eager to see me in their homes. What did I ever do to them?

I opened the lock in a few seconds. Actually, the thing on that door had no right to call itself by the proud name of "lock." I pushed the door slightly open, parted the light, airy curtains with my hands, and slipped inside Count Balistan Pargaid's house.

It's pitch-dark in here. Where am I? I hope it's not some old maid's bedroom, or there'll be shouting and screaming.

The floor in the room was covered with a carpet, so I didn't make much noise. There was a thin strip of light under the door leading into the corridor. My eyes had already got used to the darkness now, and I could see pretty well.

I was in a large room with shelves lining the walls.

A library.

If I'd been there at a different time on different business, I would definitely have checked out a couple of the bookcases. The count was keen on antiquity, so I wouldn't be surprised if there were books here from the early Dream Age, or even the Era of Achievements. On my way across the unlighted room I had to walk round a desk that stood out as a black patch against the dark gray background.

The heavy double doors of the library opened easily and I went out into the corridor.

It was empty.

That's right, you respectable people, at this time of night the best thing to be doing is sleeping.

Unfortunately for me, some diligent swine had lit the oil lamps, and the little tongues of flame were trembling under their glass covers.

Now came the most difficult part, walking the full length of the corridor in this wing and slipping through a room or two to end up in the corridor beside the balcony overlooking the reception hall, then walking down the corridor with the portraits to reach Balistan Pargaid's bedroom. Then I had to do what I'd come for, and go back the same way.

I tried to cover the dangerous stretch as quickly as possible. The thick pile of the carpet deadened my footsteps, and I didn't have to worry about anyone hearing me. The doors on my right and my left were closed, and there wasn't a sound from any of the rooms. I walked past one intersection where two corridors crossed. As far as I recalled, one of them led to the servants' wing and the basement.

Aha, here's the door I need.

I pressed down on the bronze handle, but it didn't give. I had to take out my lock picks and fiddle with the lock, feeling for the spring. To say I felt uncomfortable would be putting it very mildly. Fiddling with a lock when there are lanterns burning on every side and any lunatic can see you from the far end of the corridor is nervous kind of work.

"Ah! Don't talk n-nonsense, you stup-pid f-fool! I think what I s-said, was . . . hic! Yes . . ." I heard someone say behind the door opposite me.

"You're drunk, O'Lack, where are you off to?"

"F-for a leak, you stup-pid f-fool! Or do you prefer . . . hic! P-pref . . . pah! Do you want me to d-do it right here?"

The lock clicked and I tumbled into the room and closed the door behind me, before the drunk could open his. I listened to what was going on in the corridor. A man came out of the other room and walked away unsteadily. I stopped hearing his steps almost immediately—the carpet deadened every sound.

I was in one of the numerous guest rooms in this wing. And, to my roguish thief's delight, it was empty. All I had to do was go over to the other door and open it to find myself on the balcony, so that's what I did.

One glance was enough to make me jump back quickly into the shelter of the darkness. As the plan had shown, the balcony overlooked the inner courtyard of the count's mansion.

For those who haven't realized yet, the count's mansion was built in the form of a square, with a little inner courtyard that was entered through a door on the first floor. There was a fountain murmuring gently in the yard, and a few feeble apple trees, with branches that barely reached as high as the second floor. A man was sitting under one of the trees, smoking a paper pipe stuffed with tobacco. The flickering of the little light was the only reason I spotted him.

Until that moment my plan had been very simple. Climb down the spider web into the courtyard, run to the wall of the opposite wing, and climb up the rope onto a balcony—and I would be close to the Key.

But thanks to this damned guard, all my efforts had been a total waste of time. He was looking straight in my direction, and if I climbed down the rope, he was bound to see me, even on a dark night like this.

And running back through the corridors was pointless and dangerous; I could be spotted at any moment.

There was only one thing I could do—wait.

Should I put a crossbow bolt into the guard? In principle, it was possible, but in that kind of darkness I wasn't sure that I could hit him in the neck. If I missed, then he'd probably bellow like a hog under the butcher's knife and wake the entire house.

I sat down on the floor and started watching through the light, airy curtains. The little light flared up as he inhaled—he poisoned the air for what seemed like an eternity.

Eventually the guard stood up, stamped the remains of his paper pipe into the ground, slung his hefty crossbow over his shoulder, and tramped over to the door. I gave a sigh of relief, but I was getting ahead of myself. The guard swung round sharply and set off along the wall, then swung round again. . . .

He's patroling, the lousy dog! I really don't like overdiligent guards—they're always a big headache. And this lad certainly is.

There was no point in grinding my teeth—you only get one set. I sat back down on the floor and started counting the guard's steps. Six . . . ten . . . fifteen . . . twenty-two . . .

I didn't have much time, in fact none at all. I had to take the risk. I waited until the man turned his back to me and shot out onto the balcony.

Two . . .

The spider web took a grip and I flung myself over the railings and jumped, clinging on to the rope with both hands.

Eight . . .

It must have been the quickest descent of my life. If I hadn't been wearing gloves, I'd have ripped all the skin off my hands, and the muscle along with it. But not even the gloves could protect me against the fire scorching my palms.

Ten . . .

I tugged on the spider web and it came unstuck from the balcony, fell, and rolled up into a coil.

Thirteen . . .

I leaped forward toward the really thick darkness under a feeble, stunted apple tree.

Fifteen . . .

The guard swung round and came walking toward me. Come on now, darling, you won't even notice me until you trip over me. When the guard turned away again, I started moving toward him, making short little runs from one shadow to another.

Eventually I found myself behind the guard, who strode along like a mechanical toy, and I took my brass knuckles out of my pocket and smacked them against the back of his head.

The lad gave a grunt of surprise and started falling over backward. I grabbed hold of him and sat him down on the grass, with his back leaning against the trunk of a tree. Just to be on the safe side, I unloaded his crossbow and threw the bolt into the fountain, then after thinking for a moment, I threw his bag with the other nine bolts in there, too.

Then I set the useless weapon across the lad's knees and stepped to take a look at the result of my efforts.

That will do. From a distance he looks just like someone who's fallen asleep. I just hope that this guard will sleep all the way through until morning.

Using the spider web, it took only a minute to clamber up onto the balcony I needed. The door here was slightly ajar, and there was a light draft toying with the white curtains. I took one step into the room and waited for my eyes to get used to the darkness.

There was definitely someone in the room. I could hear them snuffling gently. The bed over by the far wall gradually took shape, emerging out of the gloom. I had to walk past it to get out. When I'd almost reached the door, a floorboard creaked under my feet.

I stopped, wincing as if I had a toothache. The person in the bed turned over and started snuffling again. Another step, and another creak from a floorboard.

I almost jumped in surprise when I heard an indecisive little yap from the bed.

A dog!

"What's wrong, Tobiander?" a sleepy voice asked.

Countess Ranter! Of all people, I'd ended up in her bedroom!

"Rr-ruff? Ruff!"

"What is it? Rats?"

The old woman half sat up, as if she was peering into the darkness, but she didn't get off the bed. Fortunately for me, her damned little mongrel wasn't the brave type, either, and he was in no hurry to sink his teeth into me.

"It's all that detestable count's fault, my little love! I told him I was afraid of rats, and his servants put us in a room like this. Even the floor squeaks here, never mind those horrible gray monsters! They're just waiting to get at my poor little boy."

"Rrr-ruff!" Tobiander agreed.

"Let's go to sleep, my little one. Those disgusting rats won't be able to reach us!"

Tobiander yapped again to calm his own nerves, and then shut up. My legs were completely numb from standing still before I heard the countess start snuffling again.

Trying to move as quietly as possible, I went out into the corridor, which was a precise copy of the one that my route had led me down in the other wing. The same carpet, the same lighting, and the same emptiness.

I moved forward, stopping every two yards to listen to the silence. One door on my right was slightly open.

"But who is she?"

"Keep your mouth shut. Some questions can put you in your grave." Paleface!

"All I did was ask . . ."

"And all I did was give you a piece of advice—less loose talk. You know the count is fond of shortening tongues that are too long. And I don't know who she is, anyway. I was told to meet her, and so I met her. The rest of it is none of my business."

"All right, all right, Rolio. Let's just forget it. How about a drop of wine?"

"No. And stop smoking that garbage, I've got a splitting headache."

"What are you getting so uppity about?" The man's voice sounded offended.

"That woman makes me uneasy . . ."

I took a cautious peep in through the crack of the door and I was hit by a weak smell of charm-weed. Paleface and another man, the one who was smoking, were sitting on a table and casting dice. Each one of them had a tall heap of assorted coins in front of him. Rolio was sitting with his back to me, and I was really tempted to put a bolt between his shoulder blades there and then and get rid of him for good.

"I'm sorry, Rolio, it seems to me that you're worrying about the wrong things. You have a Commission to complete. That lad's still walking around and more than a month's gone by now."

"You deal with your own business, and I'll deal with mine!"

I heard footsteps. Whoever it was, he was tramping like a platoon on Parade Square, so I heard him long before he reached the corridor. I jumped back from the door and looked around desperately for somewhere to hide.

"What's wrong?" I heard the smoker ask in a surprised voice.

"There's someone there."

"Where?"

"Outside the door."

I heard a chair being moved back. Seven yards along the corridor there were niches with huge vases of flowers, as tall as a man, standing in them. The niches were full of darkness, and I made a dash for them, hoping to hide behind one of the vases.

I barely managed to fit into the narrow space between a vase and the wall. I didn't dare risk moving the vase, in case it fell over.

A man walked past me along the corridor, swaying about as violently as if he were on the deck of a ship in a storm, not the floor of a corridor. In other words, the lad was drunk, very drunk. He almost ran straight into Paleface when the killer dashed out into the corridor with a throwing star in his hand.

"Idiot!" Paleface barked with a contemptuous scowl, pushing the other man away.

The man collapsed onto the floor.

"Th-thank you!"

"There, you see, Rolio, nobody was eavesdropping," Paleface's dice partner told him.

"S'right, wasn' lissening, no, not me. Honess! I've got lost!"

"Shut up!"

Paleface looked round the corridor with an expression of fury, turning the throwing star over in his hands, and then reluctantly tucked the weapon away behind his belt.

"Come on, Bedbug. And you, O'Lack, get off to bed!"

"Th-thank you."

Paleface slammed the door angrily, leaving the drunk on the carpet. I could see that Rolio's nerves were beginning to play him false. That's what an uncompleted Commission will do for you!

I slipped out of my hiding place and set off. The drunk was trying to get up off the floor and he took no notice of me at all. If I'd started doing a shaman's dance around him, singing and beating on a tambourine, I still don't think he would have understood what was going on.

The corridor came to an end, and I walked out onto that unforgettable balcony round the reception hall. It looked empty and cold now, without the music, the servants darting about, and the nobles all dressed up in silk. There weren't even any guards at the door. No candles, no torches, no lanterns. Darkness and peace, just pale squares of light on the floor from the windows. The moon had come out from behind the clouds and was peeping in through the tall arched windows.

The carpet came to an end: The floor on the balcony and in the next corridor was marble. Fortunately, it was the normal kind of stone, dark red with light veins, and not the Isilian pain-in-the-you-know-where, on which every step sets off a hundred alarm bells.

I could feel that tickling in my stomach and the call of the Key again.

There were widely spaced lanterns burning in the corridor with the portraits, and the shadows were roaming across the walls, playing hide-and-seek with each other. Balistan Pargaid's forebears gazed out at me from the portraits, and somehow I failed to spot any friendly amusement in their eyes. Strange as it may seem, the men in the pictures stared at me with positively menacing expressions.

For a moment I was overcome with superstitious fear—I remembered a story that For had told me in my distant childhood, about men in pictures coming to life and killing a thief.

What nonsense! Superstitious nonsense, that's all! I cast a quick glance at Suovik Pargaid and turned away. Sagot! Whoever the artist was that painted that portrait, the son of a bitch was certainly talented. I wouldn't be surprised if Suovik tumbled out of the picture, straight onto the floor.

"I'm here! Here I am! The bonds are calling!" the Key sang to me.

There was no guard outside the door of the count's bedroom. Yet another strange thing. Usually highborn individuals put a couple of guards outside their bedroom to defend their troubled sleep. So who was it I'd brought the sleeping spell for, then?

I took out my lock picks, put one in the keyhole, turned— It wasn't locked. The door was closed, but it wasn't locked!

I pushed it open, expecting to see anything at all in the bedroom, up to and including Balistan Pargaid's dead body with its throat torn out (I had a sudden vision of the body of Archduke Patin and the Messenger, who had just dispatched the king's cousin into the darkness). But no, there was no one at all in the bedroom. A huge bed standing against the wall took up most of the space. By the window there was a small table, with a lighted candle and massive casket standing on it.

The count was fond of ogre handiwork, and this item was no exception. It was made out of the same dark metal as the bracelet that we had presented to Balistan Pargaid. It was covered with half-erased runes, images of some wild creatures—animals or something worse than that. But right now it wasn't the chest that was important—it was what was inside it. The Key was calling, and I took a step toward it, as if I was hypnotized.

"I'm here! Quickly! Take me! The bonds are calling!"

The sound of steps in the corridor shattered the spell. Someone was coming this way, and I hadn't even closed the door behind me!

There was nowhere in the room to hide, and there were bars on the windows. . . . The bed! I took my crossbow out from behind my back and dived under the bed, hoping that the person walking along the corridor would go straight past the room and take no notice of the open door.

My hiding place was a bit cramped, but I could see the entire room (or rather, the entire floor). There was no dust, so I wasn't afraid of sneezing at the wrong moment.

A woman wearing red shoes walked into the room. She stopped beside the low table with the casket, and the scent of ripe strawberries struck my nostrils.

Lafresa!

There were more steps in the corridor, and a few moments later a pair of tall, soft boots came into the room. Red shoes and tall, soft boots—that was all I could see from my hiding place.

"Is it time?"

I recognized the count's voice.

"Yes, the stars are favorable. How does it open?"

Milord walked across to the table, there was a musical chiming sound and then several rapid clicks.

"There you are, Lady Iena."

"Don't call me lady."

"What would you prefer?"

"Madam. Or Lafresa. That is what the Master calls me."

"Oh!" the count gasped sympathetically.

"Save me! Quickly! They're taking me! Save me!" The howling of the Key exploded inside my head, and for a moment everything went completely black.

There was nothing I could do, not even if I had a hundred crossbows! I didn't believe an ordinary crossbow bolt would cause Lafresa any harm at all. All I could do was wait and pray to the gods.

"Step back, I have to concentrate."

Lafresa started singing in a language that I didn't know, and again the calls of the Key started ringing in my ears. The feet in the red shoes tapped out a strange, fascinating rhythm that wove itself into Lafresa's quiet song and drifted in a leaden-heavy spell around the room, which was frozen in anticipation.

"Save me! I don't want to go! Our bonds are strong!"

The pain in my ears was unbearable. I pressed my hands against my temples, but it didn't help.

Lafresa's song grew louder and louder, her words wove together into a magical music that chimed and thundered above my head. I could feel the bonds with which Miralissa had tied me to the Key breaking, feel it with my entire body. It was as if someone was smashing my fingers with a hammer.

"Our bonds are strong!" I whispered reassuringly, like someone under a spell.

"Strong!" I heard a voice say with a sigh of relief.

The pain receded a little, but Lafresa only had to raise her voice, and my fingers started aching again, and it felt as if someone had poured liquid lead in my ears.

"Our bonds are strong," I whispered again.

"Count! I need blood, I'm not getting anywhere!" Lafresa barked between her wails.

Searing fire spilled onto my fingers, but I knew what to do. They couldn't break the bonds while I was there. The Key was not alive, but it was still a rational being—and it was on my side:

> He meets at night with Strawberry
> But who will be helped by the key?

Wasn't that part of my best friend Kli-Kli's prophecy? But to be quite honest, I was very glad that the artifact was on my side.

"Our bonds are strong, our bonds are strong, our bonds are strong, strong, strong, strong, strong, strong . . ."

How about that magic, Lafresa? Do you like it?

The singing stopped as suddenly as it had started—the only sound left was the woman's hoarse, heavy breathing.

"What is wrong, madam?" The count's voice sounded like a crow cawing—harsh, repulsive.

"I don't know," she said in a weary voice. "That amateur put such strong bonds on it that I can't break them. Count, is that man who met me still here?"

"You mean Rolio? Yes, he's in the house."

"Remember, Player gave him the job of getting rid of a certain person, didn't he?"

"That's absolutely right."

"Then let him do so immediately. If necessary, with the help of your army. The Key is resisting me, it senses the person who is bound to it. Let your man remove this obstacle, and then I will try again."

"I will give orders at once—"

"Wait! Help me get to my room. . . . The artifact has taken all my strength. . . ."

"Your hand, milady."

"I asked you not to call me that!" she hissed icily. "But I beg your pardon. I am simply too tired to be polite."

I listened as their footsteps retreated, and then waited for a few more minutes to be quite sure there was no more trouble in the offing.

As quiet as the grave.

I crawled out from under the bed, released the string of my crossbow, and put it back behind my shoulder. I had been lucky so far that night, but I had to hurry; Lafresa could come back at any moment. And they had let Paleface off the leash. . . .

The candle standing on the table had burned halfway down, and the casket was closed. Lafresa's shamanism may have exhausted her, but the Master's maidservant had remembered to slam down the lid, and probably thrown in a bit of extra magic as well.

The chances of the casket being sealed with the magic of humans and light elves were negligible, but I wasn't going to take any risks, and decided to check things first.

I opened the window of the bedroom and looked out. There was no movement in the bushes under the window, so I could only hope that Kli-Kli was still hiding in there somewhere.

The light wind immediately blew out the candle. Well, to the darkness with it! The moon was shining so brightly that it was still quite light in the room anyway. I took the vial I needed out of my bag, and poured a drop of liquid onto the lid of the casket. It spread out and stopped moving. There was absolutely no human magic here at all, otherwise the drop would have disappeared. There was either shamanism, or nothing. . . . I would have to put my trust in Kli-Kli's medallion.

I licked my dry lips and reached out for the casket. It was terrifying, like picking up red-hot coals or a poisonous snake. . . . What if the goblin's medallion didn't protect me against any shamanic spells that were on it?

Nothing. No effect. No thunder, no lightning, no voices of the gods. The casket seemed absolutely normal, with no magic at all. Could I really have been wrong about Lafresa?

I couldn't see any keyhole, but the lid stubbornly refused to budge. This little trinket had a secret, I could fiddle with it like this until the end of time—it would be better to take it with me. I tried to lift it and gasped in amazement.

It was heavy!

So heavy that I could hardly even lift it off the table.

Trying to drag a weight like that all the way through the house could cost me my life. I felt all the projections and surfaces, hoping to find a concealed spring, but the lid remained immovable.

I recalled that when the count opened the casket, there had been several clicks. Did that mean that it was activated by two or three springs at once?

Very probably it did.

I changed my approach, pressing the figure of the half bird, half bear with one finger, and the skull at the feet of that creature with another, and trying to pry the lid open with my nail. Useless . . .

Hmm . . . and what had made the music before Balistan Pargaid opened the lock, if I might ask?

I had to examine the metal box very closely again. There it was—a harp stamped into the lid, and the half bird, half bear had a reed pipe in its mouth. Right, let's give it a try. . . . That's it!

The pipe and the harp both shifted inward at the same time, the casket gave a quiet musical jingle, and the lid opened, inviting me to feast my eyes on what it was guarding.

The Key lay on black velvet. Slim, woven out of crystal cobweb gossamer and icy dreams, it looked as if a single hot breath would be enough to break it. But that was not so; the dragon's tears that it was made of could only be carved with magic and diamond cutters, which had to act together and be guided skillfully.

I reached my hand out for the artifact, and Kil-Kli's medallion immediately seared my skin with cold fire. A yellowish haze sprang up around the Key and immediately disappeared again, leaving colored rings in front of my eyes from the sudden flash. Thank you to the goblin's trinket—if Kli-Kli hadn't found it, I don't like to think what might have happened to me.

I took the Key and clenched it in my fist.

"Our bonds are strong," it whispered to me happily one last time and fell silent.

That was it. Now it was time to be leaving the count's hospitable home!

I heard a menacing growl behind me. Trying not to make any sudden movements, I turned round to face the door in order to get a look at the newcomer.

A dog.

A big dog.

Very big.

A huge imperial dog. It was bigger than any dog I'd ever seen in my life—massive paws, a huge great head, a docked tail like the branch of a tree, ears that stuck out, a short smooth coat and . . . teeth. . . .

The hound was yellowish red, with a black face and paws. As taut as a loaded crossbow. The hair on the beast's mane was standing up on end, and there was a menacing gurgling sound coming from his throat. A dog like that wouldn't bark and call his master—he would finish the job without help.

I looked at him, he looked at me. Still trying not to make any sudden movements, I moved back to the window, but there were bars on it. The only way I could get out was through the door. I had to kill the dog, otherwise I would never get out.

I reached for the crossbow. The dog exploded into a hurricane of fangs and furiously flashing eyes, and in a split second the beast had covered the yards between us and frozen just one inch away from Harold's most precious possessions.

The dog raised its upper lip, displaying his impressive collection of teeth. Don't be so boastful, you dumb brute.

"All right, all right!" I chirped, showing the dog my empty hands. "I'm not armed! I just got an itch on my back!"

Oh, sure! I believe you all right! said the dog's piercing eyes.

He gave another threatening snarl, snapped his teeth together, and backed off a yard.

"And now what?"

You tell me. I swear to Sagot, that's what he thought!

"Listen, I got in here by accident. I'll be going now, okay?" I felt like a total idiot, talking to a dog.

The beast leaned its head to one side, gave me a searching look. A pink tongue lolled out of his mouth.

I'm not that stupid.

I decided to try a different approach.

"Goo-ood boy! What a fine, handsome fellow!"

The massive beast put his tongue away, narrowed his eyes, and gave me a suspicious look, sensing a trick. Then he lay down on the floor and lowered his head onto his front paws: *Let's see what else this two-legs has to say. . . .*

"Ah, what a handsome dog," I coaxed. The dog's eyes glazed over with boredom. "Let me go, eh?"

The dog snorted. He wasn't going to tear me to pieces, even though that would be no problem for him. The beast had decided to wait until his master came into the room and I was caught red-handed.

So where does that get us? Nowhere. I couldn't reach for my crossbow, this hound cursed by the darkness had been trained. If I tried to grab my knife, he'd probably snip off some part of my body.

So what did that leave? I had a few battle spells in my bag, in case of an absolute emergency. It was worth a try.

The beast responded to my attempt to reach into the bag with a menacing snarl. I jerked my hand away in a hurry.

"Listen, what do you want me for? Why don't I just bring you a bone?"

The hound only yawned at that. I pressed my back against the windowsill and hissed through the window.

"Kli-Kli! Kli-Kli!"

"Yes!" said a squeaky voice below me. "What's taking so long?"

"I've got problems!"

"Oh!" said the voice. "What kind?"

"A dog."

"I thought dogs were man's best friend."

Was he trying to be funny?

"Well, he doesn't know that!"

"Then get rid of him!"

The dog listened curiously to the squeaky sounds coming from the window, turning his head this way and that.

"I can't even raise my hands! Find the elves, maybe they can help!"

"Where am I going to find them now? All right, don't go away! I'll only be a moment."

What was that he said? "Don't go away"? Yes, I think I'll take his invaluable advice.

The jester was gone for a long time. A very long time. The dog was clearly bored, waiting for someone to come and praise him for cornering his quarry. I was quietly oozing sweat. When a short figure wrapped from head to toe in a black cloak appeared in the doorway, my heart dropped into my boots. I thought the guards had arrived.

"Mmm, he's a big one, all right," Kli-Kli said warily, approaching the huge beast without hurrying.

The beast jumped up, snarling menacingly, and backed off, trying to keep one eye on me and one on the goblin.

"Where are Egrassa and Ell?"

"I couldn't find them. Nice little doggy!"

The hound snarled even louder. He had obviously never been insulted like that in his life. Somehow the word "doggy" would never have occurred to me, let alone "nice." No doubt about it, goblins are strange folk.

"Do you want me dead? Don't make him angry! Where have you been roaming all this time?"

"I haven't been roaming, I've been trying to get you out of trouble," the jester said in an offended tone of voice. "Now we'll fix him."

The hound pricked up his ears and showed us his teeth. Kli-Kli just smiled at him and brought out what he had been holding behind his back.

A cat! A fat ginger cat, as sleek as a fattened hog! Where did the goblin manage to get hold of that?

The goblin opened his fingers, and the cat flopped onto the floor. I don't think he'd realized yet just what a crucial and unpleasant turning point had arrived in his catty life. The dog howled like an evil spirit that has just seen an exorcist and forgot all about us as he made a dash for his natural prey.

The cat might not have grown up out on the street (he was too well fed and pampered for that) but he was no fool, that's for sure! The ginger butterball pulled in his claws and took off like greased lightning— which was quite incredible with his figure. And the hound followed, just a few steps behind.

"Where did you find him?" I gasped in amazement.

The fool gave a cunning smile.

"In the count's kitchen, of course! You saw how well fed he was!"

"Right," I replied stupidly, still not believing that an idiotic trick thought up by Stalkon's fool could have been so effective.

"What do you mean, 'Right'? Have you got the Key? Then in the name of darkness, why are you just standing there gaping? Do you want to wait for that crocodile to eat the cat and come back for our livers? Let's get moving!"

We slipped out into the corridor, galloped past the pictures, flew out into the hall, and then hurtled into the next corridor.

"Shhhhh," I said, putting one finger to my lips.

Kli-Kli nodded and started moving along on tiptoe. We stopped beside the vases where I had hidden earlier.

"Where to now, Harold?"

I thought hard. The route I had followed on my own was no good for two. Especially since it led out onto the balcony through the countess's room. Creeping through any of the other rooms was out of the question; we'd probably run into a ferocious baron with a sword who wouldn't think twice before he ran us through.

"Kli-Kli, how did you get into the house?" I asked with a sudden flash of insight.

"Through the basement window." The goblin made a wry face. "You're too big to get through it. But I could cut you into pieces and stick you through. . . ."

"Kli-Kli, this is no time for jokes."

"It's exactly the right time. But if you can't even manage a polite 'ha-ha,' then don't bother! We can try to get through the kitchen."

"The kitchen?" I didn't have a plan of the first floor, and I only had a vague idea of its layout.

"That's where they cook the food," the little wretch explained. "It's on the way to the basement."

"Lead on."

The door of the room where Paleface and his friend had been sitting was wide open. The room was empty, apart from a faint smell of charmweed. Paleface had already received his orders to find Harold. . . .

Kli-Kli led me to a stairway that went down to the first floor. It took us into the servants' wing. The walls here were gray and not so looked-after as on the second floor. There were no rich furnishings here. No pictures, no carpets, no statues or vases in niches. Even the oil lamps had been replaced by smoky torches that left black trails on the walls.

"Now where?"

"Right."

Behind the kitchen door we could hear dishes clattering and voices talking.

"There's someone there," I said, stating the absolutely obvious.

"You think I don't know that? How easy do you think it was to steal that cat from the fat cook?"

Why hadn't I realized that the kitchen would be working? The cooks in houses like this rarely went to bed. One kept the fire going in the hearth, another one decided what delicacies to prepare for Balistan Pargaid this fine morning, and another cooked for the guests. . . . With all this fuss and bother, I'd completely forgotten about that.

"Then why in the name of darkness did you bring me here?"

"You asked me to, so I did. And don't you look at me like that, Dancer in the Shadows! As if I didn't know you've got three little bottles of muck for putting people to sleep in that bag of yours! Or are you just too plain cheap to use them? You carry that stuff around for much longer, and it'll go sour!"

One of Kli-Kli's little weaknesses is that he likes to rummage through other people's things while the owner isn't there. So it's not surprising that the goblin knew all about the contents of my bag.

I had to start clinking the bottles about, looking for the right one. Then I opened the door and flung the bottle in, catching a brief glimpse of the cooks' startled faces before I slammed the door shut again. There was an ominous-sounding *oomph!*

I'm afraid Count Balistan Pargaid will have to go without breakfast this morning.

"And now what?"

"We wait."

"Now accept it, Harold, without my help you'd never have got out of here alive."

"Okay. And now shut up!"

"Oh, how serious we are! And how fierce," the goblin muttered to himself. "Listen, Harold," he snapped after a short pause, "we can't wait any longer. We really can't."

"Why not?"

"Because," Kli-Kli grunted, and pointed behind me.

My old friend the imperial dog stood at the far end of the corridor. His face looked a bit battered, somehow. The look he gave us wasn't exactly beaming with benevolence, either.

"It looks as if he didn't catch the cat," Kli-Kli said.

The dog came dashing at us, taking huge bounds. The goblin squealed like a five-year-old girl who'd just found a live mouse on her plate.

"Hold your breath!" I shouted.

We tumbled into the kitchen and slammed the door shut right in the dog's face. The beast responded to this dirty trick by barking deafeningly. Kli-Kli slammed home the bolt and ran along the line of tables and hot stoves, jumping over the bodies of the sleeping servants.

The remains of the sleepy fumes were still swirling around on the floor, and I tried not to breathe. Kli-Kli pushed open the door at the other end of the kitchen, and we found ourselves outside.

"Well, he really went wild!" Kli-Kli exclaimed admiringly. "I wonder what's going to happen to us if he manages to break out?"

I could hear the barking even from there.

"Someone's bound to come to check why the count's dog is making such a racket. We need to clear out as soon as possible. Move it!"

We had to run across to the park in short bursts, hiding from the guards in the shadows and the bushes. Kli-Kli almost ran straight under the feet of one of the guards, and I just managed to save the goblin from disaster at the very last moment.

The gentle whispers of the night welcomed us into the dark park, with its sleeping trees.

"Where are the others?" Kli-Kli whispered, turning his head right and left.

"Let's get to the wall, we'll figure things out there."

When the count found out the Key was missing, he'd be furious—and that's putting it mildly. As for the way Lafresa will feel, I won't even try to say—she let the Master down again, so now she would be in really hot water.

Egrassa met us halfway to the wall.

"Is the job done?"

"Yes."

The elf gave a call like a night bird. There was an answer from somewhere beyond the trees.

"Let's pull out."

When we reached the wall, Arnkh and Alistan had already clambered over it, and Ell was waiting for us with his bow at the ready.

"The goblin first."

Egrassa jumped up onto the wall, I tossed the goblin up, the elf caught him and passed him into the arms of the men standing on the other side. Then it was my turn. I jumped, and Egrassa and Ell pulled me up. When Little Bee saw me, she whinnied in greeting. I took the Key out and tossed it to Alistan. He caught it and nodded.

"Well done, thief."

Oho! That was the first time I'd ever heard a note of approval in his voice.

"We have to get clear of Ranneng tonight," the count said, striking his horse with his heels to set it moving.

I offered up thanks to Sagot. In the few days we had spent in this city, I had learned to hate it with all my heart.

10

THE BLACK RIVER

By my reckoning, it was only four in the morning, at the latest, but the Learned Owl was abuzz with preparations. We rode into the yard of the inn to find Hallas and Deler arguing furiously as they loaded up the packhorses for the road.

"Harold, I knew you could do it!" said Uncle, giving me a friendly slap on the shoulder.

Thanks to the elfin shamanism, the wound in the sergeant's arm, where it had been hit by a crossbow bolt, was now completely healed.

"Well, I didn't," I said.

"Take it," said Miralissa, handing me the Key. "It's best if you have it."

The last time she had tried to give me the artifact to keep, I had refused, but now . . . Maybe it really was best to carry it around with me.

Without saying a word, I hung the Key round my neck and tucked it under my clothes.

"Lafresa tried to break the bonds, but she couldn't manage it," I told the elfess.

"That was to be expected. It's not that easy to break the bonds with the Dancer in the Shadows. The Master still does not know that the goblin prophecies have started coming true."

"So you believe in all that nonsense our jester spouts?" I asked sourly.

"Why not?" asked the elfess, tossing her braid back over her shoulder. "So far his prophecies have not misled us."

Uncle walked across to us.

"Milord Alistan, Tresh Miralissa . . . Everything's ready, we can start."

"Good. Master Quidd!"

"Yes, Lady Miralissa?" said the innkeeper, hurrying up.

"Have you done everything?"

"Yes, exactly as you told me." Quidd started counting off his tasks on his fingers. "I've sent the servants home for two weeks, taken all my relatives out of the city, I'm closing down the inn and will leave soon myself. I never saw you, or rather, I saw you, but I have no idea what you were doing, I'm too unimportant . . ."

"Precisely, Master Quidd. Don't delay, leave as soon as possible; you could get caught in the backlash. Take this for your trouble."

The innkeeper accepted the purse full of coins and thanked her effusively.

"Allow me to give you some advice, Lady Miralissa. Better leave by the Muddy Gates, they are never closed for the night, and for a coin the guards will forget that you were ever there."

"Well then, we'll do that, and now—good-bye!"

Quidd bowed once again, wished us a safe journey, and went back into the inn to conclude his final pieces of business.

"For a coin they'll forget us, but for two they'll remember us only too well," I said, not talking to anyone in particular.

"Good thinking, thief. Let Master Quidd think that we will leave via the Muddy Gates. That won't do any harm to him, or to us. But we'll try to leave the city through the Festival Gates."

Bass was sitting on the porch and watching our preparations curiously. The darkness take me, I'd completely forgotten about him.

"Your horse," said Ell, holding out a bridle to Snoop.

"Thank you, I place more faith in my own feet, I'll walk home. Harold, can I see you for a moment? I need to have a word."

Ell blocked his way.

"You'll have plenty of time for talking. You're going with us."

"With you?"

"With us?" I gasped. "Why in the name of darkness should he go with us? That's the last thing we need right now!"

"You and I are in complete agreement there, Harold. I also think your friend should be left here. Preferably buried under the pigsty. But Tresh Miralissa thinks otherwise."

"Curses!" I exclaimed loudly. I didn't really like the idea of traveling in the same group as Bass. But I definitely didn't want him to be killed.

"It's very simple, Master Bass," said the elfess from the House of the Black Moon. "We simply cannot leave you here."

"You'll start gossiping," Ell went on. "And we don't want that."

"I promise I'll be as silent as the grave."

"You men make lots of promises, but you don't keep many of them. But you're quite right; if you decide to stay, you'll be exactly as silent as the grave. . . ."

No more explanations were required—the choice was a journey on horseback with us, or a crooked elfin blade in the throat.

"Harold! You say something to them!"

"I'm sorry, but there's nothing I can do," I said, shaking my head regretfully. "I think it will be best for everyone if you go with us."

Miralissa was right, even if Snoop didn't blurt out the truth on his own, the count's men could find him. To the elfin way of thinking, it was simpler just to kill him, but since I put in a word for him and he'd helped us, the dark elves made an exception.

"This is insane! It must have been the Nameless One who prompted me to get involved with your gang!" Bass said, and spat angrily, realizing that he had no way out and now he would have to share our journey with us. "And where are we going?"

"You don't need to know that, man. Get into the saddle and keep your mouth shut. And if you get any ideas about trying to escape, remember—I'll be right there beside you."

Ell had taken a very great "liking" to my friend from the first moment they met.

"This is what I get for giving someone a helping hand!" the card-sharp exclaimed, still furious as he climbed up onto the horse. I must say, he did that rather clumsily.

"Don't take it to heart, it could have been worse," I consoled him.

Little Bee reached her muzzle out to me, looking for a dainty tidbit, but I didn't have anything in my pockets and just shrugged.

"Here," said Marmot, handing me an apple.

The horse gobbled down the treat and gave me a good-natured sideways glance, looking for more.

"Harold!" said Kli-Kli as he rode up to me, looking like a little hummock on the back of his huge black steed. "Do you think you could give me back my medallion?"

"Ah, of course." I'd forgotten about Kli-Kli's little knickknack. "Here. Thank you."

"Don't mention it." The goblin hung the trinket round his neck. "Right then, ready for the road?"

"No."

"I understand," the jester said with a laugh. "Nights spent out in the open air and gruel brewed up by Hallas aren't what you like best, then?"

I didn't get a chance to answer, because just then Deler appeared, cursing the green goblin to the heavens: "Kli-Kli! Was it you who took the last bottle of wine?"

"Harold, I think I'll get started now," the jester said hastily. "No, I didn't take anything! What would I want with your Asmina Valley?"

"Then how do you know what it's called?" the dwarf asked, squinting at him suspiciously.

"Oh, it just came to me."

"Kli-Kli, stop . . . stop, I tell you! Ah, you thieving little squirt!"

We rode through the Festival Gates without running into any kind of trouble. The sleepy guards swung the gates open for us as obligingly as they could manage and let us out of the city, without asking a single question about the reasons for our hasty departure in the night.

The gold handed to the corporal worked better than any official charters with the seal of the city council.

We covered the distance between Ranneng and the Iselina in the next two days, galloping at a furious pace all the way, in order to put as much distance as possible between us and any pursuit sent out by Count Balistan Pargaid.

The main road we rode along was very busy. There were travelers and artisans hurrying to Ranneng and away from Ranneng, and strings of carts carrying all sorts of things to be sold. We came across a village about every league, so our squad didn't have to spend the night in an open field.

Bass was gloomy. He had either Ell or Uncle behind him all the way. Luckily, my old friend didn't think of trying to escape—he realized what the risks were. When I asked if Snoop was really going to go all the way to Hrad Spein with us, Miralissa said she would find somewhere to put him.

"There are many guard posts and fortresses on the border. He can wait there until we come back, and then he can go anywhere he wants."

I didn't tell Bass about what the elfess had decided. I don't think he would have been too delighted by the news.

At five in the evening of the second day we reached the Iselina.

I caught sight of the glittering ribbon of the river when we were still in the forest—the sun was glinting on the water, and the reflections shone straight into my eyes between the trees. And the sight when we emerged into open space simply took my breath away.

Our group was standing on a low elevation, with the broad band of the river laid out in front of us. During our journey I had seen plenty of streams and rivers, both great and small. But none of them bore any comparison to the Iselina.

I was looking at the mother of all the northern rivers. Huge, wide, and deep, it began somewhere far off, where the streams flowing from the Mountains of the Dwarves came together to form a mighty hissing torrent that flowed on through the Forests of Zagraba and emptied into the Sea of Storms, away to the southeast.

We could see a large village on the road ahead. Not far from it the mighty ramparts of a castle towered up into the air.

"Marmot," I said to the Wild Heart. "What settlement is that?"

The warrior gave me a rather strange look and replied: "Boltnik."

"*That* Boltnik?"

"Yes."

Everyone remembers the bloodbath at Boltnik that swallowed up a quarter of our army during the Spring War. The men were standing on the bank of the Iselina, waiting for the orcs' storm troopers to start crossing. At the time no one knew that fifty leagues further upstream, the Firstborn had broken through the human rearguard and driven the men back to Ranneng. Then they attacked those who were waiting for them at Boltnik from the rear.

The enemy from Zagraba pinned the men back against the river, and the far bank was black with the teeming hordes of orcish bowmen. Almost no one managed to escape from this encirclement; only a tiny number got away by water or broke out of the ring. When this happened, men realized that the elves had chosen the name of this river well—Iselina means "Black River." But during those terrible days, the river was not black, it was red with the blood of men and the Firstborn.

Alistan did not lead our group into the village; we avoided it, leaving the white houses with red tiled roofs on our right. Nobody really wanted to go into a place haunted by ghosts.

Eel and Arnkh were the only ones who went to the village, to find out about the ferry to the other side of the river, while we stayed in a small spinney right beside the water, slightly downstream from Boltnik.

The air by the river had a fresh smell of damp grass. The riverbank was overgrown with sedge and reeds, and weeping willows hung their silver-green leaves right down to the surface of the water.

A pair of gadflies, which Kli-Kli called "buzzers," immediately began circling round the horses, and the goblin started hunting them.

From here the opposite bank looked very far away. I wouldn't have bet that I could swim all the way across. The trees on that side looked tiny, only half the size of my little finger.

"What are you gazing at, Harold? Never seen a river before?" said Hallas, squatting down beside me and lighting up his pipe.

"Not one as big as this."

"If you ask me, it's best not to see any. A river means a boat. And I hate boats!"

"If you haven't already realized, our gnome here is afraid of traveling on water," explained Honeycomb, who was standing close by.

"Gnomes aren't afraid of anything! It's just that boats aren't for gnomes!"

"Mattocks are for gnomes," Deler snorted. "Don't get nervous, Lucky! You'll get across without suffering too much. In any case, it's not a canoe, it's a ferry."

"In other words, just a big boat!" Hallas said morosely, blowing out a ring of smoke.

"He gets seasick," Honeycomb chuckled.

Hallas started puffing away even harder, peering gloomily at the watery expanse.

"Seasickness isn't the worst thing! I don't know how to swim," Kli-Kli informed us with insufferable pride.

"You mean not at all?" asked Hallas, looking at the jester.

"I mean I can swim like an ax! But I'm not at all afraid."

"Piffling pokers, I told you, gnomes aren't afraid of anything!" Hallas said, as Eel and Arnkh came back.

"We can't leave yet, milord," said Arnkh, his bald patch gleaming with sweat. "It's some kind of town holiday today. Nobody's working, both ferries are standing idle, everybody's drunk. We won't be able to move on from this bank until tomorrow morning."

"Ah, darkness!" our commander swore.

We moved closer to the ferries, in order to be the first to cross to the far side in the morning. The two massive wooden structures with huge drums, onto which the thick chains were wound, stood about a quarter of a league from Boltnik. They were about a hundred yards apart from each other, and owned by completely different people.

We found one of the ferrymen. The old man was sitting in his house on the bank of the river, and he absolutely refused to take us across, even for all the gold in Siala.

"The workers are celebrating, who's going to haul the chain? They'll come back tonight, sleep it off, and then why wouldn't they take fine gentlemen like yourselves across and first thing in the morning?" he croaked.

"Careful, granddad, or we'll go to your competitor!"

"Off you go, gentlemen, I'm not keeping you here, am I? Only there's no point, I swear by all the gods. It's the same thing there. Nothing works until morning. It's our holiday."

But the stubborn old-timer was only too delighted to let Markauz, Miralissa, and Egrassa use his house. The ferryman narrowed his eyes contentedly at the sound of money jingling in his pockets as he tramped off to the town.

"This is plain stupid," said Bass. "How do they feed their families? Apart from being so far from the town, he has a competitor right beside him."

"Think again," Uncle said with a chuckle. "The ferries constantly carry goods across for the Border Kingdom, and they move soldiers from one bank to the other. The army pays well. . . ."

"The nearest ford is forty leagues to the north of here, Boltnik is the last large settlement in these parts," said Arnkh. "On the other bank there are only small scattered villages and noblemen's castles."

We didn't get any soft beds, and we had to spend the night on the riverbank. The Wild Hearts took this calmly—they had spent nights in the snowy tundra of the Desolate Lands, where only a fire and a blanket keep a sleeping man from freezing to death, so what was wrong with a night out in the fresh air beside some river or other? But Bass moaned miserably: "Not only do you drag me off to some mysterious place, you make me feed the mosquitoes on the way! Ah, darkness!" He smacked himself on the forehead, flattening several of the little bloodsuckers at one go.

Snoop was right about that—the air was simply buzzing with them. The little monsters showed up just before evening and launched into a spectacular feast. Every now and then there were curses and deafening slaps. Mosquitoes were dispatched to the light by the dozen, but that evidently did nothing to deter their hungry comrades. And there was no wind to blow the tiny bloodsuckers away from the river.

Kli-Kli suggested a remarkable goblin shamanic spell that he said would wipe out every mosquito for ten leagues around, but, remembering his conjuring with the pieces of string that destroyed the house of the Nameless One's followers, we told the fool what he could do with his wonderful idea.

The bloodsuckers carried on feasting. What made me most furious was they kept trying to get into my ears and my mouth, buzzing repulsively all the time. Finally, even Ell couldn't stand it anymore and he went to Miralissa for help. When he came back, he tossed some powder into the fire we'd made with logs borrowed from the ferryman's woodpile, and the air around us was filled with a spicy, herbal smell. The mosquitoes started dying by the hundreds, and our suffering was over in literally just a few minutes.

It was getting dark, and the water in the river began to look like a black mirror, with the clouds drifting across the sky reflected in it. A few moments later the setting sun cast its final rays on the smooth surface of the water, and it lit up like molten bronze.

There was a splashing sound in the reeds nearby.

"That's the fish jumping, there must be a pike hunting small fry," Uncle said with a sigh.

"I could just do with some fish soup," said Arnkh, smacking his lips dreamily. "I'm sick of Hallas's garbage."

"Don't eat it if you don't want to!" the gnome snapped in reply.

"Don't take offense, Lucky. You probably fancy a bite of fish yourself," Arnkh replied good-naturedly, lowering his feet into the river water. "Ooh! As warm as milk fresh from the cow!"

"Never mind what I might fancy a bite of. Where do we get it from, that's the question."

"Let's just catch a whole lot of fish!" said Kli-Kli, struck by a brilliant idea. "I've never gone fishing in my whole life!"

"And where will you get the tackle?"

"Ah, the tackle's no problem. We'll take some rope, a couple of nails, some bait, and throw it out as far as we can. Maybe some fool will bite," said Uncle, stroking his beard.

"Let's do it! Come on!" Kli-Kli said, and started jigging about on the spot.

"All right. But while I make the tackle, you can find the bait."

"Straightaway! I'll do that in a moment!" the delighted goblin shouted, running off to start searching.

"A perfect child," Bass chuckled, sitting down beside me. "They won't get anywhere, with tackle like that you can't catch anything but frogs."

"Don't you be so hasty. When I was little I used to pull out bream like thi-i-is with this kind of tackle!" said Uncle, spreading his hands wide.

"That's enough blathering, come over to the fire, the food's ready," Hallas called to us.

We had almost emptied the pot when His Majesty's jester appeared beside the campfire.

"Get rid of that!" growled Marmot, moving as far away from the goblin as he could. "It stinks!"

"Of course it stinks," Kli-Kli said gleefully, holding a dead cat out in front of him.

"Where did you find it?"

"In the ditch beside the road; a wagon ran over it. A long time ago. It's even got worms in its eyes, look!"

"Don't ruin our appetites," said Mumr, pushing his plate away.

"So shall I just throw it away, then? You said yourselves, we need some bait," the little green urchin said, blinking in confusion.

"But not a dead cat! Use your head, Kli-Kli!"

"Wait, Lamplighter," said Uncle, licking his spoon. "Not risking anything, are we?"

"Only our stomachs," put in Hallas, trying not to look at the poor creature's mangy little corpse. "Tell him, Deler."

"Hallas is right," the dwarf confirmed.

"Don't despair, Kli-Kli, we'll have your bait on a hook in a moment."

"Hooray! Thanks, Uncle!" Kli-Kli exclaimed, almost dropping the cat in our pot of gruel.

This sacrilegious treatment of Hallas's cooking almost gave him a stroke, and the goblin hastily cleared off to the riverbank and waited for the sergeant there. I decided to take a look at how this strange kind of fishing would go and got up from the "table" to join the fishermen.

Without the slightest sign of squeamishness, Uncle took hold of the dead cat by the tail, attached it to his homemade tackle, twirled it round like a sling, and flung it into the river. There was a loud splash and circles ran out across the water.

"Now what? Now there'll be a bite, right?" asked the goblin, jumping up and down in his impatience.

"Maybe now, maybe in a little while. Here, you take the rope, wind it round your hand, and when you feel a tug, you tug on it, too," Uncle said gravely, handing Kli-Kli the tackle.

The goblin sat down on the bank and watched the calm, smooth surface of the water in which the first stars were already reflected.

"Listen, Uncle," I whispered quietly to the sergeant as we walked back to the campfire, leaving Kli-Kli on his own. "I can understand Kli-Kli. But you ought to know how hard it is to catch anything with a half-rotten cat."

Uncle chuckled, "Yes, I do know."

"Then why . . ."

"Kli-Kli's just like a child. Goblins mature a lot later than we people do. Let him relax and get a bit of rest. The gods only know what an effort it costs him to be a jester all the time. Over there on the other side of the river is the Borderland, and none of us will have any time for rest there."

"Is it that bad?"

"Well, of course, the Borderland isn't the Desolate Lands, but orcs can appear at the most unexpected moments. The Firstborn regularly send punitive squads into our lands, and we'll have to keep our wits about us, otherwise we won't stay alive for long. We've already lost two men. . . . Curses! What sort of sergeant am I, if I wasn't able to keep them safe?"

"A good sergeant, Uncle. You're not to blame for the deaths of Tomcat and Loudmouth." That was the only answer I could give him.

"Forget it," he sighed. "I'm too old for expeditions like this. I should have collected the money I've earned and settled down in my own little tavern ages ago. And when we get this job finished, that's just what I'll do."

"You said the same thing when we got back from the last expedition," chuckled Honeycomb, who had overheard us. "A leopard can never change his spots!"

"You hold your tongue, kid! I'm still the sergeant around here," Uncle rebuked him good-naturedly. "How could I leave you thickheads all on your own?"

And that put an end to the conversation.

There was a fresh scent coming off the water and the stars were lighting up one by one in the sky. The Wild Hearts were laying their traveling blankets on the grass, getting ready to go to sleep.

"So where are we going, then?" Bass asked, stuffing his folded-up jacket under his head.

"You just sleep, man," chuckled Ell. "When we get there, I'll be the first to tell you."

"If it's the Borderland, I'd like a chance to leave a few offspring behind and draw up a will."

"Your friend's very droll, Harold. Maybe we should make him our second jester?" Marmot chuckled. "My dear man, you were told—sleep and don't worry about a thing."

"I'm sleeping," Snoop muttered, and closed his eyes.

Ell took another close look at him and went off into the darkness—to stand the first watch.

"A bite! A bite! I swear by the great shaman Tre-Tre, I've got a bite," the jester yelled.

The goblin's shrill howls battered at my ears, driving away sleep. I unglued my eyes and swore violently. The stars were still shining in the heavens, and dawn was not yet kindling in the east. The grass, the blankets, and our clothes were all covered with a fine diamond dust of dew. I shuddered from the cold as I emerged from sleep—during the night my clothes had soaked up the moisture.

The willows were motionless shadows against the background of the sky and the fading stars. Beside one of the trees a very familiar little figure, dressed in a cloak and pointed cap, was jumping up and down.

"A bite! Word of honor, a bite!" he yelled. "Help me! I've got a bite!"

"Ah, drop dead!" I said, and dove back under the blanket.

The others who were woken up felt the same way. Hallas, who had propped himself up on one elbow and was watching the goblin perform his crazy dance, growled in fury.

"Shut up, Kli-Kli!" Mumr advised him, without opening his eyes. "It's not morning yet."

"Why can't you understand? I've got a bite! Honest, I'm not lying! Come and look for yourselves! Come quick! I can't pull it out!"

"Uncle," Deler said from underneath the hat tilted forward across his face. "You started this whole business, you go and see what kind of bite our horse-shit merchant has got. And shut him up!"

"Quick, quick! The rope's breaking!"

"Curse the moment when I decided to teach a goblin to catch fish!" the sergeant sighed. He got up off the ground, pulled on his leather jacket, and tramped off toward Kli-Kli, who was going wild.

"Uncle, look! I've caught a fish!"

No, this is just too much! I'll never get back to sleep now!

"Harold, are you going over to Kli-Kli?" Bass growled.

"Why?"

"Give him a good kick for me," Snoop said, and turned over onto his other side.

I gazed at him enviously—my old friend had always been hard to wake up.

"Let's go and take a look," growled Honeycomb, getting to his feet.

A tattered blanket of mist lay across the smooth, undisturbed surface of the river. The goblin's yells and howls echoed far across the water.

"Harold! Harold! Look! I caught it! It almost pulled me into the water! Harold, I caught it!"

The rope, stretched as tight as a bowstring, was jerking convulsively. The quick-witted goblin had done the right thing by winding the free end of his tackle several times around the trunk of the nearest willow.

"Almost pulled you in, you say?" Uncle pulled on the line with the gesture of an experienced angler. "Oh, he's well hooked! And big, too! Honeycomb, come and help!"

The sergeant and the big, beefy soldier grunted as they started hauling the line in. "He's fighting, the swine!" Honeycomb grunted, when a sharp tug from under the water almost pulled him off his feet.

The hauling-in of the unknown prize went on for a full hour. By that time the excited howling of our would-be fisherman had woken even Bass, and everyone was standing behind Honeycomb and making suggestions about what the jester could have caught with a dead cat.

"He must have hooked a water sprite," said Hallas, struggling to get his pipe to light. "Or a water nymph."

"Or maybe the king of the krakens?" Deler laughed as he helped Honeycomb. "You're a great one for making things up, Lucky."

"You ignorant bonehead!" the gnome retorted. "What kind of fish is it that takes an hour to pull out of the water? Look, it's not even thrashing its tail and it's not giving up for a moment. It's got to be a water nymph!"

"Well, the idea of a nymph is nonsense, of course, but it could be some kind of river monster," Marmot said with a yawn.

"And what would you know, scholar? Have you ever seen one?" Hallas seemed to really like the idea of seeing a naked maiden.

"No, the old men told me about them."

"Bah . . . Arnkh, take over from me," Uncle said with a tired sigh. "It would be simpler to let it go than put ourselves through this agony."

"Never!" Kli-Kli and Hallas howled in a single voice.

The battle with the water monster continued. By the time something long and black finally appeared on the surface of the water we were all fed up.

"A log!" said Deler, spitting in disappointment. "All that time tugging just wasted!"

"Ah!" said Arnkh. "And there was I thinking—"

"That's no log! It can't be a log! I couldn't have caught a log!" Kli-Kli exclaimed indignantly.

"Better accept it, my friend," Bass laughed. And just then the log opened a mouth that could have swallowed up a full-grown man.

"Oh, mother," Kli-Kli cried, and fell over on his back in surprise.

"A catfish!" Uncle roared. "What a huge brute!"

At this point the catfish realized that the Wild Hearts weren't going to be impressed just by a large pair of jaws—they'd seen worse things than that in the Desolate Lands—and it made an attempt to escape. The water seethed and Honeycomb went down on his knees, but he didn't let go of the line. Arnkh gritted his teeth as he tried to hold on to the huge fish. Everyone on the bank, including me, went dashing to help them.

As a result of our joint efforts, the catfish ended up on the bank. The massive black body was covered with waterweed and shells; its long black whiskers twitched, its great white eyes gaped at us, and the fish opened its mouth greedily, threatening to gobble up anyone who dared to come close enough. The monster had an entire arsenal of different-sized hooks sticking out of its lips. It was about seven yards long and I didn't even want to think about how much it must have weighed.

"What's going on here?" asked Miralissa, who had come out to us.

"Miralissa, I caught a fish! Word of honor! Just look how big it is, they all helped me pull it out, but I caught it! Isn't that fantastic?" Kli-Kli boasted.

"And what are you going to do with it?"

"I don't know . . ." Kli-Kli pondered for a moment. "Let's take it with us!"

"Eat this rubbish?" said Hallas, pulling a face. "It must be at least a hundred years old! Old meat, it'll have the stench of the swamp! Damn the thing. Better just to let it go!"

"Let it go?" said Kli-Kli, pondering again, and then he decided to demonstrate the magnanimity of the victor to the defeated, and said with a solemn nod: "We can let it go. Off you swim, fish, and don't forget that dead cats will be the ruin of you. Right then . . . you know . . . push it into the water, won't you. . . ."

Unable to believe its fishy luck, the catfish sent a column of water high up into the air as it plunged into the black depths of the river.

"Harold, did you see what a fish I caught? Tremendous, wasn't it?"

"Well done, Kli-Kli, you're a genuine fisherman," I said.

"You really think so?"

"Yes, really," I sighed. "Now go gnaw on a carrot and calm down."

"I haven't got any carrots," Kli-Kli said with a shrug of disappointment. "I ran out the day before yesterday."

"I'm sorry to hear that."

"Hey, Kli-Kli! Help Marmot bring the firewood," Uncle ordered the goblin.

"Straightaway! I'll do that in a moment!" And the ever-cheerful goblin forgot about the fish and rushed off on his new assignment.

By the time they had got the fire going and Uncle, who took over kitchen duty from Hallas, had cooked breakfast, and we had packed away our things, it was early morning. The sky was already completely bright, the sunlight had driven away the stars, and there was only a slim crescent, the pale ghost of the moon, still hanging just above the horizon. The ferryman came back, accompanied by six hefty hulks, and said we could set out straightaway if we wanted.

"Only, my good gentlemen, you won't all fit in at once. There are too many of you, and all the horses, too. I can take you across in two trips."

"No need for that," replied Alistan, counting out six silver pieces to the ferryman. "I see your neighbor's back at work, too, so he can take the others across."

"That won't do, milord, pardon me for speaking so plainly. It's a matter of professional pride. He won't carry my clients, and I won't take his, that's the way things are. I humbly beg your pardon, but you'll have to make the two trips."

The other ferryman and his helpers were glowering hostilely at their rival.

"Two trips then, if it has to be two," Alistan agreed. "Uncle, you divide up the men."

"I hate boats," Hallas muttered, glancing at the ferry apprehensively. The gnome's face was the color of tender young leaves in spring.

"Stop that," Arnkh laughed, and his chain mail jangled. "Look, there aren't any waves, the water's smooth, you'll get across and nothing will happen to you."

"But as soon as the ferry starts swaying up and down, up and down, you'll see what kind of stomach our mattockman has," Deler laughed.

"Shut up, pumpkin-head!" Hallas snarled, gazing at the river fearfully. "I'm feeling sick enough without any help from you."

"Then go into the bushes so you won't upset anyone, and throw up there," the kind-hearted dwarf suggested.

Hallas groaned and tightened his grip on the handle of his battle-mattock.

"Why don't you sing a little song?" Kli-Kli suggested to the gnome. "It helps me."

"Really?" An expression of disbelief mingled with hope appeared on the gnome's bearded face. "But what should I sing?"

"Well, sing 'The Hammer on the Ax.' Or 'The Song of the Crazy Miners,'" said Deler, slapping Hallas on the shoulder. "Welcome on board!"

The gnome gulped, turned even brighter green, told us all for the hundredth time that he hated boats, and stepped onto the ferry.

"Kli-Kli, you now," said Uncle, nodding.

"Oh no, not on your life! I'll go with Harold!"

"If that's what you want. Then it's you, Lamplighter. That's it, cast off, we'll follow on!"

"Put your backs into it, lads!" the ferryman called to his men.

His workers heaved on the drum, the chain clanged as it was wound up, and the ferry set off. Kli-Kli, Uncle, Arnkh, Eel, and I were left on the bank, together with the packhorses.

When the ferry had got a quarter of the way across, the peaceful silence of the early morning was shattered as Hallas started singing. I didn't envy the others who were on the ferry right then—the gnome could sing about as well as I could fly.

Lucky Hallas roared away out of tune at the top of his voice, howling so loud that they could even hear his song in Boltnik. I doubted whether the inhabitants of the village would be grateful to the gnome for this wonderful awakening.

"Just listen to him howl," Arnkh chuckled, hanging his sword's scabbard behind his shoulder. His eternal chain mail had been joined by a leather jerkin with metal plates sewn onto it, arm and leg armor, and chain-mail gloves. Arnkh caught my puzzled glance.

"It's not far to the Border Kingdom now; I have to return to my homeland fully armed."

"We still have two weeks' riding to reach the Border Kingdom . . ."

"Well?"

It would take a h'san'kor to understand these men from the Borderland. They'll happily go hungry, just as long as they can hang iron all over themselves. Living close to the eastern Forests of Zagraba—the domain of the Firstborn—does pretty strange things to people.

Meanwhile Hallas was still belting out his song loud enough to frighten everyone for miles around.

> Whether old or young your age,
> Beardless youth or hoarhead sage,
> In the autumn and the spring,
> The winter and the summer,
> You shall hear the hammer
> Set the axhead ringing!
>
> The leafy forest's cheery throng
> Will all break off their jolly song.
> All will quake in silent dread
> As the graves on every side
> Throw their dismal portals wide
> To free the restless dead!
>
> Through the battle's clamorous din
> Legions of the dead move in,
> A grim and silent throng.
> Bearded heroes block their path,
> Soldiers unafraid of death,
> Fearless, bold, and strong
>
> Frenzied clash of shield to shield
> Forces tempered steel to yield
> And mighty swords to crack!
> And then the undead host will quake,
> Their battle line will shift and break
> And they will stagger back.

The spurt and splash of undead blood
Will soak the gnomes' beards, doing good
To doughty heroes' fettle.
The argument of ax and hammer
Will ring amid the clamor,
Bracing the whole clan's mettle.

Though in the end the hand of death
Will still the soldier's heaving breath,
Whatever future time might bring,
Through winter and through summer
We shall wait here for the hammer
To set the axhead ringing!

Three times Hallas had to break off before he finished a couplet to lean over the side of the ferry and disgorge his breakfast into the water.

"Oh, he's really going through it, poor soul!" said Uncle, with a sigh of sympathy.

In a while the ferry nudged against the bank and little figures that I could barely recognize as my traveling companions started leading off the horses. One of the figures dropped to the ground and just lay there. I think it was Hallas.

The ferry started moving back toward us.

"Get ready. Arnkh, lead up the horses."

"Harold, hey, Harold! Will you hold my hand?"

"Kli-Kli, are you being silly again?"

"No, I'm serious! I can't swim! What if I fall in?"

"Sit in the middle of the ferry, and nothing bad will happen," I reassured him, still not sure whether the goblin had thought up yet another trick or he really didn't know how to swim.

"I'm afraid," Kli-Kli said quite sincerely, sniffing.

The ferry picked up speed moving toward us, and ten minutes later we were leading the remaining horses onto it. The animals were quite calm at the prospect of crossing the river and didn't balk. They took their places in special stalls, and Uncle let the ferryman know that we were ready to go.

"Put your backs into it!"

The great hulking ferry hands heaved, the drum creaked, and we set off.

The water splashed gently against the sides of the ferry, the planks smelled of duckweed and fish. The willows on the bank gradually drifted away.

"Kli-Kli, what are you doing?" I asked the goblin, who had hung his legs over the edge and was dabbling his feet in the water.

"What am I doing? Trying to overcome my fear of water."

"And what if you happen to plop in?"

"You'll catch me," he said with a carefree grin.

I sat down beside him and started watching the opposite bank approaching slowly but surely. In the middle of the river there was a wind, and the ferry started swaying gently on waves that sprang up out of nowhere.

One of the horses snorted and started whinnying and trying to kick out a wooden partition with its hind hooves.

"Hold her! I've got problems enough already!" shouted the ferryman.

Uncle dashed across to reassure the frightened animal. The horse was snorting, rolling its eyes, and trembling. The sergeant's gentle whispers gradually calmed it down, but it still squinted warily at the water.

The chain clanged, the water splashed, and the riverbank slowly drifted closer.

"Why are they running about like that?" Kli-Kli's shout of surprise interrupted my contemplation of the black water.

Our comrades were dashing about on the bank, waving their arms and shouting something. They were definitely shouting to us, but at that distance the wind carried their words away, and I couldn't make anything out.

"I don't know," I said, concerned. "Has something happened?"

"It doesn't look like it . . . ," Kli-Kli said slowly.

Just then one of the elves drew his bow and shot an arrow in a steep arc in our direction.

"Has he lost his mind?" the jester hissed, watching the flight of the arrow.

"Keep your head down!" I snapped at him, but the arrow sliced through the air above the ferry and fell into the water behind us.

"Hey, what are they up to over there? Have they gone crazy?" Arnkh roared.

"Look! On the other bank!" the jester shouted as he raised his eyes from the water where the arrow had landed to the riverbank that we had recently left.

There was certainly something to look at, and the elf had been right to use such an unusual method of pointing it out. Bustling about on the bank beside the second ferry were almost forty mounted men.

But that wasn't the worst thing. Moving straight toward us, slowly, implacably, and absolutely silently, was a semitransparent sphere the color of scarlet flame. It hung just slightly above the water and was about the size of a decent barn. Standing on the bank from which our death was approaching I could just make out a female figure, standing motionless with her arms raised in the air.

Lafresa!

"What is *that*?" the ferryman gasped in amazement.

I knew what it was. Kronk-a-Mor. Exactly the same kind of sphere, only ten times smaller, had killed Valder. Neither Kli-Kli's medallion nor Miralissa's skills would save us from this magic.

"Off the ferry! Look lively!" I roared, then grabbed the goblin by the scruff of his neck and plunged into the water.

Kli-Kli squealed in surprise and kicked at the air with his legs. I fell awkwardly, with no time to gather myself together—I was in too much of a hurry to get as far away as possible from the doomed ferry.

The water was warm and black. I opened my eyes, but down in the depths I could hardly see a thing. The floundering goblin and I were surrounded by specks of drifting sediment and hundreds of little bubbles.

I struck out as hard as I could with my free arm and my legs, trying to get as deep under the water as possible. Kli-Kli struggled and panicked, like a rabbit in a noose. I saw his eyes, gaping wide in terror, and the bubbles escaping from his mouth, but I kept moving deeper and deeper, without worrying about the goblin. I just hoped he had enough air to last until we surfaced.

Boo-oo-oom!

The shock of the explosion struck my ears, for a moment everything went dark and I was completely disoriented, not knowing which way was up and which way was down. . . . The glimmering ceiling of light above my head showed me that I was moving in the right direction.

A stroke with my free hand, a hard thrust with my legs, another stroke, another thrust. I seemed to be stuck in one spot, making no progress at all toward the blessed air. When the surface of the water finally parted above my head, Kli-Kli had almost stopped moving, but as soon as he took a breath in, he started coughing and thrashing about even more violently.

"I don't know how to drown! I don't know how to drown!" the goblin squeaked, getting his words confused.

"Stop struggling!" I shouted. "You'll drown both of us! Stop it! Do you hear!"

That had no effect on the jester at all, and I ducked him under the water for a few moments. When I lifted his head back above the water, Kli-Kli coughed, spat, and spouted foul abuse.

"Stop struggling! Or I'll let go of you! Do you hear me, you idiot?"

"Ghghabool! Yes! I hear you!"

"Relax! I'm holding you, you won't drown! Just relax, lie on the water, and breathe!"

He gurgled to let me know he had understood.

I looked around. All that was left of the ferry was a memory and scraps of wood scattered across the river. A few especially large beams were still burning and the air was filled with the smell of smoke and soot. I could see the head of someone who was swimming about forty yards away from us, but I couldn't tell who it was. One other person had survived, then. . . . But what about the others?

This isn't the moment to mourn our losses, Harold! You have to get out of the water. It was a fair distance to the bank, but I had to make it if I didn't want to feed the fishes on the bottom. I could see people swimming to help us, but it would take them a long time to cover the distance.

I set off. Stroking smoothly through the water, counting every stroke and trying to breathe as regularly as possible.

"One! Two! Three!"

I don't know how many times I repeated that "One! Two! Three!" It was certainly a lot of times. All I could see was the splashing water, the pitiless sky, and the thin, distant line of the bank.

I'll make it! No you won't! Yes I will!

One! Two! Three!

Just a little farther! Just a little bit more!

One! Two! Three!

Kli-Kli was an impossible burden, weighing down my arm; and my boots, clothes, crossbow, knife, and bag were dragging me to the bottom, too. I ought to have dumped my weapon, but I'd rather have abandoned the jester than my equipment.

Of course, what I just said wasn't true—I'm not the kind of swine who would drown a helpless goblin, but you can't just abandon your only weapon.

My boots had filled with water and were pulling me down. There was no way I could get rid of them—they were laced on, and I'm no acrobat or conjurer, I couldn't unfasten them with just one hand—it wasn't even worth trying. It was a real stroke of luck that I'd taken off my cloak. It was lost forever now, but at least it wasn't winding round my legs and dragging me down to the bottom.

After about fifty strokes, I realized that I wouldn't get very far with a load like this. If help didn't reach us, Kli-Kli and I would be glugging our final farewells as we sank under the water forever.

My arms and legs felt like they were made of lead, my strokes were getting weaker and weaker. It was hard to breathe. Often all I could see ahead was black water, with only an occasional glimpse of the edge of the blue sky above it.

I was hanging on, just to avoid sinking straightaway. I'd swallowed a lot of water and my mind was clouded.

But the riverbank—that vague, blurred line—was still a very long way off. . . .

"Kli-Kli," I gasped hoarsely. "Try to get your boots off!"

"I've done that!"

Well done, goblin!

"Then . . . why . . . are you . . . so heavy?"

"The chain mail . . ."

Darkness! That's what was pulling him down! The little shit had covered himself with chain mail!

"Kli . . . Kli . . . I'll . . . kill . . . you."

"Only . . . when we get . . . ashore! Please!"

Ashore! I'll never reach that cursed shore!

One! Two! Three! And again! And just a few more!

My clothes were pulling me down more and more heavily, I was putting my last ounces of strength into my strokes, everything was dark in front of my eyes, there was a ringing sound in my ears, and the arm holding Kli-Kli felt like it would fall off at any moment. I sank under the water three times, and three times, with an absolutely immense effort, I struggled back to the surface for at least one more gulp of air. . . .

When I felt someone's hands take hold of me, I was on the point of fainting.

"Harold, let go of Kli-Kli. Harold!" Marmot's voice said somewhere close by.

I reluctantly released my grip on the goblin's clothes.

"The bank's not far, don't struggle!" Ell was breathing heavily; the fast swim had tired him.

If I could have managed it, I would have giggled. Don't struggle! Wasn't that what I'd said to Kli-Kli?

When my feet touched the bottom and Ell and Honeycomb dragged me onto the bank, it was too miraculous to believe. I'd made it after all, Sagot be praised!

I sank down on all fours, exhausted, and puked up river water. I felt better for that. I spat out some sour saliva, and someone slapped me on the back:

"Are you alive, thief?"

"I thi-ink so, Milord Al-listan." I was shuddering violently.

Somewhere nearby Kli-Kli was coughing hoarsely.

"Take a sip," said Deler, sticking his flask under my nose.

I nodded gratefully and took a big swallow. A second later a gnomish powder barrel exploded in my stomach, searing my insides with raging flame.

A crazy thought passed through my mind: "Poison!"

Tears poured out of my eyes and I tried to take a breath, but I couldn't, I just started coughing.

"That's not beer, you know, it's Fury of the Depths! Did you feel it? Come on, Harold, get up!" said Deler, taking back his flask.

I sat up with an effort and started pulling off my wet clothes.

"Those idiots have killed all the ferrymen," Hallas hissed fiercely through his teeth, looking at the far bank through a small spyglass. "They're pushing off, I swear by the mountains!"

The horsemen were dashing about on the far bank, and fifteen or twenty of them were just setting off on the ferry with the clear intention of getting to us. I couldn't see Lafresa from where I was.

"Who are these lads? What do they want?" Hallas said, with his beard bristling fiercely.

"Balistan Pargaid's men, no doubt," Alistan Markauz replied, drawing his sword. "Ready yourselves for action. Lady Miralissa, can you do anything to help?"

"Only with my dagger and bow. That woman is blocking me."

"Ell? Egrassa?"

"It's too far, the arrows can't reach that bank. Or the ferry, yet. We'll be able to fire at four hundred paces."

"And what if the witch tries blasting us with another one of those things!" Mumr asked warily, leaning both hands on the cross guard of his bidenhander, which was stuck into the ground.

"No, a spell like that takes five or six hours to prepare," the elfess replied as she observed the approaching ferry. It had already covered a quarter of the distance between us.

"Honeycomb! Honeycomb, wake up! We'll mourn for them later! Into battle, warrior!" Alistan ordered.

The young soldier roused himself and gave a gloomy nod as he picked up his ogre-hammer.

Mourn them? Who? I thought stupidly. My head wasn't working at all, and I still had the taste of river water and slime in my mouth. "Darkness! Were we the only ones who escaped from the ferry?"

Uncle, Arnkh, Eel, the ferrymen . . . had they all been killed? It was impossible. . . . It simply couldn't be true!

I looked round desperately, trying to count the men that we still had. The first one I saw was Eel in soaking wet clothes. He must have been swimming behind me. The Garrakian warrior's chest was heaving rapidly; the swim had obviously taken its toll on him, too. He hadn't abandoned his swords, and I could only imagine the effort it must have cost him to reach the bank alone.

The elves, holding their bows at the ready, waited in silence for the ferry to come within range. It was already in the middle of the river.

"Harold, let's clear out," said Bass, running up to me. "There's going to be a bloodbath any minute!"

"He's talking good sense, Harold," said Hallas. "You're not warriors. You'd better wait it out behind us. Ah, if I only had a cannon, I'd make short work of that boat."

"A cannon!" Kli-Kli laughed crazily, and stopped wringing out his poor cloak. "Well done, Lucky! Why, of course, a cannon! Harold, wake up! Where's your bag? Get the cannon out!"

"Has fear completely addled your brains?" I asked, afraid that the goblin really had gone insane after our dip in the river. "What cannon?"

"You know the one." And without explaining anything, Kli-Kli bounded across to where I had dropped my bag, tipped everything out of it onto the ground, and started rummaging through the magic vials.

"There it is!"

Kli-Kli raised the vial, full of dark cherry-red liquid with golden sparks floating in it, above his head and then dashed it against the ground. And almost immediately an absolutely genuine gnomish cannon appeared out of thin air.

"Piffling pokers!" Deler exclaimed, gaping wide-eyed.

Hallas was struck speechless. He stood there like a statue, with his mouth wide open and his eyes staring out of his head. Someone standing behind me drew in a noisy breath through clenched teeth. And I must admit that I was pretty stunned as well.

After the hard journey and all the misfortunes we had suffered, I had completely forgotten about the minor spot of trouble I'd had at Stalkon's palace, when Kli-Kli stole a vial just like this one from me and smashed it against a cannon belonging to some gnomes, which immediately disappeared, just as it was supposed to do. The furious gnomes had almost torn the jester into a thousand tiny little green pieces for using the carrying spell on their beloved treasure. Break a vial like that on any object, and it disappears; break another one, and it reappears.

I'd been planning to use that spell at Hrad Spein, in case we discovered incalculable riches, but fate had decreed otherwise, and instead of emeralds we had a weapon.

"Hallas, come on!" The goblin's voice roused Lucky from his stupefied contemplation of one of the gnomes' greatest secrets, and he dashed across to the gun: "Is it loaded?"

"It looks as if it is."

"I'll just check. . . . Yes, everything's in order! Deler, Honeycomb! Give me a hand!"

The three of them started turning the cannon in the direction of the approaching ferry.

"Do you have many more surprises like that up your sleeve, my old friend?" Bass asked rather nervously.

I didn't answer; my attention was focused entirely on Hallas. He was hastily lighting up his pipe and at the same time giving instructions to Deler and Honeycomb.

"We need a small aiming point offset! An offset! Do you know what an offset is, you dunderhead?"

"I'll show you later who's the dunderhead!" panted the dwarf, red-faced from the effort of trying to shift the cannon a few more inches.

"Stop! Everybody get back, let the master get to work."

"Do you actually know how to work this thing?" Marmot asked anxiously.

"I'm a gnome, and gunpowder flows through our veins!" said Hallas, screwing up one eye as he peered at the ferry.

"Remember, you've only got one shot."

"Don't put me off, Kli-Kli!" the gnome growled. "Everybody plug your ears."

I quickly followed his advice. Hallas raised his burning pipe to an opening in the cannon, ran back, stuck his index fingers into his ears, and watched.

A bluish gray haze rose from the barrel.

BOOM!

The cannon was shrouded in a pall of stinking bluish smoke and it jerked backward sharply. There was a whistling sound in the air, and then, at the spot where the ferry was, a column of fire and smoke hissed up into the air, mingled with water, men, horses, planks of wood . . .

We heard the sound: *Cra-a-ash!*

"Bull's-eye!" the gnome exclaimed. "I hit them! I hit them!"

"Ye-e-es!" Kli-Kli yelled. "How about that?"

All that was left of the ferry and the people on it was rubbish floating on the water.

The count's men on the opposite bank were also looking at the spot where their friends on the ferry had been just a few moments ago. Then several of the horsemen consulted, and the entire cavalcade turned and galloped rapidly away from the riverbank.

"If I just had another ball," said Hallas, stroking the side of the cannon affectionately.

"Where are they off to?" asked Lamplighter.

"To look for a ford, where else?" Honeycomb said, and spat.

"There are twenty-eight of them," said Ell, unstringing his bow.

"Right, so it's time we were leaving. . . ."

"They won't get across here," said Miralissa, shaking her head as she gazed after the horsemen. "The Iselina is too broad and deep at this point. It's more than forty leagues to the nearest ford."

I started wringing out my shirt. The wet clothes clinging to my body felt cold and clammy.

"Honeycomb," Alistan said with a glance at the smooth, settled surface of the river. "Take command. . . . You're the sergeant now."

How could he be a sergeant, with only six men of the Wild Hearts platoon left?

"Maybe they got out further downstream?" Honeycomb asked wearily. Like everyone else, the warrior was looking at the water.

"They couldn't have got out," Eel said gloomily. "I leapt into the water straight after Harold. Uncle didn't have enough time, he was right in the middle of the ferry, with the horses. And Arnkh . . . He was wearing chain mail, and plenty of other metal. . . . Even if he did jump, he sank like a stone. . . ."

There was a somber silence. How would we manage now without our staid, gray-haired Uncle and the man from the Borderland, with his gleaming bald patch? We couldn't believe they were gone.

"May they dwell in the light," Deler said in a dull voice, taking off his hat.

Kli-Kli was sniffing and rubbing his eyes, trying to hide his tears.

We left an hour later, after the Wild Hearts had held the rites for their fallen comrades and Hallas had buried the cannon. The gnome had insisted, saying that his people's greatest secret must not fall into alien hands.

We were all feeling gloomy and depressed, which is hardly surprising. We set out, moving away from the Iselina, which would always be the Black River for us.

11

THE SOULLESS ONE

All the following week we drove our horses hard to the southeast, moving ever closer to the Borderland, the area adjoining the Border Kingdom and Zagraba.

An undulating, hilly plain extended for tens of leagues around us, crisscrossed with narrow rivers, loud-running brooks, and sparse mixed forest. There were not many villages in the area; during the last two days we had only seen one, and we gave it a wide berth, not wishing to make our presence known to the locals.

The earth in these parts was fertile and rich, and the grass reached up for the sun. But there were few people who wished to cross the Iselina and settle this part of the kingdom. Just ahead of us lay the Borderland, and beyond that the eastern forests of Zagraba and the famous Golden Forest, where the orcs lived.

Alistan kept veering more and more to the southeast, avoiding the trading routes running between Valiostr and the Border Kingdom. As I understood it, he was hoping to get us to the border between the two states in a week, and then take our group in a straight line from there to the Forests of Zagraba.

All the packhorses had been killed on the ferry, which had taken our provisions and our armor to the bottom of the river. Hallas and Deler bewailed their loss for a long time, but of course there was nothing to be done. We only had the chain mail that had been on the horses that had crossed on the first trip, and the elves had kept their armor, with the crest of their houses engraved on the chests.

Marmot and Lamplighter had been left without any kind of armor at all, apart from their jackets of stone-washed leather with metal plates sewn onto them. The provisions, spare clothing, and much else besides had been left behind forever at the bottom of the river. But we did not go hungry; there was plenty of game in these parts, and there was always meat roasting on our fire.

On the fourth day after the ill-starred crossing of the Iselina, the weather finally turned bad and the rain came lashing down. It tormented us for seven whole days, and I had to wrap myself in a cloak kindly lent to me by Egrassa.

The continuous rain poured down from the low, gray clouds, and the conditions were always damp, cold, and vile. It was especially hard getting up in the morning and lighting the fire. Our arms and legs were stiff; it felt as if we had been sleeping on snow and not on grass, with a cloak of waterproof drokr to keep off the interminable rain falling from the sky. Kli-Kli caught a cold and he coughed and sniffled all the time. Marmot treated him with herbal concoctions, which made the goblin spit and gag, saying that he'd never tasted anything so bitter in all his life.

The rain just kept pouring down.

The ground turned into a huge lake of mud, and every now and then the horses slipped and stumbled in this mush, threatening to throw their riders to the ground. The dozens of tinkling brooks and little rivers that crisscrossed the terrain all swelled up and overflowed their banks. On low-lying land there was genuine flooding, and sometimes the water was as high as our stirrups, so that we had to search for a long time to find an elevation above the plain where we could make camp for the night.

It was only after the heavy downpour stopped that the water started to recede a little, but the rain was still sprinkling down. When we approached the Borderland, Alistan gave orders for everyone to put on their chain mail. I couldn't stand any kind of metal garments—they made me feel like I was in a coffin—they were so cramped and heavy, and they made it so uncomfortable to move. But in this particular case there were no objections raised on my side—I really didn't want to take an arrow in the stomach from an orc who happened to have wandered far from Zagraba. When Kli-Kli saw me putting on the mail, he nodded approvingly.

"Kli-Kli, I thought you told me you didn't need chain mail, because you're such a small target that you're hard to hit," I teased him, remembering how the goblin's armor had almost dragged me down to the bottom of the river.

He looked out at me from under his hood and said: "I may be small, but I still have to look after my health. I got it 'specially in Ranneng . . ."

Just when does this little weasel manage to get everything done?

Bass didn't have any chain mail. During the last few days, he had been as dour as the sky above our heads. The rain was no help to Snoop's state of mind, and I could understand how he must be feeling. Being dragged off to someplace you don't even know about with a tight-lipped elf riding beside you is very definitely bad for the nerves. Ell was still following my former friend about all the time, and I couldn't spot a single spark of sympathy in those yellow eyes.

My former friend . . .

Yes, I suppose that's how it was.

There was no friendship left between us. Yes, we were still bound by a great many things, but these things were only memories, no more than that. During the time when we had not seen each other, Bass and I had both changed a great deal. We had followed different paths through life. And I still hadn't forgiven him for that trick he had pulled so long ago, when he ran off, leaving me and For, stealing the money that belonged to all of us.

Kli-Kli with his cold was not the only one who had a hard time because of the rain. Hallas's pipe refused to light, and the gnome was absolutely furious with the whole wide world. Deler huddled up under his short green cloak, muttering the ancient songs of the dwarves to himself. This really drove Hallas wild, but the weather was not conducive to arguing, and the gnome just grunted irritably and made yet another unsuccessful attempt to light his pipe.

Honeycomb was now the Wild Hearts' commander, and his mind seemed to be roaming somewhere very far away. The yellow-haired giant's eyes had acquired a thoughtful, weary look. He had been too close a friend of Uncle's and simply could not accept that he was gone. Alistan paid no attention to anything at all, he just looked straight ahead and drove his battle horse on toward Zagraba. Egrassa and Marmot stopped the squad often in order to ride back and check if there were any pursuers. But the horizon was empty, and when the elf and the soldier returned they shook their heads.

When the rain took a short break, everybody cheered up a bit. Even the horses seemed to start moving more quickly and easily, taking no notice of the clouds that had still not dispersed. But sunshine was no more than a distant dream.

It wasn't long before we saw a pillar on one of the lower hills that was overgrown right to the top with tall coarse grass. It was made out of black basalt, but not even that had saved it from the ravages of time. As far as we could tell, the pillar must have been set up at least a thousand years earlier.

"The Borderland," Milord Alistan announced, and urged his horse on again.

The Borderland was an immense territory where the land belonged to the border barons. This was where my new friend Baron Oro Gabsbarg lived—the one who had invited me to drop in to see him.

During one of the halts, when everyone was busy with his own business, I went up to Miralissa, who was sitting all alone beside the spluttering fire, and asked the question that had been bothering me for almost two weeks: "How did they manage to find us, Lady Miralissa?"

She understood immediately who I was asking about.

"I don't know, Harold. Recently there have been many things that I don't know. They shouldn't have been able to find us so quickly, I put up defenses. . . ." She sighed. "Perhaps that woman can sense the Key."

I immediately felt like tearing the artifact off my neck.

"Or perhaps that has nothing to do with it, and there is some other sign that they use to track us."

There was another question I was very curious about.

"Was the thing that hit the ferry Kronk-a-Mor?"

"Yes, the ogres' most dangerous magic, and now a human being has control of it. But Lafresa doesn't have the experience of the Nameless One, and what she created on that day should have killed her on the spot."

"But it didn't kill her."

"No. The House of Power is capable of defending its servants," said Miralissa, looking hard at me.

"I'm sorry, I don't understand," I said, shaking my head. "The House of Power is no more than an empty phrase to me. Isn't it time to stop playing at riddles?"

"The time for answers has not yet come, Dancer in the Shadows," said the goblin, who had crept up behind me unnoticed.

"I'm afraid that when the time does come, it will be too late, fool," I replied rather angrily. "I'm sick of mysteries! I'm sick of my dreams!"

"You are the Dancer in the Shadows, and that is why you have these dreams."

"Just at the moment you're not much like a royal jester, more like a fat priest spouting sacred nonsense to fleece the worshipers of a few more coins."

"What do you want to know, Harold?" Kli-Kli sighed, sitting down beside me.

"Everything."

"A praiseworthy aspiration," the goblin giggled. "But what's impossible is impossible. It's good that you're no longer a child and I think you're capable of understanding. . . . I'll tell you about the Four Great Houses and the Creation. This story was told to me by my grandfather. We goblins remember things that the orcs and the elves have forgotten; we remember things that you humans never even knew."

"Yet another goblin fairy tale?" I asked him rather churlishly.

"A fairy tale? I suppose so. But you've got nothing against that, have you? I thought not. Where should I begin? When the world was young . . . No, not like that. . . . When Siala did not yet even exist, when even the gods were carefree children, and no one had ever heard of ogres, only one world existed throughout the entire universe. Now it is called the World of Chaos. It was the First, the Primal World, and in it there lived—" The jester hesitated for a moment. "—people, probably. One day, one of them discovered a secret—that creatures were living in the shadows of their world, even if they were rather different. The shadows were the seeds, the prototypes of other universes. And if a man knew how to control them, that is, if he could 'dance' with them, he could take any shadow in Chaos and build a new world. His own world. Or at least, he could try to build it—it might not work out too well for everyone. Not everybody was capable of doing this, only one in a hundred million, or perhaps two hundred million, but in those hoary old times there were a lot more of them than now. Those who were capable of creating worlds out of shadows came to be known as Dancers in the Shadows."

I shuddered.

"Are you trying to tell me that I can take any shadow and make something like Siala out of thin air?"

"You can deny it if you like, Harold, but you are the Dancer, and there's no way you can get away from that. And as for the shadows, the answer is no, you can't. I told you. A new universe can only be created from shadows of the World of Chaos. The shadows of our world are only shadows of shadows of shadows of shadows of the Primal World. They are dead and not capable of dancing."

"But if I did end up in Chaos, then I could manage it?"

"How would I know? It's only a fairy tale, after all, and you don't know how to wander between different worlds . . ."

"And Sagot be praised for that," I said with a sigh of relief. "Carry on then, let's hear a few more lies."

"Where was I, now? Ah, yes! The Dancers took the shadows, and thousands and thousands of new worlds appeared, thanks to them. But in creating new worlds, the Dancers took away a little part of their own world, and the time came when the World of Chaos died. There were no shadows left there. It was filled with the darkness and the fire of the Elemental Time. The people left it and settled in other worlds, and the way to the Primal World was forgotten. None of the Dancers in that time tried to save the World of Chaos, although they could have done it. What for? With so many new and unusual universes all around, why bother trying to restore an old piece of junk?"

"What are you thinking about, Harold?" asked Miralissa, who had kept quiet all this time.

"About the joker who created our world. So, Kli-Kli, you say that Chaos can no longer be restored?"

"No. The way to it has been forgotten. And if there was a way to get there, you need a shadow from that world in order to breathe life into it."

I remembered the three female shadow-friends dancing on the crimson tongues of flame and asking me to save their world. I got an itchy feeling in my stomach—maybe the jester was right? Maybe there was an element of truth in his fairy tale?

"Why are you telling me all of this? I have enough trouble sleeping at night already. And just how does the House of Power fit into your story?"

"This is only the prehistory. . . . To be honest, Harold-Barold, I don't really know anything about these houses. . . . My grandfather said there were Four Great Houses, and that they were supposedly created by the Dancer who gave life to our world. But no one knows why he created these houses. The goblin books don't even hint at the reason."

"But it is mentioned in the *Annals of the Crown*," said Miralissa, joining in the conversation again. "In the very first pages of the chronicles there is a small paragraph about the houses. There were four of them, absolutely different and quite unlike each other: the House of Love, the House of Pain, the House of Fear, and, finally and most importantly, the House of Power. It is said that those who have visited them became immortal. No matter how many times you kill these people, sooner or later they are reborn in the House of Love. Someone who has been through the four houses can be killed forever only when he is in one of the houses. But I don't know which one."

"What were they created for?"

"You must understand that we know nothing for certain and can only guess. That one short paragraph in the annals, written by an unknown author, has provoked controversy among our historians for thousands of years. Entire works of scholarship have been written, based on that fragment, but how reliable are they? We only know that someone who has passed through all the Four Great Houses is no longer simply a man, an elf, or a dwarf—he is something completely different. I have no idea what they do in the Houses of Love, Pain, and Fear. The only thing we do know is that those who are in the House of Power are exceptionally powerful in magic, or rather, in its initial aspect—shamanism. And that is all I know, Harold."

"That is all you know?" I repeated like an echo. "And you hid this knowledge from me? A stupid story about how our world was supposedly created, and assumptions based on some tiny little paragraph? Is this the greatest and most terrible secret of the goblins and the elves?"

I was amused. Go into any tavern and you'd hear a better story than that. And it would sound a lot more plausible than what Kli-Kli and Miralissa had told me.

"This knowledge is very dangerous," the elfess rebuked me gently.

"Especially for certain people—when they learn that they can become even greater than the gods and create their own world."

"I beg your pardon, milady, but this is nonsense."

"I told you it was still too early and he wouldn't understand a thing," said the goblin, looking reproachfully at the elfess. "The Order would pay us a wagonload of gold for the story that we've just told you."

"That does not speak well for the wizards," I said.

"Pah, you fool," the jester said irritably, and walked away.

I thought he was reacting a bit too sensitively to my skepticism.

"Perhaps you will understand some time later, Harold," Miralissa sighed, also standing up.

"Wait," I said to her. "Why did you think that I might know something about the House of Power?"

"You are the Dancer in the Shadows. . . . But take no notice, I made a mistake."

"And the Master? Why did you decide that the Master is in this House of Power?"

"He has a distinctive magical signature. . . . You would not understand that, Harold, you have no skills in shamanism. The things that attacked us in Hargan's Wasteland, the thing that struck the ferry . . . They are quite different, nothing like our magic . . . Things like that can only be created with the help of the legendary and mythical House of Power."

She walked away, treading gently on the soaking wet grass, and I was left alone.

To think.

After what the elfess and the goblin had told me, there were even more riddles, not fewer.

Ranneng was awash with flowers. Sweet-scented roses of every possible color had invaded the entire town. The festival was in its second noisy day, and those who could still stand had spilled out into the streets, bawling out songs and dancing together in circles, gorging themselves on the free food laid out on tables and washing it down with the wine or beer that gushed out of huge barrels in torrents. It had always been this way and it always would be. Once a year, at the end of August, all the people glorified the gods.

Voices singing and yelling, the laughter and the music, the smells of wine, fine fresh bread and roasted meat—it all mingled together into an atmosphere of vital festive joy.

Djok Imargo was walking down the street with a smile on his face.

He was a tall young man with broad shoulders and a firm jaw, brown eyes, absolutely black hair, and a mischievous smile. He radiated a feeling of calm confidence and high spirits.

People recognized him and waved to him, they shouted to him, inviting him to join one group or another, to drink a mug of beer or take a turn in some antic dance. It was hard not to notice him—tall and well-built, with a quiver of arrows on his hip and a powerful two-yard bow in his hands. Who did not know Djok Imargo, everybody's favorite, the champion bowman at the last four royal tournaments?

"Hey, Djok, come over here!"

"Djok, dance with me! Oh, Djok!"

"Djok, it's the royal tournament today! Good luck."

"Hey, Djok! Let's have a beer!"

"Five in a row, Djok!"

He smiled, nodded, waved his hand in response to the greetings, but he didn't stop. Right now he wasn't really interested in mugs of beer with foaming heads, or accommodating young beauties. At five o'clock today, he would become the champion archer for the fifth time, and only then would he be able to relax and celebrate his success.

It was still too early as yet—the tournament was not due to begin until after midday, and the archery contest was supposed to take place before the final jousts between the knights, just after the general combat and the swordsmen's competition. Djok still had time to spare, and at the moment he was following the call of his heart.

The Street of Fruits was as crowded as every other part of town. People called to him a few times and slapped him on the shoulders, but he politely refused their invitations.

Djok stopped outside a large shop trading in fruits and vegetables, then pushed open the door and went inside. The bell jingled in greeting to let the owner know that he had a new customer. But then, it was a holiday, and no one was actually selling anything. The center of the room was occupied by a table, with people sitting round it and drinking beer.

"Ah, Djok, my boy!" said one of the men at the table, waving in greet-

ing. "How good to see you! Come on in, don't be shy. Someone pour the lad a beer."

"Thank you, Master Lotr, but not just now. I have to keep a clear head today."

The shopkeeper clapped a hand to his forehead.

"And I forgot, what a memory! Well then, my boy, will you show them all again?"

"I'll try my best," Djok replied.

"Plant one in the bull's-eye for me," said the scrawny Lotr, handing Djok a peach.

"It'll be tough for you today, lad," croaked the innkeeper whose establishment was next door to Master Lotr's shop. "With a challenger like that!"

"Don't talk nonsense, pudding head. Where will they find anyone to challenge Djok Imargo?" asked Lotr, raising his mug of beer.

"Nowhere, among the men, but the elves, now . . . I wouldn't put my gold piece on Djok, begging your pardon, lad. . . ."

"What are you talking about, may the gods save you? What elves?" Lotr chuckled.

"The usual kind. Perfectly ordinary dark elves, with fangs. They fire bows much better than men do."

"But what have elves got to do with the tournament, darkness take you!" the owner of a meat shop put in.

"You mean you still haven't heard? Don't you know that there's a legation of dark elves arriving today to see the king, from the House of the . . . what is it now . . . the House of the Black Rose, that's it. And who's leading the legation? The crown prince of that house, with a name darkness only knows how to pronounce. And this crown prince has expressed a wish to take part in the tournament; to be precise, in the archery competition. And that's why you'll have a tough time of it, ay, lad. You won't find an elf that easy to beat."

"We'll see," Djok said with an indifferent shrug. He didn't really believe in the rumors going round the town. "Master Lotr, where's Lia?"

"In the garden. Go and see her," the girl's father replied amiably.

When Djok left, the innkeeper grinned and said: "Did you see how upset he was when I told him about the elf?"

"Ah, nonsense. Djok's a good lad, he wasn't upset at all."

"You know best, Lotr. It's your daughter he's chasing, not mine." The innkeeper chuckled, getting up from the table. The fat man had nothing more to *do here, he had said what he had been told to say, and the Master would be pleased with him.*

Lotr had the reputation of being a rich shopkeeper. Selling fruit had proved a profitable trade; he supplied his goods to the tables of many noblemen in the capital, even to the king's. The money poured in, and there was nothing strange about the fact that the inner yard of the shop had been transformed into a flower garden with three gently murmuring fountains. A girl was sitting on a bench beside one of them.

She was busy with her embroidery, and a bloodred poppy and a sky blue harebell had already blossomed on the white fabric. A boy about seven years old was sitting beside the girl. He was launching a little boat into the fountain.

"Lia?" Djok called.

She looked up from her task, smiling the smile that he loved so much.

"Djok! How glad I am to see you!"

"Surely you didn't think I'd forgotten you?" he asked.

"No, but the royal tournament is today, and you have to be there."

"Your eyes are worth more to me than any tournament."

Lia lowered her gaze modestly and smiled. Then she put down her embroidery, got to her feet gracefully, and took a strawberry out of a huge dish of fruit.

"Do you want it?"

"Thank you, your father gave me a peach." He showed her the succulent fruit with its velvety skin.

"A pity, it's very good," said the girl, taking a bite out of the ripe strawberry.

"I'm going to win this tournament for you, Lia," Djok said, sitting down with her little brother, who was completely absorbed in playing with his boats.

"Ah, Djok! But haven't you heard what they say about the elf?"

"I've heard. But elf or no elf, I'm going to win this tournament for you. Everyone in the town knows that Lotr's daughter Lia is the most beautiful girl in Ranneng. No prince is going to put my arrow off its mark!"

Lia picked a flower from one of the beds and started pulling off its petals.

"What are you doing?"

"Fortune-telling. To see if you're going to win today."

"That's nothing but a flower."

"You're right," she said with a sigh. "I'm so nervous. Let's not trust a stupid little flower. Lun, Lun, come here!"

"What is it?" Lia's brother asked in annoyance, looking up from his game.

"Come over here quickly, Djok's going to show us how he fires his bow."

The little boy immediately abandoned his game and ran across to them.

"Here's an apple. You see that statue of a soldier right down at the end of the garden? Put the apple on his spear and run back here."

"Just a moment," said Lun, running off to do as his sister asked.

"What are you doing?" the young bowman asked in surprise.

"I made a wish—if you hit that apple, it means you're going to win the royal tournament."

"It's a lot closer than the target at the field will be," said Djok, shaking his head.

"Oh, please! Do it for me!" Lia begged him.

Djok smiled and nodded. He put on his glove, set the string on his mighty bow, and took an arrow out of the quiver. The flights were purple with gold stripes. Everybody knew what Djok Imargo's arrows looked like. Lun came running back, leaving the apple behind, a green spot on the end of the statue's spear.

Djok set his arrow on the string, pulled the string back smoothly, held his breath, and released the string just as gently. It slapped loudly against his glove and the arrow took off with a furious buzz. A second later it split the apple in two and disappeared into the garden.

"Hooray," Lun cried merrily, jumping up and down.

"Ah, well done!" cried Lia, clapping her hands happily. "You're going to win that tournament. You're bound to! Where are you going?"

"To get the arrow."

"Wait!" She grabbed hold of his hand, stood up on tiptoe, and whispered, "Leave it. I'll give it back to you later."

He gave her a look of joyful surprise. Lia smiled, kissed him on the cheek, and cooed: "And now go! We'll celebrate your victory tonight."

He was going to say something else to her, but the girl put her finger to his lips, smiled enchantingly once again, and walked to the fountain without looking back. Djok hesitated for a moment and left the garden. It was time for him to prepare for the tournament, and Lia was expecting him to win.

The girl waited for five minutes, then walked down the garden. She pulled up the arrow that was stuck in the ground and examined it carefully.

Excellent. Lun was busy with his little boat, her father was with his friends, nobody would miss her for a while.

She had to get the arrow to a certain person as quickly as possible, and then there would be a reward waiting for her from the Master. She smiled the smile that Djok loved so much.

"What do you make of this town, Eroch?" Endargassa asked.

"A barbarous place, Tresh Endargassa," the elderly guard riding beside the prince replied deferentially.

Eroch was an elf of the old school, and his attitude toward humans was highly disdainful. Endargassa did not agree with his old friend and k'lissang. The houses of the dark elves had to maintain relations with humans. No matter how strange, uncultured, aggressive, and treacherous people were—they had power, and only their warriors, acting together with the elves, were capable of annihilating the orcs.

And this was why the leaders of the nine dark houses had taken counsel together and decided that the time had come to unite the forces of men and elves into a single army to oppose those who dared to call themselves the Firstborn. This was why the eldest son of the head of the House of the Black Rose had come to Valiostr with a formal missive for the king. This was why Endargassa's younger brother had been sent on a similar mission to the Border Kingdom.

"You are wrong, Eroch; men hold power, and without them we will never finally deal with our cousins." This was not the first time that Endargassa had begun this conversation.

"Perhaps they do hold power, Tresh Endargassa, but men are avaricious, cruel, and very dangerous. We will deal with the orcs without their help."

"Thousands of years of war with the Firstborn prove that this is not true, my friend Eroch. We are equally matched, and nobody can gain the upper hand. The army of men is the force that can alter the course of centuries of war in our favor."

"Men fight in ranks, they have cavalry, they are not accustomed to fighting in the forest. Or at least, most of them are not."

"Then we shall have to drive the orcs out of the forest," Endargassa said with an indifferent shrug.

"Before he sent us on our way, your father should have remembered 'The Legend of Soft Gold,'" Eroch sighed.

"'*Best defend your own house yourself*'?" the prince cited. "*Of course, I remember that. But that is only a song. And the events in it never really happened.*"

"*Of course, Tresh Endargassa, of course. But the legend expresses the wise lesson that one should not trust men. Otherwise after the orcs they will set about us.*"

Endargassa merely grinned. Eroch was certainly no great supporter of an alliance with men.

"*Men can be dangerous. And you haven't even put on your armor!*" The bodyguard's words had a reproachful ring to them.

Endargassa was dressed in a light silk shirt with a black rose embroidered on the chest, and he certainly looked vulnerable among his forty-nine-warrior escort, with their glinting armor of bluish metal.

"*If you wish to swelter in a case of iron in this heat—that is your business,*" said Endargassa. "*And then you are here with me, so what could possibly happen?*"

Eroch did not say anything, he just assumed an even more somber expression and glanced around with his yellow eyes at the human crowd that had lined the streets in order to gaze at the honored guests.

"*And here is the reception party,*" said Endargassa when he saw a group of twenty horsemen clad in heavy armor galloping toward his party.

"*Tresh Endargassa, in the name of our glorious King Stalkon of the Broken Heart, I am happy to welcome you and your companions to the capital of Valiostr!*" declared a horseman in white and green armor. "*I am Count Pelan Gelmi, captain of the royal guard, and I have been instructed to escort you to the royal palace.*"

"*Very well,*" said the elf with a nod. "*We will follow you, Milord Gelmi.*"

The knight nodded, and they rode on. The horsemen parted the festive crowd, making way for the honored guest. Milord Gelmi reined back his horse and rode alongside the prince.

"*As you may have noticed, Tresh Endargassa, today is a holiday in our town, that is why the streets are so full of people.*"

"*And I thought they had all come out to welcome me,*" the elf jested.

"*Naturally, that as well,*" Milord Gelmi replied, embarrassed. "*Are you aware that today is the annual royal tournament? His Majesty has invited you to join him in the royal box.*"

"*Most certainly.*"

"At the end of the tournament our bowmen will try their skill. They say you are a fine shot, Tresh Endargassa. Would you care to join the contest?"

"No, thank you," said the prince, with his features set in a faint smile. "I think that would not be entirely honor—"

There was a sudden movement in the air, and an arrow struck Endargassa in the neck. The elf swayed, clutched at his throat, gasped, and fell from his steed onto the street.

The dark elves grabbed their s'kashes, the men clutched their swords, the crowd scattered wildly, trampling each other underfoot, someone dashed to the body, hoping to stop the blood, but it was already too late. Endargassa, the crown prince of the House of the Black Rose, was dead.

"The marksman's on the roof," someone shouted.

"Men will answer for the death of my lord!" roared Eroch, holding the body of his prince tight against himself.

Count Pelan Gelmi was pale-faced and frightened. He was surrounded by fifty grim and furious dark elves, who had just lost their noble kinsman.

We have to act, or swords will be drawn! he thought.

"Chuch! Cut off the street! Brakès, gallop to the king with the news. Darkness, find that marksman! Paru, summon the entire guard here! Don't just stand there! Do something!"

The men went dashing off to carry out their orders; the count dismounted and leaned down over the dead elf. Eroch was kneeling in the puddle of blood, with his s'kash lying beside him. He had broken the arrow and pulled it out of Endargassa's neck, and the two harmless pieces were lying in the blood.

"If you do not find the assassin, we shall take our own revenge for the death of Tresh Endargassa," Eroch said with bitter hatred.

The count picked up the pieces of the arrow, getting bloodstains on his expensive formal gloves.

"Chuch!"

"Yes, milord." One of the knight's men rode up and reined in his horse.

"Do you recognize that?" the count asked the lieutenant of the guard, sticking a piece of the arrow under his nose.

"Ye-es . . ." Chuch was just as surprised as the count. "That arrow . . ."

"I think we shall catch your lord's killer within the hour," Lord Gelmi interrupted, turning to Eroch.

"We will wait . . . for an hour."

———

There was still at least an hour to go until the beginning of the royal tournament, but Djok was already hurrying on his way to the field where the main competitions were due to be held. For one thing, he was curious to find out who would compete in the general combat, and for another, he needed to prepare—check the wind and inspect the area where all the competitions would take place.

There was something wrong as he walked along the street leading to the field, but Djok couldn't work out what it was. Then he realized—it was the people! There were far too few of them for the day of the royal tournament! For some reason there were no townsfolk hurrying to take their seats on the benches.

Everybody was discussing something that had happened near the Muddy Gates. Apparently one of the elves had been killed, but Djok didn't give it a thought, he was completely focused on the victory he was going to win and not concerned about anything else. For the last hour all the bowman had seen in his mind's eye was the red and white target with the bull's-eye into which he had to plant at least eight arrows.

Djok walked the final hundred paces to the end of the street and the beginning of the tournament grounds completely alone. Everybody seemed to have vanished into thin air. There was not a soul to be seen, apart from some soldiers of the royal guard standing ahead of him. Djok frowned. Firstly, what were these guardsmen doing here, when usually the municipal guard was used? And secondly, there were far more soldiers than necessary.

There were at least twenty men on foot, half of them with lances and half with crossbows. And ten men on horseback, all in full armor and looking very belligerent. Djok assumed that the knight in white and green armor was in command; at least his armor was the most finely finished.

The men waited in silence as he approached without speaking and no one moved. Djok slowed down and gasped—the tournament flags and the blue and gray royal banner had been lowered to half-mast.

"Has the king died, then?" he muttered in amazement.

That certainly would explain why there had been no one hurrying to the tournament and why the people had looked so worried and frightened.

The guardsmen's faces were dour and tense. Djok walked up to the men who were blocking his path and turned to one soldier with whom he had drunk beer a few times: "Tramur, what's going on?"

"Well, just look, he's come to us!" the soldier said with a crooked grin, taking a tighter grip on his lance. "Drop that bow, you vermin!"

"What?" said Djok, startled. He glanced at the knight in white and green, but the knight didn't speak.

Tramur struck Djok in the stomach with the handle of his lance. The young man doubled over in pain and dropped his bow. Tears sprang to his eyes and he was completely winded.

The second blow landed on his neck, and the surface of the road swayed, then leapt up and hit him hard in the face. His mouth filled up with blood, his head was full of swirling fog, he tried to get up and ask why they were beating him, but someone kicked him under the ribs and he collapsed back onto the stones of the road.

They beat him for a long time in silence. He tried to protect his head with his hands and curled up like a baby in its mother's womb, but he couldn't get away from the blows, there was nowhere to hide. The blows just kept on showering down. Powerful, painful, desperate.

The archer could no longer taste the blood in his mouth, there was too much of it. The noise in his ears was turning thick and dull, like a muddy swamp. Eventually somebody's voice roared: "That's enough! Enough, I say! The elves don't want a dead man."

Djok didn't hear any more after that. He dove into the shelter of oblivion.

He spent the next few days in a foggy daze, waking up in a narrow cell, a genuine stone box, where three men with bored faces, wearing the emblem of the Royal Sandmen, asked him strange, frightening questions.

At first Djok tried to explain, to tell them that he was innocent, but then the beatings started again. Nobody wanted to listen to him.

All the Sandmen wanted was confession, otherwise the dark elves, who were insane with fury, would turn the kingdom into a bloodbath. And then the tortures began. He broke down at the third session and confessed to all the outrages that they attributed to him. He no longer cared what happened to him, just as long as they left him in peace for at least a little while.

Djok's face had been smashed into a bloody pulp, his nose was broken in several places, his fingers had been shattered and his ribs broken and he was covered all over in bruises and cuts. He could barely even move when they *tossed him onto the urine-soaked straw in his cell; all he could do was breathe and whine and go to sleep.*

Sometimes the door of the cell would open and he would have visitors. At those moments he groaned quietly and pitifully, because they started beating him again. Then oblivion returned and for more than a week he was on the brink of death.

But they did not let him die. A magician of the Order helped to bring him back out of the dark.

Djok often had dreams. He was asleep and dreaming, somewhere far, far away from the stone box that some evildoer had had him thrown into. The archer hardly remembered any of his dreams, except for one. . . .

In this dream a guard came and opened the door of the cell and said with a cheerful smile that he knew Djok was innocent and the crime had been committed by the servants of the Master. The Master was waiting. . . . After that Djok wept and squirmed about on his straw. And then he fell asleep again.

Afterward there was a very hasty trial, which he could hardly even remember. Just bright light in his eyes, the pale blobs of lots of faces, and voices talking. They asked him about something and he answered. . . . One man showed the tall judge his quiver of arrows and then took out an arrow that was broken and covered in dried blood.

"I'm not guilty," Djok whispered. But no one listened to him and the clerk of the court scraped his pen across his paper. "It was the servants of the Master. . . ."

The court questioned Lotr, who was red-faced and sweaty, and so frightened that he stammered as he looked around and spoke. Yes, Djok was at my house that day. . . . Yes, he was upset when he heard that the elfin prince, may he dwell in the light, wanted to take part in the tournament. . . . Yes, there was something about the look in his eyes. . . . Why didn't I notice that immediately, old fool that I am?

And there were other people, too. . . . Friends, acquaintances, relatives . . . Yes, he had wanted to win. . . . Yes, he could have lost to the elf. . . . Yes, all his life he had been a vain and malicious fellow. Yes, what a terrible disgrace!

Then there was Lia. Yes, Djok had told her he would do anything to win the tournament that day. . . . He didn't listen to any more after that, he just kept on whispering one word through his broken lips: "Lia . . . Lia . . . Lia."

It was over very quickly. Everything—his signed confession, his arrow with the blood on it, the testimony from a dozen witnesses—rapidly led the Royal High Court to the only possible conclusion.

When the wooden mallet descended and the old, skinny judge in the black robe and the absurd white wig pronounced the single word, "guilty," Djok saw the elf who had sat through the whole trial as if he were made of stone look at him and smile. Djok's trousers were suddenly soaking wet—that smile frightened him far more than all the beatings he had received from men.

They did not execute him, they did something far more terrible than that— they handed him over to the dark elves. An old elf with faded yellow eyes and hair as dry as straw, the same elf who had frightened Djok so badly at the trial, took charge of him in person.

They put him on a cart with shackles on his feet and drove him out of Ranneng.

For Djok the journey to Zagraba was a single, unbroken thread of squeaking wheels, the sky above his head, the guttural voices of elves, and pain. It came every day, biting into his flesh like red-hot pincers, as soon as evening arrived and the elves halted for the night.

This was when Eroch came to the prisoner and took out a little box of steel needles. The elf never spoke, but every time after the torture, Djok thought that his time had come and he was about to die at any moment. And he waited for his death to come with joyful anticipation.

But the elves were too careful to lose their prisoner as a result of torture. When the pain became absolutely unbearable, when it threatened to expand and shatter his head open, an elfin shaman appeared and relieved his suffering. And the next evening it was repeated all over again. Day after day Djok suffered absolutely unbearable torment, dying, cursing the gods, coming back to life, weeping, and dying again. There was no end to this terrible dream. . . .

He did not remember much about Zagraba . . . green leaves, tinkling brooks, cold, and pain. . . . They took him somewhere, showed him to someone, hundreds of elfin faces with fangs, an old elf with a black coronet on his head, silence, and more pain. . . .

For some reason all the trees here grew upside down. So did the grass. And the sun set upward. The elves walked upside down on the ground with their heads downward.

For a long time he couldn't understand what was happening. He only realized the truth when he noticed that the blood oozing feebly from a cut on his cheek was falling on his forehead instead of his chin, and then dripping off onto the ground that was above his head.

It was very simple; he was hanging head down on a tree with his feet securely tied to a thick branch. How long had he been there like this? An hour? A day?

It turned dark and night came to the forest, and stars began shining through the crowns of the trees down below.

There was nobody guarding him. There was no need. He could never escape from the elfin spider web rope, and how far could a man half dead from torture run through a strange forest?

The archer plunged back into oblivion, trying to overcome the pain. He was woken by a quiet rustling in the grass, and when he opened his eyes he saw a dark female silhouette.

An elfess, he thought.

The person standing there said nothing, and neither did he. He was indifferent; he had already grown used to the fact that many elves came just to look at him. Let her look, as long as she didn't beat him. Suddenly she laughed.

"Who . . . are you?"

It was hard for him to form the words; he hadn't spoken for a long time. Most of the time he simply howled in pain.

"You poor thing," the woman sighed.

"Lia? Is that really you?" he gasped, unable to believe his ears.

"Lia? Well, you can call me that if you like," she said, walking out of the shadow into the moonlight.

She was just as beautiful as she had been in the garden, on that cursed day when the elfin prince was killed. Light brown hair, blue eyes, high cheekbones, full lips.

Lia. His Lia. The one who betrayed him.

"But . . . How?"

How could this girl be here, so far away from home, in the heart of the country of the elves?

"The servants of the Master can do much more than that."

"*The Master? I'm not guilty! I couldn't possibly have done it!*"

"*I know,*" she said with a smile.

"*You know. Then why didn't you say anything? You have to tell the elves, you have to explain to them—*"

"*It's too late. The elves won't listen to anyone, they're thirsting for vengeance. They won't try to find out if you're really guilty or not for at least a few months. But unfortunately you don't have that much time. The elves have decided to make an exception—tomorrow the Green Leaf is waiting for you.*"

Djok squirmed on his rope and started swaying like a pendulum. He sobbed in terror. He did not want to die like that.

"*But you have a choice, you fool.*" Lia walked up close to him, and he caught the scent of her strawberry perfume. "*Either the dark elves will make an example of you with a form of execution that they have only ever used on the orcs before or . . .*"

"*Or?*" Djok repeated like an echo.

"*. . . or you will become a faithful servant of the Master.*"

She spoke for a very long time, and when she finished, Djok said only a single word.

"*Yes.*"

Hatred blazed up in his eyes.

The girl took a crooked elfin knife out of the folds of her dress, stood up on tiptoe, and slit the man's throat with a gentle movement.

The hot cataract poured down onto her hair, face, neck, and dress. She stood there, accepting this terrible baptism in bloody dew . . . smiling. When it was all over, the girl looked at the body hanging in front of her and said:

"*You will be born again, born in the House of Love, and become the very first, the most devoted servant. You will be Djok the Winter-Bringer.*"

A moment later the forest glade was empty, apart from a dead man swaying slowly on a rope.

"You slept badly last night. More nightmares?" Kli-Kli asked me as he wrapped himself in his cloak against the chilly morning air.

"Yeah," I replied morosely, rolling up my blanket.

"What about this time?"

"Djok the Winter-Bringer."

"Oho! Tell me about it!" the goblin said eagerly.

"Leave me alone, Kli-Kli, I've no time for you now." After the previous day's conversation round the campfire and my new dream, I had plenty to think about.

Kli-Kli grunted in disappointment and wandered off to pester Lamplighter, who was saddling our horses.

That morning the weather turned bad again and there was a light drizzle. The drops were so fine that I could barely even see them.

At least it wasn't the kind of downpour we had had before. We were all thoroughly sick of that cursed rain. It's hard to say which is worse—stupefying heat or this kind of dank misery.

The fire had burnt out completely overnight and the fine rain had extinguished the coals left behind. There was no point in lighting a new one, it would take up far too much time. We ate a bite of the cold meat from some partridges that Ell had shot the day before and set off on our way.

The dreary plain with its low hills stretched on and on with no end in sight. The clouds and the semidarkness made us all feel very depressed. After an hour and a half of galloping, Alistan led our group out onto an old road, half washed away and barely visible under the puddles.

"There will be a village about three leagues ahead," said Ell.

"We need to lay in some stores and buy horses," Alistan Markauz said with a nod.

"If they will sell any," Ell said in a doubtful tone of voice.

"The peasants need every animal they have," Honeycomb put in.

"We'll see when we get there," said Alistan, and led the group on along the road.

We started moving more slowly, the horses' hooves slid in the mud and the puddles that were seething with rain. There was a shroud hanging over the world, and we could only see a hundred or a hundred and fifty yards ahead.

The road started going down the slope of yet another hill. Streams of water ran down past us, flowing into an immense puddle, where it looked as if we might have to swim again—the horses were up to their knees in water. We lost our way because we couldn't see the road and found ourselves at an old, flooded graveyard.

The tops of the monuments on the graves stuck up out of the water like little islands. We rode past them, trying to make the horses follow each other so that, Sagot forbid, they wouldn't fall into some deep pit that could easily be concealed under the layer of water.

"Now where have we got to?" Honeycomb asked gloomily, talking to himself.

"The land of the dead, can't you see?" muttered Hallas, who didn't understand that some questions are simply rhetorical.

"What would a graveyard be doing in a place like this, one that gets flooded?" asked Honeycomb, casting an indifferent glance at a half-submerged coffin floating past us: It had obviously been washed out of a recent shallow grave.

"The village is near now," replied Marmot, adjusting the edge of his hood to protect Invincible from the rain.

"The sooner the better," said Deler, whose hat had long ago been reduced to a shapeless, sodden mass. "I want to be inside, in the warm, with a fire and mulled wine and a warm bed and all the pleasures of life."

"I don't think we'll be able to find you an inn out here in the back of beyond. Be grateful if they let us spend the night in the barn," Marmot replied, wiping the drops of rain off his face.

"This rain's set in to last for the rest of the day," Bass said in a hoarse voice, trying to get his horse to walk alongside Little Bee.

"Do you want to end up in a grave? Either get back or move up," I told him.

He gave me an angry glance from under his hood and reined back his horse.

The graveyard ended as suddenly as it had begun. Something that looked like a road appeared from under the water, rising up to the top of the next hill.

I took an instant dislike to the village—about fifty low wooden houses standing along the wall of a black forest of fir trees. Soaking wet fields that had been cleared and turned, thick mud in the streets, smoke from the stove chimneys hanging over the roofs, and the rain into the bargain.

A boy walking toward us with a bucket dropped it into the mud when he saw our group, and ran off, howling. Bass swore through his teeth, apparently not realizing that armed men on horseback suddenly appearing from behind a curtain of rain might be enough to frighten a grown man, let alone a ten-year-old boy.

When we reached the center of the village, all the locals were sheltering from the rain and the street was deserted. The raindrops trickled down the roofs, drummed on our hoods, splashed in the puddles. We were surrounded by their quiet whispering. A big hefty man with an ax came out of one house and looked at us in alarm.

"What is the name of this village?" Honeycomb asked him.

"Upper Otters," the peasant replied glumly, toying nervously with his ax. "We don't want any trouble."

"You won't have any. Is there an inn in the village?"

"Straight on, about two hundred yards. The gray house with the sign. You can't miss it."

Honeycomb gave the man a nod of thanks and set his horse moving. We rode in the direction the man had indicated. I couldn't resist glancing back, but the peasant with the ax had already disappeared.

The inn was as dreary and unprepossessing as all the other houses in Upper Otters. There was a tin signplate hanging above the door, but I couldn't make out what was written on it—it was too old, the paint had worn off ages ago, and the innkeeper hadn't bothered to paint it again.

"Wait here," said Alistan Markauz, jumping down into the mud and holding out his reins to Marmot. "Let's go, Honeycomb."

They went into the house, leaving us outside, soaking in the rain. Deler was groaning, dreaming about a hot fire and hot food. Hallas asked the dwarf to be quiet in a most unusually polite manner.

Alistan and Honeycomb came back out looking glum and angry.

"The inn's closed, we can't spend the night here. Nobody in the village sells anything, especially not horses. They have less than a dozen of them."

"And if we insist?" Egrassa inquired.

"I think, my cousin, that that is not a good way to win the love of men," Miralissa replied to the elf.

Egrassa's face made it clear what he thought of the love of men.

"But will they let us in for the night or not?" Bass interrupted. "I'm sick to death of this rain!"

"We're all sick of the rain," Honeycomb boomed as he mounted his horse. "Milord Alistan, perhaps we could try to find a place in the houses? Someone might agree to take us in for five pieces of gold?"

"It's not worth the risk. The innkeeper said these are Balistan Pargaid's lands."

Marmot swore out loud.

"Let's get out of here."

But before we had gone a hundred yards, the street was blocked off by a crowd. A surly, angry, silent crowd. Almost all the inhabitants of the village were there, and many of them were holding pitchforks, axes, scythes, flails, or clubs.

"Oi!" the jester squealed quietly.

I immediately looked back—the road was blocked off by two wagons. Very smart.

"What is the problem?" Alistan Markauz shouted.

The man we had seen with the ax stepped forward out of the crowd.

"We don't want any trouble!"

"We are leaving the village, let us through!"

"Gladly, but first throw down your weapons and give us the horses!"

"What!" roared Hallas, waving his mattock in the air. "No gnome hands over his weapon to a pack of mangy, stinking peasants. Never!"

The crowd began buzzing threateningly and moving toward us.

"We'll break through," said Alistan Markauz, striking his horse on the hindquarters with the flat of his sword.

The massive warhorse bounded forward at the men and flattened the ones who were at the front. The sword flashed, repulsing a blow from a flail. The peasants howled and ran in all directions.

I set Little Bee moving forward, trying not to fall behind the others. Our group sliced through the peasants like a hot knife through butter. Those who were too slow to jump aside were trampled.

One lad there almost managed to stick a pitchfork in my side. But Hallas split his head open with his mattock before I even had time to feel afraid. A second later, I had broken out of the crowd, desperately pounding my heel against Little Bee's sides and leaning down low on her neck.

The menacing cries were left behind and we hurtled along the line of gloomy gray houses, keen to get out of this cursed village as quickly as possible. What had gotten into them? I wondered. There was a kind of crossroads ahead of us, with about fifteen men standing directly in our path. Unlike the peasants, though, these men were armed with lances and bows. And they were dressed a lot better, too—in wool and steel.

Alistan set his horse hurtling to the left, past the lances held out toward him. Miralissa managed to burn up one of our enemies with a spell. While the rest of them were blinking their eyes and yelling in fear, our group darted past after Alistan. I was galloping along last but one, immediately after Hallas, and I saw the sharp tips of the lances flash by just five inches from my face. Little Bee reared up on her hind legs and whinnied. It was a miracle that I wasn't thrown out of the saddle into the mud.

"Oh, bravo!" roared Bass, when he saw that the road to the left was already blocked off by men with lances.

With an effort, I managed to make Little Bee follow Snoop's horse. The two of us would have to break through together. Now we were galloping in the opposite direction from our comrades. I heard the twang of bowstrings behind me, and one of the arrows whistled past just above my ear and bit into the hindquarters of Bass's horse, which was galloping ahead of me. It reared up and threw its rider to the ground.

"Take my hand!" I shouted, leaning down in the saddle as I dashed up to him.

Snoop grabbed hold of my hand and jumped; I tossed him up onto Little Bee behind me and he clung on to me like a leech.

"We have to get out of this place! Move!"

I didn't need to be asked twice. Arrows whistled through the air again, but this time they missed. We galloped the entire length of the village without coming across anyone at all from our side or the other.

I only pulled up Little Bee when Upper Otters was far behind us, hidden behind the curtain of rain.

"Unfriendly fellows, why were they so upset with us?"

"We could go back and ask them," said Bass, jumping down off Little Bee.

"We have to find the others."

"In this rain? You won't even notice them until you trip over them."

"And what do you suggest?"

"I'd make a run for it, if we weren't so deep in the Borderland. But you can't get far on your own here."

I dismounted from Little Bee and turned toward him:

"You're wrong, we have to find the others as soon as possible. The village is over that way, we have to circle round until we come across the group."

"Two of us on one horse?" he said, turning round and looking thoughtfully in the direction of Upper Otters.

And that was when I saw it.

Two arrows were sticking out of Bass's back. Shafts as thick as a finger, with white flights—one was stuck right under his left shoulder blade, and the other was a lot lower and farther to the right. The heart and the liver. Nobody lives with wounds like that. But Snoop didn't seem to feel any pain or know that the arrows were there, and there wasn't a single drop of blood on his clothes.

"So what do you think? Harold, I'm talking to you!"

"What?"

Something must have shown in my eyes, because Bass looked at me keenly and asked:

"What's wrong, old friend?"

"You know," I said warily, "those lads are good shots, after all."

"Why do you say that? We're still alive, aren't we?"

"You've got two arrows sticking out of your back. Can't you feel them?"

Keeping his eyes on me, he felt for one of the arrows behind his back and chuckled grimly.

"Darkness! If only you knew what bad timing this is," Bass said with a crooked grin, and then, suddenly appearing right behind me, he punched me in the solar plexus.

Little Bee whinnied in fright and shied. I doubled over and fell down.

"All I had to do was watch you and tell the woman where you were," Snoop said, with a pitiful note in his voice. "Now the Master will punish me."

I felt my heart skip a beat.

Bass had no eyes anymore; where the pupils and irises ought to be, there was a sea of darkness. His eyes were like the eyes of the old man from the Master's prison.

The knife sprang into my hand of its own accord and I sank the long blade into his belly, but he didn't make a sound. I didn't notice how he hit me, the pain just exploded in my chest, even under the chain mail, and I was on the ground again.

"You know," Snoop said in a bored voice as he pulled my knife out of his stomach and weighed it in his hand, "Markun's lads really did drop me in the water under the pier that day when I stole the money from you and For. I was unlucky. Being dead is very bad, Harold. But the Master brought me back to life, I became a Soulless One, and all I had to do was keep an eye on you. Well, now what are we going to do with you?"

Zing! A black arrow hit him in the heart.

Zing! An arrow in the throat.

Zing! An arrow in the belly.

Ell was standing no more than ten yards away from us, methodically shooting arrow after arrow into Bass.

It was pointless!

"I'm not that easy to kill," Bass growled, flinging himself at the elf. "I've been wanting to do this for a long time!"

Ell threw his bow aside and took his s'kash off his shoulder. My knife was a lot shorter than this crooked blade, but that didn't worry Snoop at all, and he pounced on the elf like a spring hurricane.

Heavy breathing, flashing blades, the clash of steel on steel. Bass lost his left arm from the elbow down, but he kept attacking. Not a drop of blood oozed from the stump, and his black eyes remained impassive.

I planted a crossbow bolt in the back of his head and it passed right through. But this didn't upset the Soulless One at all.

I remembered what the Messenger had told Lafresa.

"Ell!" I shouted as I reloaded the crossbow. "His head! Cut off his head!"

Bass roared, turned away from his opponent, and came running at me with the knife. The elf dashed up to him from behind, the crooked sword whistled through the air and severed the head of what had once been my friend from its body.

The head fell into the mud and rolled away. The body, with the arrows stuck in it, waved its remaining arm desperately from side to side, trying to catch one of us with the knife. The foul beast was still alive and dangerous.

Ell jumped across to the head and struck twice at the black eyes with a dagger drawn from the top of his boot. There was a sound like an eggshell breaking, the eyes burst, and the body twitched convulsively once again before it collapsed into a puddle and lay still.

Wasting no time, the elf went across to the body and, using his s'kash again, started dismembering it, cutting off the other arm and the legs. I was still standing there with my crossbow lowered when Ell handed me back my knife. I took it warily, looked it over, and put it back in the scabbard. There wasn't a single drop of blood on the blade.

"I never did like him." Ell's yellow eyes glinted.

"What *was* that?" I asked, dumbfounded.

"One kind of ghoul created from someone who is dead. A faithful servant. They think, talk, eat, and they remember everything that happened to them before they died. It is almost impossible to tell them apart from ordinary people. Ask Miralissa if you want to know more."

"How did you find us?"

"I told you, I never did like him," Ell repeated. "Catch your horse and let's go. The rain's getting worse."

I whistled to Little Bee. It was a trick that Kli-Kli taught me. The horse was still frightened and she squinted at the dead man lying in the puddle, but she came to me when I called.

"Thank you," I said as I climbed into the saddle. "You saved my skin today."

"I hope I do not have to feel sorry about it," said Ell.

"What are you talking about?"

"I can see how you look at Miralissa."

"Isn't that my business?" I asked softly.

"When it touches dark elves then it is not *only* your business. You do realize that both of you have nothing in common? You're a man and she is an elf. You're a thief, she is possibly an heir to the throne. Our traditions do not allow anything like that. I advise you as a friend, do not overstep the line. If you do not think about yourself, then think about her. Everyone will get in trouble."

I looked at Ell and said:

"Don't worry. I wouldn't do that to her."

"Thank you," he said. "I hope our conversation will remain confidential."

"Of course," I said drily. "I promise."

He didn't answer, just nodded. I rode round the Soulless One's body and didn't look back once all the way to our group.

12

THE JUDGMENT OF SAGRA

After Upper Otters, the weather started to improve. The gods in the heavens snapped their fingers and in a single night a strong wind drove the clouds away. The sun peeped out in the morning and started drying out the land with its warm caress, freeing it of all that superfluous moisture. I was finally able to take off my cloak and revel in the glorious weather.

According to Alistan Markauz, our detachment was due to reach the Border Kingdom before that evening. With a bit of luck and some help from the gods, we ought to come across one of the garrisons—in the Borderland no one would refuse us shelter for the night.

After the incident with Bass, Miralissa spent a long time asking me questions about what had happened. The elfess nodded knowingly and exchanged glances with Kli-Kli, who rode up to join us, but she didn't make any comments; at the end of my story all she said was:

"As you humans say, you were born under a lucky star."

And that was the end of the conversation. Neither she nor the goblin condescended to explain anything to me.

I waited for the right moment and approached Ell. The elf gave me a surprised look, but waited for me to start the conversation.

"Ell . . . I . . ."

"Don't bother, Harold, your gratitude is not that important to me."

"That wasn't actually what I wanted to talk about," I said, embarrassed.

"No?" A quick glance. "Well, now you intrigue me. Go on."

"You're from the House of the Black Rose. . . . I know this question might surprise you, but do you know anything about Djok the Winter-Bringer?"

"The prince-killer? Every child in our house knows about him. A magnificent story to encourage hatred of the human race." He grinned and I couldn't tell if he was joking or serious.

"What happened to him?"

"He was executed."

"That's what you tell outsiders, but what really happened to him?"

"You are an outsider yourself," Ell replied harshly, then he paused and asked: "Why are you so interested in this?"

"I had a dream in which he wasn't executed. At least, not in the way that was planned."

"If you've had a dream, then why are you asking me?" the yellow-eyed elf asked. "That young lad was lucky; some soft-hearted individual slit his throat from ear to ear."

The elf ran his fingers across his own throat to show how it was done.

"We don't like to go into that story very much. Djok managed to slip through the fingers of our executioners just before the actual execution. A lucky bastard. We never found out who dispatched him into the darkness. There was a rumor that one of the orcs crept in and played a joke on us. But I don't really believe that."

"And . . ."

"Harold, it was more than six hundred years ago, there have been so many generations, and you want me to remember the old men's stories? I don't know any more than that."

"I understand . . . but couldn't you tell straightaway that he wasn't guilty?"

"You know the saying anger clouds the judgment? You humans looked for . . . er, what do you call it . . . a scapegoat. Why bother trying to find the guilty party if the elf was killed by Djok's arrow? Or an arrow very much like his? Your people had a choice. Either try to find the real killer and get involved in a war, or sacrifice one human life and forget the whole thing. Your king at the time acted wisely—the scapegoat was found, the arrow was shown in court, there was a confession, even if it was beaten out of him, witnesses . . ."

He pulled a wry face.

"My ancestors were no better, grief and fury clouded their reason, and we wanted revenge for what happened in Ranneng, even if the man accused wasn't guilty. We tried to question him further, but after your beatings and our tortures . . . He just kept begging us not to beat him . . . At the time he had been found guilty; it was only three months later that they started digging deeper and discovered it was a different archer and Djok was somewhere else at the time."

"A different archer?"

"You people don't like to talk about your mistakes any more than we elves do. He confessed. Voluntarily. Came and told us how it all happened, where he had been hiding. How he fired. The only thing he didn't say was why he did it."

"He?"

"The real killer."

"Did no one think that he was simply a madman with nothing better to do?"

"How would I know, Harold? Perhaps that's how it really was."

"But it was too late. Djok was already dead."

Ell shrugged.

"One human life wasn't very important."

"You're wrong," I said quietly. "You don't know what happened because of that terrible mistake."

"Oh?" He looked hard at me. "Then tell me, if I'm so stupid."

"Forget it, it's just idle talk now."

The elf nodded and immediately forgot about our conversation.

But I didn't. Now I knew who, what, and why.

Milord Alistan decided to send out scouts, and now Eel and Marmot moved off far to the right or the left, in search of possible danger. So far all was quiet, and I personally would have been perfectly happy for the peace and quiet to continue for a long, long time, all the way to Hrad Spein, but all good things come to an end. Marmot came back in the afternoon and reported that there was an armed detachment moving in our direction.

"Horsemen," he reported to Milord Rat. "About a hundred or a hundred and twenty, maybe more. All wearing armor. About half a league from here."

"Balistan Pargaid's men!"

"They don't look like his, but I could be wrong, it was too far to see."

"Did they see you?"

"You offend me, milord." Marmot chuckled. "If we hurry, we can still get away and avoid them."

"I don't think we'll be able to do that," said Ell, pointing to a horseman who had appeared in the distance. The man noticed us, swung his horse away, and galloped off in the opposite direction. They had their scouts, too.

"Then we'll see who comes off best," said Deler, picking up his poleax.

"You'll have time enough for fighting," Honeycomb rebuked the irascible dwarf. "Keep calm. And Hallas, that means you especially."

"Right," said the gnome, beating out his pipe and putting it away in his saddlebag. "I'm as silent as the grave."

Then Eel joined our group, and he had seen a little more than Marmot.

"It's definitely not Pargaid, unless he's trying to confuse us. They have two banners—a green field with a black cloud and lightning, and a yellow field with a clenched mailed fist in a flame."

"I can't say anything about the first, it's some petty landholder, but I do know the second banner. It belongs to Count Algert Dalli, Keeper of the Western Border," Alistan Markauz replied.

"What is he doing on someone else's lands, milord?" the jester asked.

"It's not necessarily him, it could just be a detachment of men who serve him."

"I can tell you who the first banner belongs to, milord," I interrupted. "Unless I'm mistaken that is the crest of Baron Oro Gabsbarg. We saw him at Balistan Pargaid's reception, Kli-Kli."

"Ah, yes, the big, shaggy one! Of course, of course, now I remember."

The atmosphere became a little less tense. I didn't really think that the warriors of the Borderland and the baron's men would hack us all to pieces. They were not like the bloodthirsty Count Pargaid, whose men had been waiting for us at Upper Otters—Ell had caught a glimpse of the nightingales embroidered on their clothes. The count's henchmen had turned the inhabitants of the village against us after someone had forwarded a message. I didn't know how the message had overtaken us—perhaps with a pigeon, or a raven, or by magic, but they had certainly arranged a warm welcome for us.

The column of horsemen appeared up ahead. They were galloping straight toward us, and I can't say I felt very happy about that. When that kind of force is moving straight at you, you can't help wanting to be as far away as possible. The banners fluttered in the wind, the armor and lance points glittered in the rays of sunlight, the horses' hooves hammered on the ground . . . The column was approaching rapidly.

"Steady, lads," Honeycomb said through his teeth and, without even realizing it, he reached for his ogre hammer.

Two knights wearing heavy armor were riding at the front. One was wearing a closed helmet in the form of a cock's head with green plumes. The other was not wearing any helmet and had a thick black bushy beard, which made him easily recognizable as my acquaintance Baron Oro Gabsbarg. These two were followed by their arms-bearers, then came the standard-bearers, and after them the warriors in chain mail and half-helmets with broad strips of metal protecting their noses. Many of them had lances and shields.

When the horsemen were only twenty yards away from our group, the man in the helmet raised his right hand with the open palm upward, and the column halted. The baron, the knight, arms-bearers and standard-bearers rode toward us.

"Name yourselves," the "cock" said as he approached. The helmet made his voice sound dull and lifeless.

"Bah!" cried the baron when he saw me. His expression was very astonished indeed. "May I be damned if I do not behold before me the Dralan Par in person!"

Oro screwed up his eyes, glanced at Eel, and asked uncertainly: "Milord duke?"

Eel didn't look like a duke at that moment, and the magic mask that Miralissa had applied to his face had faded long ago, so that Duke Ganet Shagor was now swarthy skinned and dark haired, and no longer concealed from the baron's gaze.

"Not entirely," said Alistan Markauz, riding forward. "Gentlemen . . ."

"I can't believe my eyes. Count Alistan Markauz in person, may lightning strike me! You're here, too! I am genuinely flattered! Have you decided to take up my invitation and visit Farahall after all? Lieutenant, allow me to introduce my guests. This is Count Alistan Markauz, our glorious King Stalkon's right hand and captain of the royal guard, this—"

"Please allow me to introduce the others to your noble companion, baron," Alistan said, politely interrupting Gabsbarg.

"I shall be honored," the "cock" rumbled, and removed his helmet.

Marmot gasped, because the knight was a woman—a young girl with her head completely shaved in the fashion of warriors from the Border Kingdom.

"This is the Marchioness Alia Dalli, lieutenant of the guard, daughter of Count Algert Dalli," the baron bellowed.

"Gentlemen," the girl said, bowing her head in polite greeting.

"Milady, allow me to introduce my companions to you. Tresh Miralissa and Tresh Egrassa are from the House of the Black Moon. Ell is from the House of the Black Rose."

"Ah . . . ," the baron rumbled in amazement, gaping at Eel and me, and wondering why Alistan had not given our names.

"Eel is a soldier, Harold is a thief," Milord Rat explained with harsh simplicity.

"A thief?" Oro looked as if someone had smashed him over the head with a log. "A thief?"

"Now that's a pleasant surprise, isn't it?" Kli-Kli put in. "By the way, as usual, everyone's forgotten about me. Allow me to introduce myself, the king's jester Kli-Kli. I'm on leave at the moment."

"A thief!" Oro repeated in an even more astonished voice, and then out of the blue he suddenly burst into thunderous laughter. "And does the dear Count Balistan Pargaid know about this? I wonder what all those high-society leeches would say if they knew they spent the evening in the company of an ordinary soldier and a criminal."

"That's just the beginning of it," Kli-Kli declared modestly.

Baron Oro Gabsbarg was not at all upset at being told the truth. These Borderland nobles are certainly a strange breed.

"Gentlemen," said Alia Dalli, "may I inquire what has brought you to the Borderland?"

"We'll tell you gladly. We are on our way to Zagraba."

"Zagraba? But the elves' territory lies far to the west; you can only reach the orcs' lands from here."

"That is where we are headed," Miralissa answered the girl.

"But in the name of the gods, what do you want there?" the baron exclaimed. "There are much easier ways to commit suicide."

"Yes, Zagraba certainly has little to recommend it," Alia Dalli agreed with him.

"Forgive me, milady, but we are on a mission of state importance, and the fate of all the Northern Lands depends on it. That is all I can tell you, only your noble father may learn the rest. I trust that you will take us to him."

"Of course," Alia said with a nod. "The gates of our castle are always open to you and your companions, Milord Alistan. We are on our way there at the moment and will be glad to lead you to Mole Castle."

"Then let us not delay, milady, we have a long journey ahead."

"In a few hours we shall be in the Border Kingdom, and we shall reach the castle by tomorrow evening," said Lady Alia, and put her helmet back on, once again becoming an anonymous knight. "Follow us, gentlemen."

Our group set off again, together with the column of soldiers. Alistan and Miralissa joined Alia Dalli, and all the others tried to stick together. But Kli-Kli decided to have a bit of fun, since there was so much new company. Within an hour the ranks of soldiers were ringing with raucous laughter—the jester had finally found a place to display his talents.

Baron Oro Gabsbarg rode up at the front, just behind Alistan Markauz, who was talking to Lady Alia, and sometimes he cast curious glances in my direction. To be honest I must say that they got on my nerves a little. Sagot only knew what kind of man he really was: He seemed friendly and warm-hearted, but he might just turn round and chop your head off for no reason.

Eventually he couldn't hold back anymore and he waited for me to draw level with him and asked:

"A thief, then?"

"Yes, milord."

"Hmm . . . well, you certainly fooled me. This mission of Milord Rat's . . . er, er . . . I meant to say Milord Alistan Markauz's—"

"It's the king's project," I lied, in order to make myself completely safe.

"Oh," he said, and chewed on his mustache thoughtfully. "I've never had any thieves as friends before."

Oro Gabsbarg pointed a finger at me. It was the size of a thick stick of sausage.

"I beg your pardon, if your honor has been offended, milord," I replied, choosing my words carefully.

He flashed his small black eyes at me, suddenly broke into a smile, and slapped me heartily on the back. I almost went flying off Little Bee.

"All right!" the baron boomed amiably. "The most important thing is, you're a good fellow. And it will give me something to boast about to my lady wife when I get back to Farahall."

Did I already mention that the barons of the Borderland are rather strange people?

"But I do feel truly sorry for you . . . er . . . what's your name again?"

"Harold, milord."

"I feel truly sorry for you—wandering around in Zagraba is no fun."

"I understand that."

"Not very well, I think, otherwise you'd be traveling in the opposite direction. Perhaps Algert Dalli can persuade Milord Alistan to drop this plan of his."

"What kind of man is he?"

"Hmmm?" the baron said, glancing at me. And then he told me anyway. He wasn't embarrassed by talking to the lower classes, and he liked to chat, all he needed was a willing listener.

"Made of stone, not a man at all. Algert Dalli is a bulwark of the throne, the keeper of the Western Border of the Kingdom. The soldiers have dubbed him Kind Heart as a joke. In battle he flies into such a furious rage that he lays out everyone, right and left, and in the kindness of his heart he doesn't even notice that he's not leaving enemies for his soldiers. He finishes them all off himself—a born warrior. But he does have one little oddity—he's crazy about knives . . ."

I looked at the baron in surprise.

"Well, they say that he always carries some sharp piece of metal around with him. He's always holding the knife in his hand, he eats with it, sleeps with it, takes it with him into his bath and when he goes to a woman. But these are all trifles, eh, thief? Everyone has his little quirks."

"Indeed so, milord. And what about his daughter?"

"Lady Alia? She commands the garrison at Mole Castle. Her daddy's right hand. A fine girl, plenty of spirit, but shaving her head . . . I reckon that's just sacrilege . . . Milord Algert sent her to Farahall with some soldiers. Remember, we were talking about it at the count's reception? Milord Algert has promised what Balistan Pargaid wouldn't give me, and that's why I'm riding with them now, taking twenty of my own men to Mole Castle, it's not far. . . . All right, I'm talking too much. We'll meet again, thief!"

"Most definitely, Your Grace, most definitely."

That evening we were in the Border Kingdom. We knew that from the pillar of black basalt standing by the side of the road.

The undulating plain was behind us now and the coniferous forests began, alternating with wide open expanses. The road wound between the fir trees, and the detachment spread out along it in a long column. Along the way we passed two wooden fortresses with tall stockades and watch towers. We stopped for the night out in the open, when it was almost completely dark.

We laid out the camp in an hour. A large number of campfires sprang to life and food started bubbling in the cooking pots. A dozen soldiers made a successful raid on the forest and captured firewood and long young tree trunks, from which they made an enclosure for the horses.

There was a small river flowing nearby, so we had plenty of water. Lady Alia's men put up a large tent and the elves, the baron, and Alistan were invited into it. High social standing does have some things to recommend it, after all—you can spend the night with all the comforts. Tired out after his long day, Kli-Kli slumped onto my blanket and fell sound asleep on the spot. I had to pass the night on my cloak, but that didn't really cause me any great discomfort.

It was very warm, and if not for the ubiquitous mosquitoes, I could say with a clear conscience that it was one of the best nights I'd spent out in the open during the whole of our trip from Avendoom. As I fell asleep, I realized what I had been missing all that time—a feeling of security. When you have more than a hundred armed soldiers around you, you feel as safe as if you were surrounded by a stone wall.

———

The next morning Lady Alia Dalli drove the detachment hard, intending to reach her father's castle before the evening. We moved at a good pace, and I was at the front of the column, right behind the nobles, arms-bearers, standard-bearers, and personal guards, so I didn't get too much of the dust raised by the horses' hooves up my nose, unlike the soldiers riding farther back. The heavy rainfall that had fallen in the Borderland seemed not to have touched this region at all. The road that we followed was dry and dusty.

After a few hours of riding, immediately after yet another argument between Hallas and Deler, this time over a small sour apple, a sergeant came riding up to Lady Alia from the rear of the column. I was close by and so I heard the entire conversation.

"Milady, the scouts have spotted horsemen."

"How many?"

"Twenty or so. They're right behind us, they'll be here in a few minutes. They have no banners, but they're not our men."

"We'll wait for them," said the girl. "We have to find out who the darkness has set on our trail."

"They're following us, milady," said Miralissa. "These men have been following our group ever since Ranneng."

"Enemies?"

"To us, yes."

"Then they are to me, too," the girl said with a nod. "Dron, tell the men to be ready for action."

"I don't think they will attack us, milady. The numbers are too uneven," Egrassa said slowly.

"We shall see."

Twenty men? On the other side of the Iselina there were twenty-eight of them—if Miralissa is right and they really are Balistan Pargaid's men. Where have the others got to?

When they came flying round a bend in the road and saw a horde of men dressed in metal, they were surprised and pulled back on their reins, forcing their horses to slow to a walk. The man at the head of the group spotted us and moved forward, the others followed him.

Count Balistan Pargaid in person. The Nightingale's face looked tired and angry; all trace of that mocking smile had disappeared. I also recognized two of the count's companions.

The first was the warrior who had met us at the gate—Meilo Trug, I thought he was called. A black silk shirt, a leather jacket, and not a trace of armor. And also his sword—a bidenhander exactly like Mumr's, with a golden oak leaf on the black handle. Kli-Kli had said that Meilo was a master of the long sword. Lamplighter gave Meilo's sword an appreciative glance, but he didn't say anything.

The second was my old friend Paleface. He hadn't changed, except that his face still hadn't healed up after the magical burn. Rolio spotted me and glared as if I owed him a hundred gold pieces. I smiled amiably. There was no response.

I was delighted and indescribably relieved not to see Lafresa in their group.

"Well, I swear on my sword, this is getting really interesting now. Count, are you and your men just out for a ride, too?" Oro Gabsbarg asked in amazement.

"Baron, I am glad to meet you. Arrest those people!"

"On what charge?" asked Alistan Markauz.

"Ah, so you are in this gang, too, milord? I wonder what the king will say when he finds out that one of his men has committed common theft?"

"Go gently, count, or we shall cross blades," Alistan said sternly, lowering his hand onto the handle of his sword. "I expect to hear your apologies."

"Apologies? These are my apologies! I accuse all these people of stealing my property and killing my men. Arrest them, baron!" Balistan Pargaid's voice rang out triumphantly.

"Alas, milord," Oro Gabsbarg laughed. "I am not in command here and can do nothing to help you."

"What difference does that make, darkness take me? Are you in command of this detachment, lieutenant? Good! Tie these scoundrels up and hand them over to me. Or at least do not interfere and my men will do it themselves!"

"I regret," Alia Dalli said from under her helmet, "that they are my guests and under my protection. I have no intention of handing them over to your bullyboys, count."

"How dare you? I am a count, and will not be spoken to in that manner by some ignorant young puppy."

"And I am the Marchioness Alia Dalli, milord!" She took off her helmet and looked at the startled Balistan Pargaid with a furious glint in her eyes. "You are not at home now. You are in my country! And you have just insulted me. Be so good as to apologize."

Balistan Pargaid broke out in red blotches, but he apologized. I don't think he was actually frightened—Milord Alistan had said that this weasel handled a sword like a true nobleman—but he knew there was no point in making the situation any more difficult.

"Excellent," the girl said with a nod. "Then I shall not detain you any further. Good day to you."

"But these people have mortally offended me. They must pay for it."

"Not today. Good-bye." Alia turned her horse away to indicate that the conversation was over.

"These people have insulted my lord," Meilo Trug suddenly hissed. "In his name I demand the Judgment of Sagra! In the name of steel, fire, blood, and by the will of the gods!"

The effect of these words on the warriors of the Borderland was like an exploding powder barrel. I even heard Milord Alistan's teeth grind together. Had this Meilo said something important?

"I heard you, soldier," Lady Alia said with a nod. "Do you accuse one particular person of the crime or all of them?"

The shadow of a smile flickered on Meilo's lips and he was just about to answer when Balistan Pargaid intervened:

"All of them! He accuses all of them!"

The smile on Meilo's face turned sour, as if the count had just committed some stupidity without realizing it.

"The answer has been heard," the marchioness said hurriedly. "You will be given the chance to prove your lord's case."

"We will do it here and now!" Balistan Pargaid intervened again.

"No, according to the laws of Sagra, the owner of the land on which the challenge was issued must be present at the judgment. We are now on the lands of my lord and father, and for the court to be held we shall have to go to Mole Castle, where the rules of combat will be announced."

Combat? Did she say combat? I definitely did not like the sound of that.

"But . . . ," Balistan Pargaid began in annoyance.

"You can withdraw the challenge, that is up to you," Alia Dalli said imperturbably. "The rules do not forbid it."

"No, we will go with you, milady."

"As you wish, milord. I wish to remind you that if your men dare to attack my guests before the duel, there will be very serious trouble indeed," the girl replied.

She did not offer the count and his men her protection.

We continued on our way, with the marchioness's men keeping an inconspicuous eye on the count's men, who were observing them. The count rode beside Oro Gabsbarg without speaking. Paleface's glance gave me an unpleasant, cold feeling in the back of my neck.

"Marmot," I asked. "What is the Judgment of Sagra?"

"I don't know. If Arnkh was here, he could explain the laws of this country to us."

"The Judgment of Sagra? I've heard something about that business, lads," said Lamplighter. "The court of the goddess of war . . . It used to be very common among the warriors of the Border Kingdom. When some questionable decision was made or a warrior's honor was insulted, then the Judgment of Sagra decided the matter. A duel, in other words. The lad with the big ears has challenged us to a fight, and no warrior in the Border Kingdom would deny him the right to do that."

"Is it a duel to the death?" asked Marmot, glancing sideways at Meilo Trug.

"That all depends on what the man who challenged us says to the lord of the land. If he says to the death, then to the death it is."

"You talk about it so calmly, Mumr," I said with a crooked grin. "That Meilo has turned out to be very cunning."

"It could have been worse," Lamplighter replied philosophically, taking out his reed pipe.

"How could it?"

"If the count hadn't interfered, then his servant could have chosen any opponent he wanted. But then Milord Pargaid said he accused everybody."

"And now this . . . what's his name?" asked Marmot.

"Meilo," I prompted him. "So now this Meilo will have to fight all of us?"

"No, it will be decided by drawing lots. No need to be so nervous, Harold. You're not involved in this business."

"Why?"

"The Judgment of Sagra is only for soldiers. You, Kli-Kli, and Miralissa aren't soldiers."

"I'm not a soldier?" exclaimed Kli-Kli, ablaze with righteous indignation. "Why, I'm a better soldier than any of you! I even know what the combat pension is!"

"All right, Kli-Kli, well done. Just calm down, will you," Honeycomb said in a conciliatory tone.

"Hey, goblin," called a soldier with a gray mustache, who had heard Kli-Kli's howling. "Sing us your song."

"And why not? Right away!"

And he did sing it. In fact, he kept on going for a good ten minutes.

"A good song," Dalli's man croaked approvingly. "Plenty of heart."

"Well then? Am I a soldier?"

"Sure you are!" he said quite seriously.

The Border Kingdom warriors laughed—in a single day's march they had grown fond of Kli-Kli's jokes and his songs.

How naïve they were! They hadn't yet experienced the charm of a nail in their boot or a tub of cold water in their bed.

The empty region was behind us now, and we passed a little village at least once every hour. But, unlike our villages in Valiostr, they were surrounded by stockades and they had watch towers with archers on them. Every peasant in the Border Kingdom can swap his plow for a battle-ax at a moment's notice when he needs to repulse an attack by the enemy.

"How's your health, Harold?" asked Paleface, drawing even with me on his horse.

"Just fine, thanks. How's yours, Rolio? Have you recovered after that skirmish with the demons?" I replied.

"So you . . . ," Paleface said slowly, and grinned. "I don't recall ever telling you my name."

"You were never that strong on etiquette. I had to find out for myself."

"All the more reason for you to be concerned about your health."

"Oh, I'll take good care of myself. Very good care. What brings you out on such a long journey?"

"A problem by the name of Harold. The way you stole that Key was very clever. I found that impressive, believe me."

"I feel flattered, on my word of honor."

"Well then, I'll be seeing you again soon."

"I hope not."

Paleface was not likely to try anything here. There are too many men around; he'd never get away with it if he tried to dispatch me to the light now. The moment I suddenly fall off my horse and start bleeding, they'd slit the killer's throat for him. And naturally, he didn't want that. So I could expect him to wait until I was alone before he tried his tricks.

We spotted Mole Castle easily from the distance—a huge gray bulk with walls rising up forty yards into the sky and twenty square towers set in a full circle.

The walls were bristling with ballistas and catapults, the wide moat was filled with running water; anyone who tried to take the citadel by storm would have a hard time of it.

When we stepped onto the drawbridge, the walls towered up above us menacingly. I raised my head and the men on the top looked like little beetles. The mighty gates of oak, clad with sheets of steel, quickly opened wide in invitation and the portcullis was raised, but in an attack, only the mightiest of battering rams could ever have broken through that barrier.

About twenty soldiers were on guard duty beside the gates. The head of the watch greeted Lady Alia and we rode into the castle. I found myself in a short tunnel with its walls studded with loopholes for archers.

Standing by the wall like a predator ready to pounce was a huge crossbow engine that fired forty bolts at once. And hanging on chains up under the ceiling there were basins that the defenders could fill with tar and hot oil. Yes, Algert Dalli's home was certainly a tough nut to crack, not to be taken easily.

We rode into the courtyard of the castle, but to call it a yard was a joke—it was the size of a large town square.

"Milady Alia," one of the soldiers said, bowing, "your lord and father is expecting you."

"Thank you, Chizzet," said the marchioness, jumping down off her horse. "Follow me, noble gentlemen. And those who seek judgment, too. Chizzet, arrange accommodation for our guests."

Naturally, a plain ordinary thief was not invited to an audience with Milord Kind Heart, and, to be quite honest, I didn't even suggest it. Milord Alistan, Baron Oro, the elves, Count Pargaid, and Meilo followed Lady Alia, and the rest of us set off after Chizzet, who had promised to find beds for us.

We were given rooms in the Tower of Blood, as the inhabitants of the castle called it. Good rooms, with beds, rushes on the floor, and windows overlooking the courtyard.

Eel told me that a citadel of this size could hold as many as six hundred people at once. A huge swarm of people. Kli-Kli, who never slept in a bed, laid out his blanket on the floor and ran off to stick his curious nose into every corner of the castle. Ell turned up and told us that the duel would take place the following morning.

"To the death," he added in a steady voice.

That immediately spoiled my good mood. But there was more to it than that. If we lost, then the Key that had been recovered with such difficulty would go back to Balistan Pargaid—that was the law of the Judgment of Sagra.

"And what if we leave under cover of darkness?"

"Leave the castle, Harold? The Judgment of Sagra is sacred to the warriors of the Borderland. We either win or we lose the Key. There is no third way."

"I'll smash that fancy popinjay's head open in person!" Hallas threatened. "Have they decided who's going to fight in the duel?"

"The lots will decide that. Come with me, Milord Algert is waiting for us."

"Can I come with them?"

"You're not involved in the drawing of lots, Harold."

"But can I come?"

"Yes," he said with an indifferent nod.

The hall to which the count led us rivaled the castle's courtyard in size. There were quite a number of people there—all wool and steel, swords and shaven heads. Every man in the kingdom seemed to have gathered together. Kli-Kli was running about, getting under people's feet, amusing the soldiers, but as soon as he saw us, the performance came to an end, and the jester joined our group.

"Where did you get to?" I asked quietly.

"I was touring the local sights. By the way, they have carrots in the kitchen."

"Congratulations."

Miralissa, Egrassa, and Alistan were already there, and so were Balistan Pargaid and Meilo Trug. Oro Gabsbarg clutched a beer mug in his huge paw of a hand. When he spotted me, the baron nodded solemnly.

Alia Dalli was standing behind a short man with broad shoulders, whose cheeks were covered with a two-week growth of stubble. Like all the soldiers in the castle, this man had a shaved head and was dressed in chain mail and coarse soldier's trousers. He was toying thoughtfully with a dagger that had an expensive handle of ogre bone. Count Algert Dalli the Kind Heart, unless I was very much mistaken.

We walked up to the table at which his lordship was sitting.

"And so, you have not changed your decision?" Milord Algert asked Meilo after looking intently at each of us in turn.

"No, I demand the Judgment of Sagra."

"Very well. All that remains is to choose an opponent. Bring in the straws!"

"Hey, Garrakian! Catch!" said Meilo Trug, throwing a copper coin to Eel. "I think I owe you that."

Eel caught the copper and calmly tucked it under his belt.

"Thank you. A bit of extra money always comes in handy."

"You suggested that I ought to be whipped. I shall pray to Sagra to meet you in combat."

"Whatever is your pleasure," Eel said, bowing imperturbably. Hallas muttered angrily to himself and gave Trug a dark look.

And then a soldier came in with the straws sticking out of his fist.

"Whoever draws the short straw will face this man for the Judgment of Sagra tomorrow morning," said Algert Dalli. "Let me remind you that you are free to refuse to take part in the draw, but by doing so you acknowledge your guilt. . . . I can see that no one wishes to do that. Draw lots, and may Sagra be with you!"

Ell was first. He reached out boldly and drew a long straw.

Egrassa. A long straw.

My heart was pounding as loudly as if I was drawing lots myself.

Milord Alistan. A long straw.

Honeycomb. A long straw.

Hallas. A long straw. The gnome looked disappointed. He had really wanted to take part in the duel. He wasn't bothered at all that one of the opponents would have to be carried out feet first. Like any gnome, Lucky was overflowing with confidence.

Eel. A long straw. Meilo Trug thrust out his lower jaw in disappointment.

That left only Deler and Lamplighter.

Mumr. A short straw. Short. Sagot save us all! Lamplighter's going to fight.

Algert Dalli's soldier opened his fist to show the whole hall that the last straw, which would have been Deler's, was long.

The dwarf spat angrily. He had been keen to fight, too.

Mumr did not seem at all upset that the next day he had to fight a duel to the death. He cleared his throat, shrugged indifferently, and put the straw away in his pocket.

"So be it," said Milord Algert. "The weapon?"

"The long sword," Meilo Trug replied, glaring hard at Mumr.

"The long sword," Mumr said with a nod.

"Tomorrow morning you will be sent for, but now I invite you to share bread and honey with me."

I didn't know about the others, but I couldn't eat a single bite, and I got up from the table leaving the food on my plate untouched.

"Any moment now," Kli-Kli said with a nervous little jump. He sniffed and took a large bite out of his carrot.

"Can you stop chomping for a little while?" I growled at him irritably.

"No, I can't," said the royal jester, shaking his head. "When I get nervous, I want to eat."

"Calm down, Kli-Kli," Honeycomb told him. The commander of the Wild Hearts was just as jumpy as I was.

"What do you think, Honeycomb?" asked Kli-Kli, biting off yet another piece of carrot. "What are Mumr's chances?"

"I don't know."

"It all depends on how well he handles his sword," said Hallas, puffing away on his pipe.

"Believe me, Meilo was born with that piece of steel in his hand," Kli-Kli sighed. "It's not that easy to win a royal tournament."

"Our Lamplighter's no pushover, either," the gnome replied. "You don't get an oak leaf on your sword handle for nothing."

I paid no attention to them. I wasn't interested in their arguments.

The morning had turned out cool, and the sun was hidden behind the clouds that covered the entire sky. Together with many inhabitants of the castle, we were standing round a large open area of hard-tamped earth in the center of the courtyard. There were no fanfares and no festive streamers; this was not a tournament, but a trial by duel. Milord Algert and his daughter, the elves, Balistan Pargaid, and Alistan Markauz . . . all of them were probably as nervous as I was, but you couldn't tell it from their noble features. . . . Darkness take me, I felt as if I was the one who had to go out there and fight. Oro Gabsbarg was the only one who seemed to be bored.

A whisper ran through the rows of spectators, and I turned my head and saw Meilo Trug. He walked unhurriedly out into the arena, turned to face the nobility, and bowed.

Even for this occasion Meilo had dressed like a dandy: a red silk shirt with wide sleeves, maroon breeches, boots polished until they shone, black leather gloves. The bidenhander was resting on his left shoulder. The long sword was almost as long as the man. Stick it in the ground and the massive round knob at the end of the handle would reach up to Meilo's chin.

Mumr appeared a minute later. He entered the arena from the other side of the castle courtyard and halted facing his opponent. Like Meilo, Lamplighter was wearing a shirt, but it was black wool, not silk. Coarse soldier's trousers and a pair of soft boots . . . The only thing the duelists had in common were the leather gloves on their hands and their heavy bidenhanders.

Neither of the warriors wore any armor—no armor was allowed at the court of the goddess. Lamplighter was a master of the long sword, and so was Meilo, so the duel would be fought until one of them made his first serious mistake. One good blow from a blade like that is enough to dispatch any opponent straight to the light.

Lamplighter had a black ribbon round his forehead to hold back his long hair and prevent any sweat running down into his eyes. He casually set down his sword with the point on the ground, holding the crosspiece lightly with his fingers.

Meilo glared fiercely at his opponent. Mumr replied with an indifferent glance. He looked as if he had come out for a morning stroll, not for combat. Beside Trug, Lamplighter looked skinny and puny. In his hands the bidenhander seemed absurdly huge and heavy.

"Are you ready?" Algert Dalli's voice rang out above the arena.

"Yes."

"Yes."

"Challenger, do you still wish to dispute this right of ownership for your lord?"

"Yes," Meilo Trug replied, nodding firmly.

"The trial will conclude . . ."

"In death," Meilo continued.

"So be it," Algert Dalli announced, and nodded, thoughtfully twirling his beloved knife between his fingers. "By steel, fire, blood, and the will of the gods, I declare that Sagra is looking down on you, and she will decide who is right and worthy!"

I have already told you that the sword is not my weapon. Apart from the crossbow, the only weapon I have more or less managed to master is the knife. For was a great specialist in matters of swordsmanship and he tried to teach me, but after a few lessons even he gave up.

The only benefit I did get from those painful exercises with a wooden stick was a superficial knowledge of stances and the names of the various strokes. That was as far as my knowledge of swordsmanship, and my skill in it, goes. But I am grateful to my old teacher; when I see guards fencing in a castle courtyard or warriors at a tournament, I can at least understand why one man covers himself with his sword this way and another thrusts that way.

Meanwhile, a priest of Sagra, dressed in chain mail and wool, like all the soldiers of the Border Kingdom, walked out into the arena where judgment would be given. He drew his sword from its scabbard, thrust it into the ground between the two opponents who were standing facing each other, and started reciting a prayer, calling on the goddess of war and death to bear witness to this duel, punish the guilty party, and protect the righteous. Meilo did not move, and Lamplighter, cradling his sword in the crook of his left arm, slowly chewed on the straw that had brought him to this place.

"Oh, mother!" squeaked Kli-Kli, who was standing beside me, and at that very second the priest pulled up his sword, took a long step back, and said:

"Begin!"

Neither of the warriors began until the priest had left the arena. And all the time Meilo kept eyes his fixed fiercely on Lamplighter, who gazed idly at a spot that only he could see, somewhere up above his enemy's head.

After six long heartbeats, Meilo gave a menacing growl and attacked first.

He took a sweeping stride forward, at the same time setting his left hand on the long handle of his sword, and the bidenhander flew off his shoulder as lightly as a feather. Meilo added speed to the sword's flight by twisting his body, and struck a terrible blow, lunging at the chest.

As soon as Meilo started to move, the Wild Heart defied my expectations by stepping toward his opponent. I think I gasped, expecting the flying blade to slice him in half, but the Wild Heart's huge bidenhander, which only a second earlier had been cradled in his arm like a sleeping baby, suddenly awoke and blocked his enemy's thrust.

Cla-ang! The sound echoed round the courtyard, and the count's servants took a step back.

Lamplighter grunted and attacked his opponent's unprotected flank. And this time Meilo surprised me—he moved almost right up to Mumr and turned his back on the flashing sword.

The crowd gasped out loud.

Meilo flung his weapon behind him and caught the thrust of Mumr's sword on the flat of the blade. *Cla-ang!*

Without pausing for a moment, Meilo completed his turn; his sword flew out from behind his back and started to descend, threatening to chop off his opponent's hands. Lamplighter deftly covered himself by thrusting the point of his blade at the other man's face, countered the blow, and immediately pushed his sword farther forward. My eyes were not fast enough to follow what was happening in the arena. The huge swords flashed to and fro like demented moths, whistling through the air and colliding with a loud crash, parting and then clashing again. At times all the opponents' movements fused into a single blur, and I could only tell that they were both still alive a few seconds later, when an attack from one of the swordsmen ran into a block.

"Phew-ew-ew!" *Clang! Clang!* "Phew-ew!"

"Aaah! Ooh! Oh!" the crowd sang in response to every stroke and every thrust.

Meilo began spinning like a top again and swung hard, putting his very soul into the blow. Mumr jumped back and dropped the hilt of his sword down low, so that the blade rose up vertically, and Meilo's blow ran into a wall of steel.

Cla-ang!

The swords wove cobwebs in the air, spinning round in a glittering blizzard of steel, striking against each other, soaring upward and threatening to wound the very sky and then descending, dreaming of slicing through the earth. The two warriors were not fighting, they were dancing, dicing with death, and their own lives were the stakes. Meilo's sword leapt high in the air, as if it were alive; Lamplighter dashed into the breach that opened up and tried to strike home.

But he could not . . .

Balistan Pargaid had certainly not wasted his money on this servant. Meilo stepped back quickly, while continuing the movement of his sword, and now Mumr's bidenhander went flying upward, allowing his opponent to strike.

Lamplighter squatted down and caught the blow almost on the crosspiece of his sword. Then he straightened up sharply and thrust his hilt hard forward. Meilo's sword very nearly struck its master in the face, the attack was so unexpected. To avoid the deflected stroke, the villain recoiled and started backing away as Mumr came at him.

Only a few minutes had passed since the beginning of the duel, but the faces of the two warriors were already gleaming with sweat.

Balistan's dog had been seriously startled by the sudden assault and now that Lamplighter had almost sent him to join his fathers, he was watching him with more caution and respect, noting every movement, no matter how small.

"It's time to kill him," Hallas growled. "You can't wave those wagon shafts around for very long."

The gnome was right. The immensely heavy swords might be flying around like feathers now, but fatigue would come sooner or later, and then the one who was more tired would lose.

Cla-a-ang!

With a pitiful groan, the swords came together in a fleeting kiss and immediately leapt apart again.

And then there were more lacy cobwebs woven in the air, creating a beautiful, glittering pattern that had to end in death.

Meilo jumped at Mumr, grunting as he struck blow after blow, pressing him back.

"Ha-a-a!"

Cla-ang!

"Ha-a-a!"

Cla-ang!

"Ha-a-a!"

Cla-ang!

Meilo's final blow was especially powerful. Lamplighter's sword flew upward, opening up a breach, and his enemy instantly struck at his unprotected head. Mumr pushed his sword forward, and the two blades froze in the air, with each opponent pressing against the other's sword, trying to force it back into his face.

For a few moments there was silence in the arena.

Meilo became too involved with pressing and Lamplighter ducked smartly under his sword and pushed his opponent away from him. Tumbling forward, Meilo began spinning round faster than a goblin shaman after a breakfast of magic mushrooms, turning into a blur too fast for the eye to follow. A streak of lightning, a shrill whistle in the air . . .

Lamplighter guessed what was coming and jumped up in the air.

"Oh, mother!" said the jester, covering his eyes with his hands and watching the fight through the gaps between his fingers. "Tell me that he's still alive!"

"He's alive!" said Hallas, who was clutching his battle-mattock with white knuckles.

The gnome was right. Mumr was still standing, although there was an expression of furious annoyance on his face. He had almost been caught out.

"The score's not looking good for us," Honeycomb rumbled. "It's time for Mumr to stop playing with him."

Cla-ang! Cla-ang! the swords sang.

Tick-tock, tick-tock, went the clock of the gods, counting away the seconds of life.

Meilo straightened his arms suddenly and stabbed at Mumr's neck. And then again my eyes were too slow to follow what was happening in the arena. In an instant Lamplighter's gloved left hand was clutching the center of his blade. As if he were holding an ordinary staff, he pushed his enemy's sword away from him and tried to strike at his throat with the point of his bidenhander. Surprised by this audacity, Meilo recoiled. But that didn't stop Mumr. Still holding his sword like a battle-staff, he tried to hit Meilo with the knob of the hilt, aiming at his face. Mumr's blows were "incorrect" and reckless, and Trug retreated in confusion, barely managing to avoid them.

"Ha-a! Ha-a!"

The wide-swinging movements of the Wild Heart's "staff" gave his opponent no chance to gather himself for a single moment. The very air seemed to groan as the blades clashed. The sweat was streaming down Trug's face.

Mumr resorted to cunning. He shifted his right hand onto the blade of his sword, too, setting it close to the guard, and holding the sword like a cross, then struck a hard blow at Meilo's head with the heavy hilt.

"Ra-a-a-a!" A wave of sound ran through the lines of spectators.

After that everything happened very quickly.

Lamplighter pulled back, and immediately Meilo was there beside him, preparing to attack. . . . I missed the blow that followed; all I could see was that Mumr had been quicker and struck his opponent in the chest with the heavy hilt.

The crowd gasped and started to buzz. I swear by Sagot that even I heard the crunch of bone!

"A hit!" Hallas gasped, with his eyes glued on the fight.

Meilo cried out in pain, staggered back, and pressed his left hand against his chest. Lamplighter stepped forward, hooked a foot round his ankle, and jerked it upward sharply, using a wrestling move.

The tug on his leg threw Meilo off balance. Lamplighter dropped his sword and shoved his opponent hard on the chest with his free left hand, adding speed to his fall.

Trug crashed down onto the trampled earth with his full weight, striking the back of his head against the ground. Balistan Pargaid's warrior seemed to lose consciousness for a moment, or at least he lay there without moving, although he was still clutching his sword in his right hand.

Mumr picked up his own sword, stood on his opponent's biden-hander, cast a quick glance at Algert Dalli, and thrust his weapon hard into the chest of his opponent just as he was trying to get up, pinning him to the ground. Meilo twitched once and stopped moving. A puddle of blood began spreading out under the warrior's body.

Lamplighter pulled his sword free with an effort, stepped back a few paces from the body of the defeated man, and bowed, swaying once, but still remaining on his feet.

Algert Dalli rose and his voice rang out across the courtyard.

"By steel, fire, blood, and by the will of the gods I confirm that judgment has been given and the guilty party punished! So be it!"

"What do you mean, punished?" howled Balistan Pargaid, beside himself with fury.

"Do you doubt the judgment of the goddess, milord?" asked Algert Dalli, raising one eyebrow in an expression of surprise.

"No. I do not doubt it," the count said, forcing the words out.

Whatever else he might be, Balistan Pargaid was certainly no fool.

"Good, then I invite you to a festive dinner to celebrate the passing of judgment."

"Thank you," said Count Pargaid. "But I have business to attend to. My men and I will leave immediately."

"As you wish." Algert Dalli had no intention of trying to detain him. "A safe journey to you."

Count Balistan Pargaid replied to these words with an irritated nod and left the arena without even glancing back at the body of Meilo Trug.

The Wild Hearts crowded round Mumr, fussing over him. Hallas was as pleased as if he had won the victory over the adversary all on his own.

"You know what, Harold-Barold," said Kli-Kli, chewing thoughtfully on a piece of carrot, "I'm a bit worried about our mutual friend, Balistan Pargaid, withdrawing like that after he just spent two weeks chasing us. He gave up a bit too easily, don't you think? And then Lafresa has disappeared somewhere. . . . Oh, I have the feeling they're preparing some dirty trick for us!"

"Just chew on your carrot and shut up, Kli-Kli. Let Alistan and Miralissa do the worrying," I told him.

But I had a feeling Kli-Kli was right.

B

CROSSROADS

That day Lamplighter was the hero of the castle. It's no secret that what the inhabitants of the Border Kingdom value most in a man is his mastery of a weapon, and that morning Mumr had demonstrated that he certainly knew how to use a sword. All day long the soldiers of the castle garrison treated our hero with respectful deference, as if he were made out of the finest Nizin porcelain.

In the evening Milord Algert Dalli held a feast at which all the warriors of the castle were present. Mumr was seated in the place of honor and enough food for an entire regiment was heaped up around him.

Some of Lamplighter's glory was even reflected onto me and the Wild Hearts. We sat beside him, at the same table as all the noble-born. Frankly, I'd rather hide away in the darkest corner of a hall, at the very farthest table, otherwise I felt too exposed. I think that pair of gluttons, Hallas and Deler, took the whole thing more simply than anyone else—they just gobbled up and swilled down everything that they could lay their hands on without the slightest embarrassment, belching deafeningly and constantly striking up new arguments with each other.

All the endless toasts raised to Milord Algert Dalli, his lovely daughter, Milord Alistan Markauz, the glorious elves, Master Lamplighter, the death of the orcs, the Border Kingdom, and so on and so forth had already set my head spinning.

Deler was red-faced from so much drinking, Hallas was feeling drowsy, Marmot's tongue seemed to be tied in knots and, to Kli-Kli's intense delight, he roused squeals from the lovely ladies by trying to stuff Invincible into a jug of wine. The goblin was really enjoying life, and he shared his joy with everyone else around him. The only ones displeased with his performance were Algert Dalli's own personal fools, who watched the little jester with poorly concealed envy and hatred. It looked as if they could well end up giving Kli-Kli a good drubbing by the end of the evening's festivities.

One dish followed another, one song followed another, and when it became absolutely unbearable to sit at the table any longer, Honeycomb nudged me with his elbow:

"Did you hear? Tomorrow we set out bright and early; if the gods are kind to us, we'll be in Zagraba in two days' time."

"I can't say the idea pleases me all that much. I reckon it's a lot safer sitting between stone walls than wandering through some gloomy old forest."

"There are no safe places, Harold," Honeycomb chuckled. "Death will creep in even through stone walls, it just depends what fate was written down for you when you were born. I remember there was a witch who predicted that Arnkh would drown. Arnkh just laughed at her, but now you see the way things have turned out. . . . If you're afraid of wolves, don't go to Zagraba."

"If there were only wolves there . . ."

"True enough," the giant agreed, taking a mouthful from his mug of beer. "Like I said—it's fate."

"I'll go and get some sleep," I said, getting up from the table. "I can't sit here any longer."

"Stay there, Harold-Barold, swig your wine," said Kli-Kli, jumping to his feet. "No point in tempting fate!"

"Meaning what?" I asked, puzzled.

"There's a rumor going round the guards at the gates that Balistan Pargaid has left."

"So what?"

"When he arrived here with his men, there were twenty of them, but when he left, somehow there were only eighteen. One was run through by Mumr, and that leaves nineteen. Where's the other one got to?"

"Paleface!" I felt my mouth turn dry instantly. "Maybe I'll stay and drink a little more after all."

"That's right," the goblin said with an approving nod, "wandering around the castle on your own would not be good for you."

"Have they tried to find him?"

"Are you joking? They've crept into all the nooks and crannies. . . . But in a humungous place like this, you could hide a mammoth and no one would find it until it died and started to stink. So imagine how hard it is to find a man."

"And you didn't tell me this before?"

"I didn't want to upset you and spoil your appetite," Kli-Kli said, giving me an innocent look.

"Scat, get out of my sight. You're worse than the plague."

"Don't take it so badly, Dancer, after all, we're with you. I think I'll take a drink as well, to keep you company. Do you think they'll bring me some milk if I ask?"

"Maybe . . ." The only thought in my head right now was of Paleface. For some reason I never doubted for a second that he had stayed behind after the count's detachment left in order to dispatch your humble servant into the light. Thoughts like that did nothing to improve my mood, and I could barely wait for the end of this dreary rigmarole of pompous speechifying and singing to the health of all the warriors. When I did finally get back to my room, to settle my nerves I checked the windows, the doors, and the chimney. The chimney was too narrow; there wasn't much chance Paleface would be able to get in that way. The bar on the door was a hefty oak beam, and the windows were fifty yards above the ground; there was no way Paleface could climb up that way—not unless he could fly, that is.

Kli-Kli, Hallas, and Deler had fallen asleep long ago, but I still couldn't nod off. I just lay there on the bed, staring up at the ceiling, until eventually sleep overcame me, too.

I was woken by a fiendish howl of pain that made me tumble out of bed, grab my crossbow, and squat down. I swung my head around drowsily, trying not to make myself a target and wondering what exactly was going on.

"What happened?" yelled Deler.

"Hey! Is everything all right in there?" someone shouted outside the door.

"Who screamed like that?" Deler asked again.

"Let's have some light!"

"Open the door!" Honeycomb shouted, pounding on it with his fists. There was a scraping sound and a shower of sparks, and a candle lit up in Hallas's hand.

"Why are you yelling like fishwives at the market, it's all over," the gnome grumbled, lifting the candle to light a torch.

"Hey, you! Do you hear me? Open the door!" Honeycomb shouted, straining his lungs to the limit.

"Stop yelling! Just a moment!" said Hallas, moving the bolt to open the door and let Honeycomb and Eel into the room. Some of Algert Dalli's soldiers peeped in at us from the corridor.

"What happened in here?"

"Some mountain-climber tried to get through the window and I swelped him with Deler's ax, to teach him not to go disturbing decent folks at night by climbing in their windows," Hallas muttered.

The window was open, Deler's bloody ax was standing by the wall, and there was a severed hand lying on the floor. Someone had just lost the end of his left arm.

It turned out that Hallas had woken up in the night and taken a walk to answer a gnomish call of nature. When he came back to the room, he had decided to light up his pipe, but he opened the window so that the room wouldn't get smoky. Literally a minute later a hand had appeared from outside, followed by another. Hallas had quite correctly decided that normal people sleep at that time of night, and don't go climbing up sheer walls like spiders, so he'd picked up the dwarf's ax and hit the hand that was nearest to him.

"And then you lot started yelling," the gnome concluded.

"Honeycomb, let's go and check," said Eel, making for the door.

"What for?" Hallas asked in amazement. "After a tumble from this height, he's not just going to get up and walk away."

"We'll find out who it was."

Eel, Honeycomb, and the guardsmen left. I cautiously stuck my head out the window and looked down. Just as I thought, there was no body on the ground. Soldiers were running round the castle courtyard with torches, but I could tell that they hadn't spotted anyone, only heard the screaming.

"Harold, is this Paleface's?" Kli-Kli asked, holding the severed hand squeamishly by one finger.

"How should I know? It looks like his, the fingers are slim, like Rolio's, but I can only say for certain if I see the assassin himself."

"I see," said Kli-Kli, casually tossing the hand out the window.

"And what in darkness made you take my ax, couldn't you have used
your mattock?" Deler grumbled, carefully wiping down the terrible
blade with a little rag.

"You're so possessive, Deler," Hallas said resentfully. "A real dwarf.
All your beardless tribe are the same."

"Just look who's talking," Deler retorted. "When it comes to taking
what belongs to others, you're the champions!"

"We take what belongs to others? We do?" said the gnome, starting
to get heated. "Who was it that took the books? Who was it that stole
the books of magic, you tell me that?"

"What makes you think they're yours? They're ours, we just lent
them to you for a while!"

Hallas started to choke on his indignation. The gnome was still
searching for an adequate reply when Eel and Honeycomb came back.
Alistan followed them in.

"Not a thing," Honeycomb said with a wry grimace. "No body, no
blood, as if there was never anybody there. The guards have combed
the entire courtyard—not a trace."

"Have you got the Key, thief?" Alistan Markauz asked.

"Yes, milord."

"Good," the count said with a nod, and left.

"Let's get some sleep," sighed Hallas, who was feeling chilly, and he
closed the window. "We've got another day in the saddle tomorrow, and I
still want a good night's rest. Deler, lock the door and put out the torch."

"So I'm your servant now, am I?" the dwarf grumbled, but he closed
the door, after first telling Eel: "You wake us up in the morning."

He lowered the oak beam and stuck the torch into the sandbox.

After a few minutes of peace and quiet, I heard Kli-Kli's voice through
the darkness.

"Harold, are you asleep?"

"What do you want?"

"I was just thinking, Paleface will stop bothering you now, right?"

"Maybe. That's if it was him, of course."

"Well, who else?"

"Listen, you guys," Hallas hissed. "Let's get some sleep, follow Deler's good example."

I could hear the sound of quiet snoring coming from the ginger-haired dwarf's bed.

"All right, all right," Kli-Kli whispered.

I closed my eyes, but sleep wouldn't come. Sagot! Paleface had almost reached me tonight!

"Harold, are you asleep?"

"Now what?" I sighed.

"Tell me, what do you think? Where has Balistan Pargaid gone now?"

"You'll have to ask him that."

"Jut shut up, will you?" Hallas howled.

"What are you yelling at, Beard-Face? Let me sleep," Deler muttered without waking up, and turned over onto his other side.

"I'm not yelling, they're the ones who won't let me sleep," the gnome muttered. "Kli-Kli, shut up!"

"All right, I won't say a word," the goblin whispered hastily.

I yawned and closed my eyes.

"Harold, are you asleep?" the whispering voice asked again.

Will he ever calm down? I won't say a word now, just to spite him.

"Harold? *Harold!*"

Hallas groaned and broke into a string of choice abuse in a mixture of gnomish and human language. "Kli-Kli, one more word, and I'll lose control."

"But I can't get to sleep."

"Then count something!"

"What?"

"Mammoths!" the gnome exclaimed furiously.

"All right," the jester sighed. "The first mammoth jumps over the wall. . . . The second mammoth jumps over the wall. . . . The third mammoth jumps over the wall. . . . The fourth mammoth jumps over the wall. . . ."

Hallas started groaning again.

"The twenty-fifth mammoth jumps over the wall . . . ," Kli-Kli continued. "The twen-ty sev-enth mammoth jumps . . . over . . . the wall . . ."

Something went whistling through the air above me and Kli-Kli gasped in fright.

"Why are you throwing your boots, Hallas?" the jester asked indignantly.

"You know why! If you don't shut up, you'll spend the night in the corridor!"

Kli-Kli sighed, turned over on the floor, and stopped talking. I was absolutely certain that the goblin had thought up some sly trick. But the minutes passed, and he didn't make a sound.

I managed to get to sleep after all. Perhaps I was just tired after the long day, or perhaps the sleeping goblin's snoring sounded like a lullaby. . . .

We left Algert Dalli's castle at dawn, when the waking sun had just painted the edge of the sky a pale pink. Kli-Kli was yawning desperately and muttering sleepily, looking as if he would tumble off his saddle at any moment if someone didn't support him.

At that early hour of the morning Milord Algert Dalli, his wife, and his daughter came in person to see us off and wish us success. Oro Gabsbarg was also there. I don't know what Miralissa and Alistan Markauz had told the count, but we were given an escort of forty mounted men under the command of a certain Milord Fer, who turned out to be Dalli's illegitimate son. Kli-Kli told me that in the Border Kingdom the attitude toward bastards was completely different from in Valiostr. As long as a man was a good warrior, it didn't matter what blood ran in his veins. Fer was about three years older than Lady Alia and he looked like his father—short and sturdy.

Milord Algert had generously flung open the doors of his armory for us, and the castle's three armorers had wasted no time in selecting suits for Hallas, Deler, Alistan Markauz, Lamplighter, and Marmot. So now our entire group felt more or less well protected, although the replacements were far from comparable to the armor that had gone to the bottom of the Black River with the ferry. Lamplighter received a personal gift from the count—the dagger with the precious handle.

Fer's men were supposed to take us as far as a castle where a powerful garrison was quartered, ready to repulse any sudden attack from Zagraba. This castle was the final human stronghold; beyond it lay dense thickets into which no right-minded Border Kingdom warrior would wander without good reason.

Our road lay through coniferous forests with murmuring rivers and reinforced villages. The detachment was challenged from watch towers three times, and we came across five armed patrols.

The Borderland was seething with anticipation; the soldiers told us that the orcs were on the move in the Golden Forest.

"They've attacked two villages in the last month, Master Lamplighter," one of the men told Mumr respectfully. "And they gave a detachment from the Foresty Hills a good hiding, too. Until recently, we only saw orcs once in every six months, and then in the distance, but now they're testing our strength right along the border of the kingdom, searching out the weak spots. They say the Hand is gathering an army and dreaming of finally doing what they failed to do in the Spring War."

"Could they really break through?" Mumr asked, frowning and squirming in his saddle. He had taken too much to drink the evening before, and today he had a splitting headache.

"Break through?" The soldier thought for a moment. "I don't know, Master Lamplighter. If real trouble starts, then they'll certainly try, only not in our lands. They'll move past further to the west, where there's unbroken forest, with not many garrisons and, pardon me for saying so, the soldiers of Valiostr haven't really been doing their job recently. Anyone could slip by the fortresses there, even an orc, even a crowd of Terrible Flutes—if they exist, that is."

"Sagra forbid, if there is any serious trouble, we'll be the only ones here trying to fight it," said another soldier. "Before the main forces get here, and your regulars are assembled in Valiostr . . . How long is all that going to take? I've already moved my family closer to Shamar. It's safer there, after all it is the capital."

"What about the elves? Surely the elves will support you?" Eel asked.

"Elves?" The soldier glanced warily at the dark elves riding at the head of the column. "You know what Lord Algert says about elves? He says he's sick of them and their promises."

"Hold your tongue, Servin," one of the sergeants said gloomily. "Fer doesn't like any loose talk."

"But I'm right, Khruch. I'm right, and you know it."

"Maybe you are, but I still don't like the idea of a s'kash across my head."

"The dark elves make lots of promises, but who can understand them? They're not like us."

"The House of the Black Flame promised to send six hundred warriors to our borders, but not one has arrived yet," said the soldier, spitting on the ground under his horse's hooves.

The detachment halted for lunch at a village with no name. The horses were allowed to rest and we were greeted amiably and fed without any complaints, even though there was such a great horde of us. The short break did everyone good and the detachment moved on refreshed and invigorated.

"Fir trees, fir trees, everywhere," Kli-Kli sighed, looking round gloomily at the landscape.

"What's wrong with you? Is Zagraba supposed to be some kind of flower garden?"

Kli-Kli snorted contemptuously.

"Harold, you don't know what you're talking about. Yes, fir trees grow in Zagraba, but there are other trees, too. Pines, oaks, larches, maples, golden-leafs, birches, rowans, too many kinds to mention . . ."

"So what harm have fir trees ever done to you?"

"I don't like them. They're bad trees. Dark."

"And there's some-one hi-ding in them," said Honeycomb, opening his eyes in mock terror.

"That's right, for instance Balistan Pargaid and that witch of his! She'll jump out and shout 'Whoo-oo-oo,'" Deler added.

"It's such hard work talking to fools like you," the jester muttered miserably, and he didn't speak to us again until that night.

Although it was already the second half of August, and according to all the laws of nature the morning should have been just as hot as the previous day, the weather turned bad again, and if I hadn't known it was August, I would have thought it was late October.

Hazy and cool—those are probably the two words that best describe the day. The sky was completely covered with swollen, grayish purple clouds, and I began to feel afraid that I would have to travel in the rain again, as I had done on the journey to the Borderland. The cool wind did nothing to improve my spirits, either. Deler grumbled about the ache in his bones, Hallas grumbled about Deler, Kli-Kli grumbled about both of them. I'm sure I don't need to explain what kind of a din all that created.

"Look, now we're entering the Land of Streams, as we call this area," said Dervin, the same lad who had started the conversation about orcs the day before. "We're right on the edge of the inhabited region. In about four hours we'll be in Cuckoo."

"Cuckoo?" Marmot asked. "What's cuckoo?"

"That's the castle where the garrison is."

"A-ah. How many men do you have there?"

"Four hundred, not counting the servants and magicians."

"Magicians?" Hallas asked in a very suspicious tone of voice. For some reason the gnome couldn't stand magicians of the Order.

"Yes, master gnome, magicians. We have a magician in every fortress. In case the orcs' shamans show up."

"If the orcs' shamans show up, it's simpler to just climb into your coffin than hope for any help from the Order's cheap conjurers!" Hallas snorted contemptuously.

"Come now, master gnome, the magicians are really a great help! I remember I was in Milord Fer's detachment when we were defending Drunken Springs, and a shaman did show up—he almost dispatched all hundred of us to the light. If we hadn't had a magician there, I swear by Sagra I wouldn't be talking with you now."

Hallas muttered something to himself and changed the subject.

Ell came galloping up and said that Miralissa wanted to see me, so I had to follow the k'lissang to the front of the column. The elfess was chattering politely with Fer. But when she spotted me, she reined back her horse and asked:

"Harold, can you sense anything?"

"N-no," I answered after thinking for a moment. "What should I sense, Lady Miralissa?"

"I don't know," she sighed. "Is the Key silent?"

"Yes." The dwarves' handiwork had not given any sign since that night at Balistan Pargaid's house.

"I'm worried by Lafresa's sudden disappearance. She wasn't at Mole Castle with Balistan Pargaid, but she must be somewhere, and the count wasn't too upset when the judgment went against his man."

"I also got the impression that he had the ace of trumps hidden up his sleeve."

"Ace of trumps?" She thought for a moment. "Ah, yes! Cards. Yes, you're right, he must have some contingency plan, or he would not have given up so easily. I suspect the hand of that maidservant of the Master in this, and I thought that you ought to sense her, since you're attuned to the Key."

"No, I don't sense anything, Lady Miralissa."

"A pity," she said sincerely. "Although, on the other hand, if you can't sense her, then she must be somewhere far away."

"Or close by, but the artifact cannot sense her power," said Egrassa.

I preferred Miralissa's explanation; it made me feel a lot safer.

"Lady Miralissa, may I ask a question?"

"Please do."

"Balistan Pargaid is our enemy, he serves the Master, and yet you let him leave Algert Dalli's castle without hindrance. Why?"

"Have you still not realized that the laws in the Border Kingdom are different from the laws of Valiostr? Balistan Pargaid had sat at Milord Algert's table, and to arrest him . . . Here that would require more substantial evidence than just our word. And in addition, after the Judgment of Sagra, the count was entitled to leave, and no one had any right to stop him."

I nodded, and in my heart I cursed the damned warriors of the Border Kingdom and their stupid laws.

"What was she talking to you about?" Kli-Kli asked curiously.

"Nothing important."

The jester cast a wary glance at the gloomy sky and asked:

"Did you know that we'll be in Zagraba today?"

"Today? But I thought that—"

"Try using your head when you think, Harold. It'll be a lot better that way, believe me," the jester remarked. "Time is passing, so we'll go straight from the castle to Zagraba, and it's much safer to go there at night."

The forest thinned out, the gloomy fir trees shrank away to the sides, the road took a turn to the left, and a large village appeared ahead of us.

"Noble warriors, what is the name of that village?" Kli-Kli asked the soldiers with a pompous expression on his face.

"Crossroads," Servin answered again. "From there it's only an hour on foot to the castle."

"A-a-ah," the jester drawled, gazing hard at the houses in the distance.

Fer raised his clenched fist and the column halted.

"What's happening?" asked Marmot, breaking off from playing with Invincible.

"A strange kind of village," Eel hissed through his teeth, pulling his "brother" and "sister" closer to him.

"That's right," Lamplighter agreed, hurriedly tying the ribbon round his forehead. "I'd say very strange."

"What's strange about it?" I asked, puzzled.

"Can you see any people?"

"It's still a bit far away," I replied uncertainly, peering hard at the distant little houses.

"Not too far to see the people," Marmot countered. "Look—there's no one by the houses, no one in the street, and the watch towers are empty, too. I don't know any village in this country that doesn't have archers on its towers."

The Wild Heart was right—there was no one on the towers.

"Harold, have you got your chain mail on?" the goblin asked in concern.

"Under my jacket."

After conferring with the sergeants and Milord Alistan, Fer waved his hand, and the column slowly moved toward the village.

"Keep your crossbow close," Deler advised me, putting on his helmet.

The soldiers' sense of alarm infected me, too, and I took out my little weapon, set the string and loaded the bolts. One ordinary bolt, and one with the spirit of ice. Deler pressed his poleax against his horse's flank with his foot and also armed a crossbow, which was three times the size of mine. Several soldiers in the detachment did the same.

"Make haste slowly, lads, Fer says to keep your eyes peeled," said the sergeant, Grunt, when the column entered the village.

The straight street was as empty and quiet as if everybody had died.

"Why isn't there any stockade here?" I asked.

"No point, the village is too big," Servin answered, keeping his hand on the hilt of his sword. "It would be too big a job to fence it in, and Cuckoo's just down the road—"

"Servin, Kassani, Urch, One-Eye!" Fer called, interrupting the soldier's reply. "Check the houses. In pairs."

The warriors jumped down off their horses: Two of them ran to the houses on the left side of the street, and two to the houses on the right. The first soldier in each pair carried a crossbow and the second a sword. The swordsman ran to the door of the nearest house, kicked it open, and jumped aside to let the other man in. The warriors of the Borderland worked as precisely as one of the dwarves' mechanical clocks.

The seconds dragged on, and I was beginning to think the lads must have fallen into the cellar, they were gone so long. The same thing was happening on the other side of the street. Eventually the men came out of the houses and walked back.

"Nobody!" said a soldier from the first pair.

"The same on our side, commander, the houses are empty. No damage, nothing broken, food on the table, but the soup's cold."

"I'm sure it will be the same in the other houses, too, Milord Alistan," Honeycomb shouted to the count.

"Maybe there's a festival of some kind, or a wedding?"

"We don't have any festivals," said a warrior with a lance. "And weddings aren't held early in the morning."

"Orcs?" Lamplighter asked.

"It can't be. Cuckoo's just down the road. The Firstborn would never dare attack a village so close to a garrison."

"Urch, Kassani, check the tower!" Fer ordered.

The tower was close by, only ten yards from the road, at the edge of a field. While the lads were checking the houses, three of the mounted soldiers had kept their eyes on it, holding their crossbows ready. An archer could easily be hiding up there.

One of the soldiers started climbing up the shaky ladder, with a knife clutched in his teeth, while another held his crossbow pointed straight up in case an enemy head should suddenly appear in the square hole in the floor. The soldier with the knife clambered up and disappeared from view for a second. Then he reappeared and shouted:

"No one!"

"Is there anything up there, Urch?" asked Fer, raising his visor.

"A bow, a quiver of arrows, a jug of milk, commander!" Urch replied after a brief pause. "Blood! There's blood here on the boards!"

"Fresh?" shouted one of the sergeants, drawing his sword.

"No, it's dry! And there's only a little bit, right beside the bow!"

"Kassani, what is there on the ground?"

"I can't see anything," said the soldier below the tower. "Just ordinary earth, and we've trampled it."

Ell rode across to the tower, jumped off his horse, handed the reins to the soldier, then squatted down on his haunches and started studying the ground.

"Harold," the jester called anxiously, "can you smell anything?"

"No."

"I think there's a smell of burning."

"I can't smell it," I said after sniffing at the air. "You must have imagined it."

"I swear by the great shaman Tre-Tre, there's a smell of something burning."

"Blood!" shouted Ell. "There's blood on the ground!"

The elf jumped onto his horse and galloped across to Fer, Alistan, and Miralissa.

"He was killed on the tower, probably by an arrow, and he fell."

"I see," said Milord Alistan, tensing his jaw muscles. He pulled his chain-mail hood up over his head and put on a closed helmet with slits for his eyes. As if on command, Ell and Egrassa put on half-helmets that covered the top part of their faces.

"There's something bad here, oh, very bad!" said Lamplighter, looking round nervously for any possible enemy.

But the street was as empty as the houses around us. Not just empty, but dead. There were no birds singing, no cows mooing in the barn, no dogs barking.

"The dogs!" I blurted out.

"What do you mean, Harold?" asked Egrassa, turning toward me.

"The dogs, Egrassa! Have you seen one? Have you heard them bark?"

"Orcs," one of the soldiers said, and spat. "Those brutes hate dogs and they kill them first."

"Then where are the bodies? Did they take them with them?" asked Marmot.

"Some clans do that," Kassani said, climbing into his saddle. "They make ornaments out of dogs' skins."

"Urch, come down!" one of the sergeants shouted.

"Wait, commander, smoke!" cried Urch, pointing toward the center of the village.

"Thick?"

"No, I can just barely see it."

"What's burning?"

"I can't see for the roofs of the houses."

"Come down!"

Urch climbed down the ladder and got onto his horse.

"We move forward. Stay alert. We cover our back," said Fer, and lowered his visor with a smooth movement.

"You know, Harold," the goblin said in a whisper. "I'm beginning to feel afraid that we'll run into orcs."

"Me too, Kli-Kli. Me too."

We caught the charred smell twenty houses away from the site of the fire. A huge barn belonging to a well-to-do peasant was burning. Or rather, it had already burned down. What we found was a heap of ash, still smoking slightly.

The smell of smoke and ash was mingled with the smell of burned flesh.

"Check it," Fer rumbled from under his helmet.

One of the soldiers covered his face with his hands and walked to the extinguished fire. Walking across the cold embers and stepping over burnt-out beams, he stirred the ash with the toe of his boot and ran back to us. His face was pale.

"They were all burned, commander. Nothing but charred bones. They drove them into the barn and set fire to it. More than a hundred of them."

Someone sighed loudly behind me and someone else swore.

"How could this have happened?"

"Someone will pay for this!"

"Stop sniveling! Forward, at a walk," Fer said harshly. "Crossbowmen move up into the front line."

"What about the dead, commander?"

"Later," Fer replied.

We found the other villagers on the small square, where there was an inn and a wooden temple to the gods—more than twenty-five corpses. All the bodies had been gutted, like fish, their heads had been cut off and heaped up in one big pile. The stench of blood and death hammered at our nostrils and the buzzing of thousands of flies rang in our ears. It looked as if a crowd of insane jesters had run through here, splashing blood left and right out of buckets.

One of the soldiers dismounted and puked violently. And to be quite honest, I almost followed his example. It cost me an immense effort to keep my breakfast in my stomach.

Things like this just shouldn't happen. Things like this have no right to exist in our world!

Men. Women, old people, children . . . Everyone who had not been burned in the barn was lying in the square, which was covered in blood.

"There," said Marmot, with a nod.

There were seven bodies hanging on the wall of the inn. Their hands and feet had been nailed to the planks, their stomachs were slit open, and their heads were missing. Two women had been hanged on a rope thrown across the sign of the inn, and their bodies were swaying gently in the light breeze.

I heard a chirping sound and turned my head toward it. A small creature with gray skin, no bigger than a baby, broke off from devouring flesh and raised its bloody face toward us, blinking eyes that were like red saucers. A second one noticed that we were watching it and hissed maliciously.

A bowstring twanged and the first creature squealed and fell, pierced through by an elfin arrow. The second scavenger went darting away and Ell missed it. It disappeared behind the houses, chirping viciously.

"Gkhols, a curse on them!" Deler growled.

"The corpse-eaters are already feasting . . ."

"Take down the bodies," Fer ordered his soldiers.

They started cutting through the rope holding up the two women and taking down the seven bodies off the wall.

"I don't like the smell of this place," Kli-Kli groaned.

"I don't either, Kli-Kli."

"The ears have been cut off all the heads," said Eel, examining the corpses dispassionately.

"The Grun Ear-Cutters," one of the soldiers told us. "This is their work."

"Ear-Cutters?" Hallas repeated, raising one eyebrow.

"Punitive detachments. They like to collect ears."

"I see."

"Fer, tell me, could anyone have been left alive?" Alistan Markauz asked the commander of the column.

"I doubt it," the Border Kingdom warrior said somberly, watching his men carefully setting down the dead bodies removed from the wall. "Hasal, how long ago did this happen?"

"Yesterday evening, commander. The ash from the fire is barely smoking, the blood has all congealed."

"We need to get to Cuckoo as soon as possible; we can still overtake the Firstborn and have our revenge."

"We need to check the rest of the village; the orcs could still be here," Miralissa said with a shake of her head.

"Why, Tresh Miralissa? What would they be doing here?"

"Who can understand the Firstborn, Fer? Further on the street divides, which way do you intend to lead the detachment?"

"One-Eye, you're from here, aren't you?" Fer asked a soldier with a black bandage over his left eye.

"Yes." The lad's face was greener than a leaf in spring. "My aunt, my sisters . . . Everyone . . ."

"Pull yourself together, soldier! Where do these two streets lead?"

"They run separately to the end of the village, commander. The rich people lived further on, and the orchards start there . . ."

"I'm thinking of dividing the detachment into equal halves, Milord Alistan. We need to explore both streets. What if there is someone from the village still alive, after all?"

"Dividing up your forces may not be wise."

"But even so, I think it's the best way."

"Act as you think best, you are in command here."

"Grunt, Mouth, take your platoons down the street on the left. Eagle, Torch, you come with me."

"Yes, commander."

"Ell, Honeycomb, Hallas, Eel, Harold, Kli-Kli, go with Grunt," Alistan Markauz ordered. "Lady Miralissa, Egrassa, Marmot, Lamplighter, and I will follow Fer's detachment."

"Is it a good idea to split us up, milord?" Deler asked peevishly, testing the keenness of his battle-ax blade with his thumb.

"We can't weaken one of the detachments. They might need our help."

"Let's move," Fer commanded. "Mouth, we'll meet at the end of the village."

"Yes, commander."

"If anything happens, blow your horns," the knight said, and started his horse.

"Mind your beard, Beard-Face!" Deler boomed to Hallas.

"You worry about yourself," the gnome replied good-naturedly, adjusting his grip on the handle of his mattock.

We moved into the street, following the two platoons of Fer's somber and wary soldiers.

"Crud, Brute," the sergeant said to two twin brothers, "go in front, thirty paces ahead, where I can see your backsides. Keep your eyes peeled. If you see anything, come straight back."

The two soldiers moved ahead on their horses, trying to spot enemies.

Ell also urged his horse on and rode alongside the sergeant, holding an arrow in the string of his bow.

"I reckon this is stupid," Hallas grumbled. "Why would the orcs wait about for us to come and tickle their bellies?"

"The Firstborn are capable of any filthy trick, master gnome," said one of the soldiers. "And the Grun Ear-Cutters are the worst of all."

"Harold, Kli-Kli, stay behind me. If anything happens, I'll take them on," said Hallas.

"You're our little defender," Kli-Kli giggled, but he followed the gnome's advice and held Featherlight back a little.

The two scouts moved along slowly in front of us, but the street was calm and quiet.

The neat little houses with shutters and doors painted blue and yellow looked ominous, as if there was some threat lurking in them. The street widened out and the houses and fences painted blue and yellow became larger. The gates of a house where there were sunflowers growing in the garden had been knocked down and were lying on the ground. Somebody had used an ax to good effect here. There was a human body, bristling with arrows, lying on the porch. Like all the corpses in the village, it had no head. I looked away—I'd seen enough dead bodies for one day.

The houses on the left of the road came to an end and the orchards began. The thick bushes along the road oozed menace—an entire army of orcs could be hiding in there, and archers could easily be concealed in the branches of the apple trees, with their dense greenery. The soldiers kept a careful eye on the hedges, but the only movement was a startled wagtail that fluttered up off a branch and flew away behind the trees.

We had almost reached the end of Crossroads—three houses on the right, a small field, and then a forest of fir trees. On the left there was a field of cabbage, and Kli-Kli remarked that it would be a good idea to pinch a couple of cabbages for supper, the peasants wouldn't have any use for them now. The goblin hinted clumsily that I ought to steal the cabbages, but after what I had seen in the square, my appetite had been completely destroyed, and I told the goblin so without mincing my words.

Disaster came when no one was expecting it. The immense gates of the last two houses suddenly collapsed and arrows came flying out through the dust raised when they hit the ground.

Screams of pain, the rustling of swords being drawn, the whinnying of horses.

"Orcs!"

"Firstborn!"

"To arms!"

"Sound the horn!"

A war horn sounded and then immediately fell silent when an arrow hit the soldier blowing it in the throat. He dropped the horn and fell under the hooves of his horse. Another horn sounded, and from somewhere behind the houses we heard the clash of weapons. We couldn't expect any help; the other detachment had fallen into a trap, too.

"Some thieves we are!" the jester shouted, gazing at me with eyes wide in horror.

My memory of what happened after that is not very clear, and yet only too clear at the same time. I was myself, but I could see myself from the outside at the same time, as if watching what was happening around me. The entire battle is etched in my memory forever—it was like something happening in a nightmare, in a dream that is frozen in the frost, carved with an ax on separate blocks of ice.

Bowstrings twanged again and the orcs drew their yataghans and threw themselves on us. They attacked in silence, and that was probably the most terrifying thing that happened to me that day. They say fear has big eyes—in those first seconds it seemed to me that there were a lot of enemies, far more than there were of us.

We were at the very end of the detachment, and so the brunt of the first and most terrible onslaught was borne by the soldiers of the Border Kingdom . . . and Ell. I saw an arrow lodge in the eye slit of his helmet, I saw the elf leaning back, tumbling over . . .

The small number of men with crossbows started firing, and a few orcs fell, but the others came at us in silence.

The Borderlanders met the orcs with steel, repulsing the attack with swords and lances. The raucous din that filled the air was indescribable—oaths and screams, the clash of weapons, groans. The orcs were not deterred at all by the fact that their opponents were on horseback. One of them hurled himself at me. I fired and missed, then fired again and the ice bolt hit the Firstborn's shield, releasing its magic with a ringing sound and transforming my enemy into a statue of ice.

"Honeycomb, cover me!" I roared, trying to shout above the din of the battle. I had to reload the crossbow as quickly as possible.

The orcs were still busy with the men up at the front. They weren't really expecting an attack, and that gave those of us at the back of the column an extra twenty precious seconds to shower a deadly rain down on the Firstborn.

I don't think I have ever loaded a crossbow so fast in life. Put the bolts in the channels, pull the lever toward me, take aim, hold my breath, press one trigger, then the other.

The battle moved from the street into the cabbage field, and before the orcs could reach me, I had taken down four of them, another three bolts had missed, and two had just bounced off our enemies' armor as if it was enchanted. One of the orcs tried to break through to me, but he was stopped by Honeycomb's ogre-hammer. The heavy flail caught him in the side and flung him away.

Bang! My ears were struck by a strange new sound.

Little Bee reared up in fright and I crashed to the ground. I had to roll aside in order to avoid my own horse's hooves.

Jumping up off the ground, I found myself face-to-face with a massive orc. I had dropped the crossbow when I fell and there was no time to get my knife out. The Firstborn was clearly intending to remove my curly head and cut the ears off it. His yataghan whistled repulsively. I pulled my head down into my shoulders and my enemy's blade passed over it, merely ruffling my hair.

The battle was raging on all sides, our enemies were pressing hard and the men were all busy trying to survive, so I couldn't expect any help. The orc struck again, and in reply I dropped to the ground, rolled over in the dirt, grabbed the nearest cabbage, and flung it at my opponent's head. The Firstborn contemptuously knocked the cabbage aside with his yataghan, slicing it neatly into two halves. I had to jump back again, this lad was incredibly agile and—

Bang! I heard that loud sound again.

Something went whistling past me and the orc's head flew apart as messily as a ripe melon from the Sultanate, spraying me with hot blood.

I turned toward the sound. Hallas was standing on the ground, with his precious sack now dangling on his stomach. He was surrounded by rapidly thinning, bluish, foul-smelling smoke, and he still had his pipe in his mouth. In each hand my savior was holding a short, thick object that looked very much like a miniature cannon.

I'd never seen a wonder like that before.

Meanwhile three Firstborn came dashing at Hallas, realizing that he represented the greatest threat to them. Without any fuss, the gnome threw his terrible little cannons aside, took out another two exactly the same, raised one of them to the smoking pipe in his mouth, lit the fuse, and pointed it at one of the orcs rushing toward him.

Bang!

The enemy performed a most amusing aerial kicking movement and fell down.

Bang!

A hole the size of a fist appeared in the second orc's coat of mail and he swayed and collapsed facedown in the dirt.

The third orc stopped as if he was suddenly rooted to the ground, and was immediately run through with a lance by one of Fer's soldiers.

One-Eye could barely stay on his feet as one of the orcs crashed an ax down onto his shield. I pulled out my knife and committed the most insane act of my life. I took a run, jumped up, and hit the foul creature in the back with my feet, so that I ended up on the ground again. The orc, who wasn't expecting anything like this, dove forward, fell to his knees, and immediately parted with his head.

One-Eye nodded gratefully and jumped into the next scrimmage.

Darkness, I had to get back and pick up my crossbow.

"Die, little monkey!" Two orcs in helmets had noticed the solitary, innocuous man with a knife. I despairingly flung the knife at one of them, but he playfully knocked it aside with his shield.

"Harold, behind you!" called Honeycomb, leaping over to me. "Pick up the ax!"

I sprang back to make way for his ogre-hammer. The battle-flail swung low. Honeycomb was aiming for the legs. The Firstborn jumped up smartly, trying to avoid the heavy studded club. The Wild Heart changed the angle of his blow and the flail flew upward, putting an end to the less agile of the two orcs. The second orc tried to attack, but I was already there with the dead orc's ax. I struck out clumsily, but put everything I could into it.

The ax sliced into his shield and stuck there.

"Get out of there!"

The orc took a step back, taking my weapon away with him. I took the Wild Heart's advice just in time and jumped aside. In desperation the Firstborn held his yataghan out in front of him in an attempt to fend off Honeycomb's blow. The striking head of the ogre-hammer flew higher this time, wound its chain round the orc's yataghan, and stopped, tying the two weapons together.

Honeycomb tugged, but the orc kept his nerve and started tugging, too. Honeycomb let go of the handle of his ogre-hammer, stepped forward, and stabbed his dumbfounded opponent with his dagger just below the helmet, in his chin.

"Harold, what did I tell you? Clear out, go back to your horse!"

Honeycomb had already picked up someone else's sword and was fighting the next Firstborn. The entire cabbage field was seething with clashing weapons, shouts and screams, and blood. The battle had only been going on for a minute, or maybe two, but it seemed to me like an eternity since the start of the attack.

I picked my knife up off the ground, looked round, spotted Little Bee, and made a dash for her. One of the orcs flung a spear that pierced the links of Sergeant Mouth's chain mail and stuck in his back. Another two orcs finished off Servin, who was desperately trying to hold them off. One distracted his attention and the other chopped off his arm with an ax.

I was overwhelmed by fury.

May the darkness take me, I swear by Sagot that I am a calm man, not given to suicidal acts, but this really got to my liver! Our men were being killed, and I was just rushing round the field, dodging the Firstborn's yataghans.

I jumped up on the back of the one with the ax and literally drove the knife into the back of his head. He shuddered, went limp, and started to fall.

His comrade howled in fury and rushed at me. I was saved by the shield that had fallen from the hands of the orc I'd killed. I held it up in front of me, using both hands. The Firstborn struck once, twice, three times. His yellow eyes were blazing with fury.

Somewhere in the back of my mind I realized there was plaintive singing in a language I didn't know weaving itself into the noise of the battle. With every blow that descended on the shield I took several steps back. The orc was beginning to enjoy it, and I could barely manage to raise the shield fast enough against his yataghan. Chips of wood were flying everywhere—this lad ought to have been a woodcutter, not a soldier. I trod on a cabbage, slipped, and almost fell.

Clang-bash! Clang-bash!

After the tenth clang-bash, when the accursed shield started pulling my arms out of their sockets and the orc had just swung back for another blow, I resorted to cunning: I didn't defend myself against the blow, but simply stepped aside when the next attack came.

The orc put all his strength into the blow, and when he didn't encounter the usual resistance, he went flying forward, growling viciously.

To avoid falling to the ground, the Firstborn took a few more steps, and I smashed the shield against his back. The blow distracted him and then Hallas turned up to help me out.

The back section of his battle-mattock, the part that looked so much like a punch for working metal, pierced the Firstborn's armor with a resounding *cla-ang* and killed him on the spot.

"Harold, what would I do without your help?" Hallas laughed into his bloodstained beard.

"Behind you!" I shouted to warn him of danger approaching.

The short little gnome jumped smartly to one side, spun round, and attacked the new enemy.

Little Bee was still standing where I had left her. I hadn't even noticed when the fever of battle had carried me so far away from my horse. The crossbow was lying in the dirt, close to her hooves.

Kli-Kli appeared in front of me.

The goblin lowered his hands to his belt in a fluent movement, pulled off two heavy throwing knives, which performed glittering somersaults in his fingers, so that he was holding them by the blades, and then he flung them at me.

I didn't duck, I didn't move, and basically I didn't even have time to feel scared, it all happened so fast.

One of the knives whistled past my right ear and the other past my left ear, almost slicing it off.

Amazingly enough, I was still alive.

I had enough wits to look round. The enemy standing behind me had already raised his ax. The goblin's throwing knives were sticking out of his eye sockets. The orc stood there for a moment, swaying on his heels, and fell facedown, almost flattening me.

"You'll never get even for me saving your skin." The jester already had a second pair of knives in his hands.

I couldn't think of anything to say. I felt too ashamed, remembering how we had all laughed at the goblin's skill with throwing knives.

I picked up the crossbow and loaded it hastily.

"We're losing, we only have eight against twelve!" the goblin declared.

Where does he find the time to count?

"I know!"

"Then keep your wits about you. Can you hear the shaman singing? When he finishes casting his spell, things will get really bad."

A shaman! I turned cold, finally realizing the disaster that song could bring.

"What do you want me to do?"

"Find him and kill him! He's hiding somewhere!"

Easily said—kill a shaman!

Little Bee suddenly lashed out at an orc who was being pressed hard by a Border Kingdom soldier. Her hoof caught him in his unprotected back and the soldier finished off the job.

"I told you she was a battle horse!" Even in this situation the jester could find the strength to smile. "I know the right gifts to give my friends!"

Suddenly horns sounded and the second detachment, under Fer's command, struck the enemy in the rear like an iron fist. Alistan went sweeping past me and sliced the head off one of four orcs who were closing in on Eel.

I wouldn't say the Garrakian was exactly having a hard time against four adversaries, but the unexpected help certainly did no harm. In his hands the "brother" and "sister" were fluttering about like butterflies, fusing into a single glittering blur. The "sister" thrust and the "brother" slashed. The "sister" struck from above, aiming at the head; the orc covered himself with his shield and the "brother" immediately slashed open his exposed belly.

I calmly fired a crossbow bolt into the third orc, hitting him just below the right shoulder blade. Kli-Kli ducked down and slashed the fourth one's tendons, then Eel finished the job by killing the fallen orc.

"Miralissa!" I yelled when I saw the elfess, armed with a s'kash. Her ash-gray hair was covered by a hood of chain mail. "There's a shaman here!"

She shouted something in orcic to Egrassa and pronounced a spell, flinging out her hands. Ice appeared under the feet of the orc running toward her and her enemy slipped and skidded forward across it, waving his arms in surprise. He was greeted eagerly by Fer, who brought down his mace on the Firstborn's helmet. Blood spurted in all directions.

Suddenly semitransparent, poisonous-green bubbles appeared in the air.

"Keep away from them!" shouted Miralissa, forcing her Doralissian horse to turn aside sharply. *"Egrassa sh'tan nyrg sh'aman dulleh."*

Without even listening to her, the elf was shooting arrow after arrow, aiming at the sound of the voice. It looked as if Egrassa was insane—why else would he be firing at an absolutely empty spot in the field? The arrows hummed through the air and stuck in the ground, the singing went on, and more and more of the soap bubbles kept appearing. One of the soldiers cried out in pain.

A sudden blow threw me to the ground and clattered my teeth together.

"Are you tired of living?" Eel roared.

The Garrakian was on the alert—he had pushed me out of the way of the shaman's airborne curse just in time.

The elf's next arrow stuck in midair, there was a shriek, and the chanting stopped. An orc wearing a strange-looking headdress appeared from out of nowhere, out of thin air, and fell to the ground.

"The illusion of invisibility!" Kli-Kli shouted.

With the death of the shaman, the soap bubbles instantly burst and disappeared.

The cabbage field no longer rang to the sound of clashing weapons. Everything had ended as suddenly as it had begun. I realized that we had won and by the whim of Sagot I was still alive.

"Easy, my friend, just two more stitches and I'll be done," said Eel as he deftly sewed up Lamplighter's forehead with a crooked needle.

Mumr hissed and scowled, but he bore it. An orcish yataghan had caught Lamplighter on the forehead and sliced away a flap of skin. When the battle was over, the warrior's face and clothes were completely covered in blood, and now the Garrakian was stitching the skin dangling over Lamplighter's eyes back into place with woolen thread.

"Stop torturing me, Eel, I've lost enough blood already! Why don't you call Miralissa?"

"She's busy trying to save the men affected by the shaman's spell," said Eel, putting in another stitch. "And don't worry about all the blood. It's always like that with wounds on the face. It would be far more dangerous if they'd stabbed you in the stomach and it hadn't bled at all."

"Smart aleck . . . ," Mumr said, and scowled as Eel started tying off the thread. "Now there'll be a scar."

"They say they look well on a man." Eel chuckled. "Deler, give me your Fury of the Depths."

The dwarf stopped cleaning the blade of his battle-ax and handed the Garrakian his flask of dwarfish firewater. Eel moistened a rag and ruthlessly pressed it against Mumr's forehead. Lamplighter howled as if he had sat on hot coals.

"Put up with it, if you don't want the wound to fester."

The Wild Heart nodded with his face contorted in pain and took the rag from the Garrakian.

"Are you wounded, thief?"

Milord Rat had taken off his helmet and was holding it in his hands. Naturally enough, the captain of the guard was concerned about my health. After all, Stalkon had instructed him to protect me, and today I had almost been dispatched to the light. A fine joke that would be, if Milord Alistan Markauz failed to carry out an assignment!

"I don't think so," I said apathetically.

The battle was over, but I still couldn't get over the delirious fever that is born from the clash of swords. Kli-Kli and I were sitting on the ground beside Little Bee and looking at the trampled cabbage field, scattered with the bodies of orcs, men, and horses.

"You have blood on your face."

Blood? Ah, yes! When Hallas blew the orc's head off with his wonder-weapon, a few drops of blood had landed on me.

"Not mine, milord."

"Here, wipe it off." And he kindly handed me a clean piece of rag. "Well done for surviving, thief."

I grinned sadly. I'd survived, all right, but others hadn't been so lucky. An orcish arrow had killed Ell on the spot. Marmot would never feed Invincible again—he had been hit by the shaman's bubbles, and killed. Honeycomb, too, had been hit by the bubble and now he was lying unconscious, at death's door. Miralissa was trying to help him and three other warriors, but I wasn't sure she could do anything.

The other detachment had also run into orcs, but there were far fewer of the Firstborn there, so Fer and his men had managed to deal with their enemies and come to help.

"They gave us a good mauling," Fer said to Alistan.

"How many?"

"Eighteen killed, not counting your two men, milord. Hasal, how many wounded?"

The healer looked up from bandaging a casualty.

"Slightly wounded—almost everyone. Four seriously. They chopped off Servin's arm and pierced his stomach. I'm afraid he won't last the night, commander."

"And how many orcs?"

"No one's counted them," Hasal said, with a grimace. "No more than thirty."

"Thirty orcs after an advantage of fifty. We got off lightly after all."

"Commander, what shall we do with the two prisoners?" One-Eye shouted.

"We'll deal with them in a moment," Fer said somberly.

"Come on, Harold, let's take a look," said Kli-Kli, jumping to his feet.

I wasn't really interested in looking at orcs. I'd have preferred to dispatch them straight to the darkness, it's a lot safer that way.

"Oh, come on!" he said, tugging on my arm. "What's the point of just sitting around?"

Cursing the restless goblin to the high heavens, I got up off the ground and plodded after him.

The two Firstborn had been wrapped round with so much rope that it looked as if they had fallen into some gigantic spider's web. One was wounded in the leg and the blood was still flowing, but no one had bothered to bandage the wound. Four soldiers were keeping a close watch on the prisoners, one of them holding the point of a lance right against the neck of a Firstborn. Egrassa was standing beside them, toying with a crooked dagger.

Orcs and elves. Elves and orcs. They look so much alike that at first glance it's hard for someone inexperienced to tell the two races apart. Both of them have swarthy skin, yellow eyes, ash-gray hair, black lips, and fangs, and they speak the same language. The differences are too small for a casual observer to notice.

Firstborn and elves are blood relatives. Orcs are a little bit shorter than elves, a little bit stockier, their lips are a little bit thicker and their fangs are a little bit longer. And sometimes that simple "little bit" can cost a careless man his life. The only clear difference is that orcs never cut their hair and weave it into long braids.

"If you want to die quickly, answer my questions. We'll start with you," Fer said to the wounded orc.

The orc set his jaws, jerked, and gave a gurgling sound. Blood poured out of his mouth.

"Sagra!" one of the soldiers exclaimed in horror. "He's bitten off his own tongue!"

The orc suddenly arched over sideways, and the point of the lance that was just pricking his skin ran right through his neck. The Border Kingdom soldier swore and recoiled, pulling out the lance, but it was too late—from the fountain of blood shooting up toward the sky it was clear that the Firstborn was dead.

"Kassani, darkness take you! Stop acting like a little kid!" Fer swore at the soldier.

"They're all crazy, commander! He stuck himself on it," said the soldier.

"Well then, your friend has departed for the darkness, but I won't give you the chance to do the same," Egrassa said to the remaining orc. "You will answer this man's questions, or our conversation is going to last for a very long time."

The orc looked contemptuously at the elf and spat in his face.

"I don't talk to lower races."

Egrassa calmly wiped the gob of spittle off his face and broke one of the orc's fingers. The Firstborn howled.

"You will answer, or I will break all the rest of your fingers and toes." The elf's voice was as cold as the frozen Needles of Ice.

I turned and walked away. It doesn't make me feel good watching someone's fingers get broken. Kli-Kli came with me.

"Harold, I still can't believe that we survived."

"Well then, pinch yourself on the ear," I advised him.

The soldiers who were still on their feet had already put the bodies of the fallen on a wagon found in one of the yards. They put the wounded into another one.

Honeycomb was still as pale as ever, and grim-faced Miralissa was whispering spells over him and the other warriors who had been hit by the shaman's spell.

"How is he?" Kli-Kli asked anxiously.

"Very bad. The life is leaving him, I can see that, but I can't stop it. We need a magician's help here. And as soon as possible."

"There's an experienced magician at Cuckoo, milady," said one of the wounded soldiers on the wagon.

"Crud, take some lads and harness horses to the wagons!" Fer shouted.

The soldiers set to it and led over horses that had lost their masters in the fighting. I went back to the Wild Hearts.

Hallas was sitting on the ground, carefully tipping gunpowder out of a large silver horn into his little cannons.

"So that's what you've been hiding in that sack all this time." Deler sniffed disdainfully. "What other fantastic nonsense have you lot invented now?"

"We invented what we wanted," the gnome muttered, and started hastily packing his mysterious weapons away in the sack.

"Hallas, would you mind?" Alistan Markauz asked, reaching out his hand.

The gnome gave the Rat a resentful look, but there was no way he could refuse the count, and he reluctantly handed him one of his toys. Milord Alistan turned the little cannon over in his hands and asked, "How does it work?"

"That's a gnome secret, milord," Hallas said with a frown. "I'm sorry, I can't tell you."

"Don't talk nonsense, any fool can figure that out," Deler interrupted. "There's the wick, and there's the trigger. Press the trigger and it lowers the wick, lights the powder, and the ball flies out! Tremendous gnomish cunning, my foot! It's just a little cannon."

Hallas ground his teeth in annoyance.

"You're a cannon, you thickhead! It's a pistol, our new invention. Just you wait till we turn up in the mountains with weapons like these to take our land back!"

"We're always glad to see you, call any time! If the Field of Sorna wasn't enough for you beard-faces, we can give you more, we're not greedy!" Deler's voice sounded boastful, but his eyes were fixed on the pistol in Alistan Markauz's hands.

"If we had a few hundred pistols like this, it would make fighting the Nameless One's army a lot easier," the captain said pensively, handing the weapon back to the gnome. "What do you think, Hallas, would your kinsmen fulfill an order like that?"

"Pardon me for speaking plainly, Milord Alistan," Hallas said in a flat voice, putting the weapon away in his sack. "But gnomes have never been fools. If we let you have things like this, first you'll kill all your enemies, and then you'll come after us, out of sheer boredom. You people are not all that bright, all you want to do is fight wars and let your enemies' blood. A weapon like this in your hands . . . Our rulers would never make such a bargain."

"A shame, we'll have to take it with our swords."

Egrassa came back and shook his head.

"He didn't say anything."

"Damn the orc to the darkness! Let's go." Miralissa was in a hurry to get to the castle as quickly as possible. "Are you ready, Fer?"

"Yes, milady."

The detachment set off, with the wagon wheels creaking, and we left behind Crossroads, the place that had sent another two of our number to the light.

14

ON THE BORDER

The detachment moved as fast as it could. The elfess rode along-side one of the wagons, constantly checking the condition of the wounded men.

"I hope Honeycomb's going to be all right," Hallas muttered.

"Everyone hopes so, Beard-Face," Deler replied, and took a sip from his flask. "Want some?"

"All right," the gnome replied after a moment's thought. "Since there's nothing else, dwarf swill will have to do."

Fer sent two horsemen on ahead to Cuckoo to warn the magician, the healers, and the garrison. Everyone held their weapons at the ready, in case any of the orcs we hadn't killed were lying in ambush in the forest.

"Torch!" a soldier with his left arm bandaged shouted to his sergeant. "Servin's dead!"

"May he dwell in the light," whispered one of the soldiers.

"Harold!" said Eel, holding out Invincible to me. "You keep him, the little beast is used to you."

I took the shaggy little rat that had just lost his master and tucked him inside my jacket. Ling sniffled as he settled down and then fell quiet. We could decide what to do with him later.

A horn sounded—it was the messengers sent on ahead by Fer com-ing back. A detachment of eighty horsemen came with them.

Their commander, an elderly warrior with a wispy beard, asked, "Is there anyone left alive in the village?"

"Not as far as I know. But the villagers who were killed need to be buried."

"We'll deal with that. I'll leave twenty horsemen to accompany you. It's no more than four leagues to the castle, you're expected."

"Thank you," said Fer, with a curt nod.

Cuckoo—a reddish gray hulk with three towers, double walls, and six earthen ramparts—was seething like a disturbed anthill. It was hard to believe that only an hour's ride from here the orcs had wiped out a village, and the soldiers had known nothing about it.

"Healers!" Fer barked as soon as we were in the castle courtyard.

Men came running up to the wagon, some of them brought stretchers, and first aid was given to the wounded on the spot, leaving the men who had been hurt by the orc's magic to Miralissa's care.

A tall man with a bald head walked up to the elfess, who was still whispering spells. He was dressed in the black chain mail of a simple soldier. There was a sword hanging on his belt and he was holding the staff of a magician of the Order.

The magicians in the Border Kingdom weren't all that different from ordinary soldiers. They were as skilled in handling a sword as in magic. Nothing like our Valiostrian idlers.

"A 'soap bubble,' milady?" he asked, putting his hand on Honeycomb's forehead, which was covered in sweat.

"Yes, it's the Khra-z ten'r," she replied with a nod. "To whom do I have the honor of speaking?"

"Wolner Gray, magician of the Order of the Border Kingdom, at your service . . ."

"Miralissa of the House of the Black Moon. Can you help me?"

"Yes, Tresh Miralissa. Hey, lads!" the magician called to the soldiers. "Get stretchers and carry the stricken into the hospital hall."

The magician and the elfess walked away. The soldiers carried the wounded after them.

"Young lad!" said Deler, grabbing hold of a stable boy by the sleeve. "Do you have a shrine to Sagra here?"

"Yes, master dwarf, over there."

"What's this, Deler? Turned devout all of a sudden?"

"Don't be a fool, Beard-Face. I'm going to pray for Honeycomb's health."

Hallas scratched his beard and shouted: "Hang on, Hat-Head, I'll go with you, or you'll only get lost."

"But I'm not going anywhere," said Lamplighter, who was feverish from his wound. "Eel, help me stagger over to the healers, I'm feeling a bit shaky."

Mumr leaned on his bidenhander and got to his feet. Without speaking a word, the Garrakian offered him his shoulder and led him toward the healers bustling around the wagons. Kli-Kli and I were left on our own.

"Come on, Dancer, I'll show you something," the jester called out to me.

"Where are we going?" I asked him suspiciously.

"Come on, you won't regret it."

There was nothing to do, evening was drawing in, and I didn't think we would be going to Zagraba today, so I followed the goblin. Kli-Kli walked over to a hoist beside the wall.

"Where are you going, greeny?" asked the man who was loading stones for a catapult into the hoist.

"Would you be so kind, my dear man, as to raise the two of us up onto the wall together with these most remarkable stones that match the color of your face so well?" Kli-Kli asked.

"What?" the worker asked, wide-eyed. ·

"Can you hoist us up, blockhead?"

"The steps are over there!" said the man, jabbing a dirty finger toward the wall. "Use your legs, I've got work to do, I've no time to be giving you a lift as well."

Kli-Kli stuck his tongue out at him and stomped off angrily to the steps that led up onto the top of the wall.

"Kli-Kli, can you tell me why I should climb twenty yards up a wall?" I asked the goblin.

"It would spoil the surprise. Have you ever regretted listening to what I say?" The goblin was already climbing briskly up the steps.

"Yes," I replied quite sincerely.

I followed him anyway. It was an easy climb, because the steps wound round the wall. The palace courtyard sank lower and lower below us, and the men, the horses, and the wagons all shrank.

"Tell me this," I asked Kli-Kli as he ambled along in front of me. "Where did you learn to handle throwing knives so neatly?"

"Why, did you like it?" asked Kli-Kli, glowing at this unexpected praise. "I have just as many hidden talents as you do, Dancer."

"You don't say?"

"I'm a jester," he said, and shrugged. "Throwing knives is no harder than juggling four torches or doing a triple reverse somersault."

"You've got a tough job, old friend," I laughed.

He stopped, looked down at me, and said in a serious voice, "You can't even imagine how tough it is, Harold. Especially when I have to look after fools like you!"

"So you're the one who's looking after me!"

"There, that's human gratitude for you," said the goblin, raising his hands imploringly to the sky. "Wasn't I the one who saved you from that dog's teeth?"

"Well, yes," I had to agree.

"And today? Today, whose knives stopped the orc's ax?" the goblin went on as he completed another turn of the stairway.

"Yours," I sighed.

"Oh!" said the goblin, raising one finger didactically without turning to face me. "That's exactly the point. Are you thieves all like that?"

"Like what?"

"With such a short memory for the good things that other people do for you."

"All right, calm down, Kli-Kli. I remember that I owe you for one time."

"What do you mean, for one time!"

"You saved me from the dog, and I saved you from the river, so I still owe you one rescue," I chuckled.

"Maybe I know how to swim, and I was only pretending?" Kli-Kli suggested, narrowing his eyes cunningly.

"Well, then you really are a fool."

"All right, I admit it, I can't swim. And by the way, we're here."

I hadn't realized that I was on the wall. It was broad, with immense battlements, loopholes, and blue sky. The walls gave no protection from the wind up here, and it blew straight into my back. I could imagine what it was like being up here in winter or during a storm. Invincible crept out from under my jacket and clambered onto my shoulder.

"So what was it you wanted to show me?" I couldn't spot anything interesting up there, just a catapult, a few bowmen standing watch, and one craftsman, reinforcing the stones of the wall.

"Look over that way!" said Kli-Kli, dragging me across to a loophole and almost pushing me off the wall in his enthusiasm. "Over here!"

The castle stood on a low hill, and the view was magnificent. Out there, beyond the castle's earthen ramparts and three moats, beyond a small river with a lazy current and a field about three hundred yards across, overgrown with scrubby bushes, the forest started.

Zagraba.

The massive wall of trees gazing back at me from the far side of the river was magnificent and beautiful. A forest whose size rivaled the whole of Valiostr. It stretched on for thousands of leagues.

There before my eyes was the land where the gods had walked at the dawn of time, the kingdom that had existed in Siala before the times of the Dark Age, when orcs and elves had not even been heard of. The mysterious, fabulous, magical, enchanting, and also bloody, terrible, and sinister Forests of Zagraba.

How many legends, how many myths, how many endless stories, riddles, and mysteries were hidden beneath the green branches of the forest country? How many beautiful, outlandish, and dangerous creatures roamed its narrow animal tracks?

The beautiful towns of the elves and the orcs, the famous foliage and the labyrinth, the abandoned idols and temples of vanished races, the remains of the cities of the ogres, almost as old as time itself and, of course, the wonder and the horror of all the Northern Lands—Hrad Spein.

"My homeland," Kli-Kli declared in a ringing voice. "Can you just feel that smell?"

I sniffed the air. There was a cool, fresh smell of forest, honey, and an oak leaf crushed in the palm of your hand.

"Yes."

"It's wonderful, isn't it?"

"Yes, it is," I answered quite sincerely.

The immense carpet of green stretched out in front of us all the way to the horizon, disappearing into the evening mist.

Zagraba seemed to be endless. I screwed up my eyes, and for a moment I thought I could see the majestic summits of the Mountains of the Dwarves wreathed in violet haze and propping up the sky. Of course, I only imagined it; the great mountains were hundreds of leagues away and impossible to see from there.

"Why do they call it the Golden Forest?" I asked Kli-Kli, who was pressed right up against the loophole.

"Golden-leaf trees grow there," the jester said with an indifferent shrug.

"It's getting dark, let's go back," I said, casting a last glance at Zagraba. "I don't want to break my legs on the way down."

Twilight was creeping up on the castle and torches were lit in the courtyard. There were not many men there, the bodies of the dead had already been unloaded from the wagon and carried away. I couldn't see Eel, or Alistan, or Miralissa.

"Now how can I find our group? I don't intend to go wandering all over the citadel like a fool."

"We'll think of something," Kli-Kli said cheerfully.

An old man in a baggy, shapeless robe came up to us:

"Master Harold, Master . . ."—a brief pause—". . . Kli-Kli?"

"That's right."

The old man gave a sigh of relief and jerked his head.

"Follow me, they're waiting for you."

He shuffled into one of the towers, led us through a long hallway where the walls were hung all over with weapons, and turned onto a narrow spiral staircase, from which we emerged into a hall where the Wild Hearts, Milord Alistan, and Egrassa were already eating.

"Where's Mumr?" asked Kli-Kli, sitting down on a bench and pulling a plate toward him.

"Sleeping, he's not feeling well," said Hallas, stuffing a piece of sausage into his mouth and chomping on it.

"Is he all right?"

"A slight fever," said Eel, taking a sip of beer. "He'll be fine in a couple of days. I'm more worried about Honeycomb."

"Miralissa will do everything possible to save him," said Egrassa, without raising his eyes from his plate.

The rest of supper was spent in silence.

When the elfess joined us, Egrassa jumped to his feet and moved up a chair for her. Lady Miralissa nodded gratefully, and it was clear that she was absolutely exhausted. She had dark shadows under her eyes and deep creases running across her forehead; her hair was loose and tangled.

Milord Alistan poured her some dark wine without speaking, but she merely shook her head and smiled sadly.

"Wine and food can wait, I have another job to do. Egrassa?"

"Yes, the men have already made everything ready. We can begin."

"Have you eaten?" she asked, turning to us.

"We are ready, milady," Milord Alistan answered for all of us.

Kli-Kli nodded hastily, with his mouth full.

"Let us go," she said briefly, and stood up. Egrassa dashed to her and supported her by the elbow.

"Lady Miralissa," Hallas said plaintively. "You haven't said a word about Honeycomb. Is he all right?"

"Yes, the danger has passed, the warrior will live. He is sleeping now, but I am afraid he will not be able to continue on the journey. It will be two weeks before Honeycomb can get out of bed, and we cannot afford to wait that long. We will leave him in the castle."

"Where are we going, Kli-Kli?" I asked the goblin, when Miralissa had left the hall.

"They're going to have Ell's funeral now, so hurry up, Dancer. And don't forget to pick the ling up off the table, or someone will think he's a rat and kill him."

I grabbed Invincible and set him on my shoulder. I had no idea what I was going to do with him now.

It was completely dark outside, but the gates of the castle were not locked. The detachment of soldiers that we had met on our way here had only just returned. They had four people from Crossroads with them—the only ones who had managed to hide in the forest when the orcs attacked the village.

Miralissa led us out through the gates and down to the river. On the other bank Zagraba rose up as black as an inkblot against the starry sky. A funeral pyre had been built right at the water's edge. They had been generous with the wood, and the heap was two yards high. Ell's body lay on the very top, clad in a black silk shirt. His s'kash and bow lay beside him.

We halted at a distance, watching as Miralissa and Egrassa approached our dead comrade.

"And now one more has left us," said Alistan Markauz.

"Two, milord," Eel corrected the count. "Tomorrow we shall have to commit Marmot to the earth."

"I'm afraid we shall not even have time for that; we leave at dawn," the captain of the guard said with a guilty shake of his head.

"But a funeral—," the dwarf began. Alistan Markauz interrupted him: "They will take care of Marmot's body, Deler."

Miralissa and Egrassa walked back to us.

"Sleep well, k'lissang. Egrassa and I will take care of your kin," Miralissa said, and snapped her fingers.

The fire took immediately. The flames roared up to the sky like a red horse that became a red dragon, roaring as it consumed the wood and the body of the dead elf. Reflected in the water, the magical fire strained upward toward the stars, it howled and wailed, bearing the elf's soul away into the light. The pyre was more than twenty yards away, but we all moved back, because the heat was unbearable.

The flames gave a sudden sob, the burnt-out platform on which Ell was lying collapsed down into the open jaws of the heat, and the pyre tossed a shower of sparks up to the cold stars.

Miralissa began singing in a low, throaty voice, chanting the song that elves sang over a deceased kinsman.

Nobody said a word until the pyre had been reduced to a heap of winking coals radiating heat.

"That is all," said the elfess. She made several passes with her hands and a sudden gust of wind picked the coals and Ell's ashes up off the ground and swirled them up into the air, filling the night with hot fireflies, then tossed the remains of the pyre into the river.

The river hissed and snorted in alarm, its calm waters heaved and spat out steam and then swallowed up the remains of our companion.

"Hmm . . . ," said Deler after a short silence. "I'd like to be buried so . . ."

"Beautifully," Hallas concluded for him.

"We have a belief that when an elf dies in battle, a new star lights up in the sky," said Egrassa. "Foolish, but beautiful. Ell deserved his star."

"Like all those no longer with us," Alistan replied. "Let's go back to the castle, it's late."

And the river flowed on as quietly and lazily as ever, with nothing to show that a few minutes earlier it had swallowed up the remains of a funeral pyre.

"Harold, this is yours." Kli-Kli jabbed one finger at a sack with two shoulder straps that was standing beside my bed.

It was barely dawn outside, but the group was already up. Zagraba was waiting for us, and I had a chilly feeling of anticipation in my belly. But whether what was coming was good or bad, I couldn't tell.

"What's in it?" I asked, fastening on my crossbow.

"Your things. Blanket, rations, and a few odds and ends. I took the liberty of transferring all this junk from your saddlebags, plus a few things from the general heap . . ."

"Who asked you to do that?" I asked in a threatening voice.

"Oh, Harold," Kli-Kli said dismissively. "No need for gratitude, I got up a lot earlier than you, so it was no bother for me."

"Kli-Kli, don't pretend to be more stupid than you really are. Why did you empty the bags?"

"Because you won't carry them on your back. You're not a horse, are you? It's easier to walk through Zagraba with a sack. The trappers and a few hunters who dare to go into the forests take exactly this kind of sack with them."

"Mmm . . . ," I began warily. "Kli-Kli, I thought I heard you use the word 'walk.' Did I mishear?"

"Not at all, that's right, I said 'walk.' The horses are staying at the castle."

"What!"

"Harold, I can see that you've never gone roaming through a forest before," Kli-Kli chuckled, tightening the knot on his sack. "Just you try galloping through fallen trees, bogs, and darkness knows what else on a horse. It's no fun. We're going on foot. The elfess says that from here to Hrad Spein is exactly seven days' march. That is, one week. The entrance to the burial chambers is in the Golden Forest. If the gods smile on us, we'll soon be there."

It was surprising, but I didn't want to leave Little Bee. After a month and a half of traveling, I couldn't imagine how I could get by without my own horse. And now I would have to wear my legs out dragging a massive load around on my back.

I didn't really believe that Kli-Kli had packed my things properly, so I turned the contents of the sack out onto the bed. It would have been just like the goblin to slip five weighty cobblestones in with my things out of the sheer goodness of his heart. Sagot be praised, there weren't any cobblestones, but I did find a stack of useless heavy things.

"What are you doing?" Kli-Kli asked, watching skeptically as I set the superfluous things aside.

"Sparing my back unnecessary suffering," I muttered, tossing away a cast-iron cooking pot.

The pot was followed by a collection of assorted cutlery, a candlestick and candles, a ball of string, a hammer, two pairs of boots, spare chain mail, and all sorts of other miscellaneous nonsense. When I was through, the sack was a lot lighter. Now I could take it on a journey with an easy mind, without being afraid that I might suddenly break down at the wrong moment.

"All that hard work for nothing," Kli-Kli sighed mournfully.

"You don't have to carry it, so don't whine," I said, packing the blanket.

"Let's get a move on," said Hallas, glancing into the room. "It's time."

"Let's go and say good-bye to Honeycomb," said Kli-Kli, and skipped out through the door.

On the way we ran into Lamplighter. The Wild Heart was pale and the welt on his forehead looked terrible, but he was perfectly steady on his feet.

"So you're still alive, then?" Kli-Kli asked the warrior sympathetically.

"You can't bury me yet, fool," Lamplighter said with a crooked grin, and then frowned at the pain. "I still intend to get back to the Lonely Giant. Are you on your way to Honeycomb?"

"Yes, do you know where he is?"

"Yes, I've just come from there. Go out of the tower, across the courtyard, in at the door on the left, up the stairs to the second floor, and it's the third door on the right."

"Thanks. If Alistan comes looking for us, tell him you haven't seen us. Come on, pick up those feet, Harold, time's passing!"

Mumr gave me a pitying look—when Kli-Kli gets his hooks into someone, no power on earth can shake him off.

We found Honeycomb's room without any trouble. In one night the warrior had lost as much weight as if he hadn't eaten anything for a month, and he had changed from the husky giant of a man we all remembered to a skeleton. A bundle of bones wrapped in parchment skin that looked ready to split apart, eyes with a feverish glow, yellow hair that looked as if it had been bleached by the sun. If I didn't know it was Honeycomb on the bed, I'd have thought I was looking at an old, old man. The orcs' shaman had done a really good job, and if Miralissa and the Border Kingdom magician hadn't been there to help him, our comrade would have been lying in his grave alongside Marmot.

When he saw us, he gave a weak smile.

"How are you feeling?" squeaked Kli-Kli.

"Rotten," Honeycomb chuckled. "I managed to get in the way of that shaman's free handout."

"Don't worry about that. The main thing is that you're still alive."

"Thank you, Harold, that's a great comfort," he snorted in reply. "Deler let slip that Marmot and Ell . . . Is it true?"

"Yes," I answered.

"Well then, in that case, I really did get off lightly. You're leaving, I see."

"Yes," Kli-Kli said with a quick nod.

"It's a pity I won't be able to go with you," Honeycomb sighed.

"Don't worry about that, you just get well," Kli-Kli said fussily. "Look, I brought you this, so anyway, recover."

Kli-Kli took a large ripe apple out from under his cloak and put it on the table beside Honeycomb's bed. Then he thought for a moment and added a carrot to it.

"From the heart."

"I know, Kli-Kli," Honeycomb said with a serious nod. "You're a good lad."

"Of course I am," the goblin said with a grin. Then he gave me a mischievous glance, leaned right down to the warrior's ear, and whispered something to him.

Honeycomb's eyes opened wide and gaped at the goblin in surprise.

"I'm not lying," Kli-Kli said, perfectly serious. There were demons of mischief dancing in the jester's eyes.

I don't know where Honeycomb got the strength, but he suddenly burst into raucous laughter:

"What a hoot! Well . . . and no one knows?"

"Na-ah," the goblin grinned.

"What are you talking about?" I asked, bemused.

"Oh, nothing. We're just, you know . . . ," said the goblin, baring his teeth in an idiotic leer.

Honeycomb started laughing even louder. Mmm, the goblin's really in top form today.

"Will you look after him?" I asked, taking Invincible off my shoulder and putting him on the table beside the carrot, which immediately attracted the ling's interest. "He'll be a lot better off here than in the forest with us."

"Of course, let him stay."

"Well, time for us to go, be seeing you."

"Get well."

"Hey," he called as we were walking out. "Come back with flags flying."

"Definitely. We'll definitely be back!"

I don't know why, but I felt strangely confident that despite all our enemies I was going to defy fate and get that cursed Horn for the Order.

We were escorted to the border by Fer and ten of the soldiers who had traveled with us from Mole Castle. Zagraba greeted us with the silence of a slumbering forest in which morning is still several hours away.

"You'll have to walk on from here alone," said Fer. "I don't know what it is you're looking for in this forest, but in any case I wish you luck."

"Make sure that Marmot is given a fitting funeral," said Lamplighter, shouldering his bidenhander.

"I shall see to it personally," the knight replied with a solemn nod.

"Expect us at the end of September," said Miralissa.

"Very well, Tresh Miralissa," replied Algert Dalli's illegitimate son, then he swung his horse round and set off back toward the castle.

I felt as if I'd left behind an entire familiar world that I loved passionately. And waiting ahead for me was Zagraba. Dark, unwelcoming, and alien.

When I turned back from watching the men riding away, almost all our group had disappeared into the forest.

"Harold, have you decided to stay behind?" asked Kli-Kli, hopping impatiently from one foot to another. The goblin had a small sack hanging behind his shoulders.

"All right, Kli-Kli, you show the way, I'll follow you."

The goblin grinned and disappeared into the trees. I took a deep breath and stepped forward into a place where I thought I would never go for love or money. I stepped into Zagraba.

Glossary

Annals of the Crown - the most ancient and detailed of the historical chronicles, maintained by the elves since they first appeared in the world of Siala.

Avendoom - the capital of the northern kingdom of Valiostr. The largest and richest city of the Northern Lands.

battery sword - a variety of sword with a midsized blade that can be wielded either with one hand or both.

Beaver Caps or beavers - soldiers of Valiostr, armed with heavy two-handed swords. Each soldier bears the title of "Master of the Long Sword" and wears a beaver-fur cap as an emblem to distinguish him from the soldiers of other units. These forces are used as a reserve striking force, to recover all kinds of difficult situations in battle. During military action the beavers are also accorded the honor of guarding the banner and the king, taking the place of the royal guard.

bidenhander - a two-handed sword with a blade that can be a yard and a half long. They usually are designed with a massive handle, a heavy counterweight that is usually round, and a broad crosspiece. Sometimes the armorers would add massive metal spurs to prevent the blade running right through the opponent.

Border Kingdom, or Borderland - the kingdom beside the northern outcrops of the Mountains of the Dwarves and the Forests of Zagraba.

Borg's link - named after a general of ancient times who invented the chain formation, in which every single soldier plays an indispensable part in repelling an attack.

brother and sister swords - the names of the two swords in the special school of swordsmanship that is widespread among the nobility of Garrak. During combat the weapons are held at different heights in relationship to each other. The "brother," a narrow, double-sided blade held in the right hand, is used both for slashing and for thrusting. The "sister," a shorter blade with no cutting edge, is only used for thrusting blows. The weapons are either carried behind the back or in a double scabbard.

Canian forge work - weapons made from the steel mined in the Steel Mines of Isilia. The steel is worked in the famous smithies of the kingdom's capital, Cania. Following special processing and forging it acquires a ruby color and a unique quality—on encountering steel of a different type it emits a melodic ringing sound like small bells, or a shriek of fury. For this reason Canian-forged steel is also known as Singing Steel, Shrieking Steel, or Ruby Blood.

Chapel of the Hands - the assembly of the supreme priests of Sagot.

Cold Sea - the northern sea of the Western Ocean. It washes the shores of Valiostr and the Desolate Lands.

Commission - the agreement that is concluded between a master thief and his client. The thief undertakes to supply the item required or, in case of failure, to return the client's pledge and a percentage of the total value of the deal. The client undertakes to make payment in full on receiving the article in which he is interested. A Commission can only be abrogated by the mutual consent of both parties.

Crayfish Dukedom - the only state in the Desolate Lands.

crayfish grip (coll.) - a grip from which it is impossible to escape. The expression derives from the common saying that the men of the Crayfish Kingdom have a strong grip, and once they take you prisoner, you will never get away alive.

crayfish sleigh - in the Crayfish Dukedom, men who had been executed were transported to their graves on sleighs. Hence the meaning of this phrase—if the crayfish sleigh has come for you, death is at the door.

Crest of the World - the highest mountain chain in Siala. It runs from north to south across almost the entire continent. The crest is very difficult to cross and the lands beyond it are almost entirely unexplored.

Defender of the Hands - one of the highest positions in the hierarchy of the priests of Sagot.

Desolate Lands - the forests, stretches of open tundra, and ice fields in the far north. They have been settled by beings of various kinds, several of which constantly attempt to gain entry to the Northern Lands of Siala, and only the unassailable Mountains of Despair, the Lonely Giant fortress, and the Wild Hearts hold back their invasion of the world of men. Ogres, giants, svens, h'varrs, winter orcs, and dozens of other races and varieties of creatures inhabit these vast territories. People also live here, savages and barbarians who are subjects of the Nameless One. In all the Desolate Lands there is only one human state, the Crayfish Dukedom on the Crayfish Claw peninsula.

In the far north of the Desolate Lands, beyond the Needles of Ice, lies the dwelling of the Nameless One, whom savages captured by the Wild Hearts' scouts mention only in reverential whispers.

Disputed Lands - the lands lying alongside the Forests of Zagraba, between Miranueh and Valiostr.

djanga - a rapid, rhythmical dance, very popular in Zagorie.

Djashla - the kingdom of the mountain people that lies alongside the Crest of the World.

Djok Imargo or "Djok the bringer of winter" - the man who supposedly killed the prince of the House of the Black Rose. The Long Winter began as a result of this murder.

Doralissians - a race of goat-people who live in the Steppes of Ungava.

Doralissian horses - a type of horses bred in the Steppes of Ungava and valued throughout the Northern Lands for their beauty, speed, and stamina.

dralan - a commoner who has been granted a title by a duke; the title is not hereditary.

drokr - an elfin fabric that is proof against water and odors and does not burn in fire.

D'san-dor (orcish), or the Slumbering Forest - a forest that lies in the Desolate Lands, close to the spurs of the Mountains of Despair.

dwarves - the race of short beings living in the Mountains of the Dwarves. They are quite different from their near cousins, the gnomes. It is astonishing how their short, thick-fingered hands can create the most wonderful items, which are valued highly in every corner of Siala, whether they are weapons, tools, or works of art.

E.D. - the Era of Dreams, the final age of Siala. The events described in this book take place in the final year of the Era of Dreams. This age was preceded by the Era of Accomplishments (the age during which men appeared in Siala, about seven thousand years ago), the Gray Era (the age deemed to have begun with the appearance of orcs and elves in Siala) and the Dark Era (it is not known who, apart from ogres, lived in Siala in these distant times and what happened then).

elves - the second young race of Siala. The elves appeared almost immediately after their relatives, the orcs. After living in the Forests of Zagraba for several thousand years, the elves became divided into light and dark.

The light elves were dissatisfied with what they could achieve using shamanism and set about studying wizardry, basing their approach on the magic of men.

The dark elves, however, felt the light elves had betrayed the memory of their ancestors. They continued to make use of the primordial magic of their race, shamanism.

The names of all dark elfin women begin with *M* and the names of the men begin with *E*. If an elf is a member of the ruling family of the Dark House, then *ssa* is added to the name.

Empire - following the birth in the imperial family of twin boys, the Empire split into two states—the Near Lakeside Empire and the Far Lakeside Empire. These two kingdoms are constantly warring with each other to unite the Empire under the power of one of the two dynasties that trace their descent from the twin brothers.

Eyes of Death - when dice are cast and they show two "ones."

Field of Sorna - the field on which the battle between the gnomes and the dwarves took place in 1100 E.D. Cannons and battle-mattocks clashed with poleaxes and swords. In this battle there were no victors.

Filand - a kingdom lying along the southern spurs of the Mountains of the Dwarves.

Forests of Zagraba - these evergreen forests cover an immense area. In some places beautiful, in others terrifying, they conceal within themselves a host of secrets and mysterious creatures. The Forests of Zagraba are home to dark elves, orcs, goblins, and dryads.

Garrak - a kingdom in the southern region of Siala's Northern Lands. Powerful and thoroughly militarized. The Garrak nobility are regarded as extremely quick-tempered, dangerous, and unpredictable.

Garrak's "Dragon" - King Garrak's guard.

garrinch (gnomish, literally "guardian of the chests") - a creature that lives in the Steppes of Ungava. A trained garrinch makes an excellent guard for stores of treasure.

giants - one of the races that live in the Desolate Lands.

gkhols - carrion-eating scavengers. These creatures are usually to be found on battlefields or in old graveyards. If their source of food fails for some reason, gkhols are capable of hibernating for several years.

gnomes - like their larger cousins, the dwarves, gnomes appeared in the world of Siala immediately after the orcs and elves. Both gnomes and dwarves settled in the Mountains of the Dwarves, burrowing deep into their heart. Gnomes are stunted, quarrelsome creatures with beards. In the Mountains of the Dwarves their position was that of younger brothers. Gnomes are poor craftsmen, and they have never been able to produce such beautiful and delicate wares as the dwarves. However, gnomes are magnificent at working with steel and mining ore and other riches of the earth. They are good builders and diggers.

After living in the Mountains of the Dwarves for several thousand years, the gnomes finally left their old home following a decisive falling-out with their relatives the dwarves.

The race of gnomes found itself a new haven in the Steel Mines of Isilia. For the right to live in the mines they pay the kingdom an annual tribute and also supply it with steel. The gnomes invented the printing press, and then discovered how to make gunpowder (the dwarves claim that the gnomes stole the secret from a dwarf who was on his way home from a journey beyond the Crest of the World). The fierce battle that broke out between the estranged relatives on the Field of Sorna (1100 E.D.) was inconclusive. Both sides returned home having suffered immense losses.

The gnomes jealously guard the secret of gunpowder and sell cannons.

They have no magic of their own, since their last magician was killed on the Field of Sorna, and the gnomes' books are hidden deep in the Mountains of the Dwarves, in a safe hiding place that they cannot reach because of their enmity with the dwarves.

goblins - small creatures who live in the very depths of the Forests of Zagraba. The shamanism of the goblins is regarded as the most powerful after that of the ogres, but it includes almost no common attack spells.

Gray Stones - the most terrible and impregnable prison fortress in Valiostr. In all the time that it has existed, no one has ever managed to escape.

Green Leaf - one of the dark elves' most terrible tortures, which they only use on orcs (the one exception being Djok Imargo). Almost nothing is known about it, but rumors speak of the infernal torment of the victim. The torture can continue for years without interruption.

Grok - 1) the legendary general of Valiostr who held back the army of the orcs at Avendoom until the dark elves arrived to help in the final year of the Quiet Times (640 E.D.). A statue in his honor was erected in one of the central squares of the city; 2) the younger twin brother of the general Grok, who bore the same name, i.e., the magician who was dubbed the Nameless One.

hand - an orcish military leader.

Heartless Chasseurs - units of the army of Valiostr. In times of peace they perform the functions of the police. They are employed in military actions, and also assist in suppressing revolts and conspiracies, and in capturing and exterminating dangerous gangs and individual criminals.

Hospital of the Ten Martyrs - the Avendoom municipal hospital, founded by order of Grok on the precise spot where a detachment of orcs that had broken through the defenses of the human army was halted by ten warriors from the Avendoom garrison (640 E.D.).

Hrad Spein (ogric), or Palaces of Bone - immense underground palaces and catacombs, where ogres, orcs, elves and, later, men have all buried fallen warriors.

h'san'kor (orcish), or fearsome flute - a man-eating monster that lives in the Forests of Zagraba.

I'alyala Forests - these forests lie in the Northern Lands of Siala, beside the Crest of the World. The light elves moved here from the Forests of Zagraba following the schism between the elfin houses.

imperial dog - a type of guard dog bred in the Empire.

"Innocent as Djok the Winter-Bringer" – a common saying. Djok Imargo was the man accused of the murder of the prince of the House of the Black Rose. He was handed over to the elves, who executed him. After that, from 501 to 640 E.D., the dark elfin houses of Zagraba had no contacts with Valiostr. It subsequently emerged that Djok was innocent.

irilla (orcish), or mist spider - an emanation generated by the shamanism of the ogres. To this day no one knows for certain if it is an immaterial substance or a living creature.

Iselina (orcish), or Black River - this river starts in the Mountains of the Dwarves, runs through the eastern section of the Forests of Zagraba, crosses Valiostr, then forks into a left branch and a right branch, which both flow into the Eastern Ocean.

Isilia (orcish) - a kingdom bordering on Valiostr and Miranueh.

Isilian marble - is mined in the southern spurs of the Steel Mines. Walking across this stone generates a powerful echo. It is generally used for protection against thieves, or to prevent the approach of assassins, or even simply for its beauty, despite the unpleasant sounds that have to be tolerated.

Jolly Gallows-Birds - former convicts, criminals, and pirates who have been recruited to serve as soldiers. On joining the ranks of the army of Valiostr they are pardoned for all previous transgressions. They perform the military functions of marines.

k'lissang (orcish, lit. "ever faithful") - an elf who has sworn an oath of fealty and engaged himself as a bodyguard to an elf of a more noble line for nine years. If the ever-faithful elf is killed during his period of service, his entire family is accepted into the clan of the elf whom the k'lissang was protecting.

Kronk-a-Mor - the shamanism of the ogres.

labyrinth - an ancient structure erected by the orcs, located in the Forests of Zagraba. The orcs release prisoners into the labyrinth and place bets on which of the unfortunates will survive longest.

languages of Siala - there are three main groups of languages in Siala. The first group is the orcish languages, spoken by orcs and elves. The second group is the gnomish languages, spoken by gnomes and dwarves. The third group includes all the human languages. There are also other languages and dialects, for instance, the languages of the ogres and goblins.

"Like looking for a smoking dwarf" - Dwarves do not smoke and they regard smokers with a certain degree of disdain, since the first beings to take up smoking were the gnomes. Following the gnomes, men also became addicted to the habit.

ling - a small animal that lives in the tundra of the Desolate Lands. Very like a shaggy-haired rat, but with much larger teeth and claws.

Lonely Giant - the fortress that closes off the only pass leading from the Desolate Lands through the Mountains of Despair to Valiostr.

Long Winter - the name given by the elves to a period of 140 years from 500 to 640 E.D. The Long Winter set in following the grotesque death of the elfin prince of the House of the Black Rose in Ranneng during festivities in the town. It came to an end in the final year of the Quiet Times (640 E.D.), during the Spring War, when the elves came to the aid of Grok and his men in the battle against the army of the orcs. Grok was presented with the Rainbow Horn to confirm that the Long Winter was over.

Lowland - the kingdom lying beside the I'alyala Forests.

Lowland masters - master craftsmen from the Lowland, famous throughout Siala for the dishes and tableware they make from a special lilac-colored porcelain.

Market Square - a famous Avendoom square where theatrical performances constantly take place.

Master of the Long Sword - a title that is given to soldiers who have completely mastered the three techniques for using the two-handed sword (classical grip, single-fang grip, staff grip). The hilt of the sword is decorated with an embossed gold image of an oak leaf.

mattockmen - a name sometimes used for the gnomes. Their favorite weapon is the so-called battle-mattock, which combines a large cutting blade with a war hammer.

Mirangrad - the capital of Miranueh, a kingdom located beside Valiostr.

Miranueh - a kingdom bordering on Garrak, Isilia, and Valiostr. Constantly at war with Valiostr over the Disputed Lands.

Mountains of Despair - the low but unassailable mountains that separate Valiostr from the Desolate Lands. There is only one pass through them, and the Lonely Giant fortress is located on it.

Mountains of the Dwarves - an immense mountain chain, so high that only the Crest of the World compares with it. It runs from east to west through the Northern Lands, dividing them in two. Zam-da-Mort, or the Castle of Death, is the tallest and most majestic peak in the Mountains of the Dwarves.

Nameless One - the title given to a Valiostran magician after he committed treason in the final year of the Quiet Times (640 E.D.).

Needles of Ice - icebound mountains far away in the Desolate Lands.

obur - a gigantic bear from the Forests of Zagraba.

ogres - a race from the Desolate Lands. The only old race of Siala still remaining in this world. From the very beginning the ogres were granted a very powerful and destructive magic, Kronk-a-Mor. They are regarded as distant relatives of the orcs and elves. The elves say the gods took away the ogres' intelligence. If the ogres had remained as clever as they once were, they would have captured and destroyed the entire world of Siala.

Ol's Diggings - stone quarries lying at a distance of six days' journey from Avendoom. They were named after their first owner. The stone for the city's legendary walls was quarried here. Nowadays Ol's Diggings are abandoned.

orcs - the first new race of Siala. The elves regard them as their archenemies, although they are directly related to each other. The orcs say that they were here first and should rule the entire world, and all the other races are an unfortunate mistake made by the gods. In addition to the Forests of Zagraba, orcs also live in the Desolate Lands (the winter orcs).

Order of Magicians - there is an Order in every kingdom, the only exceptions being Zagorie and Djashla. Each Order has a council of archmagicians and is headed by a Master. Within the Order there is a strict division according to rank, and ranks are marked on the magicians' staffs: magician of the Order—one ring; elemental magician (master of the specific skills of several schools)—two rings; magician with right of access to the council—three rings; archmagician—four rings; master— four rings and a small black figure of a raven on the top of the staff.

Purple Years - a period of time during which the dwarves and the gnomes waged a series of bloody wars against each other, and as a result the gnomes withdrew from the Mountains of the Dwarves.

Quiet Times - the period from 423 E.D. to 640 E.D., during which Valiostr did not wage a single war. These were times of prosperity when the kingdom flourished. They came to an end when an immense army of orcs from the Forests of Zagraba invaded Valiostr.

Rainbow Horn - a legendary artifact created by the ogres to counterbalance their own magic, the Kronk-a-Mor, if it should ever get out of control. The Horn was captured by the dark elves, who later gave it to men (in the person of Grok) as a token of their good intentions and the conclusion of an eternal alliance between the dark elves and Valiostr. Every two or three hundred years the Horn has to be saturated with magic in order not to lose its powers. Following the creation of the Secret Territory, the Horn was buried with Grok in the Hrad Spein. It is the Horn's magic that keeps the Nameless One in the Desolate Lands.

River of the Crystal Dream - a narrow little river in Avendoom. It runs through the Port City and falls into the Cold Sea.

Royal Guard of Valiostr - the king's personal guard. Only nobles are recruited to serve in it. The guardsmen wear the king's colors of gray and blue. The guard is commanded by a captain.

Royal Sandmen - the king's secret police, who defend the interests of the state and the sovereign. Their nickname is derived from their emblem, an hourglass.

Sagot - one of the twelve deities of the world of Siala. Patron of thieves, swindlers, rogues, and spies.

Sagra - one the twelve deities of the world of Siala. Goddess of war, justice, and death, and also patroness of soldiers.

Secret (Forbidden) Territory, or "the Stain" - a district of Avendoom created as the result of an attempt to use the Rainbow Horn to neutralize Kronk-a-Mor in 872 E.D. The Secret Territory is surrounded by a magical wall, through which almost no one dares to pass. Evil is said to dwell there.

shamanism - the primordial magic of Siala. It was first used by the ogres, then the orcs, the dark elves, and the goblins. The magic of men and the light elves is derived from shamanism.

Shamar - the capital of the Border Kingdom.

Siala - the world in which the events of this book take place.

Silna - the goddess of love, beauty, and nature.

s'kash (orcish) - a sword with curved blade. It is sharpened on its inner, concave edge and usually has teeth like a saw.

sklot (gnomic), or "corkscrew" - a heavy military crossbow designed to puncture the heavy armor of warriors walking the front ranks of an army.

Spring War - the war that began in the final year of the Quiet Times (640 E.D.). Men and dark elves fought on one side, and the orcs of Zagraba on the other. The War of Shame is the name that orcs use for the Spring War.

Stalkons - the royal dynasty of Valiostr.

Steel Brows - the heavy infantry of the Wild Hearts.

Steel Mines - the mountains and mines in Isilia that produce the finest steel in the Northern Lands. The race of gnomes lives here.

Steppes of Ungava - the steppes on the very southern edge of the Northern Lands.

S'u-dar (ogric), or the Icy Pass - the only route through the Needles of Ice from the Desolate Lands to the citadel of the Nameless One.

Sultanate - a state located far beyond the Steppes of Ungava.

svens, or chanters - creatures of the Desolate Lands that resemble shaggy flying spheres. When the freezing conditions in the open expanses of the Desolate Lands are at their fiercest they appear, chanting a song that kills all living things.

Thorns - the soldiers of this detachment carry out reconnaissance work and raids deep into the territory of the Desolate Lands. The Thorns have a reputation as daredevils and swashbuckling desperadoes.

tresh (orcish) - a polite term of address used by elves to an elf of noble birth. Sometimes used by other races when addressing highborn elves.

vampire - a creature of legend. Even today it is still not known if it exists in reality or only in the tales told by drunken peasants. According to the legend, only human beings and dark elves can become vampires. Vampires are credited with magical powers, such as the ability to transform themselves into a bat or mist. The Order of Magicians regards the existence of vampires as doubtful.

Vastar's Bargain - in 223 E.D. Vastar, the king of Garrak, concluded an alliance with a dragon so that the creature would assist him in attacking neighboring kingdoms. The agreement, however, proved worthless to the king: The dragon failed to engage the humans in battle and Vastar's army was routed. The term "a Vastar's bargain" signifies any similarly disadvantageous agreement.

Wild Hearts - the detachment of soldiers who serve at the Lonely Giant.

Wind Jugglers - the name given in the army to experienced bowmen, no matter to what detachment they belonged. Even when there was a strong wind interfering with the flight of the arrow, the "jugglers" almost always hit their mark.

wizardry - a higher magic possessed by the magicians of men and the light elves, based on the earlier magic, or shamanism, of the orcs and dark elves.

Zagorie, or the Free Lands - the lands beside the southern spurs of the Mountains of the Dwarves. All who are discontented with the rule of the authorities or the laws of the kingdom flee here—peasants, younger sons, courtiers in disgrace, adventurers, and criminals. Such people can always find land and work in the Free Lands.

Zam-da-mort (gnomish), or the Castle of Death - the highest and most majestic peak of the Mountains of the Dwarves.